Barlow

Redefined

By D.M. Williams

Editing- Q By Design
Cover design- D.M. Williams/Lil' A 601 Imaging
Consulting Services- Q By Design, Lil' A 601 Imaging
ISBN: 9781666403787

The Lure of the South

The Southern language is as diverse alone as the many languages of the world. I never tire of listening to the people around me as I go about my day. It's pleasantly difficult to find two people with the exact same dialect. Many will agree this is the allure of the language indeed, with a sex appeal of its own. My personal favorite is the Deep South rhythmic drawl, the sexy accent that can easily hold its own beside the romantic French Gallo. The ear tingling high pitch twang rarely goes un-noticed much like the beautiful woman you never expect to see it hurling from when you look suddenly in its direction. Then there's the melodic Cajun rhythms of creole that make your heart dance to its fast pace poetic tempo. And let's be real, the south wouldn't be genuine without the flavorful dramatic grammar that each of us seems to perfect to our own liking literally changing mundane words into lavish works of art to sculpt our beautiful way of communicating. I believe the southern dialect has a romance of its own far beyond comparison. I have tried to depict only a few of these tantalizing dialects in my works to celebrate what I believe is The Lure of the South. Y'all enjoy now!

Table of Contents

Unimagined Gift

Even though he had lost his beloved Ethel, Barlow was happy to see this eventful year come to an end. So many things had happened that he wanted to forget. They had originally planned to start their travels at the beginning of the new year. When things were settled with the Butlers, plans changed. He wanted to get away and regroup. He and Chasidy decided to skip Christmas at home and leave early for their world travels instead.

Christmas is Chasidy's favorite holiday. She enjoyed spending that day with her family. It was the one day everyone made a real effort to get together. But Barlow is the most important person in the world to her. She knew he needed a break from the norm. She knew he needed to get away, to forget and regroup.

Once on the plane however, Barlow began to feel guilty about taking her away from her family during her favorite time of year. As he stared at her sitting in the seat across from him, he noticed that she didn't look disappointed at all. In fact, she seemed quite content. Still, he felt compelled to make things right. "Are you sure yur okay with this? It's not too late to change yor mine."

D.M. Williams

"Why would I change my mind?" she asked as if she really didn't comprehend his question.

He moved over to the seat beside her and took hold of her hand. "Christmas is yor favorite holiday, da one you love most to spend with yor family. And now I've dashed you off to a part of da world where you don't know anyone. Complete strangers you once said."

"Mr. Barlow, it b'hooves me sometimes that you talk like you know nothan' at all. I'll know plenty of people when we get to Rio."

"You will?" Barlow asked, not realizing she had acquaintances down there. "Who?"

"Well, there's Rob, Robert, Mr. Barlow, and my husband," Chasidy said smiling.

"That's a lot of people," Barlow now realizing she's playing, played alone with her. "And all of them of a male persuasion.

"Well, I'm very popular with that particular set of males," she replied.

"I have a feelin', yur more popular than you realize," he told her. "That's why one of them wants to know if yur truly happy with this."

She gazed into his chestnut eyes and said, "Robert, I'm more content with you than I am anywhere else. I love my family very much, but my first commitment is to you. And you need this right now. There's no way I'd turn this plane around. Christmas will come again a year from now."

Barlow loved the way Chasidy was always able to read him. He basked in her answer and made her a solemn promise, "Thank you, but I'll make Christmas up to you."

"No," she said. 'Not this time. I'm choosan' to give up Christmas fa you. You don't owe me any restitutions." He put his arm around her, and they snuggled together for most of the flight to Rio de Janeiro.

The weather in Rio was an easy distraction of the season; near perfect being not too hot or too cold. They took advantage taking long slow walks along the beaches and sightseeing in the beautiful city. They had gotten a glimpse of the magnificent ninety-eight-foot-tall statue of Christ from afar when they first arrived. But it was Barlow who suggested they visit up close and personal for a better look. "We have to go see that," he told Chasidy with an expression of intrigue plastered to his face.

Chasidy's immediate response, "Bet!" with a huge smile of her own.

They relaxed on the sandy white beaches seven days before venturing up Corcovado Mountain to admire the massive structure. Chasidy watched Barlow gaze in admiration at the beautiful figure for several minutes. He looked as if he had entered a different place and just wanted to linger there for a while. Chasidy was quite content to allow him to have his time in the moment.

As Barlow gazed at the statue, he thought about things he had recently learned of the Christ the statue represented along with the events He had just brought him and Chasidy through. Witnessing His outstretched arms, if only in stone, gave him a realization of the real Jesus offering to all, *"come to me all of you just as you are."* Barlow imagined himself someday cradled in the loving arms of Jesus. The feeling that accompanied that thought was wonderfully overwhelming and his eyes filled with joyous tears. When he was finally able to leave that realm and return to Chasidy, he said to her with tear trenched eyes, "Thank you for introducing me to God." Chasidy was pleasantly speechless.

From Rio they made their way to the Virgin Islands where they settled for six weeks enjoying each of the sanctuary islands' crystal-clear waters; perfecting their snorkeling skills from previous island visits. They strolled along with warm sandy beaches, enjoyed exquisite cuisine, and dabbled in their sultry calypso. Barlow being a huge fan of culture, especially enjoyed learning the art of Quelbe music and dance. Chasidy enjoyed watching her rhythmless husband having the time of his life making a complete fool of himself.

But once more their travels were halted when they returned to British Columbia, to take up where they had left off on their honeymoon.

Barlow had already promised Chasidy she could stay as long as she had a desire to whenever they returned. She had freely given up Christmas with her family for his sake. That promise had twice the meaning it had before. Chasidy played her what Chasidy wants, Chasidy gets card when she asked if they could stay until Al, Mic, and AJ joined them.

D.M. Williams

Barlow rented a lovely rustic bungalow in Fairmount Mountains with gushing hot springs and rushing waterfalls nearby. Mornings were sometimes eventful when they awakened to an occasional moose playing in the yard. Barlow posed a special question to Chasidy on the mornings of the moose's visit, "Do you wanna go hikin' taday?"

The moose were huge and scary looking to Chasidy. She declared those days their getting-reacquainted-days when she replied, "This feels like a snuggling day to me."

Barlow came to look forward to the moose visiting. Usually snuggling turned into long heart-pounding talks, especially on a crisp cold day perched in front of the warm crackling fire of the fireplace. Chasidy would be content to stay here forever, having Barlow all to herself. But selfishness has never been her strong suit. She knew Barlow would miss Al a lot. And Al is probably already pulling his hairs out missing his friend too. Barlow has already spoken of the reunion in May on two occasions. He's anxious to see his friend again, though he uses little AJ as an excuse.

Six months into their world travels, Barlow and Chasidy were living in their own realm of contentment. Barlow, like every other outfit he slips into, wears retirement extremely well; enjoying his lifelong dream of travel with the woman he never dared to dream he'd ever have. Chasidy, having seen places she never dreamed of seeing, not even as a child, is completely mesmerized. Barlow has taken her places and shown her things she didn't even know existed. In his world, the teacher has become the student and loving every minute of it. Once more it was difficult to leave the beautiful serenity of the mountains in British Columbia. But she too has family she would like to get back to. That will happen as soon as they have exhausted their adventurous spirit.

AJ is finally out for summer break. Barlow and Chasidy are scheduled to join Alan, Michelle, and AJ at the Disney Resort in Tokyo, AJ's first choice to visit. Barlow was ready to reconnect with his friends. Since AJ won't be able to be with them long, they will cater to his desires until school starts up again in August. Fun was inevitable. Enjoying the world from a child's perspective partaking in things now, that they missed out on when they were children, put a new and more exhilarating twist on the travels. They willingly allowed their minds to wander into child-like wonderment as they gallivanted around with AJ and his very active imagination. They had fun that most adults forget about after a certain age, when the serious business of everyday life takes over. Chasidy embraced every moment with her nephew. Barlow was elated in the fun Chasidy and AJ were having together.

Alan took advantage of AJ's fascination with Chasidy's child-like wonderment by sharing a few overdue romantic endeavors with Michelle. Michelle has never been a winey wife. Al always admired that in her. Whenever he had assignments out of town, he packed her and AJ up and took them with him. She never once complained about being uprooted so much. During the Christmas Holiday he had the thought of doing something special for her for their upcoming anniversary. This time alone with her gave him just the opportunity he needed. He took Michelle on a ride through the park on the Western River Railroad. The gentle ride on the steam train was just what they needed to remind them of how much they are still in love with each other. As he gazed at Michelle losing himself in her perpetual beauty, he couldn't help but smile. "Did you know you've gotten more and more beautiful ov'r da years?" he asked her. "I had no idea that would even be possible. You were already da most beautiful woman I'd ev'r seen."

"Where did that come from?" A smiling Michelle asked in her slightly high-pitch southern twang that no one would imagine could come from a woman with such a soft glowing beauty. Michelle had mastered the art of facial makeup. She loved being beautiful at all times for her husband. He would argue any day that she didn't need makeup to accomplish that. Putting in the time each day to make herself more attractive was her way of showing him that she didn't take his love for granted. She wanted to look her best for him at all times.

Michelle had teased once that Al didn't know how to be romantic. Alan wanting to remind his wife of how much he cared for her set out to prove her wrong. Especially since it was so close to their special day. "From my heart," he replied in his own sultry southern drawl.

From the day they first met as teenagers, he was completely taken with her soft flawless beauty. He hasn't looked at another woman twice since she became a part of his life. In those days she always wore her long hair up in a ponytail with a scrunchie around it as if she knew she didn't have to do anything special with it to enhance her beauty. He would remove the scrunchie ever-so-often so her hair could fall freely to her shoulders. Once she met him with her hair already hanging freely expecting to please him so that he wouldn't have to release it. Surprisingly to her, he asked, "where's yor ponytail?" It was at that moment she realized it was the simple act of releasing her hair, watching it fall to her shoulders and fixing it to compliment the shape of her lovely face that was truly pleasurable to him. She has long since grown out of her ponytail, but she hasn't worn her hair down since that day. When she defied her parents and married him, Al secretly vowed she would never regret that decision promising to give her the best life he possibly could.

In his constant playful foolery, he had laxed in showing his wife how much he truly cared. Mic had become accustomed to his witty manner. She knew deep down that he loved her. He showed it every day in the way he cared for her and AJ. That was enough for her. That's why when she saw the group of people approaching dressed in fictional character costumes lead by Mickey Mouse himself, she thought it was all part of the ride. But she soon learned it was her husband's witty imagination and just a hint of romance at play when Mickey Mouse handed her two dozen long-stemmed roses as the characters began singing; *Every Little Thing She Does Is Magic*.

Michelle breathed in the soft scent of the roses, "They're beautiful, Al. Thank you." She stared at Alan with a new love and suddenly didn't want to take her eyes off of him as his gorgeous golden ambers flirted with her. He too was as handsome as the day they first met. She was blown away all over again by his sweltering good looks. His neatly trimmed curls and sharply lined edges gave him the perfectly distinguished look of the southern gentleman he is.

Al took the pin from her silky black hair highlighted with an attractive golden bronze to allow it to fall to her shoulders and brushed it with his hands to the shape of her face. He caressed her satiny soft cheek and said, "See, I haven't fa' gotten how to be romantic." Kissing her affectionately, he continued, "I'm sorry it's taken me so long to do this. It won't happen again. From now on I'm intentionally gonna celebrate you every chance I get."

"Intentionally?" she repeated.

"Very …. intentionally," he promised.

When they got back to Barlow, Chasidy and AJ, Michelle was all smiles hugged up with her roses and her husband. Barlow and Chasidy met them with their own approving smiles. She immediately told Chasidy, "I stand corrected. My husband is very romantic," remembering the night they first met in Arkansas. Chasidy remembered that night all too well for her own set of special reasons.

Little did Michelle know that Alan wasn't finished wooing her just yet. He had one more surprise planned for his wife of twenty-four years. The following day, they cruised the river on the Mark Twain Riverboat admiring the park from a different perspective. Just before returning to the starting point, Alan took Michelle's hand and pulled her close to him. "Do you know what day this is?" he asked.

"Friday," Michelle answered. Alan smiled, knowing that he was about to pleasantly remind her of a day that she usually reminds him of. He pulled a small red suede box from his pocket. Michelle looked at the box in excited anticipation. "What is this?" she asked him.

He opened the box that housed a beautiful diamond cluster ring with a diamond for each year they've been married and AJ birthstone in the center. He placed the ring on her finger counting the diamonds by two's. Placing his finger on the sapphire stone in the middle representing AJ's birth month. He asked her again, "Now do you know what day it is?"

"May 19th. Our anniversary, Al." Michelle began to cry. "I can't b'lieve you remembered, and I forgot. I'm so sorry."

"You don't need to apologize to me for anythan'. I should've been doing this every year. You put yor heart and soul into takin care of me and AJ, nev'r askin' for anythan' in return. Things are gonna be different from this day forward. A rose and a diamond for every wonderful year we've been married isn't nearly enough. But this is just da b'ginning. Marrying you was da smartest thing I've ev'r done. I intend to keep remindin' you of that. I love you, Mic."

"Rob needs to take us on more of his trips. I could get used to this," she replied.

"We don't need Rob to fly us around da world. I can take you anywhere you wanna go whenever you wanna go. Just say da word, Baby," he practically promised her. In fact, why don't we start with a honeymoon?"

"A honeymoon?" Michelle asked.

Al got down on one knee, holding his wife's hand. "You didn't get to have da weddin' of yor dreams like most young brides do. I wanna make that right for ya. I promised you one as grand as Becky's. Remember?"

"I remember."

Mic, will you marry me, again?"

Michelle answered joining her husband kneeling on her knees, "A hundred times ov'r, Al. I love you too." The patrons of the river boat ride applauded their new re-engagement. Neither of them was ready for the cruise to end. When they came to the end of the ride, they stayed and enjoyed another ride snuggled in each other's arms. When they finally got back to the gang, she excitedly announced, "We're gettin' married! Again!"

Barlow's congratulation to Al was, "Yur showin' off, aren't ya?"

Al's reply, "Yur not da only romancer in this bunch."

"Good ansar, Al," Chasidy said. Looking at an over-the-top excited Michelle, she added, "Girl, we've got a weddan' to plan!"

#

During their two-week stay in Tokyo, Chasidy begins to feel ill. She didn't mention it to Barlow because she didn't want to ruin AJ's fun. She knows Barlow would end everything and fly everybody home if he thought she was becoming ill. She willingly assumes it was due to carrying on too much like a child on all the crazy rides with AJ. What she didn't know was that Barlow is experiencing some symptoms as well. Because of that, he let them have a few rides on their own. He fears he's caught a bud and didn't want Chasidy to catch it, so he keeps as much of a distance from her as possible. It's not an easy task. They both are accustomed to staying close to each other. She didn't care for him falling asleep on the sofa in the outer room from the bedroom. She wondered what his distancing was all about, but waits as usual, for him to bring it up.

She was hoping that would be soon. She didn't like the distance between them, and she was missing their talks.

AJ's next adventure took them to the mind-boggling entertainment world of Universal Studios, a child's adventure paradise. They were two weeks into their visit at the action-packed amusement park when his little world was shaken again. Disembarking from one of the rides, Chasidy became lightheaded. She fell and hit her head on an iron bar. They were holding hands when it happened, but he was unable to stop her from falling. Likewise, it happened so quickly, Barlow couldn't get to her either because he had elected to sit this ride out. But he could see the whole thing from where he was standing. He and Al rushed to see about her. Mic rushed to comfort AJ seeing how upset he had become. It broke his little heart. She was rushed to the emergency room. Once again Barlow found himself at the mercy of God.

Chasidy lost consciousness briefly, regaining it shortly after getting to the hospital. It was during the examination that she awakened immediately asking for her husband. "Where's Rob?" expecting to see him as soon as she opened her eyes.

One of the nurses replied, "Your husband is waiting in the waiting area. You'll be able to see him soon."

"AJ? Where's AJ?" she asked also. They didn't know who AJ was. She realized that when they didn't answer right away. "My nephew. He was with me. Is he alright?"

"Oh. Yes," the nurse answered. "He's fine. Everyone is waiting for you outside."

The doctor asked, "How are you feeling, Mrs. Barlow?"

"My head hurts," she answered, "and there's pain in my stomach. What hap'aned to me?"

"Well, you have a pretty nasty bump up there. You fell and hit your head pretty hard," the doctor said. "I've given you a small dose of pain killer. You're gonna have to try to tough it out though. Too much medication would be bad for the baby."

"Baby?" Chasidy tried to rise up. "What baby?"

"Please, stay still Mrs. Barlow." The doctor ordered. "You weren't aware you were pregnant?"

"No," she said, "how is this possible?"

"It happens to be fairly common among married people," the doctor joked. "I'm assuming you and your husband never discussed the possibility of children."

"No," Chasidy answered. "Da thought neva crossed our minds at our age."

"Well, looks like you're overdue for a talk," the doctor said smiling.

"Please don't tell 'im," Chasidy pleaded, "not about da baby."

"He's bound to find out sooner or later," added the doctor. Again, jokingly and puzzled as to why she wanted to keep it a secret.

"Please." Chasidy pleaded again.

"Okay," he agreed. "They're all waiting to see you. Shall I let them come in?"

"Yes, thank you," she said anxiously.

The nurse ushered them into the room. "Mr. Barlow, you can see your wife now." Everyone followed.

AJ ran ahead of them all, giving Chasidy a long hug. "Are you alright Aunt Chasidy?"

"Completely," she answered, not wanting him to worry about her. "Are you?"

"I'm fine. I was scared though. You fell and I couldn't catch you."

"Don't be scared anymore. Aunt Chasidy's fine too."

Barlow walked up behind AJ and sat on the bed. "You scared me too," he said hugging her. "How do you feel?"

"Like I'll have a headache for a long time," she answered trying to smile. Barlow looked up at the doctor.

"Yes, she will," he told him. "I've given her a mild pain killer. I'm afraid you'll have to cut your trip short. She'll need to go home and go straight to bed, for at least two, maybe three weeks. Make sure she sees her doctor as soon as possible."

"I will," Barlow agreed. "Is it that serious?"

The doctor wanted to make certain Chasidy stayed immobile for at least the next two weeks for the baby's sake; if not the entire three. Not knowing her reason for the secrecy, he wasn't sure she would comply. To him, her husband looked like the type of man who would see to that. But he also wanted to honor her wishes in keeping the baby a secret for now. "Any bump on the head that knocks you unconscious for any length of time is serious enough to take caution," he told Barlow.

"Thank you, doc. When can I take 'er home?" He asked anxiously.

"Tomorrow. I wanna monitor that bump overnight," the doctor told him.

Chasidy was quiet all night trying to process the thought of a baby so late in life. She didn't even know if Barlow wanted children. That conversation never came up presumably, because of their ages. Or maybe it never came up because he didn't want any. He seems to like children. He adores AJ and the twins, not to mention, the Academy children.

Barlow felt like something was on her mind, but he wouldn't ask because he didn't know if it was something that would upset her. And he didn't want to do that. He preferred she concentrate on feeling better. But he was sure there was something more going on with her than just a bump on the head. He watched her toss and turn as she slept. She couldn't have been getting much rest. He buzzed the nurse thinking her head must be hurting. She was one of the nurses present when the doctor informed Chasidy about the baby. The nurse explained to Barlow that she couldn't administer medications unless it was ordered by the doctor. It was unsettling for Barlow to see Chasidy in pain, and nothing could be done about it.

Her quietness lasted the entire flight home. Completely lost in her thoughts, Chasidy came to the realization that she had no idea how her husband felt about having children of his own. That was a little frightening to her. Unsettling even. During the flight, everyone was so concerned for Chasidy they didn't even notice that little AJ had his own concerns. Chasidy made the flight home in the sleeping chamber. Barlow insisted. AJ went in to check on her. Michelle noticed he had been missing for more than the few minutes it took to go to the restroom, so she went to check on him. He wasn't there. She found him in the sleeping chamber with Chasidy. She overheard their conversation stopping just outside the door to listen. "Aunt

Chasidy, I'm sorry yur hurt. It's all my fault. I hope yur not mad at me. Please don't die."

"AJ, it's not at all yor fault! And I'm not mad at you," Chasidy corrected. "Why would you think that?"

"You and Uncle Rob were fine before I got here. I was da one who wanted to go to all da stupid parks. If we hadn't gone there, you wouldn't have fallen and hit yor head. And you wouldn't be hurt." His eyes started to tear up. "It's my fault; just like Grandma Ethel."

She reached for him to give him a comforting hug. By now Alan and Barlow had joined Michelle in listening in on the conversation. "Is that what yur thankan', Baby?" she asked him, that yor grandma died b'cause of you?"

He started to cry. "I made her die. I don't wanna make you die too."

Chasidy hugged him long and tight rocking him from side to side. "You stop thankan' like that right this instant," she scolded. "Aunt Chasidy isn't gonna die. Yor Uncle Rob and I could hardly wait fa you and yor parents to join us. We wouldn't change that fa anythan'. And you didn't cause yor grandmotha's death eitha'. It was just time fa her to leave us. Yor grandma would be so sad if she knew you were havan' these thoughts." she kissed his little forehead. "Oh Baby, I wish I could make you understand. I fell b'cause I ova-exhausted myself havan' too much fun with you. I've neva had so much fun." She kissed him again. "And I would do it all ova' again at da snap of a fingar." That's when she saw the others standing at the door. "Those old folks don't know how to have fun like that. Why do you think I was hangan' out with you?" He thought that was funny. "But just know that Aunt Chasidy will be right here with you, fa a long time. Okay. I'm not going anywhere. I promise." She thought for a second on how she could help him get past his grandma's death or at least understand it better. "In fact, I think you and I should spend more time t'gethar. Talk with yor folks to see if its ok fa you to visit me once a week. That way you can see fa yorself that I'm alright."

"Ok. I will," he said excitedly.

She beckoned for them to come in. Michelle and Alan were speechless. They now realized that AJ is still mourning and may need to see Dr. Milo again concerning Ethel's death. They embraced their little guy sharing with each other a, *we-really-need-to-talk-about-this* look. Barlow smiled an approving smile at Chasidy.

"Why don't we let Aunt Chasidy get 'er rest now?" Barlow told him.

"Okay. Goodnight, Aunt Chasidy."

"Goodnight, Sweetheart." When he got to the door, he turned and ran back to Chasidy to give her a kiss on the cheek and another hug.

"Hey, what about me?" Barlow asked him.

AJ hugged him even longer. "Sorry Uncle Rob," he apologized.

"You handled that beautifully," Barlow said to Chasidy. He sat with her for a while until she fell asleep. He was hoping she would share what was on her mind, why she's been so quiet. She reached for a hug from him. He laid down beside her and held her close. "Are you really okay Chasidy?"

"Aside from a headache, I couldn't be betta. Especially layan' here in yor arms, my favorite place to be," she answered evasively.

He knew she was being evasive. He decided to wait until she was ready to confide in him. "Take a short nap. We'll be landing in forty-five minutes." Being still very exhausted, she did just that.

#

As soon as they made it home, Barlow put Chasidy straight to bed. He made it clear to her that would be her perch until the doctor said otherwise. The very same day Chasidy made an appointment to see her doctor. It was scheduled for the following Monday. She told Barlow she couldn't get an appointment until next month. That wasn't acceptable to him. He wanted to take her to his doctor in Saint Catherine. "No," Chasidy refused. "I wanna see my doctor. I promise to stay in bed until he can see me." Barlow didn't like that but what Chasidy wants, Chasidy gets.

He still felt ill himself periodically but literally waited on her hand and foot, not allowing her to move for anything. He wouldn't allow how he was feeling to keep him from caring for her. He has tried to stop worrying about losing her so much. But it seems every time he thinks he has a grip on his fears, something happens to remind him that he doesn't.

She wondered how she would get him away from her so that she could make her appointment. She used his consistent care for her as

13

an excuse the day of, along with the assistance of little AJ to accomplish that.

They were all visiting early that morning to check up on her and Barlow, to see if they needed anything. Chasidy enlisted AJ's help in wrangling his Uncle Rob into taking him fishing. He agreed. Chasidy started the conversation. AJ was the perfect little actor. "Alan," she started. "Rob has been waitan' on me day and night. I think he needs a break. Why don't you guys go fishing or somethan'?" she tempted. "I'll bet AJ would love that. Wouldn't you Little Guy?"

"I've nev'r been fishing b'fore. I'd love to learn how to fish Dad," AJ replied.

Alan didn't say anything. "Well, taday is a good day fa just that," Chasidy encouraged. "Ya dad is slackan'. At eleven years old, you should be a pro by now."

Alan looked at Barlow, and Barlow back at him. They knew she was trying to get rid of him, just couldn't figure out why. "What if somethin' hap'ens while I'm out fishin'?" Barlow asked her.

"I'm gonna stay right here in bed," she lied. "Besides, Mic will be here with me. Won't ya, Mic?"

"I won't leave her side," Michelle promised. She too wanted to know what Chasidy was up to.

"Please Uncle Rob," AJ pleaded.

"We don't have any fishin' gear. Or licenses." Barlow argued. Chasidy gave him an *as-if-that's-really-a-problem* glance. Al and Mic were interested to see how this would turn out. They waited intensely. Barlow didn't want to leave, but Chasidy's silent glance overtook him in the end. He concluded that his wife needed a break from him, so he and Alan took AJ on his first fishing trip.

"AJ, make sure Uncle Rob takes his time and enjoys himself, ok," she coached.

"Ok Aunt Chasidy."

She beckoned for her husband to come closer. When he did, she kissed him softly and said, "I'll be alright. Have fun. You deserve a break."

When they were far out of sight, Michelle sat down on the bed beside Chasidy and asked, "Okay, what's going on? Yur not fooling anyone, ya know," in a slightly lowered southern twang.

"I know. I neva have lied very well," Chasidy admitted. "That's why I'm glad my husband won't deny me."

"What's going on with you?" Michelle asked again.

Chasidy paused. "I have an appointment this afternoon."

"I thought you couldn't get in until next month," Michelle reminded her.

"That's what I told Rob. I don't want 'im to go with me.

"Why not?" A baffled Michelle asked her friend. Her high pitch southern twang suddenly returned. "It's not like you to keep things from 'im. Are you dying?" sounding almost serious.

Chasidy chuckled at that. "No. I'm pregnant."

"What?" Michelle blurted out. "That's wonderful! Why are you keeping that from 'im?"

"I'm scared," Chasidy admitted.

"Why? Rob will be thrilled," Michelle told her.

"What if he's not? He's neva mentioned children to me. We've neva had that conversation at all." Chasidy replied knowing full well she also has another reason.

Michelle isn't stupid though. "Chasidy. I repeat. Yur not foolin' anyone." She stared her straight faced in the eyes. "You know as much as Rob loves you…" She stopped. "What's really going on, girl?"

"I know, but a baby, at my age?" she said almost in tears.

"Oh, I understand now," Michelle replied nodding her head.

"Will you go with me taday?" Chasidy pleaded.

"Girl, you know good and doggone well I will," Michelle told her.

"My appointment is this afternoon, but if we go now, he may see me early and I can be back b'fore Rob gets home."

"I'll buzz Sam," Michelle told her.

"No," Chasidy interrupted. "He can track da Bentley. We'll take my truck."

#

The doctor was able to get her in almost as soon as she arrived. She shared her concerns about the baby and her age. She wondered if she would have issues being pregnant so late in life. Point blank, she asked the doctor, "Will I be able to carry this baby to term?"

"You've taken good care of yourself, Mrs. Barlow. You're healthy, active. I see no reason why you wouldn't be able to do just that." Dr. Reed told her. "Continue with your bed rest for the next couple of weeks. That bump doesn't look like it's anything to be taken lightly. You're a couple of months along, so we need to get you on prenatal right away. You have nothing to worry about. Many women have had successful pregnancies at your age."

Chasidy felt much relieved. She didn't want to share this news with Barlow until she knew she would be able to carry his baby to term. When she looked at Michelle after returning to the waiting room, Michelle knew the news was good. "Come on, tell me!" she said excitedly, "are we havin' this baby?"

"Well, I'm two months along and there's no reason fa me not to have a successful pregnancy." Chasidy very excitedly told her exactly what Dr. Reed said. "So yes, we're havan' this baby!"

"We have to celebrate!" Michelle told her. "I'll fix a special dinn'r t'night. Okay?"

"Okay," Chasidy agreed. "I wish we could go out or do it at yor house. Afta' Rob finds out, he may neva' let me leave home again."

"And you know this!" Michelle agreed laughing.

#

They went straight home hoping the guys hadn't made it back yet. Chasidy sat on the sofa while Michelle prepared dinner. Michelle would have preferred she be in bed when her husband got home. "If Rob finds you on that sofa when he gets here, he's nev'r gonna let me babysit you again." She warned Chasidy. Trying to convince Chasidy to get back into bed wasn't difficult at all. Not wanting Rob to look at Michelle cross-eyed, she made her way slowly back to the bedroom. And not a moment too soon. They could hear the truck pulling up in the driveway just about the time she had gotten settled in bed.

Barlow went straight to the bedroom. "How was it?" A smiling Chasidy asked him.

Barlow, who hadn't seen his wife smile since the accident, was elated, even if it returned during his absence. "It was fun. AJ really enjoyed it." Wondering what her smile was all about, he asked, "How was yor day?"

"Wonderful! Aside from missan' you that is."

"Absence makes da heart grow fond'r?" He spoke in a solemn tone.

"Robert, if my heart could grow any fonda' of you, it would be a complete surprise to me," she confessed.

"Then why did you send me away?" He probed.

"For yor own good." It wasn't a lie, only a half truth. He needed a break. It did him good to take one. "You can't tell me you don't feel betta. I see it all ova yor face."

He couldn't argue with that. "I didn't like leavin' you, but I think this is gonna be somethin' special b'tween da three of us. I don't know who had more fun; AJ learning how to fish or Al teachin' him. Thank you for suggestin' it." Suddenly he had a different expression on his face. A more solemn look. "I'm glad I was able to be a part of that."

"Yur welcome," she said. Chasidy caressed his face. "What's that look about?" She asked him hoping he would say what she needed to hear.

Holding and caressing her soft hand in return, he answered, "Nothin'. Nothin' at all."

Alan found Michelle in the kitchen all smiles also. "Somethin' smells good." He said kissing her on the cheek. "What are you all smiles for? Yur that glad to see me?"

"Absolutely!" She answered, giving him a hug to prove it.

Alan thought. "Wait. We sound like Rob and Chasidy." They chuckled.

"Where's my little guy?"

"He's out on da porch with his catch. I told him not to bring 'em in da house. But he wanted you to see 'em."

"Well, let's go take a look," she told him.

As soon as she stepped onto the porch AJ pulled a huge bass out of the bucket. "Look mom! I caught this!"

"That's a big fish!" Michelle was surprised. She looked at Al and back at AJ. "You caught that all by yorself?"

"Well, not really. Dad had to help me." His tone mellowing a little. "But he let me take him off da hook!"

"Of course, he did," Michelle said, "da dangerous part."

Al laughing, replied to that, "It's all part of fishin. He has to learn it all." Then he said to AJ, "Go put 'em back in da truck, Little Guy."

"Did Rob enjoy 'imself?" Michelle asked.

"I think he did. He seemed a little distant at times. Eith'r he was thankan' about Chasidy or…"

"Or what?" Michelle nudged.

Al shared his suspicions. "I kinda got da feelin' he was wishin' he was teachin' his own son how to fish."

"You really think that?" Michelle asked smiling profusely again.

"Yeah," Alan said. "What - are - you – smilin' about?"

Michelle couldn't hold it until dinner. She had to tell Alan right away. "Rob is in fa da biggest surprise of his life t'night."

"What?" He asked. "What's hap'ning?"

Michelle began rubbing her belly. "Chasidy's pregnant."

"Are you serious?" Al asked grinning. "That's why she's been so quiet."

"Yep. And why she wanted to get rid of her husband taday. So, she could see da doctor without 'im." He picked up his wife and swung her around like they were the ones expecting.

Alan was completely excited for his friend and completely speechless. "I can't wait to see his reaction." He hugged Michelle again. "I'm so happy for 'im."

"Me too," Michelle agreed. "You guys get cleaned up. Dinner's ready." Michelle went to the bedroom to let them know that dinner was ready also.

Before Barlow could insist she has dinner in bed, she requested, "I wanna have dinna' at da table with everyone."

"Yur supposed to stay in bed," he reminded her.

"It's lonely in here. Just for dinna'. Please." Knowing her husband couldn't say no to her; she played that 'whatever Chasidy wants' card this evening.

"I can stay with you," he reasoned.

"That would be rude, wouldn't it? Mic cooked." He knew Mic would understand. He also knew Chasidy had something going on. So, he reluctantly gave in and helped her to the dining table.

AJ started right away telling her about the fish he caught. And how his dad was gonna show him how to clean it when they get home. She was very excited for him. "There's nothan' like da feelin' of catchan' yor first fish, is there?" she said looking and grinning at AJ. "Guess what?"

"What?" AJ asked.

"Your Aunt Chasidy caught a fish too." Now looking at her husband who is still wondering what's up with her. "When I was about yor age." She added to keep a bit of mystery. "What about you, Rob. Did you catch anythan'?" she asked smiling.

"I got a couple of bites but nothin' latched on." He replied not taking his eyes off of her. He didn't know what was going on with Chasidy, but he liked it. He'd much rather see her beautiful smile over anything else. This evening it was more radiant than ever.

"Somethan' latched on," she corrected. Michelle and Alan joined her in smiling profusely. Barlow noticed.

Chasidy wanted to be sure Barlow ate his dinner not knowing if he would be able to after he heard the news. So, she let everyone finish their meal before sharing. Barlow pondered her last comment all through dinner wondering what she meant by that. He also wondered what everyone's smiles were about. The thought of a child though, never crossed his mind. "Yur done with dinn'r. Are you ready for me to help you back in bed?" He asked her.

"You don't give a girl a break, do you?" she asked him.

"Not when da girl means as much to me as you do," he said seriously without smiling.

"I sure hope you don't have a daughtar," Chasidy said to him. "That child is gonna catch it."

It took a minute to process what Chasidy said. But when he finally did, Barlow asked, "Whatta you mean, 'you hope I don't have a daught'r'?"

She started smiling again. Even bigger and brighter than before. "You hooked somethan' too." She told her husband. "One day *or night* while you were fishan'." Chasidy said handing him papers from her doctor's visit.

AJ listening attentively, asked, "Aunt Chasidy, you can fish at night too?"

"Oh yeah," Chasidy replied. "Sometimes night fishan' is da best."

"Dad, can we go night fishin' next?" He asked his dad excitedly.

Alan answered playing along with Chasidy, "You have to be a little bit old'r for night fishin'. Let's work on gettin day fishin mastered first. But don't worry, Buddy, it's comin'."

Tears began to form in his eyes as he looked at the papers. Barlow was in total shock. Chasidy watched him trying to find the words to speak to her. "How long have you known?" he asked Chasidy in semi-belief. Alan with a grin that reached all the way across the table to Barlow, sat back in his chair to watch his friend's reaction.

"Since da day of da accident." She saw the tears, hoping they were tears of joy. "Are you disappointed?"

Then he looked at Michelle. Michelle knew what he wanted to ask, but his words were hiding back in a dark corner of his mind. She answered the question he was unable to ask. "I didn't find out until aft'r you guys left taday. She asked me to take 'er to her appointment."

When he finally made it around to Alan, Alan was grinning like a Chester cat. This was a Barlow he had never seen before. Too excited to be excited. Which was fine because Alan was plenty excited for him. "Did you know too?"

"No. Mic just told me aft'r we got back. Congratulations Buddy. I couldn't be happier fa ya."

He got up from his chair and gave Chasidy a gentle hug, making sure not to squeeze too tightly. "The only thing I'm disappointed about is that you didn't tell me b'fore now. Why didn't you tell me?" Al and Mic knew that was a conversation they needed to have in private. So, they excused themselves to go home. But not before congratulating them both, again. "Let me go see them out. Don't move from this spot," he ordered.

"I'll be right here," she submitted.

Barlow escorted them to the door. Alan gave him a good friend pat on the back, after which Barlow took Chasidy back to the bed where the doctor ordered her to be for the next three weeks. "Are you comfortable? Do you need anythin' at all?" Chasidy smiled at her husband who seemed to still be in shock.

"Are you alright?" She asked him. "You look like yur stuck in a place."

Barlow began to shake his head. "I am," he answered in a daze. "It's a place I nev'r dreamed I'd be." He looked at Chasidy with a new admiration; something else he never thought could happen. "Why didn't you tell me?" He asked again. "Why didn't you let me go with you to see da doctor?"

"I wanted you with me, but I had concerns b'cause of my age and my history with pregnancy when I was younger. I just wanted to be sure I could give you this wonderful gift b'fore I told you about it. I didn't wanna get yor hopes up just to have them crushed again."

Even though that made sense to Barlow, and he understood perfectly, he still preferred to be with her. "Chasidy, you know you mean da world ta me. Yur da most important person in my life. There's only one thing you could ev'r do to disappoint me. And that's if you ev'r left me. We're in this t'gether. No matter what."

"So, yur happy, right?" Chasidy needed to hear him say it.

Barlow thought about the day with Alan and AJ. He sighed just before speaking. "Taday, I watched Al have da most wonderful time teachin' his son how to fish. It was da most beautiful thing to me. AJ was so excited. And Al, well, you know him. He laughed at everythin'. And I began to think…" He stopped. "I didn't think I'd ev'r get to experience anythin' like that." Chasidy's own eyes began to fill with tears. "Chasidy, I didn't think you could make me happier than I was already. But this…" He hugged her again. "This, I don't have da words for. I didn't think I'd ev'r b'come a father. I thought those years w're b'hind me. So yes. I'm happy. I am very, very happy." Placing his hand on her stomach. "Eight weeks, da papers said?"

"Two months." Chasidy confirmed. Seeing the unspeakable joy all over his face made her proud to be carrying his child. She wanted more than ever now to give him the gift of fatherhood.

When Michelle was carrying AJ, Al experienced morning sickness with her. He realized now that this must be what's going on with him and that he didn't have a bug after all. "That's gotta be why I was feelin bad sometimes. I thought I had caught a bug. I didn't wanna give it to you," he told her. "That's why I was keepin' my distance from you." He laughed. "You don't know how hard that was for me."

"Well, you had already given me da bug," Chasidy teased. "And I know how hard it was fa me. I thought I had done somethan wrong." Wanting to be certain all is well, she asked again, "Are you sure yur alright?"

"Bett'r, now that I can hold you again. But, but… I'll let you know t'morrow for sure aft'r all this sinks in. T'night, I just wanna hold you." He gave her a gentle kiss on her belly before snuggling up close to her.

"Careful Mr. Barlow," Chasidy said to him playfully. "That's exactly da kinda thang that got us into this mess in da first place."

"What a wonderful mess to be in," he told her.

$$\mathcal{T}he\ \mathcal{M}idwife$$

For the next three weeks Barlow clung to the doctor's instructions like Velcro. Not only did he not let Chasidy out of bed, but Alan couldn't get him to leave the house for anything. Not even to come right next door to visit him. "Ya know, Rob, she's pregnant. She's not sick." He told him one day while talking on the phone.

"I just don't want 'er to exhaust herself," he told Al.

"How can she? You won't let 'er move," he teased. But then he realized Rob had just experienced a second big trauma concerning his wife. He needed encouragement not scolding. "She's a strong woman, Rob," Al reminded him. "She's gonna be fine."

"Yes, I know. But she took a bad fall and got a concussion during her pregnancy that we knew nothin' about. If I had known, she nev'r would've gotten on those rides," Barlow argued. "I just can't b'lieve I'm gonna be a dad. I've always r'gretted missin' out on that. I realized how much when we went fishin da oth'r day."

"I had a feelin' somethin' like that was roamin' through yor head." Alan could hear the state of disbelief Barlow was *still* in. "Well, believe it Buddy. I guess yur not too old aft'r all." They both laughed. "I can't even b'gin to imagine what she'll get for Christmas this year," he added. "And as for those rides. I'm glad you didn't know. She really did have da time of her life with AJ. When she said that on da plane, she meant it."

"I know she did," Barlow agreed. "And we'll have to build a whole oth'r house just for her Christmas gifts," Barlow replied laughing. Al recognizes that the scary thing about that comment is that, knowing Rob, it could very well happen.

"I'm glad he had you guys to explore his world with. It gave me a chance to woo Mic a little. I've really been slacking in that area. For far too long. We needed that rekindling. So, I for one thank her for enjoying my son so much."

"Looking at it from that point of view," Barlow said, "Maybe I wouldn't have stopped her. Mic wore a whole new expression of happiness by da time we left Tokyo. I think she had fallen in love with you all ov'r again. She must have, to agree to marry you a second time." Barlow teased.

#

In spite of all that was going on in Chasidy's life, she was still concerned about Little Guy. He hadn't been over to visit her yet and she really wanted to spend time with him. She called Mic to see if he had mentioned it to her.

"We did talk about it. And of course, Al and I said it was ok. But every time he gets ready to come, he changes his mind. It was da last place he saw his grandma. I don't think he can handle it," Mic explained.

"Actually, that's kinda what I wanted to talk to im about. I wanna teach im about Jesus and his love fa him and his grandma Ethel. See if you can get 'im ova' here say, on Thursday eve'nans," Chasidy asked.

"I'll do that. You know what, I might even join 'im myself."

"That would be great Mic." Chasidy became excited that she would have something to do while she was confined to the bed for the next three weeks. And that she would be teaching and sharing about God again.

#

Even though bed wasn't her favorite place unless Barlow was with her, the next three weeks sailed by rather quickly. Preparing lessons for her studies with AJ helped with that. Her appointment day was here before she realized it. Barlow was all too anxious to accompany her to it. "Mr. Barlow, it's good to meet you."

"Same here, Dr.," Barlow replied. With the new visit came new concerns. Dr. Reed remembered she had concerns due to her age when she was here before, so he wasn't sure how she would receive his news on today. They noticed his look of concern right off. "Is something wrong, doctor?" Barlow asked the question Chasidy was afraid to ask.

"No, Mr. Barlow," the doctor answered. "Nothin' that the three of us can't get through together," he added.

"What does that mean?" Chasidy asked him.

"Well, it appears that you two lucky folks are having twins." He smiled so that they wouldn't become too concerned. Chasidy looked at Barlow. Barlow was afraid for her. Dr. Reed could clearly see their concern. "Mr. Barlow, like I told your wife at her first visit, she's a healthy woman. And many women have carried babies to term when they were well in their early 50's. Your wife is still at a good age for childbearing," he reassured them.

"Is there anythin special we should do?" Barlow asked.

"No. As a matter of fact, I'm taking her off bed rest. She needs all the reasonable exercise she can get." Then he looked at Chasidy. "So, let's get you mobile again. But of course, nothing strenuous. Feel free to get out and enjoy the fireworks tomorrow if you desire." Dr. Reed encouraged with tomorrow being July 4th. Chasidy was happy to hear that. She had grown pretty tired of that bed. Barlow was undecided.

On the way home, they both were unusually quiet. Chasidy was still haunted by her past even though she tried very hard not to be. Barlow couldn't fully bask in his joy seeing Chasidy so riddled with fear. She felt bad for reducing this wonderful time in his life to fear. He already harbors too much of that. "I wanna hire someone to help out around here," he told her as they entered the house.

She studied him. She knew his intentions were good. They always are. She just wasn't sure how she felt about a strange woman roaming around her home and her husband, especially after what they had gone through recently. "Are you tellan' me or askin me?"

He studied her. He knew she didn't care for hired help. She preferred to take care of her own. But this is too important to both of them. He had to take charge. He reluctantly answered in a solemn tone right after a huge sigh. "Tellin you."

"Why don't you go see what Alan's up to fa a while. Send Mic back when you get there," she suggestively ordered.

He didn't really want to leave her. He'd rather she shared what was on her mind with him. "Are you askin' me or tellin' me?"

Chasidy didn't want him thinking she was upset with him, but she needed to talk to Michelle alone. She beckoned with her finger for him to come closer and kissed him tenderly on the lips. Knowing that he wouldn't refuse her, she replied, "askan' you."

When Michelle got there, Chasidy had already started dinner. She was preparing Barlow's favorite meal. The door was open, she made her way to the kitchen where Chasidy was. "Now see, this is why yor husband is afraid to leave you alone." She fussed. Chasidy chuckled. "I heard 'im tellin' Al as I was leavin' that you kicked him out." Hearing that in Michelle's high-pitch twang sounded funnier that it probably really was.

She chuckled again. "He did?" Chasidy looked up at Michelle. "I guess I did. I needed to talk to you. I didn't want 'im to hear."

"I'm hearin' that a little too much lately. You too aren't growing apart, are you?" Michelle asked.

"No," Chasidy clarified. "We're closer than eva'. I think that's da real problem."

"That doesn't make any sense," Michelle stated.

"Just when I had gotten ova my fear of carrying one child, I find out I'm carrying two," Chasidy begins to explain.

"What! Chasidy that's wonderful!" said Michelle.

"It's also more difficult fa a woman my age. I'm worried. Rob can sense that."

"Is that what da doctor said?" Michelle asked.

"No. He said da same thing as before. He sees no reason why I shouldn't be able to carry to term," Chasidy explained.

"Then why are you so worried?" a confused Michelle asked.

Chasidy sat down at the island with Michelle to explain the reason behind her fear. She didn't prolong the story. She wasn't sure how long Rob would stay away. "My first husband left me b'cause

I couldn't have children. What if I lose these babies? What if he leaves me b'cause of it?" She looked at Michelle with tear drenched eyes. "I barely made it through my first marriage's breakup and my first husband didn't come close to being da man that Rob is. If I eva' lost Rob…." She couldn't even bear to finish the sentence.

Chasidy and Michelle have never talked about their pasts to each other before. *Apparently, Chasidy has some issues she's still dealing with.* Michelle thought. Michelle didn't know how to help her with those, but she knows Robert Barlow and how he feels about her. "Chasidy, have you forgotten how much Rob loves you?"

"I can't," she admitted, "he keeps reminding me. Just before I sent him away, he told me he was gonna hire someone to help me around da house. Evan though he knows how I feel about that kinda thang. I didn't have a say."

Michelle argued, "Girl, you have a say. You know whatever Chasidy wants Chasidy gets."

"Da bible says there's a time fa all things. That wasn't da time to play that card. He was pretty adamant." Chasidy shared other fears with her as well, how she didn't really trust other women around Barlow after what they all have just been through. And how she didn't know how he would look at her after her body began to change. All of these things wrapped up in one nice big roll is keeping her from enjoying this beautiful experience with her husband. And she doesn't know what to do about it. "This should be one of da happiest times in his life and I'm ruining that fa im," she confessed.

"Then stop," Michelle ordered. She remembered Rob's television interview from before the wedding. She reminded Chasidy. "Beauty for ashes." Chasidy entered a short reminiscent thought down memory lane. "That's what you told him, r'member?"

She did remember. She smiled at Michelle. A real smile. "Thank you."

"Glad I could help," replied Michelle.

"There is anotha good thing that came out of my doctor's visit." Chasidy said relieved.

"What's that?"

"I'm not on bed rest anymore," she said, maybe some Thursdays we can meet unda old Daniel as long as weather permits."

"I thought you wanted to teach 'im about Jesus. He's not gon be lis'ning to a word yur saying out there with all those wild animals. Sometimes I swear that boy thinks he Noah," Mic warned. "You did that, Dr. Dolittle, teachin' 'im how to catch squirrels."

"Sorry," Chasidy said laughing. "Still, I'd like to try," she insisted.

"Ok, girl," Mic agreed. "Al and I are takin AJ to see da fireworks t'morrow. You guys wanna come?"

"Run it by Rob when you get there. See what he says," Chasidy replied. "He's worse than I am when it comes to his fears."

"But does Chasidy want to go?" Mic asked again for clarity.

"Yes, I would love to," she answered. "I've been stuck in this house fa three weeks."

"Great. See ya t'morrow then," Mic said knowing Barlow wasn't about to deny his wife this simple pleasure. I'll send yor husband back. He's probably pullin' all his gray hairs out by now." They both laughed.

"Please! Thank you, b'fore he does. I'm quite fond of those gray hairs."

Barlow was in a sheer state of confusion. He practically pleaded with Alan for help. "She's not talkin' to me. I don't know what's in her head. I don't know if she's happy about da babies…."

Alan interrupted. "You mean baby, right?"

Barlow looked at Alan, grinning for the first time since he's been there. "No. I mean babies. We're havin' twins."

"Aw man! Congratulation's Buddy!" he said shaking his head at his friend. "This thang just keeps getting' bett'r and bett'r," he said. "But you have to understand da fear behind that, Rob. She was worried about da one baby and now she has two."

Barlow was remembering their conversation about her first husband when they first met. "I think it's deeper than that even. Her first husband left her because she couldn't get pregnant. I'm thinkin' maybe she thinks I'll leave her too if she can't carry this pregnancy. But she won't talk to me."

"Will you talk?" Alan asked.

"Don't ask stupid questions, Al," Barlow said.

Alan laughed and then suggested. "I'm goin' somewhere with my stupid question. If she won't talk to you, that doesn't stop you from talkin' to her."

He pondered that for a second. "Yur right. You make a darn good point," Barlow agreed.

"Fair warning though," Alan continued. "Sometimes women just need to talk to oth'r women about certain things. She doesn't mean to shut you out when she asks for Mic. She just knows yur too close to da situation. And you probably just won't understand."

"Thanks. I'll try to r'member that," Barlow said gratefully.

Michelle walked in as they were finishing up their conversation. "Okay, Rob. You've been summoned home."

"How is she?" he asked Michelle.

"She's great!" Michelle answered looking him straight faced in the eyes. "She's fine. Both of you are. Twins!" She said excitedly. "Now go enjoy this special time t'gether. FYI, she really wants to see da fireworks t'morrow."

"Oh yeah, I fa'got about that," Al told him. "We're takin' AJ."

"Then I'm takin' Chasidy," he said. Text me the info. He hugged Michelle, nodded at Alan, and went home to Chasidy. She looked at Alan pleasantly and said, "You know its gonna take all four of us to get them through this pregnancy, don't ya?"

Alan replied, "Yeah, I may need to retire until she delivers." They chuckled.

"And even then. AJ will be da only sane person left in da bunch," Michelle told him.

Alan looked at her as if she was confused. "AJ's already da only sane person in da bunch," he replied seriously.

#

Chasidy was still in the kitchen when he got there. It would be another hour before dinner would be ready. Barlow wasn't exactly pleased with what he was seeing even though Dr. Reed had given her back her freedom. "Whatta you doin'?" He asked in a tender tone that suggested his concern.

"Fixin' dinna fa my husband," Chasidy said softly. "I have permission from my doctor."

D.M. Williams

"Still. You should be restin'," he scolded sweetly. "I could've fixed dinn'r."

She raised her head to see his face. "I know. And very well. You've been doing it fa da past three weeks. You wanna help?" She asked with a smile that invited him to join her.

Barlow can never resist her smile. This is definitely a *what Chasidy wants Chasidy gets* moment. "Whatta you need me to do?" He asked, walking over towards her to render his assistance after kissing her on the cheek. Like many times before, time took a vacation as they enjoyed each other's company forgetting for a moment about their concerns.

During dinner they laid everything out on the table. Chasidy began with a difficult request, getting the hard stuff out of the way first. "Rob, if somethan' was to hap'an during da next few months and you had to make a life-or-death choice between me and da twins, you know I would want you to save our babies, don't ya?"

Barlow wondered why she would even bring up something like that. They were having such a nice time. "If yur gonna foreshadow, you could at least make it positive," he said to avoid answering.

"Positive is da easy part. We don't really have to prepare fa that," she defended. "We're always ready to receive it."

Barlow thought seriously about her request. For the past two years Chasidy has been the center of his very being. The air he breathes. He couldn't imagine living without her now that he has had a taste of her. "I have to be honest with you. I don't know if I would be able to do that. Losin' you would change my very nature. It would literally be da end of me." He had said that very thing before to Ethel the night she met Vivica. "So, let's just pray that nothin' hap'ens to cause me to have to make such a decision."

What a horrible mother-to-be I am, she thought. That answer didn't affect her nearly the way that it should have. She was too relieved to know that if she lost her babies, she wouldn't lose her husband too. "Yes," she said, "Let's pray that very prayer every night. Now that that's out of da way," Chasidy said, "I'll meet you halfway."

"I'm lis'nin'," Barlow replied.

"I'll accept parttime help with chores and dinna in da aftarnoons a few days a week. But we do breakfast t'gether," she bargained. "I don't wanna have to be rushed in da morn'ans gettan' outta bed. More than that, I still need my alone time with you."

Barlow actually liked that idea. Especially the part about the alone time. "Deal," he agreed.

"Al and Mic are takin' AJ to see da fireworks t'morrow. You wanna tag along?"

"Rob, yes I do," she answered definitely.

They talked, joked, and laughed throughout the rest of dinner, test driving baby names and discussing where to put the nursery. They decided together that this is how they wanted to spend their period of expectancy, leaving all the cares to God who is best capable of handling them.

#

The fireworks are set off over the Mississippi River each year. This would be everyone's first time attending except Chasidy. They arrived early so AJ could enjoy the games and other activities planned for the July 4th celebration. Just before dark the band started playing and Al and Mic enjoyed their version of the two-step together. Mic was drowning in continuous laughter at Al actually doing a one and a half step and her trying to keep up with him. By the time the music was over, she was completely worn out.

AJ even laughed at the funny dance performance.

"Mom, Dad, I can't b'lieve y'all did that in public," AJ spoke. "I hope none of my classmates are h're."

Alan noticed a young girl staring in AJ's direction. He pointed and said smiling, "She looks like she knows you."

When AJ looked in her direction, she waved. He waved back. Then he said, "It had to be Jessica."

"An admirer?" Alan asked.

"No. She hates me cause Mrs. Tillman says I'm her best student. She thinks she's bett'r than everybody in everything. Now everyone in school will know about you guys' goofy dancin'. She'll probably make it sound worse that it really was." AJ complained. Jessica and her friend started walking in AJ's direction. "Great. Here she comes."

Alan winked at AJ. "I got cha, Buddy."

"Hi AJ," Jessica and her friend spoke. "Are these ya parents?"

31

"Yes," AJ answered.

"Hi, I'm Al and this is his mom, Mic. You girls go to school with AJ?" Alan asked them.

"Yes, Sir." Jessica answered grinning with mischief rolling around in her little head. "I have music with 'im in Mrs. Tillman's class."

"That's wonderful," Al said. "Let me introduce you to AJ's aunt. This is Chasidy," he purposely paused, "Barlow."

The girls' mouths fell open. Chasidy reached out her hand for a handshake. "Hello girls," she said smiling enjoying what Alan was doing.

"Yur Chasidy Barlow? Owner of our school, Chasidy Barlow?" Jessica asked.

"Yes, I am. And this is AJ's uncle, Robert Barlow. He built AJ's school. We hope yur enjoyan' yor tenor there." AJ was grinning from cheek to cheek. There was no way she would talk about his parents now.

"Yes mam. I love it there," Jessica answered hurriedly. "And so does Brea." She elbowed her friend to say something.

"Oh, yes Mam. We both do." She agreed.

"Wonderful! I'm glad to hear it. It's so nice to meet y'all. Maybe I'll peep in on y'all next time I visit da school."

"Yes, mam. we'd like that. We gotta go now. See ya next year AJ. That was a cool dance, by da way," Jessica said with a change of attitude.

"See ya," AJ replied. AJ couldn't wait to thank his dad and aunt when the girls were finally out of sight. "Dad, Aunt Chasidy, that was so cool. She wouldn't dare make fun of you guys now. She's scared of being kicked outta school. Yur da coolest, Dad."

Barlow and Michelle playfully ridiculed them. "Al, y'all are wrong for that. You and Chasidy are gonna have to do a lotta prayin' for that one," Mic said.

"Yeah, Chasidy. I'm really surprised at you, intimidatin' a child that way." Barlow agreed with Mic smiling. "What have you done with my wife?"

Chasidy and Al looked at each other and then at AJ who was still grinning from cheek to cheek. Chasidy pretended to be remorseful. "AJ, yor dad was wrong fa gettan' us involved in yor school affairs like that. He should've known betta. I pray that we're both fa'givan fa it." She tried to sound serious. "But if yor mom and Uncle Rob thank yor dad and I are gonna sit back and let them pick on da sweetest boy in da whole school, they have both lost their minds. Ain't gonna hap'an." Chasidy looked back at Alan using one of his favorite sayings, "Al, those sons of Sam don't know who they're messin' with, do they?" They all laughed.

The fireworks show began right after the band finished playing. Everyone got comfortable in their seats to watch the show of lights. The sky lit up in a joyful dance in rhythm to the music that was playing. They watched in quiet awe; Chasidy snuggled in Barlow's arms, Mic snuggled in Al's arms and AJ perched on the ground directly in front of his mom and dad. It was a relaxing end to an eventful evening. Chasidy simply enjoyed the evening out with her husband and friends. When the festivities were over, Barlow let the crowd thin out a little to avoid any accidents. Chasidy was fine with that. During their wait, she expressed her appreciation, "Thank you for a lovely eve'nan. I've always loved da fireworks show. I'm glad I didn't have to miss it."

"Chasidy, you know if you want something, all you have to do is say da word and it's as good as done," Barlow assured her. "Yor happiness is my number one priority."

His quest to keeping that promise continued with their two-year anniversary was just around the corner. Barlow was racking his brain trying to come up with something extra special for Chasidy that wouldn't be too tiring for her. She enjoyed the riverboat dinner cruise on their last anniversary. So, he was thinking along those lines but something more romantic. They didn't get the opportunity to travel to Alaska to see the northern lights during their travels around the world. His heart was telling him, they should do that. So, he booked them on a fourteen-day cruise through Juneau to do just that.

They took pictures as they watched the whales put on a show, it seemed, for their benefit. And the view of the mountains was spectacular from the riverboat. However, it was the silent motion-picture of the beautiful night sky that captivated Chasidy. She has wanted to see the aurora borealis up close and personal for all of her life. This is a real-life dream come true for her. Barlow was concerned about the coolness in the air for fear that she might become ill. Chasidy didn't mind the chill though. It only gave her another reason to snuggle close to him in his arms; *her favorite place to be.* "Rob," she said smiling up at him. "How did I get to be so blessed? This is da best anniversary eva'."

Barlow twirled one of her curly locks around his finger gazing into her sparkling brown eyes. "Just what I wanted to hear, Beautiful," he said just before the kiss that always followed.

#

The cruise was extremely relaxing. But traveling of any kind is tiresome. That doubles when you're carrying two small bodies around all day. When they returned home, Barlow didn't have to insist that Chasidy get her rest. The bed had become her refuge for the next couple of days. Barlow feared the cruise was too much for her. Her next checkup is scheduled for Wednesday, but a worried Barlow took her in early on Monday to be certain she was alright. "A fourteen-day cruise," Dr. Reed repeated. "Well, Happy Anniversary."

"Thank you," she replied. "Yes. I told him I was fine. Just a little tired," Chasidy informed the doctor. "But my overly protective husband insisted we come in early."

Dr. Reed, not wanting to discount a future father's concerns replied in his favor, "It never hurts to be cautious. Let's take a look at you." He checked the chart for her vitals first. "You have a slight temperature. We need to find out what that's about," he said to them. "Are you feeling any pain?"

Chasidy answered slowly, "No."

"We'll do another ultrasound to see what's going on just to be safe."

Both Barlow and Chasidy were brought to tears when they saw the two little bodies curled up in a bundle inside her. At that moment their pregnancy became very real to them. Chasidy vowed silently to become more sensitive to Barlow's concerns. She didn't know it yet but that would turn out to be a good thing because Barlow would become more adamant about Chasidy doing as little as possible until after their babies arrived.

Dr. Reed didn't find anything unusual going on. He told her to use a cold compass to treat the fever, but if it got any worse to come back. At this stage in her pregnancy, he didn't want added drugs in her system. After two days, the fever had gone away. This was a good thing, their first interview for Chasidy's Home Care Assistant is scheduled for eleven am. There will be another at one pm and the last one for the day at three.

#

Their 11 o'clock arrived thirty minutes early. Her application stated her age as twenty-nine. To Chasidy, she looked every bit of eighteen and as pretty as she is young. As far as she was concerned, that interview would be a waste of time. She wasn't having a beautiful young lady with an eighteen-year-old body prancing around her husband while her body became more deformed each day. However, she gracefully went through the motions.

Barlow was all smiles throughout the interview knowing full well that Chasidy wasn't about to have this woman parading around in front of him in their home with a body like that. He was enjoying watching Chasidy pretend to be interested. He purposely prolonged the interview process; his way of teasing his wife, grinning all the while as he questioned the applicant. Chasidy periodically glanced at Rob, but he never looked back at her. He knew he'd burst into laughter in the middle of the interview if he did.

As soon as the interview was over and the young lady was out the door, Chasidy looked at her husband who finally decided to make eye contact with her and said, "No."

Barlow gave a full bellied-up laugh at Chasidy and asked, "Don't I get a say?"

"Yes," Chasidy answered as she ripped up the young lady's application and put it back into her folder. "As long as yor say is No."

The 1 o'clock was an older lady who came off too pushy. If she was that way during the interview, she would likely be worse after she was hired. Barlow didn't need anyone adding more stress to Chasidy's already delicate condition. He escorted her to the door and turned to Chasidy shaking his head, "No." Chasidy agreed completely.

They hoped the three o'clock would be more promising. Her age was suitable, well matured. When they met, she seemed kind

35

enough. Proclaimed to be a very good cook and willing to do the light chores required for the position. But something was off about her. To Chasidy, she seemed frail. To Barlow, it appeared she wasn't telling them something. "We'll get back with you," he told her as he escorted her out. "What are you thinkin'?" He asked Chasidy.

"She's too frail. And she's not tellan' her whole story," Chasidy answered.

"That's exactly what I was thinkin'," he replied. "Bett'r luck t'morrow, I hope."

The next day Barlow prepared breakfast. Chasidy was slow about getting up and certainly not looking forward to another day of interviews. Her only comfort; *at least I'm not on the opposite side of them.* The interviews started at nine. And first off, it looked as if they would be in for another day like yesterday as their nine o'clock was not impressive at all. Even Barlow was starting to rethink this whole Home Care Assistant idea. It wasn't anything he wasn't accustomed to, but Chasidy and the babies were too important to him. There is no room for errors.

When the eleven am applicant arrived, things took a turn for the better. Immediately upon opening the door, Barlow liked her. He had interviewed many times for his company. Each time he had this perception about an applicant, they turned out to be just what the company needed. He hoped Chasidy would pick up on the same vibes. "Good morning, I'm Berta Fields."

"Good mornin' Ms. Fields. Robert Barlow." Chasidy heard the salutations. "Come in please and meet my wife." They turned the corner to find Chasidy on the sofa. "This is Chasidy."

"Nice to meet you, Mam," the lady said.

"You too, Ms. Fields. Please have a seat," Chasidy invited.

"Thank you. You have a beautiful place out here. Just beautiful," Ms. Fields told them.

"Thank you." Both Chasidy and Barlow answered. Ms. Fields is in her late sixties, a nice mature age for this type of work. During the interview they learned that she is quite knowledgeable. She had been a cook for two of the finer restaurants in Cool River Springs, her application boasted. But it was what wasn't in her application that impressed Barlow; her tenor as a midwife which she revealed after she learned that Chasidy is pregnant with twins. At that point

Barlow was sold. She was as good as hired. Chasidy was impressed as well and leaning heavily in the same direction as her husband as she listened to Ms. Fields speak. "I was a midwife for twenty-three years until the need for the occupation kind of dwindled off," she told them. "That's when I started cooking. My most favorite thing to do."

"Da position requires light housework," Chasidy told her. "Rob and I don't really make a mess, but laundry, dishes, and occasional touchups. That type-a thang. Would that be a problem fa you?"

"Not one bit," the lady responded. "In fact, I'd insist on it. Yor only concern should be taking care of yorself, yor husband and those babies yur carrying. This is a special time for the two of you. You should be enjoying every moment of it."

By the time Ms. Fields had finished talking, Chasidy had decided also that she had the job. "If hired Ms. Fields, when would you be available to start?" Barlow asked her.

"I can start today, Mr. Barlow. I was just thinking how tired Mrs. Barlow looked this very moment. Perhaps you should get some rest, Dear." Ms. Fields all but put the seal on the already sealed deal.

"Why don't you come back at three and let us try out some of that cookin' of yors," Barlow said to her, "welcome aboard."

Chasidy sat with a smile plastered to her face at her husband's unhidden excitement over this woman he had just met moments ago. "Don't your lovely wife get a say?" Ms. Fields asked.

"Yes, she does," Barlow said looking at Chasidy and smiling also, knowing that she felt the same way. "As long as her say is yes."

Chasidy was glad Ms. Fields was their eleven o'clock. She didn't feel like she could make it through another interview. An overwhelming tiredness had suddenly come over her. "Looks like we'll be seeing you at three, Ms. Fields," Chasidy concluded. Once Ms. Fields was gone, she decided to follow her advice. "Now that that's ova, I'll leave da last two interviews to you." She kissed him on the cheek. "I'm gonna go lay down."

"Are you okay?" An always concerned Barlow asked.

"Yes. Just tired. Like da midwife said. I wanna be rested up fa bible class this eve'nan with AJ." After finding such a wonderful candidate, Chasidy wasn't even uneasy about the idea of help anymore. "Thank you," she said to Barlow.

"For what?" he asked her.

"Fa always thankan' about what's good fa me. Fa gettan' me help," she confessed. "I can be set in my old-fashioned ways sometimes. Or my superwoman mentality. This really isn't da time fa eitha' one of those."

"Yur welcome," he said, "always. It was yor old-fashioned ways that made me fall in love with you." Then he thought about what she was doing when they first met. "But it was yor superwoman mentality that lured me in in da first place."

"Please wake me if I sleep too long. He'll be here by four," she said.

"Ok."

From the very first day Ms. Fields worked out perfectly. Chasidy was quite comfortable with her in the house and Barlow felt more at ease when he had to leave knowing Chasidy was in capable hands. Not only was he impressed with her immaculate cooking skills but he also more than liked the fact that she instinctively kept a close eye on Chasidy's health without either of them asking.

The fever that Dr. Reed had spoken with Chasidy about kept reoccurring. Ms. fields had concerns about that. Chasidy volunteered to spend more time in bed because of it. Barlow was happy he didn't have to argue with her about it. But he too, didn't like that the fever kept coming back. Ms. Fields wanted to keep a closer eye on her, but she needed to be there for more than a few hours a day to do it. However, it wasn't time just yet to bring up moving in with them. She had to ease into that. Or so she thought.

Some Thursdays Chasidy would cancel her bible lessons with AJ and Mic. That also worried Barlow. He knew how much she enjoys teaching the bible. Sometimes he would sit in on their class. She would get so wrapped up in the teachings she would forget about the time. AJ was just as eager as Chasidy, there were times he would get to asking questions that Chasidy couldn't even answer. She never pretended to know it all. He finally came to realize that her answer to those questions would involve homework, when she would tell him, "Let's google that and next week we'll discuss what we've found." Eventually, Michelle and Barlow got in on some of that action and they would have a real bible experience discussion. That suited Chasidy just fine. What she really liked about it was how Barlow really got into the discussion. He began to look forward to the classes also.

One evening when they were having dinner, Ms. Fields noticed Chasidy was looking flushed and tired. She felt compelled to say something. In fact, she was thinking it was time to move to the next level. "Sweetheart how are you feeling?" she asked Chasidy as she sat her plate down in front of her.

"Fine I suppose," Chasidy told her in a breathless tone. "I'm just really tired when this feva' comes ova' me. I can't take anything fa it so I just have to wait it out. It usually goes away after a couple of days. But it takes so much out of me while it's here."

"Well, what does yor doctor say?" Ms. Fields asked before realizing she may be overstepping her boundaries just a little. "I'm sorry Dear, I'm stirring in stew I haven't been asked to taste," she purposely commented to see what their reactions would be. Barlow sat quietly listening.

"It's fine. I don't mind at all," Chasidy assured her. Barlow liked that Chasidy could speak with her so freely about her health. Maybe her midwife experience had something to do with that. Or maybe it was her Ethel persona. Chasidy could talk to Ethel about anything. Chasidy continued speaking, "After a couple of visits and Dr. Reed not being able to pinpoint a cause, Rob and I decided we would just keep an eye on it ourselves. If it got any worse, we would go back."

Barlow noticed that Ms. Fields had a reaction to that last comment Chasidy made. "Whatta you think about that, Ms. Fields?" He asked her.

"Oh, I'm sure da doctor knows what he's doing," she answered.

"I'm sure he does too. But I'd still like to hear yor thoughts," he insisted. "Please sit down. Bring yor plate."

She began cautiously. "Multiple births can be tricky sometimes. Not meaning to scare you, Hun. But because there's more than one child, its sometimes difficult to see the whole story. There could be something going on that even all that fancy equipment can't see."

Barlow instincts were whispering to him. "Have you experienced that b'fore durin' yor Midwife years?"

She didn't answer that question for fear of frightening Chasidy. Instead, she said, "If it's suitable with you two, I'd like to be yor wife's caregiver also while I'm here. I'll need equipment to monitor her vitals. When she goes to see her doctor, she can take da information I gather with her. It might help 'im figure out da fever," she finished.

Barlow and Chasidy both knew she was talking around something. They both also believed she knew what she was talking about. Barlow's unexplainable trust in Ms. Fields would have him agree right away. Having her to help around the house is one thing. He could reasonably take the forefront on that. But caring for Chasidy is invading her personal space. He had to allow his wife to make that decision. "Chasidy?"

Just after Chasidy and Barlow were first married, the feeling of being his wife was surreal. Even then she had never dreamed of having his baby. She was quite content just being his wife. But now that she's faced with that very real possibility, she wants nothing more than to make him a father. What are the odds of someone showing up for a Home Care Assistant interview and turns out to be a Midwife, one of the last remaining few of a dying profession? *Perhaps this is Ms. Field's real purpose for being here,* she thought. How could she refuse such a gift sent from God Himself? "I would like that very much, Ms. Fields." That's just what Barlow was hoping she would say.

"Can we go a step further with that?" He asked Ms. Fields while looking at Chasidy. "Will you stay with us until da babies are born? That is, if you don't have family at home to take care of."

Chasidy smiled an immediate smile of relief. Before Ms. Fields could answer, she added. "Please, won't ya say yes? Rob and I are two *nearly scared outta our wits old folks* tryan' to get through this with our sanity intact. We need you." Looking back at Barlow, she added, "I need you."

"You don't have to beg." Ms. Fields told them. "I've been wanting to ask you that very thing for days now." She chuckled. "I didn't want you to think that I'm homeless or something like that and just looking for a place to stay." She laughed some more.

Barlow and Chasidy joined her in brief laughter. "We wouldn't have thought that. We would've been too happy to have ya," Barlow assured. "Make me a list of da equipment you need. It'll be waitan for you t'morrow when you get here," he told her. Both he and Chasidy were relieved.

Unlike Barlow, Chasidy has experienced the gift of expectancy. But she wasn't this nervous when she was carrying Caitlin, and she experienced that pregnancy all on her own. With the twins she has the support of her loving very overly protective husband who would do anything in his power to ensure her safety and theirs. Even knowing that, she just couldn't shake her fears; as much as she wanted to, for his sake. So, she tried her best to keep them hidden from him.

When the thought of Caitlin crossed her mind, she suddenly realized she hadn't told her the news. She had no idea what her reaction would be. Or any of the rest of her family for that matter. Not that their opinions would make a difference, but it would be nice to have the added support. Once again, Barlow picked up on her vibes. "Whatcha thinkin' Beautiful?"

Chasidy hesitated for just a moment, but then said, "You know what I haven't done?"

"No, what's that?"

"Told any of my family," she confessed.

"Why is that? You don't think they would be happy for you."

"Oh, yeah. I'm sure they would. I'm actually thanking about Caitlin."

"She would have issues with it?" He asked in a disappointed tone.

"Ugh, yeah," Chasidy said. "She's as bad as you are when it comes to worrying about me."

Barlow was reminded of the kidnapping. "Yeah, I r'member that."

"I'll call her t'morrow just in case she gets upset. I don't need that tossan' around in my head when I'm tryan' to fall asleep t'night."

"No, you don't," Barlow agreed. "I give you a hard enough time already," he added smiling. "Do you need some support?"

"Sweetheart, I've been handlan' my child fa ova' twenty-three years. "I've got it," she said in her motherly confidence.

The next morning Barlow prepared the most delightful breakfast for Chasidy of heart-shaped Belgium waffles with glazed strawberries and crispy bacon just like she likes it. He even served it in bed to her. Her smile was a tell-all when he sat the plate down in front of her. Before she could even ask, he said, "I'm just r'turnin' a favor or two." Then he gave her a good morning kiss. "Plus, I thought you might need da superpower to help with yor phone call this mornin'," he added.

"Well, I'm not all that worried about da phone call. It's been me and that child against da world for all of her life. This is not a season fa change." She took a bite of her waffle. "Fa future references, you do not need an excuse to fix this breakfast fa me. Thank you!" He crawled in bed beside her with his own plate and they both enjoyed breakfast in bed.

"Sounds like I did good," he boasted.

"Um," she added, "much betta' than good."

Chasidy called Caitlin directly after breakfast. She figured Caitlin would be at work, but that would actually work to her advantage if things went south for some unexplainable reason. "Caitlin, I've got some news. Are you sittan' down?"

Caitlin bopped down in her chair. "I am now. What's da news?"

"Yor gonna be a big sister!" Chasidy said excitedly.

"Get outta Dodge!" Caitlin shouted. "You do know yur old, right?"

"Thanks for da r'minda'," Chasidy said being every bit of sarcastic. "I'm not old. Dr. Reed said I'm still well in my childbearan' years."

"Apparently!" Caitlin shouted again. But then she caused herself to calm down, not wanting to upset her mom. "How much pregnant are you?" Caitlin asked how far along she is in a way that only she could.

"Five months."

"Five months?" Caitlin's voice rose again. "And yur just tellin' me."

"Well," Chasidy began to explain, "during da first two, we had no idea. And it's literally taken da next two for Rob and I to process it ourselves. But it's finally real to us now afta' seeing da babies during da last dr.'s visit."

"Babies?" Caitlin repeated.

"Twins," Chasidy said.

"Are you happy?"

"Very," Chasidy answered.

"Is Dad happy?" Caitlin asked.

"Who?" Chasidy wanted her to repeat what she said.

"Is – Dad – happy - too?" Caitlin repeated it but slower.

Chasidy was nearly speechless. It took her a minute to respond. "Yes, he is. More than evan I can imagine."

"Then that's all that matters, Mom. I love you guys. Take care of yorself. I'll be ov'r soon to check on ya. Gotta get back to work."

Chasidy sat in awe on the sofa for a few minutes, processing the conversation. Barlow joined her on the sofa as soon as he finished the dishes. "That bad huh?"

When she looked at him, though her eyes were teary, her expression was clearly happy. "You tell me. I told her she was going to be a big sistar. She reminded me how old I am." They both chuckled. "She asked me if I was happy. And then she…." Chasidy stopped in complete awe.

"What?" Barlow asked anxiously.

Then she asked, "Is Dad happy?"

"What?" Barlow asked her to repeat.

"That was my exact reaction. I wanted her to repeat it. She didn't mind repeating it at all. In fact, she spoke evan slower so I could really grasp what she was sayan', probably remindan' me of my age again." They laughed again.

"I knew I liked that girl," Barlow replied approvingly.

"She said as long as we're happy, that's all that mattars."

"And she's absolutely right, Mrs. Barlow."

When Ms. Fields arrived early at 1pm they settled her in Ethel's room which hadn't been opened since her passing. She didn't bring much with her, just one small bag that Barlow helped her with. "This is all you have?" He asked her.

"And plenty enough," she answered. "An old lady doesn't need much," she said as they showed her the room. "Oh my," she said. "This is an absolutely lovely room. It almost looks as if you two were expecting me." She chuckled as she spoke. Chasidy was glad the room was being used again. She missed Ethel. Seeing Ms. Fields settling in there gave her the calming feeling of their Ethel being home again. They both noticed she already looked quite at home there.

"Sorry I didn't get a chance to freshen it up for ya," Chasidy apologized.

"Now, don't you worry about that. I'll take care of it."

"I'll show you where everythan' is when yur ready."

Barlow was trying to put his own feelings into perspective. Ms. Fields had such a calming effect on him as well. A familiar calming effect like the ones he experienced with his beloved Ethel. The way that he immediately received her and trusted her; much like when he first met Chasidy and he didn't realize that the familiar part of her belonged to Rebecca. This time it didn't catch him by surprise. The conclusion that he's arrived to at this very moment is the same one he made when he first opened the door to meet her weeks ago, *Ethel is back.* "Well," he said, "if there's anythin' else you need, just let me know."

With a constant present watch over Chasidy, Barlow felt better about venturing out. He took a stroll over to Al's house to catch up with what was going on at work the very day Ms. Fields moved in.

Alan was glad to see him out and about. "Hey. Did she put you out again?" Barlow laughed a real laugh. Alan noticed. "You look great man. What's hap'ened?" He said as Barlow walked into his office.

"We've got somebody in our corner who knows what they're doin'," Barlow answered, "I hired a midwife."

"A midwife?" Alan jested. "Those people still exist?"

"I think we got da last one," Barlow joked. "But seriously, she really is a Godsend. We w're lookin' to hire someone parttime to help Chasidy around da house. When this lady came and it turned out she used to be a midwife, we had to have her," Barlow explained. "We just got 'er moved in taday."

That alarmed Alan. "You moved 'er in already? You must really trust her to leave 'er alone with Chasidy so soon." Alan spoke with his radar up, thinking about the kidnapping.

"I do. And not just me, but Chasidy trusts her too," Barlow added. "When I first mentioned I was gonna hire her some help, I thought it was gonna be our first disagreement. I told you about it. She doesn't care for her privacy being invaded. But yesterday, she practically begged her to move in to help her during da pregnancy."

"Well," Alan said half-heartedly, "I hope she works out fa you guys. I know Chasidy really wants to give you da gift of fatherhood."

Barlow could see that Alan had some reservations about Ms. Fields. He was sure that would change once he met her though. "And I really wanna receive it. I can hardly relax some nights just thinkin' about da little fellas or gals bumpin' around in there." They shared a proud father smile between them after which, Barlow changed the subject. "What's goin on with you? You looked perturbed about something when I walked in." He handed Barlow the proposal he was going over again for a perspective client. "This looks good. What's da problem?"

Alan sat back in his chair readying himself for a long talk. "Da problem is, they won't even look at it. They won't deal with me. Period. They say they'll only talk business with you."

"Did you let em know I was retired?"

"Of course."

"And you informed them that they weren't gonna get a bett'r proposal even from me."

"Yep," Alan answered, "as much as I could."

"So, Whatta you gonna do?" Barlow asked him, seeing he was baffled.

Alan sighed. "Part of me wants to reach out to 'em again. That's why I was going ov'r da proposal again. But da only oth'r thang I can do is move on. Leave 'em to pond'r da error of their ways." Barlow nodded his head once. Alan knew that meant his partner approved.

"Anythin' else on da table?"

"Yeah, I'm getting' ready to head out with a crew to New Mexico next week. We're buildin' a hotel there. Five-star luxury chain."

"And yur going with 'em?" He thought about AJ. "Does that mean that AJ is bett'r?"

"Just ta kick it off. Then I'll be back. I'm filled to da brim with meetings." Then he looked him seriously in the face, "AJ? We didn't realize he was struggling so much with Ethel's death. That kid sure knows how to hold stuff in. I think between Dr. Milo and Chasidy, he's comin' around though."

"Wonder where he gets that from? Listen out for da jokes," Barlow insinuated the resemblance to his dad. "Sounds like you might be keepin' yorself a little too busy." Barlow advised, "Even now, yor beautiful wife is home and yur in yor office mullin' ov'r a proposal," he told him. "R'member that promise you made to 'er a few months ago? Don't make da same mistake I made. You have a wife and kid at home. Work will be there whenev'r you get back to it. And it sounds like AJ needs his dad's attention for a while long'r. Dr. Milo nor Chasidy can hold a candle to you." He smiled proudly. Barlow left him a little bit of professional advice before heading home. "R'member, we're da best in da business. We don't beg. If you need to, let Bradley lighten yor load some."

"I think I'll do that. Thanks," Alan agreed. "And I haven't fa'gotten my promise to Mic. I have somethin' in da works as we speak, I think she'll be very excited about."

"That's what I like to hear," he said in approval. Then Barlow reminded him of something else, "You don't have to wait for me to make suggestions. Yur runnin' this show now. Make it work for ya. You had my back when I was there. Put somebody in place that you can trust and rely on."

"Just what I needed to hear, Rob," Al said relieved.

"Well now you've heard it," nodding once at his partner. He also wanted to put Al's mind at ease about Chasidy's new help. "I'd love for you guys to meet Ms. Fields. How 'bout dinner at our house b'fore you leave?"

"Sounds good."

"I'll text you with a day," Barlow said and then left for home.

Ms. Fields was turning the lights off in the kitchen when Barlow walked in. She gave Chasidy a thorough check over before she settled in bed, and she was about to retire herself. "Mr. Barlow, I was hoping you got back before I retired for the evening. Have a glass of tea with me? I'd like to talk to you for just a minute." Barlow was reminded of his Ethel again. *'Tea is better for talking,'* he remembered her always saying. While he was pondering that thought, Ms. Fields came into the living room with two glasses of tea.

"Nothing beats a cold talk over a good glass of sweet tea." She laughed at herself. "I'm sorry, turn that around, Dear."

Barlow laughed also. "What's on yor mind? Is Chasidy alright?"

"Well, that's what I wanted to talk with you about." Barlow began to look concerned. "No. No." Ms. Fields noticed. None of that. One of you needs to keep a calm head at all times. And by *one,* I mean you. Her emotions will be all over the place until she's holding those babies in her arms. There's nothing we can do about that," she warned.

Barlow took a sip of his tea waiting for her to continue. He believed she purposely procrastinated in order for him to contain his composure. "Okay. I'm lis'nin."

"I was concerned when I learned about the fever yesterday," she started.

"I noticed that" he replied.

"Not much gets past you, does it?" Ms. Fields commented.

"Wait 'il you get to know Chasidy," he responded smiling.

"You were right. I have seen a similar case before. I didn't want to say that in front of the Mrs. She's a strong woman, but every woman weakens during this time in their life. She has a life other than her own to consider. That's an important responsibility."

"I agree." Barlow immediately remembered Chasidy's request she asked of him a short while ago. "What is it, Ms. Fields?"

She continued. "Fevers come from infections. It's the body's way of trying to fight off the intruder. Sometimes in multiple births, a fetus doesn't mature as it should like the other one is doing. It can cause serious problems. Sometimes the body thinks the un-developing fetus is an intruder. This is the part I didn't want your wife to hear. We don't want her worrying until we find out if there's something to worry about. But one of you needs to know. And by *one,*" she stated again, "I mean you, for right now."

"Dr. Reed hasn't said anythin' about one of the babies not developin' properly. He says they're comin' along as scheduled," Barlow explained.

"Those are the two he sees," Ms. Fields told Barlow.

She had Barlow's attention even more. "What does that mean?"

"Like I said yesterday, sometimes it's hard to see things even with an ultrasound. That's such a cramped space in there. When I examined Chasidy this evening, for just a second or two, I thought I heard a third heartbeat. Very faint and very weak, but I'm certain it was a heartbeat."

"But…" Barlow looked confused. He nev'r…."

"Babies are fickle, Mr. Barlow. Even in the womb. It's almost like they want us to know right off that they're the ones who are really in charge." She chuckled. "If that little guy is hiding behind the others and not progressing the way that he should be, it would be very difficult for Dr. Reed to detect him. That goes double for the heartbeat. I only heard it for a second or two myself before it faded back off."

"But how can you hear what he couldn't hear."

"Because I was listening for it. He was relying on his equipment to tell 'im."

"Whatta we do?" Barlow asked anxiously. "I've written up a plan of action. We need to get these babies moving around before her next appointment." She reached for her notebook on the table and explained it to Barlow. "I'm going to share this with Mrs. Barlow tomorrow. She was already asleep when I finished it. I want her to take a fifteen minute walk every morning after breakfast. No more than that. And the same in the afternoon. I've noticed she's usually pretty tired after dinner so before dinner is fine. We're aiming for thirty minutes of exercise a day. Make sure she takes a warm lavender bath before bed, not a shower. She's pretty good herself about resting and I'll make sure the meals are healthy. We'll see what her doctor says when she gets back to him."

Barlow once again is in shock. "Three babies," He repeated, looking at Ms. Fields in bewilderment. "What if he can't find da oth'r baby? Can you tell 'im what you know?"

"I'm not a doctor," she kindly protested, "he's not gonna listen to me. But if the baby doesn't show his little face and he's not developing properly, Chasidy will become very sick. Possibly even life-threatening sick. That's why I wanted to be here to monitor her."

Barlow thought again about the request Chasidy asked of him. "Ms. Fields, not long ago, Chasidy said to me that if somethin' hap'ened durin' her pregnancy and I had to choose b'tween her life and da babies' lives, she wants me to choose da babies. Do you think she was havin' a premonition or somethin'?"

"That's hard to say. But I would think not. I believe she was just making sure her babies would be taken care of. That's what good mothers do. They put their children first."

Barlow could easily buy into that. She's always putting him first before herself. Even though Barlow liked that answer, he still had difficulty with her request. "Neith'r of us had seen their little bodies inside 'er at that time. I told 'er I didn't think I could do that. Now, I don't know what I would do. I don't wanna lose any of 'em."

"Well, you just leave all that up to God," she said. "And we'll do as much as we can within our power to make sure you don't." She smiled a comforting smile at him. "Now you go get some rest. We have a plan. Try not to worry."

Before he left, he gave her a head's up about inviting his family to dinner. "Pick a day that's suitable for you before Monday. He's goin' outta town next week."

"Oh, tomorrow's fine with me," she said excitedly. "I'd love to meet them."

"T'morrow it is then."

Barlow tried to relax. He had gotten an earful that he didn't need to hear just before bed. But Ms. Fields was right. He had to be strong for Chasidy's sake. He knows that she stresses when he's stress. He learned that during their therapy sessions. He had never learned how to really pray, but Chasidy told him once that it was only talking. The difference is Who he's talking to. He sat out on the patio connected to their bedroom and had a good long talk with God. He told God how much he loves Chasidy. And how he had lived contently all these years before she strolled gracefully into his life. Then he told Him, "That goes double for children." He never allowed himself to fantasize about that type of thing because he never thought he would ever be married again. And then he said to God, "Chasidy told me once that you allow things to hap'en to us b'cause you don't want us to fa'get how much we need you. I guess I still tend to fa'get that, thinkin' my money can fix everythin'. I know you brought Ms. Fields here to help us through this. She's too perfect to be from anyone but You. Thank you for that." When he came to the end of his speaking, he made a soul-searching confession and asked a heart-wrenching request, "God, I do need you. I'm realizin' that more and more each day. Please don't make me choose b'tween my wife and my children."

He lingered a while longer enjoying the still peacefulness of The Grove. The cool Autumn night air was just what he needed to help him regroup. When he finally climbed in bed with Chasidy putting his arm around her thinking on how blessed he is, in her natural reflexes she immediately snuggled up close to him, never awakening.

The following morning, she woke with a burst of energy she hadn't felt for a long time. The fever had gone. Ms. Fields had suggested she take a bath in place of a shower to see if it made a difference in how she felt. It did. She left her husband sleeping like a baby and proceeded to the kitchen to fix breakfast. Ms. Fields wasn't even up yet. But she did rise before Barlow. "Good morn'an Ms. Fields," Chasidy said.

"Good morning, Dear. Looks like that bath worked a small miracle," Ms. Fields told her commenting on how different she looked from last night. "Why didn't you wake me? I would've done this."

"Yes, it did. Thank you, fa suggesting it. And I didn't wake you because I still very much enjoy doing thangs fa my husband. When we made this deal to allow him to hire someone to help me, he promised that breakfast would be our special time. Breakfast doesn't take much outta me." Chasidy had just put the last of breakfast on the island and was going to go check on Barlow when he walked into the kitchen. "Hi sleepy head! I was just coming to see about you," Chasidy said greeting him with a smile.

"Hi," he replied with an extra-long hug. Pausing time, as he stared down at her twirling one of her curly locks around his finger and giving her the kiss that comes with it. "Looks like you had a good rest last night." He complimented her on how refreshed she looked.

"And you have that same look." She complimented in return. "Sit down. I'll fix yor plate."

"No, both of you sit," Ms. Fields told them. "You've done the hard part. I'll fix the plates."

Barlow looked at Chasidy's radiant face smiling his handsome smile. He kissed her passionately on the lips. "Thank you for breakfast. FYI. I wouldn't miss our special time for nothin' in da world," he said hinting that he had heard her comment about breakfast.

She didn't see that coming at all. "Yur so welcome," she said pleasantly surprised, "I feel da same way."

Ms. Fields could see they were in a mood to be left alone so after placing their plates on the table, she prepared her plate and started out of the kitchen. "Where're you going?" they both asked almost simultaneously.

"I was just gonna leave you two to your privacy."

"Nonsense," Chasidy told her.

"You'll sit right h're with us," Barlow added.

And then Chasidy, "I promise we'll behave."

During breakfast Ms. Fields went over her care plan for Chasidy. She didn't tell her about the third heartbeat. She wanted her to stay as upbeat as she is this very minute. So did Barlow for that matter. Chasidy especially liked the walks with her husband. They hadn't really done that since she became pregnant. Barlow was afraid it was too much for her. And she didn't want to put any added stress on him. For such a strong man, he weakens so much when it comes to her. "Did you hear that Mr. Barlow?" she flirted. "We're ordared to spend thirty minutes a day frolickan'. I expect those ordars to be carried out."

"Mrs. Barlow, I was just about ta say, I won't be stood up."

Ms. Fields picked up her plate and stood up from the table. "So much for behaving." She told them shaking her head and grinning as she left the kitchen. "Leave the dishes for me. You two just take care of that frolicking stuff." They laughed. "Don't forget to tell her about dinner tonight."

"Dinna'?"

"I told Al yesterday I wanted them to meet Ms. Fields. And she said tonight was a good time to do that."

"Great! Company," she exclaimed. "And I'll get to see AJ too. With this fever off and on so much, we haven't been consistent with our studies. But he's been reading to me ova' da phone. I enjoyed that."

Ms. Fields prepared a delicious oven broiled steak smothered in an onion and green pepper gravy with creamy mashed potatoes and steamed French green beans. It was the golden garlic bread that set the real aroma at the table. AJ was so taken with Ms. Fields, Alan had to keep reminding him to eat. Extremely untypical of the eleven-year-old, especially since steak and potatoes is one of his favorite meals. This one is very similar to how his grandma Ethel used to fix it. After the third time Alan insisted he eat, Michelle decided she would try a more direct approach. "AJ. Stop staring. Yur being rude. Eat yor dinn'r."

"Oh, he's alright, Dear. He's not hurting anything," Ms. Fields told Mic. "It's been a long time since a handsome gentleman looked at me like that." Then she winked at AJ, and he became even more intrigued with her. "I can fix his plate to take with him if he's not up to eating right now."

Barlow and Chasidy watched him in awe. Barlow had invited them over because he wanted to see Alan's reaction to Ms. Fields. But AJ's reactions said it all. AJ is seeing what he and Chasidy sees in her, Ethel. When Barlow walked out with them after dinner, he asked Al what he thought of her. "I could tell you had concerns when I told you about Ms. Fields. Are you still leery?" His answer didn't surprise him.

"Actually, no," Alan said. "It's weird, but she feels like family." Barlow laughed. "Did you see her wink at AJ?"

"Yeah, I saw that," Barlow answered.

D.M. Williams

"Did you see how AJ's little face lit up?"

"I noticed that too." There was a pause.

"Don't think I'm crazy, Rob." He still hesitated. "Ethel used to do that when she was takin' his side against Mic.

"She did?" That was something Barlow didn't know.

"Every single time," Al told him. That put a warm feeling in Barlow's spirit.

After dinner, Chasidy felt so good, she helped Ms. Fields with dishes before her walk with Barlow. Having her there made a huge difference in the atmosphere. Chasidy didn't worry about the pregnancy nearly as much as she did before.

Family Reunion

With AJ's birthday approaching September tenth right after the start of school, Alan wanted to celebrate before the school term began. None of them had ever seen a rodeo before. He was sure AJ would enjoy one. But Alan had another plan in play also for AJ's twelfth birthday. One that he hoped would be pleasing to Michelle also. In actuality, he wasn't sure how she would feel about it. With Ethel gone and AJ missing her so much; and Alan's temporary parents always off on worldly adventures, Alan thought maybe it was time for AJ to meet his biological grandparents. And perhaps in the process reunite Michelle with her parents. He was hoping Barlow and Chasidy could come along.

He's second guessing himself so much by now, he's not even sure exactly how to bring it up to Barlow. It was now only three days before they would have to leave. He and Chasidy were relaxing in the rockers on the porch when Al walked up. Barlow could see right off that Alan came with a mission. He didn't even have to ask what was going on. Alan began immediately. "This is a nice eve'nin' for that," he started, referring to them enjoying the rockers. "Rob, I need to talk to you."

"I'll go get you guys some tea," Chasidy said, seeing the seriousness in his expression.

"Bring three glasses," Alan said. "I'd like yor thoughts too."

"I'll be right back," she said.

Barlow hadn't seen Alan this up tight since the kidnapping. He could hardly wait for Chasidy to get back with the tea. Alan relieved her of the tray when she returned. "What is it? You look like yur on da run from somebody," Barlow spoke.

"I might be, in three days," Alan replied, "from Mic." He sat down at the table with his glass of tea. "I did somethin' I thought was a good idea at first. But now I'm not so sure. I don't wanna hurt Mic."

"What did you do?" Barlow had become concerned.

"Let me explain first," he said. "When I found out AJ was havin' a hard time with Ethel's death, I got ta thankin'. Kelly and Stan are always off with their travels. He doesn't get to see them much. But he has oth'r grandparents he's nev'r met."

Barlow sat his glass down on the table beside him. "You didn't," he said projecting what Al was about to say next. Chasidy listened attentively.

"I did," Alan replied. "I thought it would be good for 'im and well, Mic too. It's been twenty-four years since she's seen her parents. I know she misses 'em."

"Wait," Chasidy finally spoke. "Mic's parents are still alive?"

"Alive, well, and kickin'," Al told her.

"But she neva talks about them," Chasidy continued.

"That's why I wanted you to hear this too. I'd like yor opinion when I'm done."

"Ok, I'm lis'nan'." She sat back positioning herself for the long haul.

"I'm takin' AJ and a few of his friends to a rodeo on da Natchez Trace on Saturday for his birthday. I thought it would be an added surprise for him to meet his grandparents for da first time. But I'm really hoping that they can make amends with Mic too. They w're really close b'fore I came along and ruined everythin'. I should've done this a long time ago, but I didn't have da guts."

"Sounds like they're slippin' away from you now," Barlow told him.

"They are. I've nev'r done anythin' like this without talkin' to Mic first. But I don't wanna hurt 'er, Rob, thankin' I'm doing a good thang when I'm really not. What if it blows up in my face?"

Everyone was quiet for a moment. Chasidy broke the silence. "Why are they at odds with each otha'?" she asked Alan.

Alan spoke solemnly. "I wasn't their first choice of marriage for their only daughter. They thought she could do bett'r. She felt differently. They vowed to nev'r speak to her again if she married me." He spoke with a hint of regret in his voice.

"That's a horrible thang fa a parent to do," Chasidy said. "When you spoke with them, did they sound like they had changed their mind about you or Mic?"

"I only talked with her dad. I couldn't tell. And I don't really care what they think of me. But Mic is their daughter." He paused. "Anyway, he was very excited about meetin' AJ." Al glared a pleading glance between his friends. Barlow until now had sat quietly listening to them. "Rob, whatta you thankin'?"

"I was just about ta ask you that?" Barlow replied.

"Chasidy?" Al asked for her opinion.

"What's botheran' you more? This meetan' or you not tellan' Mic about da meetan' b'fore hand?" she asked him.

Alan hadn't thought about that. "I don't know," he answered.

"Does AJ know this story," Chasidy asked Alan.

"No. We nev'r told 'im," Al answered.

"I know I don't have to tell you this, but AJ's plenty crazy about his mom," Chasidy said. Once again Al looked at both she and Barlow. This time with a bit of clarification. He knew what Chasidy was suggesting.

"Yur not sayin' much," he told his friend.

"I agree with Chasidy. I think you do too," Barlow said. "You know what you need to do."

Alan pulled out his phone and called Michelle. "I'm ov'r to Rob's. Can you and AJ come ov'r?"

When Michelle arrived, her first thought was that she hadn't seen that much sadness on the porch since the day Ethel was rushed to the hospital. She jokingly asked, "Did somebody die?" Nobody laughed so she tried another way. They were all staring at her with pitiful faces. "Al, what'd you do?" Somehow, she knew her husband was the culprit.

Al gave a slight grin at that. "Come sit down, Mic." He invited her to the table with him. AJ perched on the step as his dad began talking. When he told Michelle about inviting her parents to meet AJ, she just sat there in silence. She has never understood how her parents could turn against her for loving someone who made her so happy. She thought it was every parent's wish that their child lived a happy and fulfilled life.

AJ got up and walked over to her very excited. "Mom, you have parents?"

Michelle started to cry. She pulled AJ close for a hug. "Yes, Baby. I have parents. And you have grandparents."

"I have grandparents. That's cool!" AJ didn't understand his mother's tears. "Why are you crying Mom?"

She wiped her face with her hand and regained her composure. "Well, yor dad opened this can of worms. I'm gonna let him sort 'em out for ya."

Alan explained that his grandparents were upset with his mom for marrying him and that they hadn't spoken to her since they were married. AJ didn't understand that either. As far as he is concerned, he has the coolest dad in the universe. "I'm sorry I didn't talk to you both about this first. I thought it might turn out to be a nice surprise for you to meet them and maybe get to know 'em. But then I realized it might not be so nice for yor mom. Mic, if you don't wanna see 'em, we don't have to."

"Then what about AJ's birthday party?" she asked. "We can't cancel that."

Alan all but promised, "AJ will have his birthday party. I haven't invited them to that yet." We w're gonna meet for dinn'r first to see how that went."

Michelle and Alan both saw the excitement in AJ's face when his grandparents were mentioned. They had no choice but to consider his feelings from this point. Michelle sat him down next to her and asked him, "Do you wanna meet yor grandparents?"

AJ didn't hesitate in answering. "No." They were surprised by that answer seeing how excited he was before. All but Chasidy that is. She remembered Caitlin's feelings towards her father when she found out he walked out on her. AJ's sentiments were very similar. "Mom, I have da best dad in da whole world and da best mom. If they can't love you guys, how can they love me?" Michelle started crying again. "Don't cry Mom. Yur happy with me and Dad, aren't ya?"

Michelle was crying too hard to answer. She simply nodded her head vigorously, trying to smile. She hugged her little man for a long time. Alan pulled out his phone again to call Michelle's dad. He had to know for sure if they only wanted to see AJ and not Mic also. He talked with the speaker on. "Hi Mr. Peterson. How are you?"

Alan could feel Mr. Peterson's excitement through the phone. "I'm so glad you called. Val and I can hardly wait to meet our grandson." AJ heard his grandfather's voice for the first time. They could hear his grandmother's voice in the background as well.

"That's why I'm callin', Sir. There's been some change in plans. We're gonna have to cancel. Mic can't make it," Alan told them.

The conversation slipped into silence. Michelle heard her mother's voice ask, "Michy can't come." She sounded saddened by that. Her voice sounded just like Michelle's. AJ's senses were piqued again.

"You sound like my mom. Are you my grandma?" He asked the voice on the phone.

"Yes. I'm yor grandma Valerie," she answered. "I've thought of you ever since yor grandpa mentioned you da oth'r week."

"Grandma, how come you and grandpa don't like my dad?" Nobody saw that coming. Chasidy again, however, wasn't surprised. But now that Pandora's Box was finally opened, they were forced to answer.

"Is that why your mom can't make it, why plans have changed?" she asked her grandson.

"No," AJ answered. Sometimes his honesty can be a little intimidating. "I told my mom I didn't wanna meet you 'cause you don't like my dad and you make my mom cry."

His grandmother was at a dismay. "AJ can yor mom hear me?" she asked.

"Yes," AJ answered.

"I've nev'r disliked yor dad. I've always thought he was a very charming young man. I b'lieved Michy was very blessed to have met 'im," she spoke sincerely. "And I've been sending yor mom letters for years asking for her forgiveness for the way her father has acted towards him. But I've nev'r received a reply back from 'er."

Michelle immediately looked at Al with hope in her eyes. Alan smiled and nodded, encouraging her to speak. "Mom," she started, "I've nev'r r'ceived any letters from you."

"Michy! It's so good to hear yor voice Baby. I've missed you so much. I started writing to you after yor first year of marriage. I couldn't find yor phone number. You weren't at the old house anymore. But I knew mail could be forwarded. The letters never came back. I just assumed you were still upset with us."

"No. I nev'r got them," Michelle said. "I nev'r would've kept you outta AJ's life, or mine. I've missed you too. I've sent you a family photo every year since AJ was born for Mother's Day. Even this year."

"You sent me pictures of AJ. I don't have them." Her mother was confused. "I don't know what could've hap'ened to the letters. If they didn't reach us, where are they?"

Mr. Peterson listened to their conversation riddled with regret. Hearing his grandson's voice made him want to meet him even more. But hearing his daughter's voice, sounding like her mother, made him realize how much he had missed her also. "They were nev'r mailed," he confessed. "I took them out of the box before the postman could get them. And I hid yors from yor mother. I'm so sorry, Michy. This is all my doing. My stubbornness and stupidity have caused us all a lot of unnecessary pain. I've missed you too somethin' awful. And I really wanna meet my grandson. Please forgive me. Please," he pleaded.

"You should be askin' Al that," Mic told him. "You said some ugly things to him that…"

"Mic, that's not necessary," Alan said. "This is about you and AJ."

"Yes, it absolutely is necessary, Alan," Valerie said. "I've missed twenty-four years of my daughter's life and all of my grandson's life b'cause of my husband's foolery. And I have pictures of my grandson that I've nev'r seen. He owes us all an apology. Especially you." Michelle's dad didn't respond. "Go ahead Jeffrey. We're waiting," she said sternly.

"I am sorry for da way I treated you, Son. Will you forgive me?" Mr. Peterson asked. Everyone could tell it was done half-heartedly, but the effort was there.

"I've already fa'given you, Mr. Peterson. I had to in order to invite you into my son's life. It's all water under da bridge," Al told him.

Once more the tears started rolling again. But this time everyone shed a few drops. Even Barlow and Chasidy. They were happy for their friends that this bump in the road was being removed from their life. Michelle took a minute before answering. "Then I forgive you too. Whatta you say AJ? Are we havin' dinn'r with yor grandparents Friday in Natchez?"

AJ was excited all over again. "I can't wait to meet 'em." Alan was happy now he had made the call that day and this one.

"Don't hang up yet," Mr. Peterson said. He went to the antique credenza and pulled out the huge stack of Mrs. Petersons' Mother's Day cards. "These are da cards she's sent you."

She hurriedly opened one to see Michelle and her family. "Oh Michy!" she said crying. "Michy, you and yor family are so beautiful. AJ, yur as handsome as yor dad. I'm gonna go through and look at every single one of them. When I'm finished, I'm gonna have a long talk with yor father. He may not be able to make it to Natchez. But I'll be there." The smile on Mic's face was priceless, even if only to Alan.

Quite naturally, they wanted their friends to join them. Michelle suggested a *I'm not taking no for an answer* question to Chasidy and Barlow, "Y'all comin' with us, right?"

"We wouldn't miss meetan yor mothar fa da world, friend," Chasidy answered. "Or yor fathar; if he's still alive."

They all noticed Barlow meditating on something. He spoke when he noticed them all staring at him. "I'm glad you found out some truths and Little Guy will get to meet his grandparents."

"Why do I feel a 'but' comin'?" Alan asked.

"When da adrenalin dies down, there might be a lot more questions. Be prepared for more talkin b'tween now and Friday. It hasn't all hit Mic right now," he told them.

"Do you think I made a mistake contactin' them?" Alan asked.

"Absolutely not," Barlow answered. "Did you see da smiles I saw on yor family's faces? That made every bit of yor effort worth it. I'm just sayin' it may take more than one visit for da wounds to heal. If that's da case, just hang in there. It'll all work out."

"I understand what yur saying, Rob. Some of those questions are already surfacing. Like, he saw me and my mom tryin' to reach out to each oth'r, why would he keep us apart?" Michelle turned to her husband. "Al, if you hadn't reached out to my dad, I nev'r would have found out da truth. All these years, I thought my mom didn't wanna have anything to do with me. That she had sided with Dad against me. But I told myself I'd keep sending her cards each year anyway. You've opened da pathway for me to have my family back and for AJ to have a relationship with his grandparents. I can't thank you enough for that. If we botch it up again, it's on us."

"FYI," Alan said, "you didn't botch it up da first time. And apparently yor moth'r eith'r. But we won't ev'r let it get this far outta hand again. We have AJ to think about now." Then he looked at AJ. "I'm just sorry I couldn't surprise you."

Just then, Ms. Fields came to the door. "Oh my, there's a whole porch full out here," she said chuckling. "Dinner's ready."

"What's for dinner?" Barlow asked.

"Spaghetti and meat sauce with a tossed salad," she replied.

Barlow told his friends, "You guys have to stay for dinner."

"Yeah," Chasidy added, "Ms. Fields makes a mean spaghetti and meat sauce. And fa some reason, she always makes a delicious apple cobbler fa desert along with it."

AJ didn't wait for his parents to answer. "I'll stay!" he said.

"Then I guess we'll all stay, Mic added. "Spaghetti and apple cobbler. You can't beat that with a stick."

#

Alan rented a cottage for AJ and three of his friends at French Camp. They met his grandparents nearby at the Council House Restaurant. Michelle was as jittery as a schoolgirl meeting her boyfriend's parents for the first time. "I don't know why I'm so nervous," she told Al. "They're my parents for Christ's sake. Do I look alright? What about AJ, is his hair good?"

"Mic, yur always beautiful. AJ is beautiful. I'm beautiful. Everybody's beautiful," Alan teased. AJ and his friends were exploring the restaurant when his grandparents walked in.

Michell saw her mother right away and beckoned for her to come over. She couldn't wait for her to get to the table, so she hurried towards the entrance to meet her. She hugged her mother, long and tight. "Mom, mom," was all she could say at first. "I've missed you so much."

"I've missed you too, Sweetheart. I can't explain how much. I'm sorry yor father did this to us," Her mother said crying. The two of them stood there for not nearly long enough in each other's arms.

"Where's Dad?" Michelle asked.

At the same time, Valerie asked, "Where's AJ?" They shared a laugh. "Your dad stopped by the men's room. He's nervous about seeing you."

"I'm nervous too," Mic admitted. "AJ and his friends are looking around the restaurant. I'll call him in a minute." She saw Alan coming towards them.

"Mrs. Peterson, you look exactly like I r'member you. You haven't aged a bit." He told his mother-in-law. "Where's Mr. Peterson?"

"I'm right here. Michy, baby!" He answered as if Michelle had asked. He reached for a hug from her before shaking Alan's hand. "Where's my grandson?"

"Our grandson," Valerie corrected.

"Let me call 'im," Michelle said.

"No, no. I'll go get 'im. Take them to da table to meet Rob and Chasidy."

Michelle had just finished the introductions when Alan and the boys walked up. "Mic, you wanna do da honors?" AJ was standing directly in front of his dad. His eyes were glued to his grandparents and theirs to him. But mostly to Mrs. Peterson.

"AJ," Michelle called him. He walked slowly to his mother. "Mom, Dad, meet yor grandson. Alan Jr. AJ this is Grandma Val and Grandpa Jeff."

AJ looked at his grandma and then at his mom. Alan smiled because he knew exactly what AJ was thinking. "Dad," he said.

"Yes Son."

"She looks just like mom."

"Well, actually, yor mom looks like her. But yeah, she does." AJ was frozen in Michelle's arms. Alan gave a bit of a nudge. "Why don't you go say hello."

"Yes, come give yor grandmother a hug," Valerie said.

"Don't forget about your old grandpa. I wanna hug too," Mr. Peterson added.

Chasidy could see where Michelle got her ageless beauty from. Michelle and her mom looked like sisters instead of mother and daughter. Mr. Peterson wasn't short on good looks either. Alan ushered everyone to the table. "Mic introduced you to Rob and Chasidy?"

"Yes. I remember Mr. Barlow when he was a young man. The two of you were always t'gether," Mrs. Peterson said.

"And apparently they're still t'gether," Mr. Peterson added. "Who are these oth'r young men?" He asked referring to AJ's friends.

"This is AJ's birthday crew," Michelle answered. "This is Tyler, Jacob, and Rye. We're all going to da rodeo t'morrow. Would you like to join us?"

"I'd love to," Mrs. Peterson said.

Mr. Peterson teased, "You don't even like horses, Val."

"Cut it out. You know full well I do. But even if I didn't, I wouldn't miss spending this day with AJ for anything. I just can't get ov'r how handsome he is." She reached in her purse and pulled out an envelope. "Look I brought all da pictures you sent me over da years. I'm gonna make a special frame for them when I get home."

"May I see them?" Chasidy asked her. She reached them to her. Chasidy was all smiles as she flipped through them. "These are beautiful," Chasidy agreed.

AJ wanted to stay with his grandparents, but he and his friends had made interesting discoveries during their exploration of the restaurant. He was somewhat tossed between his friends and is grandparents. He wanted to spend time with them all. Alan devised a solution. "Mr. and Mrs. Peterson let's give AJ time with his friends this eve'nin and you two can play catch up with Mic. T'morrow b'fore da rodeo starts, you can hang out with Mic and AJ while I keep his friends entertained. That'll be about four hours to spend with him."

AJ had a different idea. "You won't be with us?"

"No, I thought I'd give you some time alone with yor grandparents. Yor mom will be with you." Al could tell AJ didn't like that idea. "What's wrong Little Guy?"

"I've never had my birthday party without you b'fore," AJ spoke sadly.

Barlow and Chasidy were interested to see how this would turn out. They knew AJ wasn't giving up his dad for anybody. Not even his newly discovered grandparents. "It's only four hours, Buddy."

"Yeah, but," AJ said.

"It's not da whole day," Alan continued.

"Yeah, but…," AJ spoke in a very low tone looking at his dad with sad eyes, "It'll sure feel like it."

"And you and I can do somethin' special on yor real birthday," Alan bargained.

"And Mom?" AJ added.

"And absolutely mom," Alan agreed. AJ was thrilled with that idea but still torn between his dad and his grandparents.

Chasidy couldn't stand it any longer. "Mic, Al, may I make a suggestion?"

"Always," Michelle answered.

"If yor parents don't have to be back home b'fore Monday, why don't you invite them to yor house to spend time with AJ? Let 'im have this time with his friends and his dad. A twelve-year habit is kinda hard to break all of a sudden."

AJ perked up immediately. "Would y'all be able to do that?" Michelle asked her folks, seeing the spark returning to her son's face.

"We've got no reason to hurry back," Mr. Peterson said.

"Al?" she asked for his approval.

"Whatev'r you and AJ decide," he said.

"Great!" said Michelle. And then AJ. Michelle continued, "Chasidy has a beautiful Pecan Grove that's a must see this time of year," she added.

"Dad, let me show you da hundred-year-old horseshoe in da back," AJ said excitedly whisking his dad away from the table.

Then AJ remembered something. "Wait dad." He ran back to the table to give Chasidy a hug. "Thanks Aunt Chasidy."

She kissed him on the cheek. "Not evan necessary. Go have fun with yor dad."

As soon as Alan was away from the table, Mr. Peterson voiced an unwanted opinion. "Alan has him a little spoiled, doesn't he? What twelve-year-old boy wants to spend that much time with his dad? And why are we visiting Mrs. Barlow's Pecan Grove? I thought we w're invited to yor place."

Michelle didn't particularly care for his comment about her family which included Chasidy. She answered simply, "My twelve-year old boy. And you are invited to my place."

"It doesn't seem normal…" Her father tried to continue.

"Jeffrey," Valerie scolded, "be quiet. Alan must be doing something right for his son to wanna spend so much time with 'im. Maybe you should take some notes."

Michelle never imagined she would still be defending her husband after all these years. "Alan is a wonderful father. He cherishes AJ and AJ feels exactly da same about him. Just r'member, it's his love for AJ that brought you h're taday."

Barlow didn't know much about the Petersons growing up. He only had one encounter with Mr. Peterson in the early days. He wasn't very nice to them. But he was forming a definite opinion about Mr. Peterson with every word he spoke. It wasn't a pleasant opinion. He wanted to go see what AJ and his dad were into, but he wasn't about to leave Chasidy and Mic alone with this wolf in wolf's clothing.

Mr. Peterson thought for a moment about what Michelle said. "Yur right. I'm sorry. I guess I'm still just a little upset about 'im takin' my only daughter away from me and maybe a little jealous they didn't invite me along."

"Alan didn't take me away from you. You pushed me away. And you kept me and Mom away from each oth'r. There were times when I needed her ov'r da past years. When I found out…" she paused. Michelle was about to mention her medical history but decided it wasn't time to talk about her heart condition just yet. Instead, she said, "I was pregnant. You prevented me from having da support from her that I really needed."

Barlow who has sat quietly this whole time finally spoke. "Mr. Peterson, I'd like to go spend some time with my nephew and his father as well. Alan has given you a second chance at a r'lationship with yor daught'r and a new one with yor grandson. That was a very selfless act on his part. I'd be glad to have ya walk ov'r with me if give me yor word you won't ruin my nephew's birthday celebration by upsettin' his father. That way Mic can enjoy some makeup time with 'er mother." Just then his phone rang. "This is AJ h're," he said.

Before he could speak, AJ started talking. "Uncle Rob, you gotta come see this, dad's gonna ride a bull!"

"Yor grandpa and I are on da way," Barlow told him.

Michelle could hear AJ very clearly. But still wondered if she heard correctly. "Did he say Al is about to ride a bull?"

Barlow laughed. "That's exactly what he said and very excited about it too."

"Chasidy, you up to walkin'?" Michelle asked. "I think if my husband is gonna kill 'imself for his son's birthday, I should at least be there to say goodbye."

Agreeing completely with Michelle, Chasidy said, "Mic, stayan' h're is not an option. Cause I should be there to console my dearest friend."

"All da bett'r," Barlow said escorting Chasidy to the backroom arena. Alan was waiting his turn when Barlow and the rest of the family walked up.

Michelle was only a little relieved to see a mechanical bull instead of a real one. "Al, I had to come see this. I thought for sure you w're tryin' to get yorself killed for yor son's birthday."

Alan smiled wittingly at her and said, "He and his friends are goin' after me."

"What!" Michelle yelled. Before they could discuss it, the buzzer sounded, and it was his turn to ride Bucking Blu.

He kissed her on the lips and said, "Wish me luck."

AJ was all smiles. Michelle looked down at her son who was clearly proud of his dad and asked, "Did you put im up to this?" AJ just kept grinning.

Alan was having a ball on Bucking Blu. AJ and his friends could hardly wait for their turns. They were having so much fun, Barlow decided to try his hand with the mechanical beast. Chasidy reminded him that he isn't as young as he probably feels. "Rob, r'membar, you got sevan years on me. Sevan…. Sevan," she lip-synced the last time. Barlow laughed.

Mr. Peterson watched attentively at the men interacting with AJ and his little friends. His spirit filled with even more jealousy as he experienced the closeness between AJ and Alan. But jealously was forming into sheer hatred for Barlow as he watched AJ and Michelle cling to him when they weren't clinging to Alan. He envied the strangely close-knit relationship between them as well. And he wondered how it didn't seem to bother Chasidy at all. But he was determined to spend this birthday celebration with his grandson, so he kept his opinions and his feelings to himself.

The rest of the weekend was uneventful. AJ and his friends had declared to become official cowboys by the time the rodeo was over. Alan had even arranged a horseback ride for them through the park. None of them had ridden a horse before which made that the highlight of the event. They enjoyed the real horses even more than the mechanical bull. Barlow wouldn't leave Chasidy alone, so he let them enjoy the horseback ride without him.

#

Michelle rode with her parents on to her home on Sunday while Alan dropped the boys off at their homes. Mrs. Peterson was completely awestruck with the place, especially Chasidy's Pecan Grove. All Mr. Peterson could find to say was, "You guys live awful close to each other." Even Mrs. Peterson was becoming tired of his constant negativity. All she wanted to do was enjoy her family. She was determined to do that even if he wouldn't.

She made good use of her time catching up on her daughter's life. Michelle asked if she had heard about the kidnapping and told her the whole horrible story when she said she hadn't. But it was when Michelle told her about her heart condition and how much she needed her when she first learned of it that she began to rethink her forgiveness towards her husband. They made a vow that now that they have each other back, nothing would come between them again.

AJ developed a special closeness with his grandma during the five days he spent with her. He couldn't quite connect with his grandpa because he could still feel the resistance he felt for his dad. As much as Mr. Peterson tried, it just didn't click between the two of them. Alan and Michelle noticed the difference in the relationships between him and his grandparents. They knew the fault was on the side of his grandpa and not AJ.

Mr. Peterson still couldn't see the error of his ways even up to the day they were scheduled to leave. Nothing Alan did made any sense to him. He didn't mind sharing that with Alan at all. Especially when Alan told him that he and Michelle were renewing their vows. "Why do you have to get married again? The first time has an expiration date or somethin'?"

"Of corse not," Alan spoke to him extremely patiently in spite of his constant criticism. "I just wanna give Mic her dream weddin' we w'ren't able to have when we w're young. I promised 'er one. And I was hopin' you would escort 'er down da aisle this time. I know that would mean a lot to 'er."

"So, yur gonna waste thousands of dollars on a fancy weddin' to marry the woman yur already married to," he said shaking his head. "It doesn't make a lick-a sense to me."

Alan knows by now that there's no getting through to him, but he needed him to understand one very important point. "Mr. Peterson, any amount of money I spend on yor daught'r or yor grandson is money very well spent. They're da reason I work so hard. I'm just a trussle rat, r'member? I don't need money."

Not only did Mr. Peterson remember, but he purposely never let himself forget. It was a perpetual thorn in his side that his beautiful daughter who could have married any prominent young man in that town had chosen to marry a homeless boy who lived under a railroad trestle. But he could see that Alan had become perturbed with him, so he thought he'd stop while he was ahead. Afterall, he did appreciate Alan introducing him to his grandson. "Well, I did miss out on that the first time. I'd be a fool to miss out on it again. When's this second weddin' 'pose to take place?"

"Next May. Our twenty-fifth anniversary."

"I'll be there, Son," Mr. Peterson finally agreed.

Mrs. Peterson and Michelle touched briefly on the subject of AJ and his grandfather before their departure. Mrs. Peterson was concerned that it might hinder their relationship a little. "AJ and yor father haven't really hit it off since they've met. I hope that doesn't stop you and Alan from inviting us back. Or coming to visit us on occasion."

"Mom, you will always be welcome here. And Dad too as long as he behaves himself. AJ is very sensitive. He senses how Dad feels about Al. As long as he senses that resistance, he'll nev'r be able to connect with Dad. But he adores the heck outta you," Mic said with a huge smile.

"I'm sure that has nothing to do with my striking resemblance to the only girl he's in love with right now," Mrs. Peterson said jokingly remembering the comment he made to his dad when he first saw her. "I've really enjoyed myself with you. Yor dad was so wrong about Alan. It's so obvious how much he loves you… and his son."

"I just wish Dad could see it," Michelle added. "I don't understand why he's still so set on being against him."

"Jealousy," Mrs. Peterson answered. "We nev'r told you, but you have a brother."

"What? I do?" Michelle was shocked.

"He was born three years before you. But he died when he was three-years old. It hurt yor father terribly. He nev'r spoke of him and forbade me from it." Michelle couldn't believe what she was hearing. But now she understood her father's reactions toward Alan and AJ better. Her mother continued. "Jeffrey wanted so badly what Alan has with AJ, he can hardly stand to watch them t'gether."

Michelle was speechless. "I don't know what to say. I'm glad you told me. I thought he was just being hateful. Now I understand, all of this is comin from da pain of losin' his own son."

"Well," Mrs. Peterson started. "Maybe not all of it. There may still be some hatefulness lurking about." She giggled to lighten the mood. "But yes. That's the only reason I'm still with him. Every time I think about da time I missed with you; I get angry. But then I remember da pain he suffered when he lost his son. He never got over that." They shared a warm hug. "I have something for you." She reached into her bag and pulled out the stack of letters she tried to mail to her. "I didn't want you taking any time away from us, trying to read all of these. I know when I got your cards, all I wanted to do was sit and read them all day long, staring at my lovely family. I hope you share da same enthusiasm with my letters."

"I can't wait to read 'em. I love you, Mom. I'm glad you w're able to come."

"Mama loves you too Baby," Mrs. Peterson said, "very much."

"Oh!" Michelle remembered her engagement to her husband. "I've been so preoccupied with AJ's birthday and catching up with you, I forgot to tell you."

"What?" her mom asked.

"Al proposed to me again. We're gettin' remarried. He wants me to have the big weddin' I missed when we w're young."

"That's so romantic!" Mrs. Peterson said.

"This time you and Dad can be there, I hope?" Mic added.

"When?"

"Next year for our twenty-fifth anniversary."

"I'll see to it," she promised.

Third Heartbeat

It's been six glorious weeks and Chasidy's next appointment is in just a few short days. Ms. Fields hadn't encountered the faint heartbeat since, and Chasidy hasn't had the fever or that tired feeling. Strangely enough Barlow never wavered in his trust in Ms. Fields. Instead, he asked, "Should I mention about the third heartbeat?"

"No," she answered, "let's wait until it pops up again." Then she added. "Who knows, maybe the little tykes have shifted enough for 'im to show 'imself."

"Or her," Barlow added smiling.

Chasidy watched her husband and Ms. Fields conspire over the past month or so. Many times, she wondered what that was about. Barlow never mentioned it to her, so she never asked. She had a strong suspicion it was about the pregnancy, and it possibly wasn't good.

That reason along was enough for her to leave it between the two of them. Ms. Fields was doing a splendid job taking care of her and she trusted her husband with her life. And her babies' lives. Not to mention, she trusted Ms. Fields to a strange degree also. During this course of time, they all decided that a first name basis between them would be appropriate.

During her studies with AJ, they especially enjoyed the comfort of Old Daniel when the weather permitted. The animals weren't a distraction to AJ at all. He relished learning about Jesus's love for him. Barlow wouldn't let Chasidy walk all the way back there by herself though. Chasidy didn't mind that at all. The means to the end provided two things very dear to her: more time with Rob and Rob learning more about God.

Days later at her doctor's visit, after answering the usual questions. Dr. Reed asked Chasidy if she had experienced any more fevers. "Not for about four or five weeks," she answered.

"Did you have any pain in the abdominal area?"

"Honestly, Dr. Reed, my back hurts so bad sometimes, I can't feel any pain but that," Chasidy told the doctor.

Barlow interrupted the conversation. "You nev'r complained about back pain."

"There was no need. Nothan' could really be done about it. Da warm baths have been helpan' though," she defended herself.

Barlow didn't like her keeping things from him but refrained from scolding her in the doctor's office. "Is that true Dr.? There's nothin she can do about da pain."

"Basically." Dr. Reed paused. "Unfortunately, it's one of da things that comes with childbearing."

"Is there somethin' wrong Doctor?" Barlow asked. Dr. Reed was taking much too long to answer. Barlow looked at Chasidy and she back at him.

"There's nothing wrong that I can tell right now," he finally replied. "I just thought I heard another heartbeat. Very faint so it could be an echo." He paused once more. "I have another appointment in five minutes but I wanna see you back next week, Mrs. Barlow. We'll do another ultrasound."

The ride home was quiet. Barlow was upset that Chasidy didn't share with him about the pain she has been in. Chasidy was wondering why Rob wasn't surprised about the third baby. She came to the only one conclusion it could be. He helped her out of the truck and into the house. Stopping at the door, he said, "Chasidy, I don't like it when you keep things from me. You should have told me about the pain you've been in. How can I take care of you if yur not completely open with me?" He spoke to her in a tone as unpleasant as it was unfamiliar.

"Yur right," she agreed to make a point. "It's not at all da way you and Ms. Berta have treated me for da past month."

"What does that mean?" He asked knowing full well what it meant. Just not wanting to admit to it.

"I watched you and her whisper around me for da past few weeks. I didn't say anythan' b'cause I trust you Rob, literally, with my life. You w'ren't at all surprised when da doctor mentioned that third heartbeat. You knew about da third baby already. It makes me wonder what else yur keepan' from me." She spoke in her own unfamiliar, unpleasant tone.

"That was for yor own good, Chasidy," he defended. "We didn't want you worrying. It's not good for you and da babies."

"I knew that" she argued. "I also knew nothan' could be done about da pain, and I knew that wouldn't stop it from being a concern to you. Why is it ok for you to protect my health but it's not ok for me to protect yors?"

"B'cause yor health…" he stopped to fully register the question she had just asked.

She waited for him to finish. For him to tell her that her health is more important than his is right now. For him to put her before himself, again. He didn't. So, she continued. "Robert, for all of our relationship, you and I have been puttan' each oth'r first in just about everythan' that we've done. I don't see that changing any time soon. If it did, I would b'come very concerned. So, get used to it, Rob. That's da world we live in." He stared defeatedly at the woman he loves more than anyone else in the world. She had never spoken to him that way before. He had no choice but to hear her. To really hear her. "Robert." She continued. "Don't eva' speak to me in that tone again. I don't like it," she ordered. And then said, "I'm hungry. Fix me somethan to eat please."

"Yes Mam," he answered, "right away." She retired to the patio outside their bedroom passing and acknowledging Ms. Berta on the way. She waited there for him to come with lunch.

Berta heard the whole conversation. She felt partially responsible. "I'm sorry," she said apologetically. "This is my fault. I'll fix her something to eat and you too," she said to Barlow.

"No. I've got it, Berta." He turned from the direction of the bedroom to face her. "She wants me to do it."

"Well, why does it matter who fixes lunch?" she asked him, baffled.

"B'cause we just had our first argument. I have to make restitution." He smiled as he said it.

Berta chuckled at that. "That was the cutest darn argument I've ever heard."

He concluded tomato soup and grilled cheese sandwiches would smooth things over. It was a nice day for just such a lunch. He kissed her gently after he sat the tray on the table. "Yur lunch, Me Lady." She smiled approvingly. Then she dipped the tip of her sliced sandwich into the warm tomato soup and gave him first bite. He knew then all was right in the universe again.

As he watched her eat her soup and sandwich, he thought how beautiful she looked. How motherhood agreed with her so. Then he thought of Ethel and her warning about his fear of losing her. He thought also how Ethel scolded him for treating her like a porcelain doll. '*Robert Barlow doesn't fall in love with porcelain. He falls in love with brass*', Ethel told him. He decided at that moment to change his overly protective ways towards his wife. *She is* a strong woman. As strong as she is beautiful. As strong as brass. Also, their first argument prevented them from celebrating the news about the third baby even though nothing was actually confirmed yet. He came around to her side of the table, kneeled down beside her and hugged her gently. "I'm sorry. Yur right. I know I am as important to you as you are to me. I was being such an idiot; I didn't even ask how you feel about da third baby?"

He didn't even need to apologize. Chasidy had already forgiven him and forgotten about the whole thing. "Like you w're justified in keepan it from me," she answered partially jokingly.

"Try not to worry. Okay. I'll be right back." Then he went into the house to get Ms. Berta.

She came and sat down at the table with them. "Are you two love birds alright?"

"Ms. Berta," Chasidy replied, "we will always be alright. I won't have it any otha' way."

Barlow liked that answer. "Neith'r will I," he agreed. "That's why I asked you to join us. Chasidy made a very valid point to me a few minutes ago. I've been basing our relationship on double standards. That stops today. She and I can endure anything that comes against us if we do it t'gether." He looked at Chasidy. She nodded in agreement. Then back at Ms. Berta. "I want you to tell 'er what you told me da night you heard da third heartbeat."

"Everything, Mr. Robert?" she clarified.

"Everythin," he confirmed. She did. She told how she only heard the heartbeat for a second or two. And explained the possible danger that the hidden baby could cause if he or she isn't developing properly. How it could be life threatening if the doctor didn't catch it in time. And how she felt that could be the cause of her recurring fever. She explained that was the reason she put her on a daily regimen, hoping the baby would shift so that the doctor could detect it. "It was all for your good, Hun. I didn't mean any harm."

Chasidy wasn't angry. Not even at Barlow. "You did a splendid job, Ms. Berta. It worked out just like you planned. He wants me to come back next week for an ultrasound."

"That's wonderful, darling!" she said to her. "But what was wrong with today?"

"He had another appointment directly after me."

"Oh. Ok. I guess we'll just have to wait," she said, "and your husband is exactly right. Together or not at all."

Chasidy and Barlow looked at each other and then at Ms. Berta, saying simultaneously, "*T'gether* is da only option."

Barlow felt like he needed to give Chasidy some time to herself. She hadn't really had any since he found out she was carrying his child. He feared he might be stressing her out even more than the babies. "Maybe I should give you lady folks some girl time. So y'all can talk about this multiple birth thing?"

"Whatta you thankan'?" Chasidy asked him.

"Flying out to New Mexico to see what da site looks like."

"You can do that on a whim like that?" Berta asked.

"Yes Mam. I have my own plane," he boasted.

"Nothan' like going back to work to take a vacation from yor moody pregnant wife," Chasidy teased.

"My wife has conducted herself perfectly," he corrected. "Her husband is da one who's been da idiot."

"No. Yur no idiot," she argued. "Yur too cute for that."

"Oh. Well, what would you call it?" he asked.

"Hmmm." Chasidy studied. Thinking back on a conversation they had early on in their relationship, she answered, "Mental Stupidity." Barlow bellowed his energetic iconic laugh that Chasidy hadn't heard since before he knew she was pregnant. It was long overdue.

"And you w're right about that too. I do need Him more now," he confessed. "I'll be back b'fore yor appointment next week," he promised.

"I'll miss you," she told him as he gave her a long hug.

"I'll miss you more, I'm sure." He turned to Ms. Berta. "Take care of her."

"Of course. That's why I'm here," she answered.

#

When Barlow got to Al's office, the door was open. He could see that he was on the phone engaging in an irritating conversation. He waited right outside the door until Alan beckoned for him to come in. "You should have the proposal in your email. If not, I can have Patricia email it to you again. It's a good offer. It's yor choice to accept it or not. But there won't be another one, not even from Mr. Barlow. If I don't hear from you by noon tomorrow, I'll assume you decided against doing business with us. Passing up this opportunity will be yor loss. Good day, Mr. Miller."

"Is that da same person you w're tellin' me about b'fore?" Barlow asked Al.

"Yes. He's still askin' for you. Whatta you doin' h're? Did she put you out again?" Alan asked grinning.

"I put myself out. I figured I'd bett'r leave b'fore I drive that poor woman crazy."

"What did you do now?" Alan asked disapprovingly.

"She had a doctor's visit this morning. We had our first argument right afterwards." Barlow confessed solemnly.

Alan still grinning, said, "Welcome to da real world, Buddy."

"I don't like da real world, Al," Barlow quickly replied.

Alan, seeing that his friend was truly distressed put on a more serious face. "Well, it must have been big for you to fly all da way out h're to talk about it. We couldn't have hashed this out ov'r da phone?"

"I felt like I had to give 'er a break. I've been crowdin' her so much with my porcelain doll syndrome." Al remembered Sarah using that description of Chasidy when she had her held captive. "You w're right. You told me she's a strong woman. Not that I didn't know that already. I guess…" Barlow paused.

"You guess what?"

"I guess I just need her to need me more," he finished, "especially now."

Alan was looking at Barlow, studying, trying to figure out how to reply to what he'd just said. "Do two thangs fa me." He finally said to his friend. "Think about da woman you met ov'r two years ago and what she was doing when you met 'er. And while yur doing that, tell me what hap'ened to cause this first argument."

Barlow explained every detailed event from a month ago even up to the very argument. Alan, once again, couldn't believe what he was hearing. "First things first," he told him, "Congrats again. Second thing. I clearly need to get you a dictionary to define da word 'argument.' And lastly. She's absolutely right Rob. She's yor wife. Not yor employee. Not yor property. Not yor porcelain doll meant only to be played with."

"I know that Al," Barlow said intensely. "I nev'r meant for any of this to come off that way. I have da utmost r'spect for Chasidy. I would nev'r treat 'er like my property."

"On purpose," Alan added. "R'member when you took her phone, and she didn't turn you a word? Or when you chastised her in front of her class giving her an order and she submitted gracefully. Or when you *suggested* she and Ethel stay around da house b'cause you w're afraid for them and she willingly obeyed. And just a very short while ago, you told her that you w're gonna hire her some help around da house, her house, not giving her, any say so about it, knowing how she feels about her privacy. Nothin' you have done to that woman has caused her to rebel against you or disrespect you. I'd say this was da straw that broke da camel's back."

"Hey, cut me a break on that house arrest thing. I was justified in that," Barlow defended himself. "I agree. I have been a jack," Barlow told him. "And I apologized to 'er and promised I would be bett'r.'"

"That's good. B'cause da woman that was buildin' her own house when you first met 'er is still lingerin' deep down inside there somewhere. It's da love and r'spect she has for you that keeps her buried down in there. Rest assured; she needs you plenty. She's adapting to this new way of living just like you are." Barlow hadn't thought about it that way. Alan continued with that Chester Cat grin plastered to his face again. "I'll tell you what Rob. I would have loved to hear her tell you *don't ever use that tone with me again.*"

Barlow joined him in grinning. "Al, it's da sexiest thing she's ev'r said to me. Then she ordered me to fix 'er some lunch." They both laughed.

"And you went right on and fixed it, didn't ya?"

"Darn skippy," Barlow happily confessed, "and with great pleasure.".

"Yur pathetic," Alan teased. "You can hang it up now, partner. She knows she's got you right where she wants you."

"Right where I wanna be, Al," he said to him, "right where I wanna be."

Barlow stayed for two days and helped out on the site. It felt good keeping his hands busy again. So good, he had to keep reminding himself that he's retired. On the day he was planning to leave, Mr. Miller showed up at the site to speak with Alan in person just in time to interrupt his lunch with Barlow. Alan had never met Mr. Miller in person because he wouldn't see him. He saw some of the guys pointing him in his direction. "Mr. Ferguson?" He asked to see who would respond.

"That would be me," Alan answered.

"Hi. I'm Dirk Miller. We've spoken on the phone a few times."

"Just da oth'r day as a matter of fact," Alan added. "What can I do for ya?"

"You can accept my apology for one thing," Mr. Miller spoke reaching for a handshake. Alan accepted. "Allow me to explain. Do you have a minute?"

D.M. Williams

"Alright," Alan said, "let's step into the office." Then he said to Barlow, "Come inside to finish yor lunch." Mainly because he wanted him to hear what Mr. Miller had to say. "It's okay to talk in front of 'im. I don't keep anything from 'im."

Mr. Miller began as they were all getting seated. "The hospital I'm building is a special establishment. For special needs children in commemoration of my grandson who died a short while ago. He had Cerebral Palsy. When I inquired about the best company to take on the project, I always got the same answer. Barlow. Not the company, the man. Everyone said he had a knack for reading into people and pulling out from them what they were trying to convey to him even if they were having difficulty explaining themselves. I meant no disrespect to you, Mr. Ferguson. But everyone says that Barlow is the man behind the designs. I need this place to be like no other anyone has ever seen or visited. I want the absolute best for these children. Can you make that happen for me? If you can look me in the eye and answer yes; I have the proposal right here, I'll sign it right here in front of you." He held Alan's proposal out in front of him.

Alan knew he could do a good job. He had no doubt of that. But Barlow had a way of working magic with that mind of his. He honestly wasn't sure if he could present a design that would meet Mr. Miller's expectations the way that Rob could. "Yur right. Mr. Barlow has a mind that surpasses all oth'rs in this field, including mine. I didn't lie ta ya. He is retired. Not only that, but he and his new wife are expectin'. But I suppose I could ask im and see how he feels about it. He does hold a special place in his heart for children."

"Thank you, Mr. Ferguson. Please let me know as soon as you know something." Mr. Miller turned to leave. "Well, I've disrupted your lunch long enough, gents."

Barlow looked at Al and nodded once. Their signature form of communication. "Mr. Miller, I'd like you to meet Robert Barlow."

Barlow extended his hand for a handshake. "How do you do Sir?"

"But you just said…"

"It's all true," Barlow confirmed. "I just flew in to check out da project. I have to get back to my wife today. She's carryin' triplets." He spoke proudly.

"Oh! Congratulations! Mr. Miller told him.

Barlow handed him a pen. "You can sign those papers. I'll be glad to work with you on this project. It'll keep me from gettin' on my wife's nerves so much."

"Thank you, Mr. Barlow."

"No. Thank you, Sir," Barlow corrected. "Al will pass on all yor information to me. I'll be in touch." He left right after Mr. Miller to head back to Chasidy.

"Say hi to Chasidy for me."

"Will do."

"Oh, before you go." Al stopped him. "I've been meaning to ask. Do you think you and Chasidy will make da Annual Team Advancement Celebration this year?"

"I certainly would like to, if there's any way she can pull it off. We'll be there even if we can't stay for da entire event."

"Great! Just what I wanted to hear. See ya at home."

#

Chasidy and Ms. Berta had a heart-to-heart talk about her pregnancy. Ms. Berta reassured her again that there could very well be nothing to worry about. And that she was monitoring her to help make sure that nothing happened. She relaxed a little more when they talked about baby names, but Chasidy was missing Barlow. Her fifteen-minute walks felt like exercise without him. Not that Ms. Berta wasn't good company. But Barlow was her missing half and she missed him something awful. She had to conjure up strength just to get up to go for the walks. If Barlow was trying to teach her a lesson, it was working. But she had decided to keep that little bit of information to herself. The one-day AJ joined them helped a lot. If there was anyone whose company Chasidy enjoyed as much as Rob's, it was AJ's.

#

On the flight back, Barlow realized just how much he missed Chasidy now that his hands were no longer busy. He wondered how things were going without him. When he spoke with her on the phone, she sounded lively and energetic. As much as he liked that, deep down he wished she missed him just a little bit more. But he wasn't going to be a baby about it. He kept what Alan told him dear to his heart. He was determined to be the man his wife needed him to be during this special time in their lives; even if that meant he had to give her some space more than he cared to. So, he decided to man up and keep his wishful thinking to himself.

#

Chasidy watched the clock profusely in anticipation. One while she argued with Ms. Berta that it must be stuck. "Time has fa'gotten to move," she said to her. "I really need it to r'membar."

Ms. Berta chuckled, "why don't you take a warm lavender bath to calm ya'self down. He'll be here before you know it." She didn't argue. She and Barlow hadn't spent this much time away from each other since they've been married. Aside from the kidnapping that is. The lavender bath worked its magic. Not only did she calm down, but she was able to take a short nap before Barlow made it in.

He watched her sleeping peacefully for a minute or two, not wanting to disturb her rest. But he had missed her so much. He decided he *would* be a baby this one last time before he became her superman. He kissed her softly on the lips until she awakened. "Hi beautiful," he said smiling. "I've missed you."

She rose quickly to receive him with a hug and kisses of her own. "Not as much as I've missed you. You w're gone much too long," she said as she concluded once again that *there should be no secrets in marriage*. "If that was yor way of teachan' me a lesson, I'm well learned. Don't leave me again."

"Nev'r," he agreed. Thinking on what Alan had told him, he concluded, *maybe she does need me plenty.*

Ecstatic to have her husband back where he belonged, she clung to him like cold molasses on a piece of ice. That didn't bother Barlow one bit. She was right where he wanted her to be. Needing him. "How do you feel?" He asked her."

"Fine," she answered.

"No back pains?" he asked.

"Don't be silly?" she replied. "Always back pain."

He chuckled. "Do you feel like dinn'r at Smitty's tonight?"

"Saint Catherine?" she asked intrigued.

"Da only one I know." She tried to read him, figure out what he was up to. He knew she was mapping him out. "I just wanna enjoy a nice eve'nin showing off my radiantly glowing expecting wife."

82

"Oh, since you put it that way, how can I refuse?" she answered.

"I'll let Ethel know," Barlow said without realizing.

"Rob. You mean Berta," Chasidy corrected.

"What?" looking back at her. "What did I say?"

You said Ethel."

"I did?"

"You did."

"Huh?" He said, then continued on to let Berta know that she didn't have to prepare dinner.

Chasidy enjoyed the ride to Saint Catherine in her favorite place to be and her favorite mode of transportation. Barlow wanted her to be as comfortable as possible and the massage worked wonders for her back pain. That gave him an idea. "Do you want a chair for da house?"

"A massage chair?" she asked excitedly. "Rob that would be wonderful! Cause I could take up residence in da Bentley right now." They laughed softly.

"That will be our business t'morrow. First thing," he promised.

#

Everyone at Smitty's was excited to see Barlow and Chasidy. They hadn't been back since they settled in the new house over a year ago. It was a nice change for them. Just what the doctor *should* have ordered. They hung out there for a while even after they had finished their dinner. Barlow was surprised at how much Chasidy had eaten. He had never seen her eat that much before. He thought to himself what he dared not to say out loud. *I hope you don't get sick eating so much.*

The two of them have developed an amazing knack for reading each other's minds. By the time Chasidy put her fork down, she was stuffed. "I don't think I've eva' eaten that much before," she told Barlow, "I hope I don't get sick." Barlow laughed softly at his wife reading his mind.

Soft music was playing that caught Barlow's attention. "You didn't have yor walk this eve'nin. Would you like to dance?"

Chasidy was thinking *what has gotten into my husband.* Whatever it is, she approves. "I'd like that very much. Now I know why you really flew down to New Mexico," she added.

83

D.M. Williams

"Why?" Barlow asked curiously.

"To find my husband and brang 'im home to me." He smiled at that.

When Smitty saw them dancing, he dimmed the lights just a bit and kept the music going for a few more minutes. Chasidy's head rested on his chest. He twirled a patch of her curly locks around his finger. Knowing what followed, she raised her head in anticipation. He didn't disappoint her.

"Every time I think you can't get any more beautiful, you prove me wrong." He kissed her again. "I don't know what I did to deserve you, but I'll do it a hundred times ov'r to keep you." She smiled and placed her head back on his chest.

Then he thought about what Al asked him concerning the yearly event. "Do you think you might be up to attendin' da annual celebration in a couple of weeks?' Barlow asked.

"Rob," she said, "I'd love to go. I thought that was gonna be off limits to me this year."

"Nothin' will ev'r be off limits to you, Chasidy. We may have to make adjustments with some things, but I've told you b'fore, I nev'r want you to miss out on any of life's little pleasures."

"Thank you," Chasidy said looking up at Barlow and seeing the new man he is becoming. "Fa this eve'nan and da eve'nans to come. I'm proud of you."

As much as he was enjoying this evening, he knew he had to get her home to get some rest. She had become tired. She fell asleep as soon as the Bentley hit the highway. So, Barlow sat back, relaxed, and enjoyed the ride.

The next day Chasidy was back on her routine, enjoying her walks with Barlow and the new addition to the routine, her very own recliner with massage features. It had become her new *favorite place* in the house. She groaned and moaned when she sat down expressing the sheer joy of its comfort. Barlow and Berta both would laugh watching her lose herself in the relaxation it rendered. She enjoyed it so much, Barlow wished he'd bought it sooner for her. He teased her otherwise however, "You keep carryin on like that, I might get jealous."

"Or get one of yor own," she teased back. "Then we can cheat t'gethar."

Ms. Berta had become accustomed to their corky way of keeping the romance alive between them. Even though she's never seen anything like it before, she thought it was the cutest thing ever. "You two are too adorable," she told them.

#

Ever since the first dinner at Uncle Rob's house with Ms. Berta, AJ hasn't been able the get sweet Ms. Fields out of his mind. And his walk with her and Aunt Chasidy just a couple a days ago didn't help with that at all. One day after school he had the brilliant idea to pay her a visit without consulting his mother first. When the school bus dropped him off, instead of going home, he cut through the Grove to Uncle Rob's house. He could smell the food cooking, so he entered the kitchen where he found her, dropping his backpack with his phone in it just outside the door. "Hi Ms. Berta!" he spoke excitedly.

"Well, hello there," she said in her own excitement. "What a lovely surprise. What brings you by here?"

"You," he spoke definitely.

"Me?" Ms. Berta said laughing. "You flatter an old lady."

"What's that mean?" he asked.

She laughed some more. "That means you make me feel good."

"Oh," he said, "in that case, you flatter me too."

They had talked for about thirty minutes when he heard his mom's voice in the living room near hysteric. "I can't find AJ," she told Rob and Chasidy. "He didn't get off da bus and he's not answerin' his phone."

Ms. Berta stared down at AJ compassionately. "You didn't ask your mother if you could come over?"

"No," he answered slowly. "I wanted to see you so badly, I guess I forgot."

"Come on, Dear," she told him, "Let's go fix this."

Barlow was already on the phone with the police and Michelle was talking to Alan when AJ and Ms. Fields entered from the kitchen. "AJ!" Michelle yelled. "Boy you scared da crap outta me! Whatta you doing ov'r h're?"

"I just wanted to say hi to Ms. Berta," he spoke solemnly, knowing he was in trouble. "I'm sorry Mom."

"I'm sorry, Mrs. Ferguson. It's my fault. I didn't even think to ask the child if he had been home yet." She winked at AJ like she did the first night they met. "Please don't be too hard on 'im. He was perfectly safe."

"That's not da point, Ms. Fields. AJ knows bett'r than to go anywhere without askin me first. Even Uncle Rob's house." Then she looked sternly at her son. "What w're you thinkin'?"

"I hadn't seen Ms. Berta since the oth'r night. I just wanted to say hi."

Michelle looked back and forth between AJ and Ms. Fields. "He certainly is taken with you. I guess I should've known he was here. Yur all he's talked about since we had dinn'r h're a few weeks ago. He speaks of you more than he does my mom." After calming down, she raised his little head and asked him, "What's up with that?"

He answered, "she flatters me." Michelle never hung up the phone from Alan. He laughed hysterically at his son's adorable answer. They all did. Even Michelle's anger was dwindled after that.

"If it'll help you out any at all, Little Guy," Barlow said, "she kinda has that effect on me and Aunt Chasidy too."

"I'm really sorry, Mom. Will it be alright if I came ov'r to visit with 'er sometimes?"

"Ms. Fields works h're, AJ. You may get in da way," Michelle replied sympathetically.

"Nonsense," Chasidy told her. Michelle looked at Barlow.

"What she said," agreeing with Chasidy.

Ms. Berta defended AJ again, "he could never get in my way. And besides, I don't work all the time."

"This how y'all gon do me? Ganging up on me like this. You hear that don't ya Al?" she asked seeking his assistance.

Alan was still laughing a little. "Sounds like yur outnumbered, Sweetheart. I'll be home in a couple of days. We'll talk to 'im about this then."

#

Alan made it home from New Mexico about fifteen minutes before AJ's bus arrived. Not long enough for Michelle to get her point across to him. "Why are you having such a hard time with this Mic? It's innocent."

"It's not innocent Al. Our son thinks his grandmother has returned from da dead. That's not something to take lightly." Michelle was determined to make Alan understand. But for some reason, he just wouldn't. "His real grandmother can't even keep his mind off this woman."

"It'll break his heart if he can't visit 'er." He and Mic have never disagreed about anything concerning AJ until just now. "If you wanna break his heart and tell'im he can't visit her, I'll support you. But I just can't tell 'im."

Michelle didn't wanna break her son's heart either. "Maybe we should take 'im in for an emergency visit with Dr. Milo. See what she says about it."

Alan didn't think it was that serious. After all, everybody sees something in Ms. Fields that reminds them of Ethel, except apparently Mic. But if she thinks it's that serious, he won't argue with her. "You've done a wonderful job raising AJ. You know I'm gonna always support yor decisions concerning 'im."

"Thank you," she said relieved. She saw AJ running towards the house from the bus full speed. "Maybe I'll wait until aft'r he sees Dr. Milo. Look at 'im. He can't wait to get to 'er."

Alan grinned. He knew what that really meant. "You couldn't break his little heart eith'r, could ya?"

Michelle slapped him across the shoulder. "Shut up," she said playfully.

"For da record," Al said, "that's not a Ms. Berta run. That's a *'my dad's at home'* run." Michelle smiled at Alan. He could be so cocky sometimes when it came to his son. That didn't bother her in the least. He had every right. True enough, AJ ran into the house yelling for his dad.

#

Chasidy's doctor visit had a different feel to it this time. Much like the first visit when she was riddled with concern. They anxiously wait in the waiting area for Dr. Reed to see them. Barlow senses that Chasidy is nervous. He puts his arm around her for comfort. Their fifteen-minute wait had the feel of an hour by the time the receptionist ushered them in. "Mrs. Barlow, Dr. Reed is ready for you."

He went through the normal routine, checking vitals, asking questions, and listening for concerns. He didn't see anything in vitals, nor did he hear anything from Chasidy that concerned him. "Now then, let's get you on the table, see if we can find this little guy hiding back there." Sure enough, there was another small body trying to emerge from behind his or her siblings. The baby's position still made it difficult for Dr. Reed to check his growth. That was his major concern, that the child was developing as he should be like the other two. His little heartbeat was still very faint. That bothered Dr. Reed also. With the doppler, his heartbeat should be much stronger.

Chasidy could see the concern in his face. Barlow could see it in hers. "I don't like secrets Dr. Reed," she told him. "What's going on with my babies?"

Dr. Reed looked at Chasidy and then at Barlow. "I'm concerned about the weak heartbeat," he said first and foremost. "And he's in a position where I can't really monitor his growth. I don't like that either. I need to know that he's developing properly and on schedule." He paused for just a moment. "I don't want to alarm you, but if he's not developing as he should, it could cause problems.

Barlow and Chasidy remembered Berta having that same concern. "How can we find out if the ultrasound doesn't even show it? Chasidy asked.

"Until he shifts, we can't. Unless…"

"Unless what?" Barlow asked.

"If you develop symptoms like the fever, excessive pain, nausea that doesn't go away in a day or two, then I need to see you right away." Chasidy couldn't help but notice that Dr. Reed wasn't as optimistic as he usually is. "The upside is that you look great. Whatever it is you're doing, keep it up. I'd like to see you in two-week intervals until I'm comfortable with the other little fella," he told them.

On the way out of the doctor's office, Barlow asked her, "Are you alright?"

"No," she said to her husband needing his support more than ever. "Are you?"

Remembering their promise to be truthful with each other from now on, he answered, "No," as well.

#

At home, Chasidy, bound and determined to think only good thoughts, pulled out her list of baby names. "Whatda you think about these?" She asked handing the small notebook to Barlow. He noticed right off there were no boy names.

"These are all girl names. What if one is a boy?" He asked her a little disappointedly. They didn't know the sex of their babies. Chasidy and Barlow being very traditional people chose to wait when Dr. Reed asked if they wanted to know.

"I thought that would be a given to you, Rob. I wouldn't dream of naman' yor son anythan' oth'r than yor namesake," she spoke most matter-of-factly.

"How could I not know that?" he asked apologetically. "But what if there's more than one?"

Chasidy teased, "We could always do like George Foreman."

Balow bellowed his iconic laugh. "No, let's not do that. We'll come up with one or two more just in case." He was impressed with the girl names though. Very bias towards two of them, he was now hoping that two of them would be girls so that they wouldn't have to choose only one.

"Which one of these do you prefer?" She asked after he didn't volunteer his opinion.

"Which two?" He corrected. "I would be disappointed if we only had one girl." Chasidy was okay with that answer. She actually expected it. "Are you serious about this?" He wanted to be sure.

"Absolutely," she assured.

"Rose, I'm assumin' is taken from your mother's name," he asked.

"No, actually, my grandma. Her name is Rose Marie."

"That's pretty," Barlow complimented.

Chasidy gave him a fair warning. "Don't say them out loud before you decide, or you'll be fa'eva' stuck. I made that mistake and now I wanna to use 'em all."

Barlow laughed again softly. "But we're only havin' three babies."

"Who knows, there may be anotha' one hiding back up in there somewhere," she said playfully. "God forbid." Barlow hadn't answered her question yet. "Yur not gonna get out of it, Mr. Barlow. I'm still waitan' to hear yor choices."

He smiled before answering. "Obviously Chasidy Rose is my first choice. Rebecca Rose, Ethel Rose and then Liberty Rose in that exact order. They're all very beautiful names," he said to her. "And yur right, saying them out loud would make them difficult to choose from." The first three names he understood. And she had just explained 'Rose' to him. Now he wondered about the last one. "So, does Liberty have a special meaning to you also?"

"Yes," Chasidy answered quickly. "I was thankin I would be free again after birthing these young'uns." She laughed. "Therefore Liberty! Liberty! kept coming to mind." Barlow joined her in laughter. "So, what are you thankin' in terms of boys?" she asked, "since we can't borrow George's idea."

Barlow didn't even have to think about it. "Alan," he said definitely. Chasidy wasn't the least bit surprised about that. "Alan Lewis." She liked it.

The names made her smile profusely. She confessed to Barlow, "Now that our children have names, I can't wait to meet them."

"My sentiment exactly," Barlow agreed. "I think it's time we start on that nursery, though."

"Oh yeah," Chasidy agreed, "we've waited long enough fa that. And it should fit right in with yor nature of doing thangs."

"How's that?" Barlow asked.

"Big," Chasidy teased.

It seemed that before Chasidy could get the words out, the Annal Team Advancement Celebration was upon them. Barlow was thrilled and all smiles to show for it as he mingled with people he hadn't seen since the last celebration. Making sure to keep Chasidy close to his side, he proudly announced to everyone he greeted that he was about to be a father as if they couldn't see that by looking at her. If she didn't know how much this event meant to him, she would've sworn that was the only reason he came.

He's always proud of his team members, but there was one in particular that made him especially proud this time. He was glad Al had recognized his talents and benefits to the company. Javier Gonzales had only started with the company four years ago and already he had surpassed some of his counterparts who had been there for many years in performance, trustworthiness, dependability, and knowledge. Everything that Barlow expected from every member of his team. This young man, however, went above and beyond Barlow's expectations. Alan had gained his own set of brownie points with Barlow for recognizing Gonzales' talents and promoting him to site manager. Barlow felt compelled to reflect on his achievements during such a short run with the company.

Patricia was reading off a list of names like at previous ceremonies. When she announced his name and new position, Barlow stood up to approach the podium. Al, Mic, and Chasidy watched in anticipation wondering what he was about to do. He whispered something to Patricia. She then said, "Will Mr. Ferguson and Mr. Gonzales please approach the podium?" Then Barlow motioned to someone on the floor, and a man came fourth with a large plaque. Once they were all present and accounted for, she released the stage to Barlow. Fellow team members, he's only been retired from us a couple of years, so I'm sure I don't have to introduce to you Mr. Robert Barlow."

"Good eve'nin, everyone. "You don't know how happy I am to be h're t'night. As I've always said, this is my favorite time of year. Please accept my apology for interrupting da announcements this way, but unfortunately, my wife and I have to leave early. I just wanted to extend my personal congratulations to this young man. I asked Mr. Ferguson up h're cause I didn't wanna overstep my boundaries. I may not be able to come back next year." The audience laughed. That was the cue for the man from the audience to hand the plaque to Alan. Barlow walked over to Gonzales and shook his hand. "Young man, I'm proud of you," he said to him. Then he turned to the audience. "This young man started with da company at age nineteen. He didn't know a thing about carpentry, but he said he wanted to learn. I encouraged his co-workers to take 'im under their wings, teach 'im what they know. When I was around, I taught im a thing or two also. He soaked in every bit of information that was poured into 'im. He worked hard and proved 'imself to be a valuable asset for Low-Bar Construction. And now look where he is at da young age of twenty-three. That's an accomplishment to be proud of, Son. And I wanted to make sure you knew that. Mr. Ferguson, I also wanna thank you for recognizing his talent. That lets me know I made da right choice in you as well, makin' you my partner. Please do da honors."

Alan read the engravings on the plaque; "*Javier Raimundo Gonzales, for performance of excellence and service that goes above and beyond, I present to you this Greatest Achievement Plaque for the Best Performing Employee in the History of Barlow, Inc. awarded by Alan Ferguson and Robert Barlow.* Congratulations," Al said.

Barlow had one more order of business with the young man before he left them to their celebration. He pulled out an envelope and extended it towards Gonzales. "One more thing to encourage you to keep up the good work and go on to be the best you can be, here's a bonus personally from me. Keep up da good work, Son. I see you doin great things someday."

"Thank you, Sir. Both of you. This means a lot to me. You don't know how much," Gonzales said emotionally, when he saw the fifteen-thousand-dollar check.

#

Back to the business of babies, once again, the Little House which isn't so little any more goes through a welcoming transformation. Not wanting to combine any rooms that they would use later as the children grew, Barlow extended one of the bedrooms to the outside for a nursery large enough to accommodate three babies. He didn't hire extra help for this project. It meant too much to him. He and Al worked on this one together. Chasidy chose a calming sage for the walls accented with a soothing antique white. Beautifully crafted chestnut furnishings added the style and elegance that children of Robert Lewis Barlow deserved. He made it clear to her they would have only the best. She expected nothing less from a man who had built a multi-billion-dollar empire literally from the ground up.

AJ used every excuse he could come up with to get to Uncle Rob's house to see Ms. Berta. Al's help with the nursery was the perfect excuse as far as he was concerned. He never even saw the nursery during most visits. He made his way straight to Ms. Berta every time. Chasidy sometimes heard them talking and laughing like he did with his grandma Ethel. She, like Michelle was beginning to become concerned about their relationship. It was one thing for an adult to take pleasure in her seemingly familiar persona, but AJ was at a very impressionable age. She didn't want him to have mental backlash behind this.

93

Enjoying the warm Autumn Day out on the patio, she decided to give Michelle a call to see if she still had concerns or if she had just taken up where Michelle left off. "Hey girl, Whatcha doing?"

"Wondering if I should even start dinn'r since both my guys are ov'r there," She answered in a jealous kinda tone.

Chasidy giggled. "So, don't. Come have dinna with us," Chasidy suggested.

"Girl, I ain't even gonna argue with you. It's a date." Chasidy doesn't call much so Michelle was wondering about the call. "Is that why you called, to invite me to dinn'r?"

"No." Chasidy paused for just a moment. "I was just wondering what yor thoughts on AJ and Ms. Berta are."

"Has somethin hap'ened?" Mic asked hastily.

"No. Lord No," Chasidy replied. "I just r'member you havan' issues with him visiting her. Are you ok with that now?"

"Well, since you asked, no. I'm not. But I can't get Alan to understand. He thinks I'm ov'r re'acting. So, he won't talk to 'im about it. He says he doesn't wanna break his heart."

"Ova' reactan' about what?"

"I believe that AJ thinks his grandma has come back. And that's why he can't stay away from 'er." She gave a big sigh. "Alan doesn't see anything wrong with it. He thinks it's cute."

"Have you guys spoken to Dr. Milo about this?"

"We took him in for an emergency visit. She had some concerns, but she wanted to see him again before concluding anything. But then she got sick, and she hasn't been back in 'er office."

Chasidy wanted Michelle to know she wasn't alone. "Mic, stand yor ground with Al. I hap'an to agree with you on this one. When I lis'an to them talk, it's almost as if he's really talkan' to Ethel."

Michelle was glad to hear that someone other than herself shared her concerns. "Thank you, Chasidy. That means a lot to me."

"No problem. I'll keep an eye on 'im fa ya." She assured her, putting her mind at ease.

"What time's dinn'r?"

"I don't know, usually around five. But just come on ova' now since everybody else is here."

"You ain't said nothin' but a word," Michelle said accepting her invite.

Barlow became well-adjusted at giving Chasidy her alone time. By now, he and Mr. Miller had spoken, and he knew exactly how to accommodate him. So, between the two projects, Chasidy had more time on her hands than she knew what to do with. She didn't mind as long as he was within hollering distance.

Her pregnant mindset would sometimes convince her that her husband stayed away because he couldn't stand to see how big she's getting. Even though Berta kept assuring her that wasn't the case; it wasn't until Barlow confirmed it every once in a while, in that tone that she deems her own that she would be convinced. He was excited about the progress of the nursery. She had been wanting to see it, but he didn't think it was safe enough yet. Today she would get her wish. When he stepped out on the patio where she sat looking out over The Grove, he couldn't help but take a stare break. "What is it, Mr. Barlow?"

"Have I told you how sexy you look carrying our babies?" He asked looking into her deep brown beauties that actually looked a little tired to him.

"Yes," Chasidy answered, "but tell me again anyway."

"You are da sexiest woman in da world to me this very moment," he told her in that tone she loves so much.

She remembers the first time she heard it. Her thought was the same as it is right now. *If it is a lie, I don't care. I would listen to it over and over as long as he said it in that voice.* "You do know how to make me smile, don't you? Flatterer," she told him.

He held his hand out for hers. "Come with me." When he took her hand, it felt a little warm to him. He took her to a nearly finished nursery, safe enough at least for her to see. She was learning her husband well. It was just like she had envisioned it, beautiful. She had no doubt that it would be.

Alan, remembering the story Rob told him about the Little House, asked her, "He didn't mess it up, did he?"

She chuckled a little. "No," she answered, "it's perfect." When the tears started to flow, Barlow knew she was truly pleased. That made Alan pretty happy too.

"Let's get you outta this dust," he said to her reaching for her hand again. "I think you should lay down. You look tired and you feel warm." He wasn't as worried when he suggested it as he was when she didn't disagree with him.

"Just for a little while. Mic's coming fa dinna," she told him and Alan.

Barlow asked Berta right away to check on her.

"She does feel warm," Berta agreed. "But there's no temperature yet. I'll keep a close eye on 'er. Go. Finish your work," she ordered. She didn't want Chasidy picking up on how worried Barlow was becoming. She had to get him out of the room. She was a little concerned herself. Her skin felt clammy. After Barlow left, she gave her a thorough check up. Nothing was abnormal as of yet. But Berta wasn't satisfied with that. By the time Berta had finished checking her out, Michelle had made it there.

"Hi Ms. Fields. Chasidy, what's going on?"

"Rob is worried. He asked Ms. Berta ta check me out," Chasidy answered.

Ms. Berta chuckled. "I thought I had gotten him outta here before you picked up on that," she said to Chasidy. "Are you two joined at the hip?"

"Ms. Fields," Michelle said, "they've been like that since they first met. Nothin' concerning da oth'r one gets past eith'r of 'em."

Alan could tell something was wrong as soon as Barlow made it back into the nursery. The winds of time had changed in just the few moments it took to get Chasidy back to the bedroom. "What's wrong?" he asked Barlow.

"I don't know," Barlow answered quickly. "But somethin' is. Berta hurried me outta da room for some reason. Maybe I should go back and see."

"Or maybe you should wait h're with me for a minute or two," Al coached. "If it's serious, Berta will call for ya." Barlow was comforted by that answer, but it wasn't what he wanted his friend to say to him. He wanted him to tell him to go be with his wife. He wanted him to say she needs him more than she needed her midwife. He had to remind himself, he's not going to be a baby about this, *for right now.*

Al could see that things had instantly gone from happy to worrisome so he called Michelle to let her know he would hang out with Rob a little while longer. He didn't hear her come in just a few minutes ago.

"I'm h're with Chasidy now," she told him. "Chasidy invited me to dinn'r a little while ago. I just got h're."

"Rob's worried," he confessed. "Berta put him outta da room. He wants to go back. I said he should wait. Is it safe for im to come back?"

"I'll let you know in a few minutes," she told Alan.

Berta began wiping Chasidy's face with a cool towel when Michelle hung up the phone from Alan. "Yur scaring da dickens outta Rob, ya know. How is she? What's going on?" Since the few short minutes that Michelle entered the room, Chasidy had drifted off to sleep. She didn't hear her tell Ms. Berta that she was scaring Rob.

"She's sleeping already," she told Michelle. "I think the fever is coming back. Her body is warm but it's not registering on the thermometer." Berta told her in a whisper not wanting to wake Chasidy. "I should've let him come in before she fell asleep. But she picks up on his vibes so easily."

"What can I do to help?" Michelle asked her.

"Get me some ice outta the kitchen. I'll try to cool her body down." Then she commented on the statement Michelle made about them a few minutes ago. "They certainly do have a special relationship," Berta acknowledged. "I've noticed that since I've been here."

"Yes, they do," Michelle agreed. "What do I tell Rob before he starts pulling his hairs out?"

"You might as well bring him back with you. I'm gonna check her blood pressure again. She'll probably wake up while I'm doing that. That way he won't wake her when she goes back to sleep."

Chasidy did in fact wake up while Berta was checking her blood pressure. Barlow walked in just as she was finishing. Michelle was still getting the ice. Ms. Berta looked straight away at Barlow. Then at Chasidy. "It's high," she told the both of them about her blood pressure. "Your temperature reading isn't registering, Sweetheart, but your body is way too sweaty. It shouldn't be. I've heard of instances where a temperature is so high that the thermometer can't pick it up." By now, Alan, Michelle and AJ have joined them in the room.

"I have da whole calvary here," Chasidy said softly. Then she looked at Berta; "Am I alright?"

"Are you in any pain at all, Hun?" Berta asked her.

"No, I mean, otha than my back." Chasidy was beginning to worry now. She looked at her equally concerned husband.

"Here's the ice," Michelle said handing her the bowl with the ice in it. Berta continued, setting the bowl on the table, looking again at both of them. She couldn't quite put her finger on it. After all she isn't a doctor. But something isn't right. Chasidy needs the real deal, she's sure of that. "Thank you Dear," she told Michelle. And then Chasidy, "I think you need to go to the hospital, Hun." Barlow and Chasidy knew once more that she wasn't telling them something. When she said, "I'll go with you." They knew it was serious.

Barlow immediately picked her up and carried her to the truck wrapped in her bedding. The whole gang went with him. She clung to him for dear life as he carried her out holding back her tears for his sake.

#

Dr. Reed met them at the emergency room. Barlow introduced him to Berta. He let her explain what was happening with Chasidy. Dr. Reed was glad she had come along. It saved him a lot of speculation time. He too was concerned with the first sight of Chasidy. She looked drained, weak, and very tired. Her face was flushed and her body hot by now and even more sweaty. Upon examining her, he immediately ordered that she be prepped for surgery. "Dr., what's going on?" she asked him.

"That's what I'm going to find out," he told her. "One of the babies is in distress. We need to know exactly which one and why." He was saddened to have to tell her the rest of the story. "I may need to help your babies into the world a little sooner than they're expected."

"Wait," she interrupted, "Isn't it too early?" Barlow was wondering that same thing."

"We may not have a choice, Mrs. Barlow." Then he said as delicately as possible; "It could save your life." Barlow turned to the Doctor never speaking a word. In fact, he hasn't spoken a word since he introduced Berta to him. Dr. Reed began again. "I believe the third baby, the one I can't get a good look at may be in distress. I'll know more in a few minutes when the ex-ray results get back."

"Ex-ray," he finally spoke.

"I had no choice Mr. Barlow The sonogram isn't giving me enough information." Dr. Reed gave him a minute to process that. "If the ex-ray reveals my suspicions, I'll have to give the babies a little boost."

Barlow's eyes were latched to Chasidy's as he sat down on the bed to be close to her. "Rob," she said softly, "r'member our conversation."

"NO!" He said sternly. "Don't do this to me!" He hugged her. "I can't lose you. I won't… lose you." Chasidy knew it was more than he could deal with right now. But something in her spirit told her that it had to be dealt with.

The technician brought the ex-ray results in. Dr. Reed studied them and explained them to Chasidy and Barlow. His suspicions were confirmed. "I'm sorry Mr. and Mrs. Barlow, in order to get to the little tyke causing the problem, I have to take the other two."

"Will Chasidy be in any danger?" Barlow blurted out.

"In any surgery, there's always a minimal risk of danger to the patient. Until I get in there and see exactly what's going on…" He paused. "You'll need to fill out some paperwork, Mr. Barlow. They need you in admissions."

Can they bring da papers here? I don't wanna leave her."

"Of course." The doctor agreed signaling to the nurse to go get them.

While they were waiting for the papers and getting Chasidy prepared for surgery, Barlow thought about the request Chasidy asked of him months ago. The very same request she reminded him of a few minutes ago. He wondered even at that time why she would ask such a thing of him. *Did she know this would happen somehow? Was that her way of trying to prepare me? Is this God's way of showing me that I need Him? I already admitted that. What does God want from me now? Does He want me to beg for the life of my wife and my children? Or does He really expect me to be able to choose?* Barlow was completely torn. If God makes him choose this may be the one time that Chasidy doesn't get what Chasidy wants.

When the papers came, much to Barlow's surprise, that very question was embedded in the questionnaire. *What's wrong with these people?* He thought. *How can they expect someone to make a choice like this?* He couldn't answer it, so he left it blank.

As he glanced over the papers, Dr. Reed explained briefly about the lengthy procedure. After skimming over the papers looking specifically for that answer, the Doctor saw that he hadn't answered it. "Mr. Barlow," he said to him, "I need to know. If you don't tell me and I become faced with the decision during surgery…" Chasidy listened.

Barlow didn't let him finish. "You save them all," he demanded.

"If I can't save them all?" Dr. Reed insisted.

This was the decision he didn't want to have to make. He couldn't make. Losing Chasidy would change the very nature of him. There was absolutely no doubt about that. There's an old saying *you can't miss a friend you never had.* Barlow imagined that applied to anything. He has loved Chasidy for over two years. He's held her, laughed with her, cried with her, missed her. He hasn't experienced any of those things with his babies. The fact remains, he can't miss what he's never had. But even in this short time of expectancy, he yearns to get to know his children, their personalities, their likes, and dislikes. Chasidy watched him struggle with the decision. "Rob," she said to him, "save da children. They're yor legacy." They were her last words before surgery as the drugs began to take effect.

"But you are my life," he replied. She didn't hear that either.

"Mr. Barlow, I need an answer now."

"You won't get it from me. If God is gonna take any of them from me, it'll be His choice, not mine." Dr. Reed stared compassionately at Barlow. "Save them all," he said one last time.

Dr. Reed handed the paper back to the admissions clerk. "Try not to worry. Most times we never even need this," he told Barlow in an attempt to reassure him.

Barlow made his way back to the others after they wheeled Chasidy to the operating room. They all were waiting anxiously to hear what was going on. "They've taken her to surgery," he started.

"You were right Berta. Baby number three is causing da problem. But he has to take da two in front in order to get to 'im."

Al encouraged him, "I'm sure everythang is gonna be fine."

Michelle agreed, "Yes, Chasidy is a strong woman. Strong women carry strong babies." Barlow liked that.

Berta added, "That's right Mr. Rob. That's why that little one is trying so hard to hang in there. He's refusing to give up."

Barlow liked that scenario even better. It brought a warm smile to his face. He added, "Or she." They all joined him in a comforting smile.

Once again, everyone was so preoccupied with Barlow that no one noticed AJ's sadness. Except Ms. Berta that is. She held her arms open for him to come to her. "You wanna talk about it, Dear Heart?"

He ran to her grabbing hold of her tightly. "I don't like it when Aunt Chasidy's sick," he told his part-time grandma.

"Don't you worry about Aunt Chasidy. You'll see her soon enough. And when you do, she'll have a surprise for you."

He became excited. "What surprise?"

"Well, if I told you that, it wouldn't be a surprise, would it?" Ms. Berta told him. Alan looked at Michelle for her expression. She looked back at him in approval. Ms. Berta does appear to be a special lady in the right place at the right time.

#

As soon as Chasidy fell asleep, she began to dream. She saw four children happily playing in The Grove. The sunshine beamed down from heaven on them as they ran and jumped around in endless fun and laughter. Chasidy could feel herself smiling at the children in contentment. Shortly thereafter, she had a visit from a familiar friend. "Hello Chasidy."

"Rebecca?" Chasidy was glad to see her, but curious. "Why are you here? Is Rob alright?"

Rebecca laughed affectionately. "You have a one-track mind. You're as bad as he is sometimes. Rob is fine. I told you before he's a strong man."

"So why da visit?" Chasidy asked again.

"I was just admiring the children. Rob will be so pleased."

"Those are his children?" Chasidy asked and then corrected. "Our children?"

"Yes." Rebecca told her. "So don't be frightened during this surgery. You and the babies will be fine. God is with you."

"Why is He putting Rob through this again?"

"God has special plans for Robert. He wants to make sure He has Robert's full attention."

"What plans?" Chasidy was curious.

"I'm afraid that part is between God and Robert. He just wanted you to know that He is with you. And that you and your babies, Robert's legacy, will be fine." Rebecca told her and then left her.

It's been an hour into the surgery already. Barlow was concerned about that. He was so concerned for Chasidy's safety and that question he regretted having to answer that he missed hearing Dr. Reed say it was a four-to-five-hour surgery. "Why is it taking so long?" He asked Berta.

"It's only been an hour, Dear. He's just getting started," she explained.

"Just getting started?" Barlow repeated. "How long does it take?"

"Well, without any complications and we're all praying that's the case here, four to five hours or better." Berta clarified.

"Why does it take so long?"

"Doctors aren't God," Berta told him. "Dr. Reed is trying to save four lives. He can't rush that. The time frame is just a guess from previous similar surgeries. Each surgery is different. It could be much longer and that could still be perfectly normal."

That was *not* what Barlow wanted to hear. He wasn't sure if he could survive another four hours of waiting. "I'm gonna go find da chapel," he told everyone.

"You want company?" Alan asked.

"No," he told Alan, "I need to be alone."

Alan didn't want to leave him to himself at a time like this. But he wouldn't push. "I'm h're if you need me," he simply said.

Barlow couldn't believe he was in this place again. Trying to lean solely on this Entity called God. Looking back over the recent past, he acknowledges that He did help him find Chasidy and bring her back to him. He healed her when he confessed his belief and trust in Him. He's no theologist. Not by a long shot. But he cannot deny his personal experience with God in the recent years, how God has helped him when he asked Him. Nevertheless, he is filled with questions again. Having spent more time with Him recently, it didn't dawn on him how much easier it is to talk to God now. He started speaking from his heart. "Lord, here we are again. I suppose this is another lesson to show me how much I need you. I know that I need you. Why does it have ta always be Chasidy? She loves you and trusts you so much. I'm afraid for her. I'm afraid for them. B'fore you gave them to me; I was ok with being alone. But now that I have them, I wanna keep them. All of them. Beauty for ashes, Chasidy said that's what you've given me. I thank you for the beauty you've given me. Please allow me to enjoy it a while long'r."

He sat quietly in the chapel with his eyes closed. It was a different feeling from his first visit to a chapel when Chasidy was recovering. He felt the presence of God with him this time. He knew he wasn't alone. Aside from the presence of God, someone else was there. "Hello Robert."

He opened his eyes to see Ethel sitting next to him. "Ma!" He spoke in relief. "I'm so glad yur h're."

"Of course, I'm here. I'm so proud of you, Son."

"For what, Ma? What have I done?"

"You're trusting in God. That's exactly what He wants."

"Why is God making me choose between Chasidy and the babies? If He's all powerful, why can't He save them all?"

"When Chasidy was kidnapped, that wasn't about her, it was about you. This is the same story. This isn't about Chasidy, Robert. It isn't about what God can do. It's about what *you* believe God can do. Do you believe He can save your family? All… of your family?"

Without hesitation. Without even doubt. Barlow answered, "Yes I do."

"Then stand on that. And believe that He will." Ethel told him. "No matter how bad things appear. Stand on what you believe."

Then he heard Alan's voice and turned to face him. "I know you said you wanted to be alone, but you w're in h're so long, I had to check on ya."

When Barlow turned back, Ethel was gone. "Did you see…?"

"See what?" Alan asked.

"Nothin'." He decided to keep Ethel's visit to himself. "How long have I been in h're?"

"Ov'r an hour," Alan answered, "but apparently, it's good for ya. You look peaceful."

"I feel like things will work out alright." He nodded once at Alan. "I believe that."

"I believe it with you, Buddy. We all do." They sat a few more minutes in the tranquility of the chapel. It was a good place to be at a time like this. Alan thought he'd strike up a conversation to try to keep his friend in this peaceful mood he was in. "I know this was kinda sudden, but have you guys come up with names yet?"

That brought an immediate smile to Barlow's face. "Aw man, she came up with da most beautiful names for girls."

"For girls?" Alan asked curiously. "She's not expecting any boys outta this deal?" He asked jokingly.

"I had da same reaction. You know what she told me?

"No, what?"

"Rob, I wouldn't dream of namin' yor son anythin' but Robert." They both chuckled at that.

"Of course, she wouldn't." Alan paused. "She loves you so much, man." Barlow agreed. "But what if it's more than one boy?"

"We're gonna do like George Foreman." Barlow teased. Alan thought that was hilarious. "I bet that was her idea too."

"It was." Barlow purposely didn't tell him about the name he picked if there was a second boy child. He wanted Alan to be completely surprised.

"Ok, girl names?"

"Chasidy Rose and Rebecca Rose," he proudly announced.

"Are you serious? Chasidy came up with Rebecca Rose?"

"Yes, she did. And I had that same reaction as well." Barlow thought for a second. "She's perfect, Al. She just keeps makin' me fall in love with her ov'r and ov'r again."

Al gave him his good friend pat on the back. "We should get back in case da doctor comes lookin for ya," Alan suggested.

Michelle met Barlow's eyes when he reentered the waiting area. He extended his signature one nod to her. She knew he was alright. After about another forty-five minutes, the hospital liaison came out to talk to Barlow. "Hello Mr. Barlow. I'm Teresa."

"Teresa." Barlow stood. "Good ta meet you."

"And you as well." Please take your seat. Let's stay comfortable," she directed. "I'm here to give you an update on the surgery. Everything is on schedule. The procedure is going as expected."

"Chasidy is alright then?" Barlow asked.

"Chasidy is doing great. You should be proud of her," Teresa told him.

"I am. Very proud," Barlow confessed.

"Then you'll be even more proud to know that as of right now you have a handsome little boy and a beautiful little girl," she added, "in that order. Are these your first born?"

Barlow immediately looked at Alan and the others. Joy beamed from him like radiant energy. "Yes, they are. Are they alright?"

"Aside from being a little early, their perfectly fine. All fingers and toes accounted for." She stood up to leave him to his thoughts. "I have to get back, now. The next face you should see is Dr. Reeds. Congratulations on being a brand-new dad!"

There wasn't anything for Alan or the others to say. The look on Barlow's face said it all, for all of them.

Berta asked AJ, "Did you hear that? Uncle Rob is a dad now."

"How?" The curious child asked.

"Remember that surprise I told you about from Aunt Chasidy?" She asked him. "Aunt Chasidy just had babies. You have cousins to help take care of. Isn't that wonderful?"

"Cool!" he answered.

Just as Barlow sat back in his seat to get ready for round two, a nurse came over to him. "Mr. Barlow, would you like to see your new bundles of joy?"

"Absolutely!" he said. Can we all go?" An excited Barlow asked.

"Children aren't allowed on the nursery floor but the rest of you, sure," the nurse told him.

"You three go ahead. I'll sit with AJ," Ms. Berta volunteered.

Barlow marveled at how tiny they are. "They looked bigger than that when they were inside", he said as he peered through the window at them. "They're beautiful," he added.

"Yes, they are," Al and Mic agreed.

"What are their names?" Michelle asked.

"Robert and Chasidy," Barlow proudly answered.

"What was I thinkin'?" Michelle asked, not surprised at all with his answer. Alan giggled.

#

In the waiting area, Ms. Berta took this opportunity to talk with AJ to prepare him for wat was coming next. When all the babies are here, their time together will come to an end. She didn't want that to catch him by surprise. Or for him to come looking for her and she wasn't there. "I've enjoyed this time with you Baby."

"Me too, Grandma Berta," he said proudly.

"I need to share something with you," she started. "I won't be going back home with Uncle Rob and Aunt Chasidy. So, they're gonna need as much help from you as they can get. Taking care of four babies isn't gonna be easy," she told him.

"Four babies?" AJ repeated.

"Can you help them out for me?" She asked.

"I wanna go with you Grandma."

"Oh no, Baby. You don't know what you're saying. You still have too much to do here. You're gonna be a big brother yourself in a short while," she confessed.

"I am?" he asked excitedly.

"You are. Your brother's name will be Charlie and your sister's name will be Grace. So, you're right where God needs you to be." She added smiling, "besides your parents aren't ready to let you go just yet. You bring them much too much joy." She started laughing. "Especially that dad of yours. He is something crazy about you."

"I'm pretty crazy about him, too," AJ replied. "But I'll miss you so much."

"And I you." She gave him a long tight hug. "One last thing. You mustn't tell anyone about this conversation. They may not understand."

"Not any of it?" He asked.

"Not any of it," she clarified. "Well, maybe about the babies later."

"Grandma Berta, what about Uncle Rob? You said he thinks you're Grandma Ethel. Can I tell him who you really are?"

"When the time calls for it," she told him.

"How will I know?" he asked one last question before saying goodbye.

She laughed softly again, "you'll know."

"I love you, Grandma."

"I love you too, Baby." Michelle walked up just in time to hear the, *'I love you's'*. That disturbed her. She held out her arms for AJ to come to her. He didn't until Ms. Berta gave the okay. That bothered her even more.

"How are the two Mini-Me's, Robert and Chasidy?" Ms. Berta asked her.

Michelle wondered how she knew what their names are. *Maybe she and Chasidy talked about it*, she thought. "In Rob's own words, beautiful."

"Of course." They shared a smile. "Four little ones." Ms. Berta said slightly out loud. "They're gonna need your help for a while," she said much louder.

"Four?" Michelle repeated. "There are only three babies."

"Oh," Ms. Berta said chuckling a little, "I'm sure that's what I meant." Barlow and Al walked back into the waiting area. "I didn't think they'd be able to get you away from the window," she teased Barlow.

"They ran him off," Alan told off on him.

"They had to take them away," Barlow said to her, "but they said I could come back later after they brought them back in."

"That's wonderful, Dear." Ms. Berta told him. Barlow couldn't help but notice how much she sounded like Ethel just then.

Another hour later, Dr. Reed came out. He wasn't smiling. "What is it Dr.?" Barlow asked him immediately, "Is Chasidy alright?"

"During the last delivery Mrs. Barlow suffered hypovolemic shock. She slipped away from us briefly. We were able to resuscitate her. She's in recovery now. Resting," Dr. Reed told Barlow.

"And da baby?"

"Well, you might wanna sit down." Dr. Reed approached cautiously.

"Just tell me Dr." Barlow pleaded bracing himself to hear bad news.

"They're a little underweight. They'll need to stay in neonatal until their weight is up. One of them has a heart palpitation that needs to be monitored. It may clear up on its own. But for the most part, all four babies are doing well."

"Four?" Barlow asked in complete shock.

"You have four beautiful babies. Two boys and two girls."

He looked at Al and Mic who were all smiles and then back at the doctor. "When can I see Chasidy?" He asked anxiously.

"When we get her settled into a room and she wakes up, the nurse will let you know."

"Thank you, Doctor!" Barlow was so happy he gave Dr. Reed a hug. And then Alan. And then Michelle. And then AJ. He was about to give Ms. Berta a hug but she wasn't there. "Where's Berta?" he asked. Nobody knew except AJ, and he wasn't telling.

Michelle went to the restroom to see if she was there. She wasn't. She asked the nurses if they had seen where the elderly lady went who was with them earlier. They didn't remember seeing an elderly lady with them. During this search, Michelle remembered that Ms. Berta mentioned the four babies just over an hour ago. When she returned, the guys noticed the confused expression on her face. "What is it?" Alan asked.

"She's gone," Michelle answered. "I asked da nurses at da desk if they saw where she went. They said they nev'r saw an elderly lady with us." She paused for a moment and then said, "Rob, she told me about da fourth baby before it was born. Just before you guys got back."

Alan looked at Barlow, and Barlow back at him. Then they all looked at AJ. "Do you know where Ms. Berta is?" Alan asked him.

"Yes," he answered.

"Where is she?" Barlow asked.

"I can't tell you. She said you wouldn't understand," AJ told them with a very serious tone.

"I understand," Barlow said to him.

"Me too," Added Alan.

Michelle gave AJ a hug. "I understand now too, Baby." AJ was glad that they understood, and he didn't have to break his promise to his grandma.

Barlow took a special moment to thank God when he closed his eyes reverencing Him in a silent prayer. *Father God, thank you for this honor and for helping me to believe and trust in You to bless me with da lives of my entire family.*

It had gotten late. Barlow released his friends to go home and get some rest. And AJ had school tomorrow. But they promised they would be back tomorrow to visit the new mother. Even though it was late, Barlow called Caitlin to let her know she was a big sister. She nearly busted his eardrum when he told her there were four babies. He hadn't seen the new babies yet, neonatal was off limits to him for now. He had no idea what Alan and Rebecca looked like. But he could hardly wait to find out.

Barlow went back up to the nursery to peek at the babies. He perched there until he was allowed to see Chasidy. He was proud of his children, proud to be a father, but his fullness of joy would be abated until he held his beloved Chasidy in his arms. Patience is a virtue that he had wheeled like a pro on today of all days. He was completely captivated by his two firstborns when the nurse approached him. "Ok proud papa. Let's get you in to see mama," the perky nurse said.

"She's awake?" Barlow asked.

"Almost," the nurse said, "she's getting there."

Chasidy was still coming out of sedation when Barlow sat down in the chair beside the bed. He held her hand while he waited. When she was finally fully awake, he teased, "That's da hardest you've worked in months."

A weak Chasidy answered, "Blame that on my husband. He wouldn't let me lift a finga' to point. Da babies?"

"All present and accounted for."

"Have you seen them? Tell me about them," she pleaded.

He caressed her cheek. "Robert and Chasidy arrived first. They're downright beautiful. I haven't seen Alan and Rebecca yet. They're in neonatal."

"What's wrong with them…" Chasidy paused. "Wait. Alan and Rebecca?"

"That's right," he said. "Da four of us in mini form."

"Just like in my dream," she said smiling.

"What dream?" Barlow asked.

"When I dozed off, I dreamed there were four children playing in da Grove. Then Rebecca came and said they were yor children." Chasidy explained. "They're gonna be fine. But why are they in neonatal?"

"They're underweight and Alan has a heart palpitation they're monitorin'," Barlow informed.

"Alan's started already," Chasidy teased. They both laughed. "Get some rest, Sweetheart. You look tired."

"Now that I've seen yor beautiful face, I think I'll do just that." He hugged her and then kissed her softly. "Thank you for da greatest gift a man can ask for."

"R'member that when they're takan' turns cryan' in da wee hours of da morn'an'." She teased some more. "Good night."

Barlow slept through the night. Chasidy's sleep was interrupted each time the nurse came in to check vitals. Each time she asked about the babies. "They're fine Mrs. Barlow," The last nurse told her. "They're planning to bring the first two in later this morning so you can feed them."

"That's wonderful!" Chasidy replied. "But what about the otha' two. They must be hungry too."

"I'm not supposed to share this with you, but they're having a little difficulty feeding. Try not to worry about it now. They're in the best of care here. You get some sleep so you can be ready for your babies. We won't bother you again until about seven and then the babies will be brought in." Chasidy thought she was too excited and worried at the same time to sleep. In actuality, she was too tired not to. She easily drifted back into a sound sleep.

She felt a soft kiss on her forehead. She could feel herself smiling, thinking it was Barlow. The voice startled her. "Nice job, Sweetheart," the voice said.

"Ethel?" Chasidy asked softly.

"No," the voice answered. "It's Berta."

Chasidy became more alert. "Ms. Berta have you seen da babies?"

"Of course. They're beautiful. I didn't expect them to be anything but."

"Why are you in my dream? Is everythan' alright?" Chasidy asked her.

"Everything is fine. That's why I'm here, to let you know that I won't be going home with you and the babies," Berta told her. "My season with you was only to get you and Robert through this pregnancy. My job is done."

"Are you Ethel's spirit? Cause AJ was sure fascinated with you. Well, so was Robert. He even called you Ethel once," Chasidy told her.

"No," Berta said, "I'm not Ethel's spirit."

"Then who?" Chasidy insisted. "Rob latched onto you da moment he opened da door and saw you. There was no way he wasn't gonna hire you that day."

"I'm his mother. I'm Roberta." That's the familiarity he felt. But he was so young when I passed away. He just assumed he was feeling Ethel's presence," Berta confessed. "He loves Ethel so much. He was so happy thinking he had her spirit with him. I couldn't ruin that."

"But AJ?" Chasidy was confused.

She chuckled a little. "Yes, little AJ. He knew exactly who I was. At first, he thought I was Ethel too. But I explained it to him."

"He knew all along?" Chasidy asked her.

"After about the second visit I think," Berta said. "It made him want to spend more time with me," she confessed.

"Rob would've welcomed you too."

"Things like this are a little more different with adults than they are with children. It would've affected him differently."

"How?"

"He doesn't know me. Not like he knows Ethel. He would've had too many questions. But when the time is right, you're welcome to share with him that I visited him. He'll accept it easier from you and AJ."

"How will I know when da time is right?"

"You'll know. Will you do something for me with my grandbabies?"

"Absolutely."

"There's a love song I used to sing to Robert when he was a baby; *Hear the Wind Blow*. Do you know it?"

"Yes, I do. It's beautiful." Chasidy remembered singing that very song to Caitlin when she was a baby.

"Will you sing that to them for me? Tell them it's a gift from me."

"I'd be honored," she agreed.

"Thank you, Darling. Remember when the time is right. Tell him, I wouldn't have missed this for anything."

#

Having four babies took a lot out of Barlow. He slept like he had birthed them himself. When the nurse came in at seven-thirty the next morning for Chasidy's vitals, he slept through the whole routine. When her breakfast was brought in at seven-forty-five, that didn't wake him either. Chasidy hadn't seen him this tired since her recuperation from the kidnapping, so she let him sleep. Directly after her breakfast, they brought the babies in. "Change of plans, Mrs. Barlow. I was told to bring your youngest ones in first," the nurse told her joyfully. "The doctor wants to see if they will feed with you."

Chasidy was all smiles, and one or two tears accompanied the smile when she saw her tiny two. "They're so little," she told the nurse.

"They are, but when they start sprouting, they're gonna grow like mustard seeds," the nurse told Chasidy as she handed one baby to her.

"Hello there. You must be Alan. Yur too tiny to be causing so much trouble." As hard as Barlow was sleeping only a few minutes ago, he could hear the babies' little voices calling for his attention. "Look, yor sleepyhead daddy is awake." Chasidy teased. "Rob, meet Alan, yor youngest son."

Barlow has been short on words since the babies first started coming. They haven't caught up with him yet. He caressed his little head not wanting to disturb his feeding. The nurse brought his sister to Barlow asking, "Then who might this be?"

"This would be Rebecca," he finally spoke. "Rebecca Rose," he said proudly cuddling his daughter in complete awe. He held her until Chasidy was finished nursing Alan. The nurse assisted in the baby swap. "Hey Little Al," Barlow spoke to his new son. "I'm so glad you made it h're safely."

Chasidy was admiring little Rebecca as she nursed. "I don't know Rob. I think she looks more like a Rebecca Michelle to me." She then looked up at Barlow.

"I think she looks exactly like a Rebecca Michelle," Barlow agreed.

The nurse was thrilled to see that the babies accepted their mom so well. She was happy to report that to the doctor. As Rebecca was finishing up, the other two babies were wheeled in. The nurse explained that the babies didn't have to be nursed at the same time once she gets them on a regular routine. Or one could have a bottle while the other nursed when she had help. "Whatever works for you and the babies," she told her.

Chasidy corrected, "You mean da babies and me."

"Right," the nurse agreed. "These two shouldn't be hungry. They were cutting up so, 'til they had to be fed before they were brought down to you. But we knew you were anxious to meet them," a smiling nurse told her.

"I most definitely am anxious to meet Robert Barlow Jr. and little Chasidy Rose." She held them both together for a spell because the nurse put them both in her arms since they didn't need to be nursed. Staring back and forth at her babies in admiration, she gleamed with joy. She gave an affectionate smile at her husband, who was ready to experience his own bonding with the two Mini-Me's.

"Hey, do I get to hold one?" he asked solemnly. Chasidy was sure he would reach for his daughter first. But he went straight for the gold, reaching for Rob, Jr instead, with the proudest new dad smile ever plastered to his face. It was a moment that would be permanently etched in her mind. He lost himself in the moment with his new son not finding his way back until he heard Chasidy's voice.

"We know who yor favorite is gonna be," she teased. "Little Chasidy is already gettan' jealous." Chasidy didn't have the heart to take Rob Jr. from him, so she invited him to sit on the bed and she put baby Chasidy in his other arm. "This is a Kodak moment," she told him.

The nurse hated to break up the meet-the-family party, but they had to get the babies back to the nursery. And Chasidy had to get her rest. "They'll be back around noon after you've had your lunch," she said.

By lunch time, once again Chasidy had a room full of people at her bedside. Her room was beginning to look like a florist's shop. Alan and Michelle arrived first right after visiting the nursery. They both had big Chester cat grins on their faces. Michelle didn't stop until she was giving Chasidy a huge gratitude hug. But it was Alan who spoke first when he met his buddy face to face, "Changed yor mind, huh?" He asked Barlow referring to the George Foreman idea.

"Un Unk. This was da plan all along," Barlow told him in the midst of their own hug.

"Sounds like somebody stopped by da nursery on da way here," Chasidy commented. "But I thought Alan and Michelle w're in neonatal."

"They w're all t'gether when we w're just up there," Michelle told her.

"That's a good sign though, right?" Alan asked.

"Yes, it is," Chasidy answered happily. Timing was flawless when the nurses wheeled all four babies in, and Alan and Michelle could get a look at their little namesakes up close and personal.

Each held their own namesake which worked out really well for feeding. They played pass the baby whenever Chasidy was done nursing one of them. By the time nursing was over, each of them had held and cuddled all of the babies. When the nursing was over Chasidy commented, "Guys, my grandma always told me, 'don't start nothan' ya can't finish'. So, I'll see you guys in about four hours to do this all ova' again and every day thereafta."

Michelle, who by now was holding little Al bargained with her, "Or you can just let us take our half home and that'll solve half yor problem."

"Not an option," Barlow replied, "I'm lookin forward to seein' Huck and Tom get into trouble again."

Alan appreciated the humor in that but had to warn him, "Careful what you wish for. Have you forgotten da devilment we got into?"

"No," Barlow answered grinning, "and I wouldn't change a thing."

While they were reminiscing, Caitlin and Antonio came to join the party. After the hugs, the pass the baby game started all over again. It was Caitlin who reminded them how close it is to Thanksgiving. "Holding her mother's namesake, she said, "Ms. Michelle, I guess you and I will be cookan' Thanksgiving Dinna'. My mom's gonna have her hands full for a while."

"Thanksgivan'?" Chasidy repeated. "I neva got a chance to decorate da house. Rob and I w're supposed to start this weekend."

"Don't you worry about that," Barlow spoke. "Thanksgiving is Thanksgiving whether da house is decorated or not."

Caitlin added, "Besides, you know how I love to decorate. I can hook it up for ya if you want me to."

"And I can help 'er," Michelle added.

"Thank y'all," Chasidy said, "That would be wonderful." During all this time Antonio said hardly anything at all. Chasidy could see his fascination with the babies, but he was completely speechless. "Toni, you haven't said a word since you've been here. Whatta you think of yor new in-laws?"

Holding Rob Jr., he commented. "Oh, they're beautiful," he said to Chasidy. "I'm just wonderin' how yur gonna pull this off, four whole babies at one time. Man!"

Chasidy answered playfully. "Well, we've got feedan' times figured out. That's da important part. Mic and Al will be ova' every two to four hours to render their assistance. Rob and I will draw straws fa everythang else."

"Sorry to break up the party, folks," The nurse said as she came into the room. "But we have to get the guests of honor back to their quarters."

One of the other nurses added, "Yeah, before y'all have 'em so spoiled that we can't do anything with 'em."

"The little ones aren't in neonatal anymore?" Chasidy was excited to ask.

"No," The nurse spoke. "Dr. Reed will give you a full report when he comes in. But they're already progressing quite well. Visiting with mommy was the medicine they needed, it seems."

"When will they be able to stay with me?" Chasidy asked the nurse.

"That will be up to Dr. Reed," she answered. "When he feels you're up to fulltime motherhood. But you look like you're doing good also. It may be soon."

"Mom," Caitlin asked after the nurses left, "What was that about?"

"Nothan' to worry about," Chasidy answered. "I just had a small incident duran' surgery."

"It doesn't sound like it was so small," Caitlin argued.

She had to fess up. She knew Caitlin wouldn't let it slide. "I went into hypovolemic shock, but as you can see, I'm fine now." Chasidy tried to make light of the incident.

But Caitlin, looked at Barlow and then back at her mom. Neither of them looked worried at all. Knowing how much Barlow loves her mom, she trusted his look at the moment more than her mom's. "Well, Dad doesn't look too worried, so, alright."

"Dad?" Chasidy protested, "What about me?"

"Sometimes you try to hide things from me to keep me from worrying. But if Dad isn't worried, I won't either." Barlow accepted that with great pleasure.

"Thanks a lot, Daughter." Chasidy pretended to be insulted.

"Yur welcome," Caitlin played alone. "We have to get back to work. Let me know about Thanksgiving. It's only two weeks away."

When they left, Chasidy posed a question for thought, "Have you guys noticed that Thanksgiving is becoming a mile marker for major events? Before long, I'm gonna start expec'tan' somethan' to hap'pan this time of year."

Barlow shared his thoughts on that, "at least this year, it was somethin' good." Then he added, "And you can, birthday parties."

Soon after Caitlin and Antonio left, Alan and Michelle followed suit. Chasidy and Barlow were alone again for a short while. She invited him to sit with her on the bed.

He held her in his arms while they sat quietly for a moment. Holding her had a different feel to it. Not like many times in the recent past when it was shared with fears of losing her. This time it was comforting, loving and romantic like when they first met. The gift of fatherhood she had just given him was incomparable to any gift he could ever receive from that day forward. She drifted off to sleep in her favorite place to be while Barlow daydreamed of the coming days ahead with his new family.

His mind settled once again on God and the things He has brought them through over the past two years. He was meditating on those thoughts and what they meant to him when the doctor came.

She had only been sleeping thirty minutes when Dr. Reed knocked. Upon entering the room, he commented jokingly, "Well, I have two patients now."

"Barlow grinned at him and said, "Doctor, you've always had two patients."

"How's our girl doing?" He asked Barlow.

"Good," Barlow answered. "She's been sleeping about thirty minutes."

"I'm sorry I have to wake 'er," Dr. Reed apologized. "I'll be the first to admit that a hospital is the worst place there is to get any rest. But we gotta do what we gotta do."

Dr. Reed didn't have to wake her though. As soon as Barlow moved to allow the doctor to get closer to her, she immediately awakened. "Dr. Reed is h're," Barlow told her.

"How are you feeling today?" He asked high-spiritedly.

"Really good," Chasidy answered in the same manner. "Thank you for delivering my babies safely."

"And you," Barlow added.

"And me," she agreed.

"I'm happy everything worked out the way it did," the doctor told them. "Let's take a look at ya," he said before he checked the incision area. "Nothing outta the ordinary. So far so good."

"Da babies. They're outta danger?" Chasidy asked.

"Nurse Jonnie said they fed really well with you. That was good news. Little Alan's heartbeat is still a little irregular but slowly becoming more like normal. If both of you keep progressing like you're doing, we'll have you home in time for Thanksgiving dinner. But Mr. Barlow will have to do the cooking," he joked some more.

"Mr. Barlow is actually a very good cook," Chasidy bragged. "Can they stay in da room with me now?"

"Why don't we give that incision one more day or two to heal. You don't want it to break open on ya and risk getting an infection. You wouldn't be much good to those babies then.?"

"Ok," Chasidy agreed.

"Any more questions?" Chasidy didn't have any. He turned his attention to Barlow. "Mr. Barlow?"

"None," Barlow answered. "Thank you again for takin' care of 'em all."

"That's my job, Mr. Barlow. I love it as much as the next person when it turns out like this," Dr. Reed said speaking very solemnly. "Very good then. I'll see ya tomorrow, Mrs. Barlow."

Chasidy, staring at her husband in hopefulness said to him, "Thanksgiving… at home."

"That's what the doctor said," Barlow clarified. "Should I have Caitlin and Mic commence with da decoratin'?"

"Definitely," she answered. Then she remembered the nursery wasn't finished. "What about da nursery? You didn't get to finish it."

"There's not much left. Al and I will have that done b'fore you and da babies get home." Once again, he climbed in bed with Chasidy and enjoyed holding his wife a short while before they brought the babies back in.

Later that day Barlow informed Alan that Chasidy and the babies may be released in a few of days. Alan didn't even wait for him to mention the nursery. He volunteered. "Don't worry about da nursery. It'll be ready for y'all."

"Thanks Buddy. I'm gonna order anoth'r set of furniture, keep a look out for that too," he told Alan. "Tell Mic she and Caitlin can start that decoratin'."

"Will do, Cap'n," Alan responded playfully.

As soon as he finished his phone calls, he returned to Chasidy's bedside. He sat down with a look of accomplishment on his face. "I guess you got everythang sorted out?' Chasidy asked.

"Yes, Mam. I did at that." Barlow smiled a mischievous smile. "Thanksgiving, nursery, more baby furnish'r, all done."

"Wonderful!" Chasidy responded.

Someone knocked on the door. "There's just one more thing and I'll let you get your rest." He opened the door for the visitor. The man rolled in a cart with sixty red roses on it. He explained as he handed them to Chasidy preceding each bundle with a kiss. "This dozen is for Rob Jr. This dozen is for Chasidy. This dozen is for Rebecca. And you get twice as many for Little Alan for all da trouble he's caused."

Chasidy was tickled pink. "Where are you gonna put all these roses?" She asked him. "Da room already looks like a flower shop."

"And yor da prettiest flower in da bunch. I'll nev'r stop thanking you for this, Chasidy. There's no way I can explain how much it means to me."

"I need this in writing so that I can show it to you years from now when yur removing all da doors in their rooms that lead to da Grove cause they're sneaking out after dark to get into devilment. Isn't that what Al called it?" Chasidy foreshadowed.

Barlow thought about that for a minute. "You know what? I'm gonna start r'movin' those doors as soon as we get home. I can't even begin to explain da devilment me and Al got into. We almost drove poor Ethel crazy." They both laughed.

Chasidy had been thinking about the babies' names. She's always been fond of nicknames. Caitlin and the twins had so many, they have their pic to this very day. She ran the thought across Barlow. "You know, with so many of the same names that will be bouncing around now, how do you feel about nicknames?"

"I love nicknames. They're very personable. Whatta you thinkin'?"

"Well help me choose." She gave him choices as she explained her reasoning. "Robbie or Rob Jr.? Robbie sounds a little feminine, but Rob Jr is so formal."

"I agree. What about LJ?" he suggested.

Chasidy had never thought of that. "Lewis Jr." She spoke out loud. "I like it, Rob. LJ it is." She moved on to little Chasidy. "I already kinda have my heart set on Rose for Chasidy. She's a perfect little flower."

"Then Rose it is," Barlow agreed. "Why do I feel like those two are da easy ones?"

"B'cause yur readan' my mind again. You know how we do that," Chasidy said. "I feel like we've already jinxed Alan, poor little fella. I mean, what if he turns out to be as goofy as Al?"

"Then we'll nev'r have to worry about a good laugh." Barlow defended his friend.

"You are so right about that. He is the entire life of da party," Chasidy agreed. "You go first."

"I'm stomped. Al is all I can come up with. Unless we go with AB or LB or something like that."

"I actually like AB and LB. I suppose one of those would be betta than what I'm thankan' since we've already deemed 'im our little jokester."

Barlow chuckled at that. "So whatta you thinkin'?" he asked chuckling.

"Al-3 or Third Al" she replied.

Barlow laughed full-heartedly. "Al-3? Why?"

Chasidy explained. "When I look at that little guy and thank about da struggle he's already had tryan' to make it into this world, all I can see is da laughter he's gonna brang to us. He will be the entire life of da party just like his Uncle Al. But I don't know why I'm reachan' all da way ova' to Alan when his dad can be quite da prankster himself. R'member that stunt you pulled with that pretty young applicant." Chasidy reminded him. "I'm still working on a payback fa that one." Barlow laughed remembering that day very well. "A fun little fella like him needs a fun name to compliment him."

Barlow thought back on when he first met Chasidy and how she first used her name association theory to describe him. And how her analogy of Rob was very different from her analogy of Robert Barlow. He liked the way she carefully matched names with each of their children. He especially liked her analogy of Al-3. "Only you would come up with something like this. Al is gonna jump through hoops when he hears this. Third Al is cute too though."

"Well, that's wonderful. But I'm more interested in what Rob is thankan' right now," she said.

"I like Third Al. He does have a happy-go-lucky feel about 'im already. I think we should encourage that as much as possible."

"Wonderful!" Chasidy exclaimed. "Comical little Third Al he is.

"You got me really curious to hear what you've come up with for Rebecca," Barlow told her in anticipation.

"That one," she said, "is da real hard one. I noticed a few times already you called her Becky. And that's fine. That can be yor own personal name fa her. But I'm thankan' fa everyone else, I would like fa Mic and Becky both to be represented. I know how much Rebecca meant to you. And I certainly appreciate her fa keepan' you off limits until I came along." She smiled. "But Mic has been here fa me through so much. Before her, I've nev'r really had a friend. Someone I could call any time of day or night and she'd be there. Her friendship means a lot to me. That being said, Whatta you think about Remi?"

"Remi?" Barlow repeated. "How do you get that?"

Chasidy picked up the note pad off the table and wrote both names down underlining the first two letters of each name. "Hence, Remi." Once again, Barlow was speechless. He sat quietly for so long Chasidy feared he didn't care for the name. "Or...," she added, we could just go with Becky."

"You really put a lot of energy into name analogy, don't you? When we first met, I was extremely impressed with that. And now, you've sat h're and thought out each of our children's names literally down to da lett'r, and what you would like for them to mean ov'r their lives. I don't know anyone else who does that. Most people just pick names b'cause they like them."

"No. There are still a few of us weird people left who b'lieves in da significance of a meaningful name," she told him and then added. "In da bible, people didn't give their child a name unless it had a meanan' b'hind it." There was another pause. "Does that mean you like it?"

"Absolutely. Every single one of 'em," he answered, repeating them all out loud trying them out for the fun of it. "LJ, Rose, Third Al, and Remi."

Caitlin and Michelle were busy getting the house ready for Chasidy, the babies and Thanksgiving. It gave them a chance to get to know each other. They never really mingled during previous gatherings due to the crowd, so this was a nice change of pace. Caitlin grabbed them a glass of tea from the fridge. Reaching a glass to Michelle she said, "Let's take a break and see what else needs to be done."

"Thanks," Michelle told her. "What's on yor mind, young lady?"

"So, is it by nature that all old folks know how to read young folks' minds?" Caitlin blurted out.

"Watch you callin' old girl. And yes, it is," Michelle answered, "so out with it."

"My mom and I don't talk a whole lot. She prefers visiting in person. But just about every time we talk, she mentions you b'fore we'd hang up. I've neva known my mom ta have a close friend," Caitlin said sincerely.

Michelle added her own sentiment. "Yor mom and I have been through a lot t'gether with da kidnaping and all. With our husbands being best friends, there's no way we couldn't b'come as close as we are. She's a good person. I'm glad Rob had da good sense to marry 'er," she ended in a tease.

Caitlin hadn't intended to include Barlow in the conversation but since Michelle had opened that door. "Rob," Caitlin spoke, "I thought God had stopped making men like him. He's absolutely amazing."

"Don't let yor husband hear that girl or yur gon be in trouble," Michelle warned playfully.

Caitlin responded, "My husband is a rare breed also. He's well aware of that." Caitlin admitted proudly. "B'lieve me when I say, he has his own stack of admirations fa our new dad. And my brother!" she exclaimed, "He thinks yor husband is da funniest man in da universe!"

"Well, that makes him AJ best friend," Mic said.

Caitlin returned to the subject of Chasidy. "My mom has lived most of her life alone. And now she has a wonderful husband, a brand-new family, and good friends. I guess what I'm trying to say is I'm happy fa 'er. And thank you fa being there fa her. B'cause yur my mom's friend that makes you my friend too," Caitlin spoke sincerely. "If you eva need me fa anythan', just ask."

"Awe," Michelle told her, "Come here girl. Gimme a hug. FYI, it's called family."

Alan heard the conversation from the nursery and smiled approvingly. "Since you two are in here goofin' off, why don't you come see how da nursery looks."

"Wow," Caitlin said, "this looks great!"

"Yeah," Michelle agreed, "but…"

"But what?" Alan asked.

"Why don't we move this chest by this bed," she answered.

"Yeah, and da basinet should go b'side da rocking chair," Caitlin added. And so, the conversation went on until the entire room was rearranged completely.

Alan, totally dumfounded said, "I thought y'all said it looked great."

"It did," Michelle said.

"It just works betta this way," added Caitlin.

Alan just shook his head, grinning. Then he glanced at his watch. "I'm goin to meet AJ at da bus stop and let you ladies do what you do."

#

God must be smiling down on Barlow and Chasidy because in exactly two days Dr. Reed gave Chasidy and Third Al the green light to go home but not without some restrictions and stipulations. Third Al's heart was becoming stronger each day, but Dr. Reed arranged as a condition of his release that a nurse visits him a couple times a week for at least until after Thanksgiving. Neither Barlow nor Chasidy had an issue with that. Barlow was ready for his family to be home, and Chassidy was ready to go.

The Fall decorations were welcoming from the gate all the way up to the house. Caitlin had a mind like her mom when it came to holiday decorations. Chasidy could easily point out Michelle's special touch to the scene. She had an art that was all her own. The mixture of the two decorators gave the place a special feel that Chasidy never could've accomplished on her own. "Look at it, Rob. It's mesmerizan', isn't it?"

Barlow was taken also with the holiday feel of the place. Just as they expected, the Fergusons were waiting for their arrival with arms wide open and smiles that stretched all the way through The Grove. Once they had gotten through the usual hugs and how are you's; they headed straight for their little namesakes to help them into their new home. Chasidy reached for Rose, but Barlow refused her. "I've got them both, but you can walk with me." He told his wife sweetly. Right behind them was another small truck that had all of Chasidy's flowers and gifts from the hospital in it. Michelle and Alan were taken aback when they saw the truckload of gifts that came with Chasidy and the babies. "Are you serious?" Alan remarked.

"Foreshadowing Christmas." Barlow responded grinning.

"Please tell me that all of this is not from you," Alan pleaded.

Chasidy didn't help at all. "Of course not. Don't be silly," she started, "everythang on da front seat is from somebody else. Da rest is from Rob." They all went into the house laughing.

"Well," Alan said, "Let's get everybody settled inside and I'll help get everythang in da house." He entered a continuous motion of head shaking when he saw dozens after dozens of roses being brought into the house. "I knew you w're happy, but did it really take all this?"

"Absolutely," was Barlow's one word response.

Chasidy stepped in to defend her husband. "He paid double restitution fa da present and future devilment that comes with Little Alan whom by da way is Third Al now," she said. Then she took a good long look around the house. "You guys did a splendid job with da house. Thank you so much."

To everyone's surprise, it was Barlow who suggested a peek at the nursery. "Are you up to one more walk?" he asked Chasidy.

"Where are we walkan'?" she asked in return.

"Da nursery," he said quickly.

She followed suit with his one word answered, "Absolutely." They both were at a loss for words when they saw Caitlin's addition of each child's name in their special part of the room separating their space from the others. "That is my child's touch, isn't it?"

"Yep," Michelle confessed. "She said you may as well start marking their stuff now b'fore they start arguing ov'r everythin' lat'r." Chasidy started laughing whole-heartedly.

"What's so funny?" Michelle asked.

"I'm visualizan' in my head exactly what she's talkan' about. We had a time with those twins fightan' ova' everythang. Everythang was 'mine, mine, mine'." She looked at Rob. "We've gotta get some cameras in here when they start movan' around or we're gonna miss some funny stuff."

"I'm lookin' forward to it," Barlow said joining her smiling.

Caitlin showed up just in time to help with feeding. Michelle prepared dinner. Barlow and Alan played catch-up on work stuff. "Mr. Miller was pleased with da hospital design. He said it was just what he was hopin' for."

"That's good news," Barlow told him. "What's da plan now?"

"Right aft'r Thanksgiving, I'm gonna drive down to Jacksonville to check out da site. He's meetin' me there. You wanna hitch a ride?"

"I would like for 'im to see my face," Barlow answered. "We'll see where Chasidy is by then. I promised her I wouldn't leave 'er again though, aft'r da New Mexico run."

"She was emotional then," Alan explained. "She's got 'er babies now; it won't affect her as much this time."

Barlow trusted that. He nodded once in his response. "You takin' da plane?"

"Naw. You know I like to drive," was Alan's reply.

"Yeah, but I do wish you'd use it sometimes."

"Maybe next trip," Al told him.

Alan had been sensing that his friend was a little off ever since before the first babies were born. He was hoping he would've opened up to him by now. "Are you okay, Rob?" He asked sincerely. "You've been in this odd frame of mind for days now. Do you need to talk about somethin'?"

Barlow kept quiet for a moment because he couldn't really explain what was going on with him. "I don't know Al. I don't know what to talk about. I can't tell what's in my head right now," he tried to explain.

"Yur happy about da babies, aren't you?" Alan asked.

"We talked about stupid questions b'fore," Barlow replied quickly. Alan laughed. "Did you feel differently after AJ was born?"

"Definitely," Al told him. "Proud, happy, scared, excited. All tied up in one big knot."

"Maybe that's what's going on with me," Barlow said to him. "All that mixed in with da shock that I'm actually a dad at fifty-two years old."

"Oh," Alan said, "that's it right there."

"What's it?" Barlow asked for explanations.

"Yur fifty-two years old with four brand new babies. Yur wondering how long yur gonna be around to enjoy them. A bit of advice." Alan coached, "Enjoy them one day at a time. I've noticed you and Chasidy both talk about the future a lot. And that's not a bad thang. But don't let it take away from today's present joys. None of us knows what da future holds fa us. That's God's business."

Every word made perfect sense to Barlow. He has learned that God is well capable of taking care of his own business. "Yur absolutely right, Buddy. But since when did you get so knowledgeable about God."

"I've come to know a little bit about Him ov'r da years. I'm not where I should be but, b'lieve it or not, AJ's helpin' with that."

"Oh yeah?" Barlow replied, "how's that?"

"He's been sharin' with me what he's learnin' from Chasidy."

"I've sat in on a few of those classes. He really loves learnin' about Jesus's love for 'im," Barlow added.

"Yes, he does," Alan agreed. "I'm gonna go see if Mic needs any help with dinn'r. Go enjoy yor babies."

He made it back just in time to help the sleeping babies to the nursery and Chasidy to the bedroom. Once her mom was settled in bed, Caitlin cut out on the old folks to go see about her own husband.

Chasidy slept through dinner. Barlow cleaned up the kitchen and sent his friends home. Then he sat in the nursery for a while watching over the babies. He tried to concentrate on what Al told him and just enjoy the moment. That became easier when Rose woke up crying and he changed his first diaper alone. "Let me see if I can r'member how to do this b'fore you wake up da whole gang." He said to his daughter. "Chasidy thinks LJ will be my favorite. I'm gonna try not to have a favorite. But if somehow that did come about, I think yur in close runnin' for just that." He held her for just a minute after he changed her diaper, rocking her back to sleep and putting her back into her marked territory.

When he finally settled himself and crawled up in bed with Chasidy, she made her signature move snuggling close to him. This time she was awake. "I thought we w're gonna have to move them to da bedroom fa a minute there, just to get my husband back," she teased.

"Nev'r. Da bedroom is ours alone," he promised. "You didn't have dinn'r. You want me to fix you a plate?"

She grabbed his hand that hung across her and kissed it. "I have all that I need right here," she said before going back to sleep. Barlow assumed baby duty throughout the night so Chasidy could get her rest, only disturbing her when one of them needed nursing. For that reason, she insisted on relieving him of his duties during the daylight hours. That arrangement worked out well for the new parents, even better when they incorporated bottles into the feeding routine.

Barlow enjoyed the feedings. Diapers were a different story. He tried to negotiate a deal with Chasidy. "If I let you sleep through da feedings, can I wake you for da diapers?"

Chasidy pretended to think about that. "Ugh …, no," she reminded him, "remember' da good, da bad, da ugly." Then she added, "and da stinky."

#

Shortly after Chasidy returned home from the hospital, Michelle received an invite from her mom for Thanksgiving. As much as she wanted to go, she wanted just as much to stay and help Chasidy with the babies. She hoped her mom would understand. "Mom, I'm sorry. Chasidy just had the babies. She needs my help around here." She and Rob had quadruplets. Isn't that great!"

"Oh, it is!" her mother agreed.

"Y'all can come here if you'd like. We're havin Thanksgiving at Rob's and Chasidy's."

"I would love to, but wouldn't it be a little crowded?" Mrs. Peterson asked, thinking of Chasidy and the new babies.

"Not at all," Michelle answered, "da more da merrier."

"Well, yor father will act out, I'm sure," Mrs. Peterson told her. "I'd hate for him to ruin everyone's holiday."

"Is he still keepin up foolishness?" Michelle asked.

"Ever since we left," she confessed. "He says Al acts more like AJ's friend than his dad. He can't wrap his head around da two of you renewin' yor vows. And for some reason, he's developed a pure dislike for Mr. Barlow. I simply don't understand that. Mr. Barlow seems like such an eloquent man. I don't know what to do with yor father."

"Well, he'd bett'r get his act t'gether if he wants AJ ta have anything to do with him." Michelle warned. "As far as AJ is concerned whatever his dad can't make right in da world, his Uncle Rob can. He doesn't play when it comes to those two."

"Maybe we can aim for Christmas?" her mom suggested.

"Let's do that," Michelle agreed.

#

Before they knew it, Thanksgiving was here. Chasidy and Barlow had gotten a pretty good routine in place. Barlow couldn't possibly leave now and disrupt that. He told Al they could do a virtual meeting when he got there. Alan understood that. He was glad Barlow was putting home first. He had worked all his life thinking of nothing but. This was a nice change of pace for him.

The new members to the family were the center of attention on Thanksgiving Day. The twins marveled at how small they were. "Y'all were that small," Jasmine told them.

"We were?" McKenna asked.

"Yep," Chasidy confirmed. "You were so small I was afraid to hold you at first. But I got ova' that fast, quick, and in a hurry," she said smiling at them. McKenzie fussed at her grandma for naming one of them after AJ and neither of them after her. Chasidy played the passed the blame game. "That was yor Grandpa Rob's doing. Not mine. Maybe da two of y'all should have a little talk."

"Hey! What hap'ened to standin' by yor man?" he rebelled.

"That doesn't apply to da three musketeers," Chasidy defended playfully.

"Well, if it makes a difference, da name came from AJ's dad and not AJ," He explained to the petite queen. "His name was Alan first."

"Oh. Ok then." McKenzie replied. "Hey! I get it now!" She pointed to each one as she spoke. "1st Alan, 2nd Alan and 3rd Alan. "That's cool grandma!"

"Thank you, Baby. That was Grandpa Rob's idea too," Chasidy added.

"Does that mean we're still ok?' Barlow asked playfully.

"Yea. We cool," she answered.

Chasidy enjoyed watching Barlow play around with McKenzie. He's been much too serious since before the babies were born. She wishes she could figure out the reason behind his change of demeanor. Not only is he way too serious but he's much too quiet. She misses his crafty smile and his playful mannerism. She's decided, *I'll have to see what I can do to fix that after Thanksgiving.*

The aroma coming from the kitchen was screaming at Chasidy. She wanted to offer her assistance, but she wasn't sure how her husband would react to that in this serious mood he's been in. She's thankful that he's a lot calmer than he was before the babies came. She decided she would give it a shot and see what happens. "Rob, I'm gonna go see if Mic and da girls need any help in da kitchen. You got this out here?" She asked him concerning the babies. Alan immediately looked in his direction. He didn't seem affected by the comment or the question.

He smiled at Chasidy and said, "Go ahead. We're good h're. I've got plenty of help."

Though extremely surprised, she liked that answer. So did Alan. He was expecting a reaction about Chasidy wanting to help in the kitchen. When she walked in the kitchen, Michelle questioned her right away, "Does yor husband know yur in here?'

"Yes, he does," Chasidy answered proudly.

"Is he feelin' alright?" she continued, "has his body been snatched by aliens?"

"Now that, I'm not sure about," Chasidy joked, "but if it has, we're gonna wait 'til afta Thanksgiving to go get it back." They all laughed. "I came to see if y'all needed help. Y'all got da whole house smellan'."

There wasn't really anything major left to do. Dinner was just about ready. But Michelle knew Chasidy was missing doing this herself. She and Caitlin could tell she wanted to be a part of the preparation. "I think da sweet potatoes are ready for da marshmallows," Mic told her.

"Then you can slice up da cranberry sauce and we're done," Caitlin added, "Dinna is ready to be served."

"Awe. I should've come earlier," Chasidy wined.

"You came in plenty enough time," Mic consoled. "You have Christmas to show off with. Provided you don't take off on another world tour," she teased.

"Not this time," Chasidy played along, "My arms are full."

"Will you help us set da table?" Mic asked her.

"Yes! Thank you," Chasidy answered excitedly.

But her mother Rosalee warned, "don't pick up anything heavier than ya smallest baby."

Chasidy joked, "No wonder my husband loosened me. He knew he had backup." Barlow watched her attentively, never taking his eyes off of her as long as she was in his eye's view. Chasidy felt him watching over her, so she was careful not to lift anything heavy or do anything too strenuous. While Barlow was watching Chasidy, Alan was watching Barlow. He was proud of his friend for giving Chasidy the freedom to enjoy the holiday in her own way.

When they sat down for dinner, Barlow sat at the head of the table. Chasidy sat in the chair closest to him. He looked out over his family for a good minute. Then he held his hand out for Chasidy's. "Let's say grace," he said. When he said grace, he called everyone by name, thanking God for each and every member of his family. Praying for blessings over them the way that he has been blessed this past year. He even added a special blessing for Michelle's parents. He blessed the food and ordered everyone to enjoy. He continued to hold Chasidy's hand as the food was passed around.

She commented, "It's gonna be difficult to fix yor plate if you don't let go of my hand."

Caitlin stood up. "Um, y'all good. I got both a y'all." She fixed their food for them before going back to her own plate to enjoy her meal. He was forced to let go in the end because it was Chasidy's right hand that he held. She needed it to eat with. Even the babies cooperated with her. She was done eating and enjoying the after-dinner conversation when one of them started to whimper.

Someone had the bright idea to play guess which baby it is. Chasidy responded. "Y'all can play. I know who it is," she bragged.

"You can tell them apart already?" Antonio asked. They all started blurting out names. Chasidy grinned and shook her head playfully at them.

"Well, we know one of you is right," she said grinning. "Whoeva' said Remi pat yorself on da back." She finally said on her way to receive her. Barlow sat back in his chair and watched his wife walk slowly over to the baby, still not saying a word. It was the darndest thing. Alan couldn't make heads or tails of it. Barlow has mastered one of Chasidy's expressionless faces and he's been using it all evening. He could only hope that was a good thing.

"I'll go warm a bottle," Barlow told her, "Somebody else is bound to be hungry too."

"That will be Third Al," Chasidy responded. "He and Remi always eat t'gether." Sure enough, Chasidy was right. Third Al asked politely for his dinner. Barlow was about to feed him when everyone else begged to do it. Needless to say, he beckoned for McKenzie to sit beside him, and he helped her with his feeding. He had no choice but to promise the other two to McKenna and AJ. About thirty minutes later, they got their chance when LJ and Rose invited themselves to dinner.

Everyone pitched in cleaning up the kitchen. Even the men. That was a good thing because Chasidy was worn out in a perfectly good way. Barlow escorted everyone out because he could see that Chasidy was tired. Alan was the last one to leave, on purpose. He wanted to make certain his friend was alright. He's still a little concerned about Barlow's quietness. "You good, Buddy?"

"Al," he spoke, "I've nev'r been bett'r. Beauty for ashes," he said to him. Alan gave him a good friend pat on the back. "Give me a head's up b'fore you get on the road," Barlow said referring to his trip to Jacksonville.

"Will do. I forgot to tell ya. Since AJ's outta school, he and Mic are goin with me," Alan informed him.

"That's even bett'r," Barlow agreed.

Once the babies were settled, Chasidy began to settle down herself. She sat for a minute out on the patio to wait for Barlow. She didn't go straight to bed because she didn't want to fall asleep before thanking him. He found her on the patio enjoying the stillness of The Grove. "There you are," he said, not even mentioning how cool it is. "Whatta you doing out here?"

"Waitan' fa you," she answered.

"Thank you," he said smiling.

"That's what I wanted to do," she said to him.

"You could've done that before I got here," he said being silly.

She laughed. "No. I wanted to thank you, Silly, not me. That's why I waited out here. I didn't trust da bed."

"Whatta you thankin' me for?" he asked her.

"Fa lettan' me participate in Thanksgivan' dinna."

"You don't have to thank me for that. I know you miss yor holiday routines. And I know yur gonna be careful, for da babies' sakes," he told her.

"Is that why you watched my every move?"

"No. I watched yor every move b'cause yur still da prettiest woman in da room and I can't get enough of you." She gazed into his handsome chestnuts. He returned the favor, twirling a curly lock around his finger. Chasidy never gets tired of that knowing the reward that follows. This time, the reward was long and passionate accompanied by a long hug. If she had any doubts before, which she didn't, Chasidy knew at this moment that her husband was still very much in love with her. However, hearing it was even nicer, "I love you beautiful."

"I love you more."

"Impossible. Let's get you to bed. Rest is callin."

"And you," she added, "b'fore duty calls." Neither of them had to persuade the other. The bed called them out by name.

A Different Al

Early Friday morning Alan headed out with his family to Jacksonville, Florida. He knows Barlow has night duty with the quadruplets, so he waited until later that morning to call him. They stopped for breakfast in Alabama. He called just before getting back on the road around ten thirty. "I didn't call soon'r 'cause I didn't wanna wake you up. I know you're runnin' graveyard."

"Thanks. But I'm gettin' used to that. Where're you guys?" Barlow asked.

"Halfway through Alabama. We'll be there by late eve'nin," Alan told him.

"You could've been there soon'r if you had taken da plane," Barlow scolded. He had told him when he made him partner that the plane was at his avail at any time that he needed it.

"I could also be there soon'r if you let me load up and get outta h're too," Alan argued. "Besides, you know I like to drive."

"I know. Handle ya business." When he hung up, he went to the kitchen to help Chasidy with breakfast.

"After you rest, do you think we could take da babies fa a short walk in da Grove?" Chasidy asked him.

"You feel like walking?" surprised at her question so soon after giving birth.

"Yes," she smiled at him, "if we walk slowly. I miss frolickan with my husband. Don't thank yur gonna wiggle yor way outta that just b'cause we have company."

"I don't wiggle that well," he told her jokingly. "B'sides, nothin could make me wiggle out of frolickin' with you." Halfway through breakfast, they were summoned by the new masters and mistresses of the house. Since they were awake, Barlow put his rest on hold. They had their walk right after feeding.

When they got to Ol' Daniel, they sat on the bench Barlow put under him for Chasidy. She had mentioned when they first met that she was going to do that one day. He took it upon himself to do it for her. "I've been worried about you lately," Chasidy told him.

"Why?" he asked, "I'm on cloud nine without any drugs."

She chuckled at that. "You've been so quiet since da babies w're born. Evan b'fore we left da hospital. That's not like you."

"I'm sorry. I nev'r meant to worry you." He kissed her forehead. "I've had some things on my mind. But not worrisome things."

"What thangs?" she asked inquisitively.

He paused, staring intently. Then he said, "I wanna be baptized." He just blurted it out. Chasidy never saw that coming. "I wanna be a Christian, learn more about God, like you, raise my family in church." Chasidy was speechless. She just sat staring at him lovingly, wondering what brought this on all of a sudden, which is exactly what she asked him. "It's not all of a sudden. I've been thinkin' about it occasionally since Ethel died. But it's really weighed on my heart more recently during da pregnancy and especially since their arrivals."

"Then we should talk to Pastor about it. We'll go to church Sunday." Chasidy suggested. "How 'bout that? And talk with him afterwards."

"Perfect." He was glad that they had finally talked about it. He wasn't sure how to bring the subject up. It's a good thing Chasidy is so observant of him. When they got back to the house, he made his way straight to the bed and slept like one of the babies.

#

Alan arrived in Jacksonville around ten pm much like he planned. His meeting with Mr. Miller was scheduled for nine am Saturday morning. He had no choice but to call Barlow possibly waking him. Both men had declared to check in at the meeting. Alan called traditionally first to make certain Barlow was up. Then he switched to a video call.

Barlow wanted to see the location in case adjustments needed to be made to the design. Alan scanned the area as they walked. There were certain areas Barlow wanted him to take pictures of to send to him.

Once his meeting with Mr. Miller ended, Alan spent the rest of the day enjoying the city with his family. They started at the zoo. AJ has developed a love for animals since he was introduced to The Grove. It was interesting enough but not nearly as captivating as the wild cats at the Catty Shack Ranch. AJ was having a ball admiring the big cats. It was the first time he had ever seen a fully grown lion. "Wow Dad!" he said, "Look at his mane. He's huge."

"Yeah, you wouldn't wanna meet him in da jungle *any time* of day," Alan warned.

"I wouldn't wanna meet any of' 'em," Michelle added. As excited as AJ was, it was a little too close for comfort for Michelle.

"Come on, Mic. You gotta admit. They're beautiful creatures."

"Un hun," she agreed, "but they'd look even more beautiful if we w're farther away from 'em." Alan thought that was funny.

"Mom. Stop being a baby," AJ told her, "they're locked up. They can't get to us."

"Un hun, but if you call me a baby one more time, I'm gon' throw ya little butt ov'r da fence to 'em. We'll see who da baby is then," Michelle told AJ reminding him who the parent is.

Alan figured he'd better play interference before things got ugly. He thought Christmas would get them back in a jolly mood. He decided a little Christmas shopping would clear Mics mind of the wild cats, so they found their way over to St. Johns Town Center where they ended their visit after shopping and an early dinner before heading back to Mississippi. "Are you sure you don't need to rest up first? You've been goin nonstop since early this morning."

D.M. Williams

"Thanks for da concern." He kissed his wife. "But I'm good."

"Thanks for invitin' us along," Michelle replied, "I've missed our road trips. That reminds me. When are we takin' da motor home out?"

"You know what?" Alan asked. "We should make plans for that soon. I'll talk to Rob about it when we get home. I'm always open to yor suggestions though."

"I'm gonna be thinkin' about it," she told him.

A little over three hours into the ride, Alan stopped at the pump for a top-off so he could have a steady travel through most of the evening. AJ settled in the ride with his snacks and video games. Michelle enjoyed a snuggle like she used to always do when they accompanied him on his trips. Alan simply enjoyed the ride having his family with him.

Just at the hint of dusk, he noticed a vehicle coming up close behind him at a crazy fast speed. There was also a vehicle meeting him from the opposite direction. The car behind him didn't appear to be slowing. It zoomed past him without breaking. The vehicle approaching from the opposite side swerved to keep from hitting the car head on. But it spun out of control and was headed straight for Alan, also head on. His immediate prayer is that he would be able to save his family. There was no missing the vehicle, so he turned so that his side would absorb the most impact from the collision. Upon impact, the truck flipped a full cartwheel over the car before setting back up on all four wheels. The other vehicle left the road to hit a tree.

Michelle miraculously walked away from the crash with a fractured collarbone and whiplash. AJ seated closer to Alan on the driver side of the truck suffered a broken arm and complained of neck pain also. Alan was knocked unconscious and taken away immediately because of his serious injuries. When Michelle regained her composure, she called Barlow to let him know.

#

Barlow was helping Chasidy with a diaper change when his phone rang. "Its Mic." He told Chasidy after glancing at his phone.

"Go ahead, I got this," she told him. Mic was crying hysterically. Chasidy could hear her through the phone. Barlow tried to calm her.

"Mic, I can't understand you. Calm down Honey and tell me what's hap'ning." She tried to calm herself, but started up again, no better than she was before. But he could hear AJ yelling to him.

"Uncle Rob, we were in an accident! Dad's hurt bad!"

Barlow tried to get Michelle calm again. "Mic, where are you?"

"I don't know. I was sleep. I don't know," she spoke in confusion.

"Ask da nurse…" He began to say, but then OnStar contacted him. "Mic. OnStar is on da line. Let me call you right back." When he hung up from OnStar, he looked at Chasidy and asked, "You up for trav'lin?"

"What hap'aned?" she asked in return.

"They had an accident. Al was hurt bad." Then he called Sam to make ready for the trip. "Have the plane fueled. Get us as close as you can to Lansing, Georgia."

"All of Us?" Sam asked.

"Plus, one," Chasidy added, "I'll need help with da babies while you tend to yor family. I'll see if Caitlin can take some time off."

"Thank you," he said sincerely.

Chasidy had her on the phone even before Barlow hung up from Sam. "We have an emergency. I need you to go to Georgia with me. Can you take a few days?"

Barlow said in a raised tone, "If they won't let you off, you can quit and come work for me."

"It's fine," Caitlin told them, "I don't miss many days. I'm sure its ok."

"They're gettan'' da plane ready. We'll pick you up in …" she looked at Barlow.

"Thirty minutes," he spoke answering her unasked question.

"Thirty minutes," she told Caitlin.

"You got that Sam?" Barlow asked.

"Got it Sir."

Once loaded in the Bentley, Sam informed Barlow, "Lansing is just outside of Savannah, we'll land there. The hospital is less than twenty minutes away."

"Lodging?"

"Savannah-Hilton. Three rooms. Two adjoining."

D.M. Williams

"Thank you, Sam."

"At your pleasure, Sir."

Barlow sat up front with Sam after they picked Caitlin up to allow her to sit with her mom. She took full advantage playing with the babies. "They've gotten cuter since Thanksgiving," she told her mom.

Chasidy smiled. But even chatter about the babies couldn't keep her from worrying about Mic and Al. She had to call to see if she had calmed down. AJ answered the phone. "Sweetheart, how are you doing?" Barlow gestured for her to put him on speaker.

"I'm hurting Aunt Chasidy. Everywhere. My head, my shoulder, my back. Even my chest hurts. They gave me some medicine. They say it's too soon to get more."

"Hang in there, Sweetheart. We're coman'. Where's yor mom?"

"They had to make her sleep. She wouldn't calm down. They said somethin' about her heart. I don't know what that was though."

"AJ," Barlow interrupted, "Whatda you know about yor dad?"

"Nothin'. I'm scared Uncle Rob. They told my mom somethin' about 'im and then they had to give 'er da medicine. She didn't get a chance to tell me. And they don't talk to kids here."

"You lis'en to Aunt Chasidy, Little Guy. Hang in there. We're on our way," Barlow told him. Then he called the hospital to find out what was going on with Alan and Michelle. The nurse at the nurse's station was reciting hospital rules to him about not being able to give out patient information over the phone.

The nurse who was just in the room when AJ was on the phone walked up to the desk in the middle of the down-spiraling conversation. She interrupted, "I'll take that." The nurse handed her the phone. "Uncle Rob?' she asked Barlow.

"Yes Robert Barlow. I'm tryin' to find out how Alan and Michelle Ferguson are doin'. We're on our way there from Mississippi."

"I can help you with that. I was just in the room when you and your wife were talking to your nephew."

"Thank you," he said relieved. "He said she had to be medicated ta calm 'er down. Is Al ok?"

"Mr. Barlow. Let me first say that Mr. Ferguson is still alive. That being said, the reason we had to sedate his wife is because during the operation, he coded. It took the doctors so long to bring him back, we thought we had lost him. Obviously, we didn't tell Mrs. Ferguson all of that. We didn't have to. Once she heard the code blue, she became hysterical. That's why we had to calm her down. Quite naturally we didn't share any of that info with AJ."

"Thank you, Nurse …?"

"Tammy."

"Nurse Tammy. We should be there in two hours. I'll look you up when I get there."

"My shift will be ending just about that time, but I'll stick around to give you an update. Plus, I'm the only familiar face your nephew knows right now until his mom wakes up. I'll sit with him until you get here."

"You don't know how much we appreciate that. Thank you." Before he hung up, he remembered Mic's heart condition. "Nurse Tammy, is da doctor aware of Mic's heart condition?"

"Yes, that sharp nephew of yours made sure we knew before we gave her any medications."

"My little man," Barlow spoke proudly. "See ya in two hours."

#

Once they settled at the hotel, Barlow made haste to leave for the hospital. "I'll call you with an update." he said to Chasidy.

"You won't have to. I'm going with you," she replied.

"What about da babies?" He questioned.

"Caitlin can handle them for an hour. I promise I'll come back afta that." She searched his eyes for compassion. "I won't get any rest until I look in Mic's face and give AJ a hug. Don't you dare keep me away from them Rob, not when they need me."

He turned for a quick confirmation look at Caitlin. "Go. I got this."

#

By now, hospital scenes were becoming second nature to Barlow. Like a second home of sorts. Nurse Tammy was indeed sitting with AJ when they entered the room. He was so glad to see familiar faces that he started crying. "Uncle Rob, Aunt Chasidy!" He yelled. "I'm so scared. I haven't seen my dad since I've been here, and mom is still sleeping. I don't know what to do?" he spoke non-stop.

141

"Don't worry about yor dad. They're takin' good care of him. You just concentrate on feelin' bett'r. I'm gonna talk to da nurse, see what I can find out about yor dad, ok?"

"Ok. Uncle Rob."

Barlow extended a gentle kiss on Michelle's forehead before leaving the room to speak to the nurse. Chasidy followed suit with her own kiss to the forehead before she climbed into bed with AJ holding him in her arms. "We're here now. You try to get some rest." The medicine made him sleepy, but he fought it diligently because he didn't want to leave his mother alone. He felt more at ease knowing his Uncle Rob and Aunt Chasidy were there. By the time he was fully asleep, Michelle had awakened. "Shh, Chasidy told her easing out of bed. "He just went to sleep."

"How long have you been here?" Michelle asked.

"Only about twenty minutes."

"Da babies?"

"Caitlin has them. She's here with us."

"Rob?"

"He's checking on Alan."

Michelle sat up a little. "I'm such a terrible mom. I just left him hangin' to deal with this all by himself. I was so scared, Chasidy. I think I lost him. I think Al is gone."

"I know. The nurse explained. But you didn't lose 'im. He's still with us." Chasidy consoled, now giving her a hug. Chasidy tried to lighten the atmosphere a little. "Girl, we just can't stay away from these hospitals, can we? Every time we go to a new city, we have to try it out."

Michelle tried to laugh. "That would've been a lot funnier if Al was here to hear it too." She burst into tears again. "When is Rob comin' back? I need to know how Al's doing."

"I'm right h're." He heard her as he opened the door. "I was just getting' da full story from nurse Tammy. First of all, Al is alive. He's in a coma though. When da truck flipped, he hit his head a few times."

"Da truck flipped?" Michelle asked.

"Yes. It made a full flip b'fore it sat back up on da tires." B'cause of that he's pretty traumatized."

"But how is he hurt so badly and AJ and I …?"

"Well, a'cordin' to a witness, when Al saw that y'all w're gonna be hit head-on, he turned so that he would get da biggest impact. If he hadn't done that, none of you would've come outta this alive. A'cordin to da highway patrolman."

"What hap'ened to da person who hit us?" Michelle asked. "I'll bet they were drunk."

"No. It wasn't her fault. She was hurt really badly also. She had her two-year-old son in da car with 'er. It's a modern-day God-given miracle that he wasn't hurt. Nurse Tammy said it's a miracle they're even alive aft'r hittin' Alan and a tree."

"Then what caused da accident?" Chasidy asked.

"An idiot speedin' and passin' when there was no clear right of way. He was too close to Alan and da approachin' car. He nev'r stopped."

Chasidy looked at her phone. She promised to only be gone for an hour. It would take twenty minutes to get back to the hotel. Barlow noticed her checking the time. "Are you ready for Sam?"

She nodded yes. Then she said to Michelle. "I wish I could stay. I promised Caitlin I'd be back in an hour. I just had to see you fa myself. I'm glad you woke up b'fore I had to leave." She gave her another hug. "Be proud of that son of yors. Nurse Tammy said he really did you a solid."

"I am proud of 'im," she said in her weakened voice, "he's so much like his dad. Especially in times like this."

"Get betta, sistar. I'll try to get back t'morrow."

"I'm gonna walk 'er to da car. I'll be back," Barlow assured Michelle.

"Is there any way I can peep at Alan before I go?" she asked once they were in the hallway.

"You could." Barlow said not so confidently. "He's in ICU. Will you trust me that you don't wanna do that just yet?" he asked her as they entered the elevator.

Looking away in tears, she nodded her head sadly. He turned her face back towards him with his finger. "He's gonna be alright. It's just that he's an Alan we're not used to seein'. I don't want you to see 'im like that."

"Lis'en at you," she said with a half-smile, "I should be encouraging you. But you sound like you truly believe that."

"I do." Ushering her into the car, he said, "kiss da babies for me."

"Yes, sir, Mr. Barlow. And you try to get some rest. I'll brang lunch t'morra."

#

In the Bentley, Sam expressed his interest in the family. "How is everyone, Mrs. Barlow?"

"I didn't get to see Al. Rob felt I should wait until I could handle it betta. He's in a coma in ICU. Michelle is on da verge of a nervous breakdown but physically she only has a fractured collarbone. And little AJ. He's just a trooper. He's all banged up, has a broken arm and still takan' care of his mom. But Rob believes Al will be ok, evan though he wouldn't let me see 'im."

"Thank God they're all as well as they are. I've been worried," he said to her. It never dawned on Chasidy that he might be close enough to them to be worried. But he had worked for Rob for many years. There certainly must be some emotional connection to them, just like there is between the two of them in the short time they've known each other.

Briefly, Chasidy's train of thought changed. *I'll bet Rob doesn't have a clue how Sam feels about his family. All these years, he's been seen as only an employee. He's as much a part of his family as the rest of us. That's why he told him about Mic when we were kidnapped.* Chasidy felt like she should share her and Sam's conversation with Rob.

#

The room was quiet. Caitlin and the babies were sleeping. Chasidy saw a note on the table: *All fed by 9:30.* That was thirty minutes ago. She let Caitlin sleep as she prepared herself for bed. She suspected tomorrow would be a long day. And prayed it would be a better day. She is indeed proud of her husband though. She thought he would be torn apart over Alan's condition. Perhaps his growing belief in God and His goodness has something to do with that. She pondered those thoughts as she dozed off to sleep.

Ironically, Third Al was the first to wake around 12:30am for a diaper change and nursing. She couldn't easily settle him down even when he began to nurse. It was as if he expected his father to be holding him in her stead. Chasidy scolded as she warmed a bottle for him, "Lis'en, little fella. I'm mama. I can care fa you any time of day." She smiled at him. "But it's quite all right to miss daddy I suppose." She kissed his little forehead. "There. There's a kiss from 'im." He stopped pouting his little lips and smiled at the feel of her kiss. That brought a smile to Chasidy's face. "Wait 'il Rob hears about this." She chuckled. It was amazing, each child reacted the same way to her late-night feeding. They had all gotten used to Rob on the late shift. They knew the feel of his firm but gentle touch, the sound of his sweet sultry voice and likely the smell of his wild woodsy scent. That's what they were expecting after midnight. That's what they wanted. *Well, I'm glad mom is an acceptable second choice.* She thought to herself. She sang for the first time *Hear the Wind Blow* to each of them and rocked them backed to sleep, one by one, of course.

They awakened again around three thirty, ok this time with mommy's loving touch. Feeding time went by much quicker because she didn't have to warm bottles. Once more, three hours later they were at it again. Chasidy had no idea what Rob went through on the night shift. *No wonder he's so tired in the mornings.* She thought.

Chasidy wanted to go back to the hospital but didn't want to leave Caitlin on baby duty alone this time. Not to mention, she didn't want to have to rush back. Caitlin wondered if the hospital would be safe for the preemies. She and Caitlin were discussing that when Barlow phoned her. "Good mornin', Beautiful."

"Good mornan', Sir. Everythan' went ok last night?"

"Nothin' eventful eith'r way. That can be interpreted as ok. What about there?" He asked.

"Oh! She said excitedly. "Let me tell you about here," she started. "Every one of those little boogers woke up in da middle of da night wantan' you. They knew I was not their daddy. I had to use da bottle to feed 'em like you do and give 'em a firm talking to. I had to let them know that I am still their mothar evan afta midnight."

Barlow laughed, "My babies!" he said proudly.

"Caitlin and I were just discussing brangan', 'em with me at noon," she shared with him. "She's concerned about them being preemies in that environment."

Barlow thought, "she's absolutely right. I'll check on gettin' 'em a private waitin' area. I'll let you know b'fore noon."

"Wonderful. One more thing," she continued.

"What's that?"

"Sam."

"Sam?" Barlow asked surprised.

"This has had a real effect on 'im. He's very worried about all of them," she informed him.

"He is?" Barlow asked, even more surprised.

"Think about it, Rob. He's worked fa you a lotta years. Yor family was bound ta b'come his family too. And who was it that told you that Mic was in trouble when I was in trouble?" she reasoned.

"Sam," he answered.

"Sam," Chasidy confirmed, "Maybe you could invite 'im up to visit with 'em?"

"Thanks Beautiful, I'll do that. Mic and AJ told me to say hi."

"Say hi, back. I hope she's betta since yur there."

"She seems to be."

"You have that effect on people. Do I need to come now and bring you some breakfast?"

"I can have somethin' delivered."

"Ok. See ya at noon."

Barlow isn't as strong as Chasidy thinks. When he first visited Al, he could only stay a few minutes. He was unable to handle seeing him all bandaged up, hooked up to machines and wearing a brace on his neck. That was the reason he didn't want her to see him just yet.

This morning, he tried again. He knew Michelle would ask about him. He wanted to be able to tell her something positive. He took a deep breath before stepping into the room followed by a short prayer. He stood at the entry way for a few seconds to get his composure. Then walked slowly towards Al's bed. Touching his hand, hoping he could feel his touch. He began to speak hoping he could hear him also. "It's been a long night, Buddy. You haven't been this quiet since I've known ya. All it took was yor truck doin' topsy turvy one time. Next time yur takin' da plane. No arguing. In case yur wonderin', AJ's doin' fine. Mic is drivin' herself crazy worryin' about ya. Chasidy wants to see ya, but I asked her to wait a day or two. I can't hardly stand to see ya wrapped up this way ma'self." He took a short breather. "Here's somethin' you nev'r would've guessed. Sam is worried about y'all too. I'm gonna see if he wants to come up when he brings Chasidy taday. I know I don't have to tell ya all of us are rootin' for you to pull through this."

Barlow decided to change the one-sided conversation to something more pleasant. "Chasidy had to do graveyard shift with da babies last night. I was h're with you guys. She said this mornin' all four of my little ones missed me. She could barely calm 'em down and she had to bottle feed them like I do. Isn't that funny, how they get used to routine like that? I'll tell ya, I missed being on duty last night. Those little fellas really grow on ya, don't they?" His phone rang so he stepped outside the room to answer it. It was Mr. Miller. "Mr. Miller, how are you?"

"I'm well, Mr. Barlow. I just heard on the news about Mr. Ferguson. How is he?"

"He's in a coma. But he's hangin' in there."

"And his family?"

"They're bett'r than he is. But he's gonna be alright. He's gonna get through this."

"I'm praying for him and his family," Mr. Miller told Barlow. "I feel bad that he was down here on business with me when this happened."

"Now don't you go beatin' ya'self up. It's Al's job to do just what he did for ya. That could've hap'ened at any given time. And don't you worry about da project eith'r, it'll begin and end on time," Barlow told him before he asked.

"Well, you all take care, now," Mr. Miller said and then hung up the phone.

His phone rang again as soon as he and Mr. Miller disconnected. Barlow was a little shocked. "Terrence. Good mornin'."

"Hey Dad. Cait told me about the accident. How's Uncle Al doing?"

"He's in a coma, son. But he's gonna be fine. You just help us believe that."

D.M. Williams

"I will. Let me know when he wakes up."

"Will do, son." When he got back to the room, he was elated to tell Al Terrence had checked up on him. "I think you have an admirer," he concluded.

Barlow wasn't quite ready to leave his friend. He knew Mic would be expecting a report. He never imagined he would be in this place again and especially with his best friend. His brother even. But for whatever reason. He's not afraid. He trusts God that his brother will make a full recovery. But what would he tell Mic? That he believes Al will be alright. Or would he tell her the truth; that he looks like he's barely hanging on by a thread. *That's foolishness, Barlow.* He told himself. *Are you trying to send her to an early grave? You know her heart can't take that.* Not being able to figure out what to say to Michelle. He stayed with Al until Chasidy came with lunch. "I love you, Buddy," he said to him before he left, "Get bett'r soon."

#

He helped them bring the babies in bragging about last night and teasing Chasidy at the same time. "Mama just thinks she's the head of this outfit, don't she? You showed her who da real man in charge is." Chasidy just smiled and shook her head. "Nothin' ta say?" he asked grinning.

"Nothan', real man in charge. Just don't look at me cross-eyed when I brang 'em up here to you t'night," she retaliated. Then she asked, "Any change with Al?"

"Not yet. I don't know what to say to Mic," he admitted.

"You want me to help?" Chasidy volunteered.

"If you can," Barlow agreed.

"I can. We have to tell 'er somethan'. Knowan' a little bit of da bad news is betta' than not knowan' anythan' at all. She needs to hear somethan' about his condition. R'membar when she and I were missan'. Not knowan' anythan' was da worst part. Wasn't it?"

"Yeah. Yur right," he agreed.

#

They settled Caitlin, Sam, and the babies in the private waiting area. Then proceeded on to visit Mic and AJ. Chasidy stopped him. "Rob. I'll need to see him first."

148

All of a sudden, he remembered Al and Ethel warning him about treating her like a porcelain doll. "Alright." He reached for her hand. "Come with me."

She braced herself for the worst. But she had to do this for her friend. She needs her. And so do AJ and Rob. Tears immediately formed in her eyes, but she held them back as she approached the bed. She hugged him for a long time and kissed him on the cheek. "If I had known you were gonna do all this for a kiss, I would've defied Rob two years ago." Barlow chuckled at that. "Yor wife and yor son are going stir crazy. They miss you. They're scared b'cause they haven't been able to see you since y'all been here." She touched his hand to hold it. "Now I'm gonna go tell them that yur doing betta'. Don't make me a liar. Ok?" He squeezed her hand. She shrieked.

"What is it?" Barlow asked.

"It felt like…" She looked at Barlow smiling. "He squeezed my hand." Barlow came over to the bed. Chasidy told Al, "I'm gonna put yor hand in Rob's hand. If you can hear me, try to squeeze his hand."

At first there was nothing. Barlow shook his head. "Al, if you can hear my voice squeeze my hand." He looked at Chasidy smiling. "Go get da nurse."

He was still holding his hand when the team came in. "He squeezed your hand, your wife said?"

"Yes. Hers' first and then mine," Barlow explained.

"Step back please, let us get to him," One of the nurses said.

"I can't. He won't let go of my hand," Barlow told them. "Hey Buddy, these fellas need to take a look at you. They need me to move outta their way. You need to let go of my hand so I can do that. I won't go anywhere." The staff watched as Al loosened his grip.

Chasidy was ecstatic. "I'm gonna go tell Mic and AJ."

"Wait for me a minute. Barlow stopped her. "I wanna go with you. I wanna hear what they say first." Chasidy waited very impatiently by the doorway. The team conducted verbal tests with Al trying to see if he understood them. He responded slowly only once, but never opened his eyes. When Barlow and Chasidy tried to get him to respond to them again, he didn't. One of the staff members explained that Al might be drifting into a vegetative state. "This could go on for weeks," they explained.

On the way to see Michelle, Barlow elected to stay true to his trust in God. "I understand what they're sayin'. Their educational background makes them more dependent on medical circumstances," he told Chasidy. "But I'm understandin' this God thing more and more with each trial I'm faced with. I b'lieve that was God's way of lettin' us know that he's gonna come through this with a full recovery."

I'm b'lievan' that with you," Chasidy agreed.

"You b'lieved it first. I didn't know what to tell Mic. But you knew you would once you saw Al for ya'self." He stopped to get in a quick hug. "I'm also learnin' yur more than just my porcelain doll. Yur da missin' piece that makes me whole. My brass fittin'."

"Porcelain doll," Chasidy repeated in confusion.

"I'll explain fully lat'r. But, in short, I've had a porcelain doll syndrome about you ever since we first met. I'm learnin' yur tough'r than that," he told her.

Chasidy knew that Rob wanted to be the one who shared the good news with Mic and AJ, so she went to check on the babies and retrieve Sam. Rob wanted to start Sam's visit with Mic and AJ. From there he would take him in to see Al. By the time he had finished telling them about the movement he and Chasidy witnessed, Sam entered the room. "And here's that surprise I told you about," Barlow told them. "They both squealed, "Sam!" At the same time, holding each of their one arm out for hugs.

"Me, first, Sam!" AJ begged, "Me first."

"Oh, go ahead. That means I get da longest one," Michelle said giving in.

"I'm happy yur all alright," Sam said in his human voice, "I was quite worried. I'm grateful to Mr. Barlow for allowing me to see you."

"So are we, Sam," Michelle agreed. "For future references, you don't need Rob's permission to come visit us. Anywhere. Yur always welcome. Al told me how you w're da one who let them know I was missin'. I'll nev'r fa'get that. Thank you."

"What else could I do? The three of you mean as much to me as Mr. and Mrs. Barlow." Sam becoming emotional, immediately changed the subject, "I'll bet little Remi is missing you make a fuss over her too," Sam added.

"Well, that makes two of us," Michelle added smiling.

"If you need anything, Mrs. Ferguson, just let me know," Sam told her. "And that goes double for you, Little Guy."

"Ok," AJ spoke.

And then Michelle. "Well, all I need right now is for you to stop calling me Mrs. Ferguson. Aft'r a sentimental confession like that, we're not fixin' ta go back to that formal stuff. I'm Mic from now on. You know that anyway."

Sam chuckled, "Mic it is," he agreed.

Barlow added, "That's a good idea, Sam. You can call me Rob from now on."

"That might be a little more difficult, Sir," Sam told him, "I'm on yor payroll."

Barlow teased, "I can stop payin' ya."

Sam answered immediately, "I'll give it my best shot, Rob." They all laughed. "That was easier than I thought it would be."

Michelle got another surprise when Chasidy and Caitlin rolled the babies in for her to see them. "Remi! Babies!" Michelle squealed.

"Nice save, girl," Chasidy warned, "I was starting to feel like my otha' babies w're invisible to ya."

"Well, fa'give me for being biased," Michelle apologized. "But you shouldn't have given her my name if you didn't want me to have favorites," she reasoned reaching her one good arm for little Remi.

"We have thirty days to change a name," Chasidy hinted at a quick solution to that problem.

"You wouldn't dare," Michelle argued. "B'sides, it wouldn't matt'r now. I'd still call her Remi anyway." Chasidy laughed shaking her head at Michelle.

"Rob explained about Al well enough?" Chasidy asked on a more serious note.

"Yes. I'm with you and Rob," Michelle said as she played with the baby. "I have to side with you guys. I don't know my husband any oth'r way."

"You may need to get to know 'im differently," Chasidy said to her.

"Whatta you mean?"

"Yur da otha' half of his strength. Just like he's da otha' half of yors. You need to be in that room with him Mic. He needs you more than he needs anyone else right now. He needs to hear yor voice, feel yor touch, smell yor perfume. Every one of his senses needs to absorb you. So, all of that fear yur harboran' right here," she touched her heart, "needs to be channeled into yor strength so you can get betta' and go see about yor husband."

"Rob said he's all bandaged up. I don't know if I can take that."

Chasidy thought back to a conversation they had during their first visit at the little house. "You told me once Mic, that Al was only serious during football season. Here's a news flash girl, Al is serious about you and AJ all da time. You've known 'im far longa' than I have. I don't know why I have to tell you that."

"That's nothin' but the truth," Barlow agreed. "His whole world evolves around da two of you."

"It wasn't until I told him I was coman' to tell you and AJ that he was doin' betta and to not make me a liar that he squeezed my hand." Chasidy continued. "If you and Al were in opposite places, where do you think he would be?"

"He'd be right there with me. 24/7," Michelle answered.

"That's right," Chasidy agreed. "Now get ya'self betta so you guys can be home by Christmas. Cause you know Rob gon' act a fool ova' those babies knowan' doggone well they can't play with nothan' at one month old. I know you don't wanna miss that. Cause it won't be possible to explained it with words."

They all laughed. "Yur right. If he'll build his seven-year-old nephew a whole amusement park, these kids are doomed. Al will definitely need to see that for 'imself."

Shortly after Barlow finished his lunch, the next ICU visitor's period was beginning. He took Sam down for a short peek at Al. He too began to tear up. None of them had ever seen Alan as weak and helpless as he is now. The bandages made him look weak. The bar holding his head steady, made him look fragile. Sam touched his hand, holding it for only a few seconds. "Hang in there, Mr. Al.

You'll be making fun again in no time; likely of all this. We won't have it any other way."

Barlow took mental notes of how much attention Sam had paid to everyone. He called AJ Little Guy. He knew Michelle has a soft spot for Remi. He even knows Alan makes light of everything through his jokes. Barlow came to the realization that Sam has been a silent part of his family for a long time, just like Chasidy said. If there was a positive side to all of these events other than his growing faith in God, it was that his family was growing as well, one trial encounter at a time. He certainly would be looking at Sam in a new light from now on.

#

Caitlin and Chasidy took the babies back to the private room for feeding and a nap. Once Sam was back with them in the waiting room, Barlow made his way to the chapel, again. This time he started with the gratitude he felt in his heart. "Thank you, God first and foremost for my family. Family I didn't even realize I had. Thank you especially for sparing the lives of my brother and his family. I don't understand why these things hap'en to da people I love, it seems, almost back-to-back. But God, I trust you. And I will continue to trust you. Have yor way, Lord. Test me until yur satisfied."

Chasidy had come to check on him to make certain he was ok. He loved Al as much as he loved Ethel. He said he was fine, but she had to see for herself. She didn't hear all of the prayer he spoke out loud, but she heard enough. She thought on his desire to be baptized as she listened. He didn't ask God for his brother's life. He believed Him for it. She was proud of his growing faith in God, learning to trust Him in spite of what circumstances appeared to be. She turned quietly and walked out of the chapel, leaving her husband in the best place possible, the company of their God.

#

Michelle called her mom to tell her about the accident. They took the next flight out to Savannah to be with them. They got in just before the last visiting hours. Mr. Peterson was expressing his disappointment at Michelle for not calling them sooner. "We're your parents. We should have been the first one you called. Not this Barlow fellow."

"Jeffery. Stop it." Mrs. Peterson spoke. "This is exactly why she didn't call us." Mrs. Peterson, who was sitting on the bed holding AJ, turned her attention from her husband to Michelle. "How is Alan, Dear?"

"He's in a coma. I haven't seen him yet," replied Michelle.

Barlow heard the conversation from outside the door. He elected to ignore Mr. Peterson's comments for now. He was more concerned for his family's health. He did, however, address Michelle. "You ok, Mic?"

"I'm fine," she answered. "Anything else on Al?" Barlow shook his head.

The initial doctor who cared for Mic and AJ came in late evening to check on them. AJ checked out fine. The doctor told them he could be released tomorrow if he had somewhere to go. Barlow assured him he did. Michelle promised she would stay calm if they didn't give her any more knockout pills. "My husband needs me," She told him, "I can't be with him if I'm sleeping all da time." The doctor agreed. Visiting hours in ICU was over. She made a date to visit him first thing in the morning. Chasidy allotted Barlow time to clean up and change and she too left for the hotel to get some rest. It had been an eventful day. A very good eventful day.

Once again, Mr. Peterson voiced his opinion. "Why don't you go with your wife, Mr. Barlow. Val and I will watch over Michelle and AJ."

"And who's gonna watch over AL?" Barlow asked him.

"I never thought about that," he admitted.

"Of course, you didn't," Barlow agreed.

At the car, Barlow stared long and hard at his wife, remembering how things changed for the better the moment she arrived. "I wish you didn't have to go."

Rendering him a tender kiss, she said, "Me too. But t'morra will be here b'fore we know it."

"He joked, "Aft'r midnight when you bring da babies?"

"Yep." They laughed softly.

"Good night, Sweetheart." She wanted to say it was too early for good nights, but she could see he was tired.

She gave him a long *I'll miss you* hug. "I love you. Don't let Mic's dad upset you. Get some rest."
"And you," he said slowly closing the door.

Chasidy was tired too but she had trouble winding down from the day. Until now she was the one who needed everyone else's support. She didn't realize how much supporting someone takes out of you. She was thrilled that Alan chose her to speak to. She was glad that she could convince Michelle to be with her husband. She was oh so happy that Little Guy might be released tomorrow. And she was proud that Sam had been officially inducted into the family. However, the one thing she was most excited about was her husband's new walk with God. He had developed a zeal for God. A heartache even. He was determined to learn more about Him and become closer to Him regardless of the tests being thrown at him. There's nothing sexier than a strong Christian man steadfast in his faith in God. Chasidy was falling in love with her husband all over again.

The one thing that bothered her though was leaving her husband in the clutches of a man whom everyone could see hated him for no apparent reason. She prayed they would survive the night together. She took a warm lavender bath to calm herself so that she could get some much-needed sleep. It worked too well. She didn't hear the babies wake through the night for their feedings. When she awakened at seven the next morning, she learned that Caitlin had taken care of them all night long.

"I'm so sorry," she apologized to Caitlin. "Why didn't you wake me?"

"Because you obviously needed da rest. You had a long day yesterday," Caitlin scolded. "We're not gonna do that today," she ordered.

"I thought I left my husband at da hospital," Chasidy spoke insinuating the resemblance.

"Well, Mom. Dad is right most of da time. You just had four babies. Yor body isn't healed yet. You don't wanna end up back in da hospital for Christmas, do you?"

Chasidy knew her daughter was right. She agreed to slow her pace today. She would stay at the hotel today unless Rob absolutely needed her. He became concerned when she told him she wasn't coming today unless it was absolutely necessary. "My daughter has put me under house arrest."

"Are you alright?"

"Yes. I'm fine. Really."

"Let me talk to Caitlin," he ordered.

"Hi Dad."

"What's going on with her?" he asked.

"I think she ova-did it a little yesterday. She didn't hear the babies last night, not even once when they woke up. But I took care of 'em. I just don't want 'er movin' too fast. Her body is still healin'."

"I agree with you one hundred percent. Thank you, Baby for looking out for her."

"Whatta you talkin' about? That's my mom. We've been lookin out for each otha' all my life."

Barlow chuckled. "Put 'er back on da phone."

"You two done talkan' about me like I'm not evan here?"

"Chasidy, you know she's every bit of right. All is good here. If da doctor releases AJ today, I'll bring 'im by da hotel to y'all."

"And if he doesn't, will I go a whole day without seein' you?" she asked pathetically.

"No," he said firmly. "I'll come by there anyway. Go back to bed. Caitlin will call you if she needs you." Mr. Peterson took mental notes of that entire conversation.

Mrs. Peterson was concerned. "Is yor wife alright, Mr. Barlow?"

"Cait thinks she ov'r did it a little, but otherwise, yes. Thank you for askin'," he answered.

Chasidy, actually feeling like she wasn't completely rested, didn't argue with her husband. She went straight back to bed. "Wake me if they get to be too much for you," she ordered.

Chasidy slept until two o'clock. She was still asleep when Barlow arrived with AJ. "He can rest on da sofa. I'm gonna ord'r him a rollaway on my way back out," he told Caitlin.

"No need for that. I haven't been in my bed since I've been here. I've been in here with da babies."

"Then I'll get da rollaway for you," Barlow told her. "Has she been sleepin' all day?" he asked about Chasidy.

"Yes. Yesterday was too much for her," Caitlin told him. "You can't be superwoman having just gone through a forced labor of four babies. And at her age." Caitlin protested.

"I'm glad you came along. This won't hap'en again," Barlow declared. He peeped in on her and was about to leave without waking her.

Caitlin showed him the error of his ways. "Dad," she started. "Da only thing that would be worse than Mom gettin' sick afta having these four beautiful babies is if you walked back out that door without wakin' her to say hello. No matter how good yor intentions are."

"Yeah," he thought, "Yur right again young lady." He immediately turned and went back into the room to say hello. Wanting her to stay as relaxed as possible, he crawled in bed beside her and put his arms around her. She awakened smiling at the welcoming scent of her husband holding her. "Hi beautiful."

"You keep that up and I'm gonna thank that's my name."

"It is, as far as I'm concerned. I didn't wanna wake you. But Caitlin said if I left without wakin' you, I'd come out bett'r facing a F5 tornado."

"That child is in da wrong profession. She needs to be an advisor," Chasidy told him. "She just saved yor marriage."

Barlow chuckled at that. "How are you feelin'? Really?" He asked her, touching her forehead for warmth.

"Otha' than being tired. I feel fine. Really," she answered.

"Ok," Barlow said accepting her answer. "AJ's h're in Caitlin's room. She said she hadn't been using it. I'm gonna have a rollaway sent up for 'er."

"Yeah, she stays with da babies," Chasidy told him what Caitlin had already shared with him.

"She's wonderful, Chasidy," Barlow complimented. "But then how can she not be with a moth'r like you." Chasidy smiled at his flattery. All of a sudden, he wasn't in such a big hurry to get back to the hospital. "I didn't tell you, Terrence called to check on Al."

"He did?" Chasidy replied. "I don't know why that surprises me. Caitlin says he's absolutely crazy about 'im."

"He is? I'm jealous." Barlow pouted.

"Don't be. You have yor share of adoration in this family. Terrence is as goofy as Al is. There's no way he wouldn't have connected with him." They shared a giggle. "How did Mic's visit go with Al?" she asked him.

"When she first went in, she couldn't stay. As soon as she saw him, she burst into tears and left da room."

"You know, that's everybody's initial reaction. It's like that should be anybody else but Alan." Chasidy explained her own reactions when she first saw him. "But she went back, right?"

"Yeah. Immediately," he continued. "She went back in and didn't stop until she was kissin' all over whatever part of his face she could get to. She only left him long enough to bid AJ farewell. Then she went right back in."

"That's wonderful. He really needs 'er right now."

"Well, he has her and it's all yor doin'. But now I need you to take care of you. You follow Dr. Caitlin's ord'rs, or you'll be in big trouble, Missy."

Chasidy hated to change the subject, but she was curious. "How did Mr. Peterson feel about AJ leavan' with you instead of him?"

"Bad, I hope," Barlow said without thinking. "I really feel sorry for his wife. She has to live with that."

Chasidy was in complete agreement with her husband. "You'll be here for a while?" she asked him hoping he said yes.

"Sure. Mic and Al are t'gether. Her mom is watchin' ov'r her. If she needs me, she can call. I think I'll lay right h're with you for a spell."

She heard Rose crying in the outer room. "Sounds like a spell is ova'. "Will you bring 'er to me?"

As he was getting up, he said to her, "I still don't know how you can tell them apart like that. They all sound da same ta me."

Little Rose stopped crying as soon as her dad picked her up. As he laid her in Chasidy's arms she wined, "If y'all keep this up, mommy's gonna get very jealous."

Barlow giggled. "You may as well let me feed her. Caitlin started warming a bottle already."

That was fine and dandy with Chasidy. She knows Rob enjoys his time with them. But she got her opportunity to bond when LJ awakened right after. The other two slept for at least another hour and the process began all over again.

Caitlin took it upon herself to order room service since the family was together and not even Little Guy hadn't eaten yet. Barlow invited Sam to have dinner with them. That would become a norm since his family induction. Barlow celebrated each member of his family. They were all special to him. He has officially become a *family man*. And he was loving every minute of it. Things are very different for him now. Life is different for him now, full of love, pain, joy, fear, expectations, and contentment. The good, the bad, and the ugly Chasidy once told him, were all rolled up in this wonderful thing called family. And he wouldn't change any of it.

During dinner, Chasidy's phone rang. "It's Michelle," she announced as she checked to see who was calling. "Hi Mic."

"Chasidy!" she said excitedly. "Yur not gonna believe this. No. Wait. Yes, you will. You were right." Michelle was carrying on so that she was doing more rambling than talking.

"Mic. Calm down and talk slowly in full sentences," Chasidy ordered.

"Ok." Michelle did. "Are you near Rob and AJ?"

"Yes, I am. Should I put you on speaka'?"

"Yes," she said definitely.

"Ok. Talk to us girl."

"You were right about Al. He did need me with him. I stayed with' im all day talkin' to 'im, holdin' his hand, caressin' his face. About three hours ago he started respondin'. First with a hand squeeze like with you guys. And about an hour aft'r that his eyelids began to move. Aft'r that, they called da doctor to check on 'im." She stopped, likely to catch her breath for she had begun to cry again. Then she continued. "He's not awake just yet, but they're movin' him to my room so we can be togeth'r. Chasidy, da doctor said he could be comin' out of da coma. I just had to call and thank you."

AJ started crying also. "Mom, does this mean I can see him now?"

"Yes, Baby. That's exactly what it means," she told him. Her dad listened to that conversation also, taking more mental notes.

"Uncle Rob. Can you take me t'morrow?"

Barlow was concerned about that. He remembered the effect the first glance of Al had on them. He wasn't sure if AJ should see that right now. "Mic are you sure that's a good idea. R'member how you reacted when you first saw 'im?"

"Rob. Bring him to see his dad. Please," she insisted. Chasidy had approached her with an epiphany, but Michelle made it a plan. "If Al would wade through hell and high waters to save me, he would pry open da Pearlie gates to come back to his son."

Barlow couldn't argue with that. They had only the day before agreed on Al's strong will towards his family. "Ok," Barlow agreed, "I think we'll all come. See ya t'morrow."

"Good night y'all. I love you guys." Michelle, in her excitement, hung up before any of them could respond. The rest of the dinner was all smiles. AJ, who was only nibbling before the call, developed a whole new famish afterwards and ate like a soldier thereafter.

#

The next day at the hospital, AJ ran straight past his mom to his dad, giving him a long hug. It was as if he didn't even see the bandages or the neck brace. All he saw was his dad whom he hadn't seen in four days. He immediately began talking to him. "Dad, I've missed you so much. I didn't know if I was gonna see you again.

161

Nobody was telling me anything about you. It was like I didn't matter until Uncle Rob and Aunt Chasidy got here. They told me what happened to you. They told me you couldn't move. I hope I didn't hurt you when I hugged you. I love you, Dad. I miss you. Please come back to me. Please."

Mic put her arms around him to comfort him. He turned to hug her. It didn't matter to AJ that his dad wasn't able to talk back. Every so often he would strike up a conversation with him. In fact, they all fell right in place behind AJ and had their own conversations with Al.

Barlow talked about their Tom and Huck days when he fell out of the big oak tree trying to catch a cat who had taken his lunch. "I knew you had a hard head that day when that cat outsmarted you. You w're bound and d'termined to catch that rascal. She was bound and d'termined you wouldn't. I declare man, I saw that cat laughin' at you as it was walkin' away. Now I'm only gonna tell what hap'ened to you back in those days. If you want'em to know about me, yur gonna have to wake up and tell 'em ya'self," Barlow encouraged.

"That's ok Baby. I got cha. I r'member yor Tom and Huck days, but I know 'bout yor time on da grill bett'r. I know he really should've let you have da grill that day. We w're too hungry for him to be burning up food. Did you see Chasidy trying to chew that stuff? And she said her husband did a fine job. He sure did. We had plenty of time to talk 'cause we couldn't eat nothin'." Barlow laughed. Everyone joined him.

Chasidy listened as they reminisced fondly. All she could really think about was how Al teased Rob about being too old to perform and the babies they now share. "Well, all I have to say to you, Al, is that you owe my husband an apology. Before we were married you said he was too old to enjoy me. We have proof that he enjoys me extremely well."

"Ewe!" Caitlin reacted. "T.M.I!" Close yor ears, Baby," she said to AJ, "Old folks doing their business is not for us to hear."

"Careful who you call old," Barlow warned. "Me and ya mom got a lotta youth left in us yet," he defended.

"Yeah!" Please don't make us prove it again," Chasidy pleaded pretendedly. "We have to wait until Al apologizes da first time."

Mic's parents listened as the happy chatter filled the room sporadically until well into the evening. Mrs. Peterson wished she had happy chatter to contribute. Mr. Peterson was simply wishing it would all be over with. Everyone else were enjoying their time with Al and hoped he was enjoying them too.

"It sounds like you all have a wonderful time together. I can see the closeness between you. I'm happy Michy is surrounded by so much love," Mrs. Peterson shared. "Especially since I couldn't be there for her."

"Well, yur h're now, Mrs. Peterson," Barlow said. "That's all that matt'rs at this moment."

Except for lunch, AJ stayed perched on his dad's bed the whole day to be close to him; making up for time missed over the past few days. No one heard Alan's extremely weak voice say to AJ, "Tell 'er I apologize. Stop talkin' ov'r me like I'm not h're."

"Hey Aunt Chasidy," AJ called.

"Yeah Baby," she answered.

"Dad says he apologizes," AJ said to her smiling.

"What?" She asked for clarification. They all looked at AJ and Alan. His eyes were still closed.

AJ repeated, "Dad said he apologizes and stop talkin' over 'im like he's not here." Everyone made their way closer to the bed.

Michelle was already on the other side of the bed opposite AJ. She gave him a stern look. "Boy you had bett'r not be playin'."

"He is playin'. But I did say that" Alan said weakly.

She buzzed the nurse's station, squealing with joy and hugging her husband at the same time. "Yes, you need something?" the nurse asked.

"He's awake!" Michelle said. "Al is awake!"

When the nurse came in Al's eyes were still closed. "Why do you think he's awake?" She asked skeptically.

"He was just talkin to us," Michelle told her. "Everybody heard 'im."

"Mr. Ferguson, how're you doing?" the nurse asked. "Can you hear me? Say something if you can hear me." Alan didn't respond. AJ was still grinning from cheek to cheek. Everyone else waited for

Alan to say something. "Well, he's not saying anything now," The nurse said as if she didn't believe her.

Michelle knew that Al was being his usual prankful self even moments out of a coma, "Al if you don't say somethin' to this woman makin' her think I'm crazy, I'm gonna have Rob make you walk home."

"And I'll do it for makin' all of us look crazy," Barlow agreed.

The room was quiet. The nurse glanced around the room at everybody. She wasn't expecting to hear Al say anything, that's why he startled her when he did. "They're all crazy. I nev'r said a word."

AJ bellowed with laughter, "Nice Dad!"

Relieved that she wasn't surrounded by a bunch of lunatics, she began examining Alan. "Mr. Ferguson can you open your eyes?"

"No," he said, "They hurt."

"Can you feel my hand?" She touched his hand.

"Yes," "What about now?" She touched his leg and then his feet.

"Yes," he said both times.

"Ok. You just relax," she said. "I'll get Dr. Pelonoski."

It took another forty-five minutes before the doctor came in. During the wait, Michelle must've kissed his cheek fifty times.

"So, if I keep my eyes closed, yur gonna continue to kiss me like that?" he asked her.

"Yes," she answered, "But if you open them, I'll give you a big juicy one on da lips."

"See Rob. We're not old eith'r," he spoke softly.

Barlow laughed. "Not by a long shot, Buddy."

Mrs. Peterson made her way closer to Alan. "Hello Son."

"Mrs. Peterson?" Alan asked.

"Yes. Jeffrey and I both are here. "I'm so glad you came back to us. I haven't had a chance yet to get to know the man my daughter fell in love with. I'm looking forward to that."

"Me too, Mam." Michelle shared the smile Alan didn't, not knowing that he was unable to at the moment.

When Dr. Pelonoski arrived, he could barely get to the bed for the room full of people. Chasidy helped Caitlin roll the babies out into the hallway until he was finished.

Sam joined them there. AJ refused to move from his dad's side. Dr. Pelonoski explained that he couldn't properly care for Alan until he did. AJ reluctantly went to sit with Uncle Rob.

Mr. Peterson asked AJ to join him in the hallway. "No thanks," AJ said, "I'm gonna stay with my Uncle Rob."

Once he finished his examination, he had learned that not only could Alan not move his eyelids to even blink but had limited movements with his lips. He couldn't even perform a simple task like a smile and his breathing was sometimes difficult. This was why his words were muddled and he spoke in a whisper to AJ. Dr. Pelonoski gave them a few theories. He began with the worst-case scenario. "Mr. Ferguson this could be one of three things. Let's start with the bad stuff first. The head trauma you suffered could have damaged the nerves connected to your eyes. If that's the case," he paused, "then this is likely permanent. Nothing can be done about it. However, I don't believe that's the case here. I just have to mention every possibility. I'm leaning more towards the second possibility due to your breathing issues and limited mouth movement. A fracture could've affected your nerves in some way and that is completely fixable with surgery. Now, let's hope for the last possibility. The brace we're using may be causing too much pressure on your facial nerves disabling them from functioning properly. The downside to that is, this one needs to stay on for at least three more days before we can switch it out."

"How soon can we know which one it is?" Michelle asked.

"I'm gonna order an x-ray for him first thing in the morning. That will either rule out or in one of the first two. Then we can proceed from there."

While the doctor was explaining his next plan of action, Barlow sent AJ to his grandmother and stepped out of the room. Meeting Chasidy in the hallway, he made acknowledgements. "The doctor's finishin' up now. You'll be able to go back in in just a moment. I'll be right back." Before she could ask, he explained, "I need to fill Bradley in on what's going on. Let 'im know Al will be out for a while."

Chasidy nodded. She knew that was only a half truth. He could've done that in front of her. She had her suspicions as to where he was really going. She was more than ok with that. Sure enough, Dr. Pelonoski walked out right behind Rob. Chasidy and the gang reentered the room. She didn't know if Mic's tears were of joy or sorrow and was almost afraid to ask. Especially with Rob running off to the chapel again. She walked over to Mic and began rubbing her back. "Good news?"

Michelle replied, "More like, not bad news."

"I'll take that," Chasidy replied, "Give it to me." Michelle explained all that the doctor had explained to them. That news does leave one with a bit of melancholy. Chasidy thought. But she's believing God for the latter. She knows that everyone else is also. Especially Rob. She leaned over and kissed Al on the cheek. "You keep hope alive. Yor gonna be home in no time. We're all believan' that. Right AJ? she asked, who by now had made his way back to his dad's bed.

"That's right Aunt Chasidy!" he answered excitedly.

Turning back to Mic, she said, "I hate to leave you, girl. But I got into trouble da otha' day for ova-doing it. Caitlin and Rob double teamed me and wouldn't let me out yesterday," she explained.

"That's why you didn't come?" Mic asked.

"Yes," Chasidy and Caitlin answered at the same time.

Now looking at Caitlin. "You did exactly right," Michelle told her. "You do that as often as you need to for her to take care of 'erself. Those babies need 'er. And so does Rob." She paused briefly, then said, "And so do I. We all need you, Chasidy."

Barlow walked in on the end of Mic's comment. "Yes, we do," he added.

"Great!" Chasidy spoke loudly. "Now I'm being triple teamed." She wasn't at all offended by that. She gave Al and Mic hugs getting ready to leave. AJ didn't make a move from his dad's side. Chasidy commented. "I guess Uncle Rob is gonna have ta arm wrestle you to get you away from Al."

"Dad, can I stay?" he asked his dad because he knows Al can't say no to him.

Michelle intervened, "Da hospital won't let you stay unless yur sick, Baby."

"I can break my oth'r arm," he said. Everybody laughed. Everybody except Mr. Peterson that is. They were sure Al was laughing inside too.

"Boy, get outta here b'fore I break it for ya," Michelle scolded.

Al helped her out a little intervening again, "Go Little Guy. See ya t'morrow. I love you."

"I love you too Dad." He said as he gave him a hug. Then he went around to his mom, giving her a hug too. "I love you too, Mom. Call me if dad needs me."

"What about me?" she asked jealously.

He answered like she should already know. "Of course, you too, Mom." Then he hugged his Grandma Valerie.

"What about Grandpa?" Mic asked him. He didn't want to hug his Grandpa Jeffery. But he knew his mom wanted him to. So, he did for her sake only.

<h1 style="text-align:center;font-style:italic;">Orphans Unacceptable</h1>

Mr. and Mrs. Peterson were preparing to leave as well. He suggested to AJ during their hug. "You know, your grandma and I would love for you to come visit with us tonight. We could take you out to dinn'r anywhere you wanna go."

"I'm gonna stay with Uncle Rob. But you could come have dinn'r with us in his room. Couldn't they, Uncle Rob?"

"They can if they want to," Barlow answered.

"Maybe next time," Mr. Peterson said with a snarl.

#

For several days Barlow had been lingering in an even more intense state of quietness that far surpassed before when Chasidy first had the babies. It doesn't bother Chasidy now. She's learning that these days, the quietness is significant of a definite train of thought. Usually pertaining to his walk with God. She loved that her husband was finding his own way to the Lord and not depending on her to do it. As the Christmas holiday draws closer and closer, she now knows exactly what she wants to give him for a holiday gift.

Just before bed that evening, he received a call from Bradley. He stepped out of the room to keep from disturbing her. "Go ahead Bradley."

"I'm sorry to bother you so late, but I need another field guy. Al left Gabe in charge in New Mexico and Henderson is on the West Coast. Al was looking forward to handling the Miller project himself. We're coming up on that two-week start date. I don't know who to send."

Barlow remembered his conversation with Mr. Miller right after Al's accident. "I did promise him we would start as scheduled in spite of Al's accident," Barlow confessed.

"Sir, you know I've been wrapped up in paperwork since day one. I don't know anything about field work."

Barlow laughed. "I know Bradley. You just do what you do best. Make sure all the paperwork is in order for us to get started," Barlow told him. "We're not gonna pull Gabe. Al's been hoppin' him around all ov'r da place. Let's give somebody else a chance to spread their wings. Put Gonzales on da radar for this project. I'll check with Al t'morrow to see what his thoughts are. I don't wanna go ov'r his head."

"He's that alert?" Bradley asked surprised.

"I think so," Barlow told him, "B'sides I think talkin' about work will do 'im a world of good. I'll get back with ya aft'r we talk."

"Thank you, Mr. Barlow. Say hello for me."

"I'll do that, Brad. Goodnight."

Barlow visited Al and Mic early that Sunday morning. He wanted to make sure he was there when the x-ray results and the doctor were in. They were still waiting for the techs to come get Al when Barlow got there. Al, as usual, lead with teasing. "Did you come early so you could leave my boy at da hotel?"

"No." Barlow chuckled. "Rest assured, he'll be h're with Chasidy lat'r," he defended.

"Oh, you and Caitlin lettin' 'er out da cage today?" Mic teased also.

Barlow chuckled again. "Actually, by her own doin, she's only comin to bring AJ. She said she would stay about an hour and then go back to da hotel. Cait and I didn't have anythin' to do with that decision."

"She's alright, isn't she?" Michelle sounded concerned.

"I think so," Barlow told her. "I think she's just a little more comfortable now that Al is awake and talkin'. Like da rest of us are." Then his phone rang. He shared with Al and Mic. "This is Terrence. He's already called once to check on ya." Barlow answered the phone. "Good mornin', son. Yur up awful early."

"I hope I didn't wake ya. Caitlin says Uncle Al's awake."

"He is at that. I've got ya on speaker. He's lis'nin right at ya. He can't talk very loud or very much. But you can say as much as you want to him."

"I'm not gonna hold you guys. I just want 'im to know I'm glad he's back with us. Things would be kinda boring without ya Unc."

Michelle agreed whole-heartedly. And everyone else. "Yea, but I'll be a lot more comfortable when I see his gorgeous ambers again," she added. Neither of the guys had a chance to comment. The tech came in right after to roll him down to x-ray.

He wasn't there long but Barlow took the opportunity to sort out some details with Mic while he was away. "You mentioned going home yesterday. Have you thought about that much when that time comes?"

"Rob, I've thought about nothin' but that," she said in an uncertain tone.

"Sounds like you need to talk about it," he noticed.

"It so close to Christmas," she started.

"Yeah, a couple of weeks or so," Barlow added.

"If he gets released before Christmas, …" she paused. "Last Christmas was da first Christmas he'd spent away from you. He tried to pretend like it didn't both'r 'im. Like AJ and I w're enough. But with Ethel gone and you off on yor travels, I could tell he wasn't completely happy. Let's be honest, Rob. There's a place in his heart that no one can fill but you."

"For da record, I have a matchin' place in my heart for him. Tell me yor thoughts," Barlow encouraged.

"I would hate to intrude on Chasidy and da babies. But maybe, just until da holidays are ov'r, we could bunk with you guys?" she pleaded.

"First of all, if you think you would be intrudin' on Chasidy, you don't know 'er as well as you think you do. What's that word she uses? 'Nonsense.' She would love havin' you guys there. In fact, she's probably already had that very thought 'erself. You guys can stay as long as you need to. Secondly, I believe he will be home in time for Christmas." That made Mic smile. "We'll all talk about it when Chasidy gets h're."

Before they knew it, Al was back in the room. "Rob, are you still h're?"

"Right h're, Buddy," he answered.

"Good," Al told him.

Since they were on the subject of Christmas, Barlow thought about AJ. "Mic and I w're just thinkin' about Christmas. It's close. Have you settled up with AJ yet? Is there anythin' I need to do?"

"Part of it," Al answered. "Some fellas w're comin' out aft'r I got home from this trip to start on a stable for me."

"A stable," Barlow asked smiling.

"Yeah." Michelle helped to keep Al from trying to talk so much. "Since he's developed this newfound love for animals and being outdoors, courtesy of yor wife and my friend, and there's so much room out there, Al decided to get 'im a horse for Christmas. He even hired someone to teach 'im how to ride and care for 'im."

"Man! That's a great idea," Barlow said excitedly. "He and his friends really enjoyed da horseback ride for his birthday. I'll make sure that stable is ready for 'im. Where're yur puttin' it? You already have da horse?"

"Yeah, a beautiful black Friesian, ready and waitin' for delivery Christmas Eve. He's so pretty, he could make me like animals," Michelle answered.

"I'll get right on that stable," Barlow promised.

"Da spot is already marked off," Al said.

"It is?" asked Mic.

"By da big pecan tree," Al told her.

Mic looked at Barlow. "He would give 'im da best spot on da property, wouldn't he?"

"Well, we are talkin' about AJ." They laughed. "Chasidy's gonna love this," he told them.

"She will?" Asked Al.

"Yeah. She loves horses," Barlow shared. "I found that out during AJ's birthday trip."

"Why am I not da least bit surprised about that?" Mic asked. "That woman is all about anything associated with da country. She nev'r would've pulled off a Greystone life."

Barlow smiled. "She actually fit in there pretty good. But I did know her heart wasn't fully in it. She was only doin' it for me. She was so much happier at da Little House, so much more herself."

"Well, I for one am glad. I like seeing AJ being *one with nature*." She smiled. "But lis'en, da fella already has da plans. He just needs to know where to start. Right AL?"

"Right."

Barlow thought. "So would you mind if I asked Cait to see if Antonio can show them around so they can get started?"

"That would be wonderful. Do you think he'll do it?" Mic asked.

"I think exactly that," Barlow said.

Mr. and Mrs. Peterson stood just outside the door. Mr. Peterson wanted to listen in on the conversation. Mrs. Peterson tried to get him to enter but he wouldn't. Finally, she knocked herself, and entered the room. Mr. Peterson was becoming more and more envious of Al and Barlow's relationship with his daughter for no apparent reason.

"Good morning, Sweetheart," her mother said.

"Good mornin, Mom."

"How are you feeling this morning, Alan?" she asked.

"Hopeful," Alan answered.

"Good. Stay that way." His mother-in-law replied.

"Did you sleep here last night?" Mr. Peterson asked Barlow before even speaking to anyone.

"Good mornin' ta you too, Dad." Michelle said before Barlow could answer him. She had been paying attention to the tension building between them. She knew Rob wasn't going to let that continue for much longer. Especially if it's upsetting to Alan. It wasn't only upsetting to Alan but to all of them.

Al had been talking quite a bit since Barlow's been there, so he purposely didn't bring up work just yet. He wanted to give him a chance to rest. He let him eat his breakfast in peace. He didn't eat much though. Other than orange juice and a couple of spoons of grits, he didn't really care for much else. Barlow thought it might have been too hard for him still with his limited mouth movement. Al loves to eat.

But Barlow's conscience was put at ease when Al brought up the subject himself. Being limited in speech, he got right to the point. "Tell Bradley ta put Gonzales in charge of da Miller project. Barlow chuckled an approving laugh.

"I'll do that, Buddy. Now you get some rest. AJ and Chasidy will be h're shortly." Al didn't need to be told that twice. A simple thing like talking takes a lot out of him. Eating was tiresome also. He encouraged Michelle to get some rest too. She felt compelled to watch over Barlow and her dad. She stared with a pleading glance at Barlow and her mother. She really was tired.

Barlow knew what she was thinking. He was pleasantly surprised that her mother knew also. "Get some rest, Michy. I'll put a muzzle on your dad's mouth." Michelle chuckled at that. Mr. Peterson, however, didn't think it was funny.

Dr. Pelonoski had the day shift on Sundays, so he had already come and gone by the time Chasidy and AJ made it. "What time will da doctor be in?" she asked.

"He's already been here," Mic told her.

"Good new then?" she asked.

"Well, he doesn't need surgery. That's good news," Mic told her.

"Why do I feel a *'but'* coman'?" Chasidy anticipated.

Barlow took over the explanation. "That is good news. Doctor believes changin' da brace will be da solution. He says there's nothin' else he can really do. He's talkin' about sendin' 'im home."

"That sounds good to me," Chasidy spoke carefully.

"Yeah, I think so," Barlow agreed. "We'll fly out in a day or two. Mic will go with us to get da house ready for 'im. Let me know what room she wants his equipment in. Then we'll come back to get 'im."

"You mean which room in our house, right?" Chasidy asked for clarification.

"No." Barlow purposely manipulated his conversation with Chasidy to show off how well he knows his wife. "Mic doesn't wanna intrude on you and da babies."

Chasidy looked at Mic disapprovingly and then back at Barlow. "What did you tell 'er?" Chasidy asked on the verge of being upset.

D.M. Williams

"I said OK," he lied.

Mrs. Peterson was curious. She didn't remember the conversation going that way. But she was standing outside the door. *'Maybe I missed something,'* she thought.

"Nonsense!" Chasidy squealed. "Has everybody lost their minds? Well, da real adults here have already talked about this, right AJ?"

"Yes, Mam," he answered.

"Would you kindly tell everyone where we're all going when we leave here?" she instructed him.

"Aunt Chasidy said that since Mom has a fractured collarbone, I have a broken arm and Dad can't see past da back of his eyelids; we're all comin' to stay with her and Uncle Rob at their house until everybody's bett'r."

Al said to Chasidy, "You can't see me, but I'm crackin' up ov'r that eyelid comment."

"I thought you might appreciate that," she joked and then scolded her husband, "Rob, I'm surprised at you."

"Don't be," Mic came to his defense. "He was just showin' his butt and provin' a point to let us know how well he knows his wife. I did say I didn't wanna intrude on you and da babies. And he said you'd say exactly what you just said. Almost word for word. That's scary y'all. Y'all need to get that checked." Mic teased. Barlow sat proudly in the corner smiling and staring at Chasidy. Suddenly, she felt like joining him in the chair. So, she did, bringing a special hug and delicate kiss with her.

Mr. Peterson had had about as much as he was going to take by now. He had to say something before he burst, splattering his insides all over the walls. "Michy, didn't you promise your mother that you would spend Christmas with us? And now you're gonna let this kingpin and his wife dictate to you where to spend the holiday."

"Jeffery, cut it out!" his wife tried to stop him, "that conversation was before Alan got hurt."

"Not this time Val. I've watched the whole scene play out since I've been here. I've done my research on you Barlow. I know you're some type of Big Wheel or something."

"Or somethin'," Barlow said.

"It appears to me like your word is law around here. Alan and Michy don't make a move unless you approve of it. You've even got little AJ wrapped around your finger. He thinks you're some type of demi-god. They get into a serious accident and the first person Michy calls is you. And now your Mrs. Kingpin is ordering my daughter around like she doesn't have the good sense to make her own decisions. I won't have it. Michy promised her mother a holiday visit…"

Barlow interrupted him, speaking slow and deliberately. "First of all, second to Al, Mic has called me for da past twenty-four years or more when she's needed help. And I've been there for 'er unlike ya'self." Barlow slapped him in the face with a bitter reality. "Secondly, Do you really think Mic's gonna leave her family at Christmas or any oth'r time for that matt'r? Cause as you can see for ya'self, AJ's not leavin' his dad's side for anyone," Barlow asked very calmly. "And there's no way I'd let Alan go anywhere with you, knowin' how you feel about 'im." He just put it all out there.

"Maybe your wife can answer that since she has all the answers." Mr. Peterson spoke with a harsh tone. Barlow prepared for the battle ahead of him. One thing Mr. Peterson wasn't going to do is disrespect Chasidy. Mic, Chasidy, and Alan knew this already.

Mrs. Peterson had a very strong suspicion. She tried to save her husband from some embarrassment. "Jeffrey that's enough!" Mrs. Peterson said. "Stop this now!"

"Barlow may have his own little cult situation going on here, but you're still my wife and you'll do as I say. His word isn't law with me." Mr. Peterson was full steam angry by now. The entire room is spinning in emotions. AJ and Mic are in tears. Her mom is extremely disappointed in her father and has become very angry herself. Chasidy is furious at the way Mr. Peterson is talking to Barlow. And Barlow is certain that Mr. Peterson is upsetting Alan.

Even in all the commotion, he could hear his buddy call to him in a whisper, "Rob." Mr. Peterson's rejection of his kindness had reached its extremes. Alan had had enough of his nasty treatment of his family. He needed Barlow to handle that for him since he couldn't at this time.

Barlow knew exactly what was Alan's asking of him. He wanted an end put to this foolishness. He kissed Chasidy on the cheek, gently pushing her up from his lap and said, "AJ, why don't you and yor mom go introduce yor grandmoth'r to little Remi?"

"But Uncle Rob, I wanna stay with Dad," he resisted.

"Yor dad will be alright. I've got 'im," Barlow assured him.

"Come on, Little Guy," Michelle said. They began to leave the room.

"You stop right there, Val. My wife's not a part of your cult, Barlow. She doesn't have to do what you say." he protested.

When Mr. Peterson looked at his wife, he saw a different woman. "I'm ashamed of you, Jeffrey." she said.

"He's right, Mrs. Peterson," Barlow told her. "You don't have to leave. In fact, all of you should stay. I was only tryin' ta spare him da embarrassment of you watchin' him being escorted outta h're." Barlow wasted no time. "Peterson, Al gave you da perfect opportunity to make amends with yor daught'r and get to know yor grandson. You've screwed up both of those opportunities by being a complete jack ever since Al invited you back into yor daughter's life. I'm not sure how that turned into sheer hatred for me, frankly I don't care. What I do care about is my family. Yur upsettin' 'em. All of them. That stops right h're, right now or I will ask you to leave. No. I'll see to it that you leave."

"You have no right. Michelle is my daughter. I'm her real family. You can't ask me to leave," Mr. Peterson argued.

"I can and I will. My friend requested it. And I *will* make it hap'en," Barlow declared.

"I think you're making that up to hide behind Al as a cover."

"I don't hide behind anybody," Barlow told him.

"Yes, he did, Dad. You w're so busy barking your insanities at Rob, you couldn't hear 'im," Michelle corrected. "He *can* make you leave. He has every right." She looked appreciatively at Barlow. "But I'm not gonna let 'im do that."

Mr. Peterson boasted, "See Barlow, blood is thicker than water." He was so blinded by his hatred for Barlow and his jealousy for Alan, he couldn't even see that his own daughter was about to have him tossed out.

"Rob, I can't let you put my dad out. He's right, it's not yor place. I know Al asked you to. I heard 'im." Michelle took hold of Alan's hand for support. She smiled softly at her mom silently asking for forgiveness before continuing. "Al is my husband. I support him one hundred percent. It's my place to do that."

"Michy." her dad said.

She gave her dad a stern look, slightly squeezed Alan's hand and said, "Dad, I'm askin' you, no I'm tellin' you to…"

Her mom stopped her. "Michy, if you do this, it will lay on your heart for a long time," her mom explained to her, "This isn't who you are. I won't let you get sick again behind this."

"I won't let 'im keep upsettin' Alan and AJ this way. Nor will he continue to speak to Rob like this. Rob hasn't done anythin' to him. None of us have," Michelle reasoned.

"I know Baby. That's why you don't need this hovering over your head." Her mother hugged her and held her in her arms. Then she looked at her husband and told him, "Leave Jeffrey."

"What!" Mr. Peterson exclaimed. "I'm your husband, you can't ask me…"

She interrupted, "Yes, I can, Michy can, Mr. Barlow can, and Alan can. And we're not asking you to leave, we're telling you. These people are Michy's family. And they have been nothing but kind to us. Your actions lie on the verge of unforgivable."

"And whatta you gonna do? Go home with the kingpin and his wife so they can order you around too?"

"Yes," she answered sternly. "If that's all you get out of this Jeffrey, then yes. But from where I'm standing, I'm going with my daughter and her lovely family if there's room enough for me on his plane. I'm gonna help Chasidy take of them. Can't you see the love that's shared between them all?"

Mr. Peterson didn't answer her question. "So, what am I supposed to do?" he asked his wife.

"Go home and waddle in your misery. You seem to like doing that. But I'd suggest you think long and hard about your actions. Because I'm still trying to forgive you for keeping my daughter away from me all these years. I'm lingering on the verge of not forgiving you at all right now."

Mr. Peterson could see that his wife meant exactly what she was saying. His tone changed from angry to solemn. "When will you come home?"

"That's not even something I wanna think about right now. My family needs me. I'm gonna stay with them as long as they need me to. Chasidy can't take care of them and four newborn babies too." Then she turned to Chasidy, smiling, "though I thank you so much for loving them enough to do it."

"Mic is my best friend. Al is practically Rob's brothar." Chasidy said, "They would do da same for us."

Mr. Peterson reluctantly admitted defeat when he quietly left the room, stopping only to give his wife a kiss and a hug.

#

Over the next few days, they made preparations to make their trip home. Barlow had made arrangements for all the equipment to be delivered and set up before they got there. Antonio helped out with that. He had scheduled a quick run for Wednesday over to Jacksonville to meet with Gonzales about the Miller project that was scheduled to begin the week just before the Christmas Holiday. He was glad Mic's mother was there with her and he didn't have to leave her alone.

Al's accident made him rethink the decision to start just before the holiday. The men should be with their families during the holiday. Al asked Rob to delay until the first of the year. "We'll play catch up to meet deadline," Al told him.

"This is Gonzales' first rodeo. You sure you wanna start him off with a delay. Him being da new boss, da *young* new boss. They might give 'im some resistance playin' catch up," Barlow said.

"Maybe I'll show my face for a day or two for support," Al said.

"Or maybe you won't," Mic protested. Her mother thought that was funny.

Al didn't argue with her. Not that he could anyway. But she had been through enough, he felt. They all had. "We'll see how I'm doin' by then," he told her.

Mic and Al were alone at the hospital anticipating their trip home. Barlow was headed back from Jacksonville and AJ was at the hotel with Chasidy and now his grandmother who shared his room with him; all waiting anxiously to go home. Even though Al's eyes were still closed, Mic could tell he was at an unrest about something. He looked to be having nightmares and he was waking up upset. She first thought he was worried about being able to see again. Her concern had become overwhelming. "Al, baby, what is it?"

"I keep seein' da accident," he said without hesitating. "What hap'ened to those people who hit us?" he asked her.

"Last Rob told me; da young lady was in surgery. She was eight months pregnant. She had her two-year-old son with 'er. It's a miracle, he came outta da accident without a scratch."

"You don't know where they are now? If da young lady survived."

"I don't. I suppose I could try to find out," Michelle suggested. "But why is this important, Baby?"

"I don't know. They're just weighing on my heart. This wasn't her fault eith'r, ya know. I'm just wonderin' if they need any help. If there's somethin' I can do to help," he explained. "I'd hate to leave h're and find out there's somethin' I could've done and didn't."

"Ok. I'll see what I can find out," she promised.

"Find out about what?" Barlow asked walking through the door.

"Da young lady that hit us. Al is wonderin' if he can help 'er in some way since this wasn't her fault either."

"I'm afraid not," Barlow answered, "she died in surgery."

"Rob!" Michelle asked sadly, "why didn't you tell me?"

"You had yor own problems to deal with."

"Did da baby die also?" she asked.

"No. Da baby and da boy are with da state," Barlow told them.

"Where's her family?" Al asked.

"So far, they haven't located any."

"So, da babies are orphaned," Al asked him.

"As far as they know right now," Barlow informed. That hit home to Al, too hard. He knew his friend. He knew what he was thinking.

"I won't have those babies in a state facility, Mic. Especially at Christmas."

"Are you sayin' you wanna take them with us for Christmas?" Mic asked him.

"Yeah. No. I'm sayin', I wanna take 'em with us for good," he said. Mic looked at Rob in confusion. Al could sense something in the quietness. "Mic," he said, "You know my background. I don't know where I came from or who my people are." He stopped for a rest break. "I was all alone until I met Rob and Ethel. That's a horrible feelin' for a kid. I was twelve years old by da time I met them. I was so messed up emotionally, I couldn't even see da love Ethel, or da Marshalls were showin' me until years later." He rested some more.

"Al stop talkin', Baby. Yur wearing yorself out," Mic urged.

"No," he protested. "I can't see those babies livin' like that, Mic. Likely separated. Growin' up nev'r getting' to know each oth'r. This wasn't their mother's fault. It was da idiot who passed me and put all our lives in dang'r."

Michelle was speechless. Troubled in thought. She and Al decided not to have more children because of her heart condition. They were blessed to have AJ. They wouldn't risk her health again. But that conversation was concerning childbirth. Childbirth wouldn't be a factor with these babies. Michelle pondered the idea briefly. "I'll tell you what," she bargained. "You get some rest. Sleep on it. I'll see what I can find out about 'em. And if you still feel da same way *t'morrow* when you wake up, we can see about getting' custody of 'em."

"Thank you, Baby. This means a lot to me."

"You should get some rest too, Mic," Barlow suggested. "I'll find out what I can about da children."

"Thank you, Rob. I'll try. I don't know how successful I'll be after this."

"Yur tired," Barlow told her, "It'll come naturally."

"I don't mean to cause you unrest, Sweetheart," Al said. "Please try to sleep."

Barlow's gut instinct told him that when Al got better, this conversation would come up. Once he found out those babies were orphaned, he kept a close watch on their situation. He knew Al would want to know what was going on with them. Sure enough, adopting them never crossed his mind, but he figured he'd want an active part in their lives from a distance. If he could get the information he needed to get custody of them, that would be his Christmas present to him. When he got back to the hotel, he talked to Chasidy about it.

"Rob. Are you serious?" she asked. "Is he mentally capable of makan' a d'cision like that right now?"

"Chasidy, if he hadn't made this d'cision, I would be challengin' his mentality. You don't know how much being an orphan tormented him. Thinkin' every day that his parents didn't love him. Or wondering what hap'ened to his people and why it didn't hap'en to him also." Chasidy listened with compassionate ears. "That's why I stayed on top of their situation. I knew Al would react this way when he found out." He stared pleadingly at Chasidy. "I've already spoken with someone about this. Chasidy, I can bring those babies with us. Da question is, are you ok with that?"

"So? You don't know yor wife as well as you say you do," she replied.

"I do," he responded. "But da Kingpin wouldn't dare make a move like this without consulting Mrs. Kingpin first." They shared a giggle.

"Thank you for that. I've been consulted," she agreed. "Don't we leave day after t'morra'?"

"We'll all be ready," he promised.

"Rob. It would be nice if it could be a surprise on Christmas Day."

"My sentiment exactly." he said smiling.

Until Christmas

Michelle kept her word and agreed to take the babies after Alan was adamant about doing so. She actually had become very excited about having babies in the house again. Barlow told them both he would take care of it for them. They were all set to leave on Saturday. Both Al and Mic questioned his progress. Wanting it to be a complete surprise he had to tell them a half truth. "The state has to keep them in their custody for thirty days to see if any family members will claim them. But if no one claims them, they will be with you the day after Christmas. That's as close as I could get," he apologized.

"Thanks Buddy," Al said. "That's close enough."

Michelle agreed, "Yeah thanks Rob." Giving him a hug.

Mrs. Peterson was there while the talk of babies was going on. No one had mentioned the babies to her. She was confused. "What's this talk about babies?" Michelle took great pleasure in explaining Alan's wishes to her. Mrs. Peterson's admiration for Alan grew another inch or two. "It's so wonderful that you can put others first even at a time like this," she said to Alan.

"That's the man I fell in love with, Mom," Michelle told her. "He and Rob are the most compassionate men I know. Dad would see that if he gave them half a chance."

"Well, let's not ruin the moment bringing him up," her mother said.

#

Barlow made sure the babies were boarded on the plane first so that Mic and Al wouldn't know they were with them. Sam and Caitlin agreed to tend to them. It was the ride home that was tricky. Barlow sent Caitlin and Sam on ahead with the babies in a rental car. With Alan, Mic, and AJ in the ambulance, Mrs. Peterson rode in the Bentley with Barlow and Chasidy. Likewise, Sam agreed to house the babies in the bungalow until Christmas Day. Barlow hired a sitter to help Sam care for them. The plan is set in action. All there is to do now is wait for Christmas.

Chasidy was beaming with Christmas spirit. Her house was filled with loved ones and wonderful expectations. She began decorating the very next day after they arrived home. Still being very limited physically, when Mrs. Peterson asked if she could help, she quickly accepted her offer. That was two glorious weeks before Christmas. Since cooking would be a little too much for Chasidy this year, everyone agreed to an old-fashioned potluck dinner. Barlow volunteered to cook the turkey. Al felt some type of way about that.

"Buddy, maybe you should leave that to somebody who knows what they're doing. I can't really help you out this time."

Barlow wallowing in self-confidence, stated "I've watched Ethel do it many times. I got this," he assured.

Michelle looked at Chasidy to come to the rescue. Her mother was curious as well. "Don't look at me. I have seven babies to tend to. Everybody's gotta chip in with somethan'. He said he's watched Ethel do it." She teased in support of her husband.

"He watched Al barbeque too but that didn't stop 'im from burning that up," Michelle reminded her.

"I'm crackin' up ov'r h're, Baby," Al told Michelle. They all laughed.

She really did have a lot to do, with the babies in the bungalow, her own babies, and her friends all under her care. Even though Al had his own nurse and Michelle's mom was there to help, Chasidy showed everyone special attention all the while trying to make certain she was keeping her own body healthy.

The babies were just turning a month old. And she was missing her husband. Actually, for a long time now. Although his integrity wouldn't let him say anything about it, she knew he was missing her too. When mommy and babies went in for their checkup on Wednesday, she asked Dr. Reed about her own health when Barlow stepped out to change one of the babies' diapers.

"You're all doing very well, Mrs. Barlow," Dr. Reed told her. "There's no reason why you can't give your husband some special attention for Christmas. That is what you're asking, isn't it?"

She smiled profusely. "Yes, doctor. That's exactly what I'm askan'. Thank you fa everythan'."

"I thought as much since you waited for 'im to leave the room before asking me. Take your family home and enjoy your holiday. Merry Christmas."

"Merry Christmas ta you as well." Chasidy met Barlow just outside the doctor's office. "We're all set, Mr. Barlow," she told him happily. He had no idea she was speaking of 'talking' again. She was anxiously looking forward to having an early Christmas morning conversation with him.

#

There's nothing like a busy home for the holidays. In the midst of the happy chaos, Barlow never forgot about his desire to be baptized. He reminded Chasidy after the doctor's appointment while they were picking up the turkey from the grocer. "Do you r'member da conversation we had right b'fore we had to leave for Georgia?"

"About you gettan' baptized?" she asked.

"That's da one. We nev'r got a chance to talk to yor pastor about it. Do you think he would come ta Christmas Dinn'r?"

"Sure. As long as you don't burn da turkey," she joked.

"I have no intentions of burnin' da turkey, but, if that's yor way of offerin' to help, I accept," he said volunteering her services.

"My pleasure," she said getting back to the subject of baptizing. "I'm glad you didn't change yor mind about that."

"There's no way I can change my mind now," he told her. "God has shown Himself to me so many times lately. I'm sure He's tried to do it before but, …"

"But what?' Chasidy coached.

"Well, I was in such a dark place. Lost in my pain. I wasn't open to Him then. Now, I can't learn enough about Him fast enough."

"Rob. Hearing you say that is da best Christmas present you can give me," she told him staring at him with an admiration she didn't think could get any greater. He returned the favor with his own admiring gaze. At that moment they forgot they were in the frozen food section of the supermarket with four babies waiting to go home. That is, until one of them reminded them. "Maybe we all can attend Christmas Day Service. I would love to go on Sunday, but I think that's too soon for Al, and the babies wouldn't be able to come. I'd like all of us to be there. But I'll call Pastor ahead of time to be sure he can make dinna," Chasidy said.

"Thank you. Let's get our young'uns homes," Barlow said.

Chasidy became real creative with gifts this Christmas since she didn't really have a chance to shop. She has never cared for the crowd that comes along with Christmas. She always had her shopping done by this time of year. Even the twins would have to accept a compromise. She decided to put together something different this year for gift exchange and hoped everyone would enjoy it.

Each day she went to the bungalow to check on the new babies and Sam. Sam was having the time of his life. He and the sitter got along really well. Chasidy was glad of that. Baby Jane, which is what they called her because her mother didn't get a chance to name her before she died; was flourishing. Her big brother Charles seemed to be doing fine also. He had developed an attachment to Sam already. She hoped that wouldn't be a problem come Christmas Day.

The same evening, Barlow walked over to see how the stables were coming along. To his pleasant surprise, they were finished. He noticed there were several stalls and room enough for an entire herd. He just assumed Al and Mic were getting horses also. It was a crisp winter night. He enjoyed the quiet solitude of the short walk home. So much so, he decided to visit Ol Daniel and sat a spell. He had come to enjoy his time alone with God. In fact, he looked forward to it. The more time he spent in the presence of God, the more peaceful he became in his spirit. Just thinking about having a conversation with the pastor about being baptized made him even more anxious for Christmas to arrive.

When he walked through the door Chasidy smiled at him and he her. "Al's been askin' fa ya."

"Ok," he said, kissing her cheek. "I'll go check on 'im." When he made it to his room, he stood a second to make certain Al wasn't sleeping.

Al sensed he was there. "Come on in Rob."

"How did you know it was me?" Barlow asked.

"Cause Chasidy smells bett'r," he answered.

Barlow laughed. "She does at that, doesn't she? What's on yor mind?"

"Da babies," he answered quickly. His speech has gotten much better. His voice was much stronger. Barlow was sure, if only just from that, he would be able to open his eyes real soon. "Do you know their names?"

"Da boy's name is Charles. They call the newborn Baby Jane. Her mom didn't get a chance to name 'er. I guess you and Mic have that honor now."

"Thanks for helpin' me out with that. It means a lot to me. Often, I think about what I missed out on not lettin' Ethel into my life before I did. I've beat myself up ov'r that too many times. I don't want these kids to do that."

"Well, stop beatin' ya'self up. Ethel nev'r held it against you. She loved you just da same. And as far as those babies are concerned, you'll get yor chance to make a difference."

"I hope so. I wanna fine out everythang I can about their mom. I want them to know who she is and that she loved 'em. They'll know she didn't abandon them. I'll see to that."

"I know you will, Buddy. It's late. You get some rest. I see Mic is already knocked out."

"Good night, Rob."

"Good night, Al."

Chasidy waited for him. "All is well?"

"All is well." he replied.

"I'll see you in da mornan', Mr. Barlow."

"Good night, Beautiful."

Before everyone could say Christmas at The Barlows, an entire seven days had passed and there were only three days left before Christmas. Chasidy had begun to put her game plan into action. After she finished cooking and serving breakfast, she made ready for her special after dinner family gift swap. She hid her family's gifts around the house and wrote out notes for clues as to where to find them. It would be a first Christmas Scavenger Hunt. She was looking forward to it. After she finished hiding her gifts, she checked to make sure Rob's gift and some of the other things she'd ordered would be delivered on time. Then she went over to check on the little ones in the bungalow before her own bundles of joy woke up. She was so excited for Al and Mic, having Mic's mom and the babies with them. This was going to be the best Christmas ever. She was sure of it. She only hoped Mr. Peterson would come to his senses. *Well, we are in the Christmas Miracle Season,* she thought.

Upon her return, Barlow asked, "Everything ok?"

"Darn near perfect," she told him.

"I need to run out for a short while. Are you good?"

"Darn near perfect," she said again. "Take yor time."

Anxiousness had over-taken Michelle in her excitement for the babies. She found herself talking more and more about them. She was having a cup of coffee with Chasidy and her mom when she finally brought the subject up to her. "Rob told Al that the baby girl doesn't have a name. Does that mean we get to name 'er?" she asked Chasidy.

"Yes. You got any ideas?" Chasidy replied.

"Al likes Grace. I like Lois. So, we're leanin' towards Lois Grace. But I think he really wants to know her mom's name," she shared with Chasidy. "He wants to name 'er aft'r her mom."

Chasidy immediately called Rob to see if he remembered the young lady's name. When she disconnected from him, she said, "Katherine."

"Katherine," Michelle repeated. And then again. "That's pretty."

"It is. Very pretty," Mrs. Peterson agreed.

"I think Al will like that," Chasidy added.

"I know he will," Michelle concluded. Catherine Grace with a C because her brother's name starts with a C."

"Perfect," Chasidy replied.

"I'm gonna go tell 'im right now," she hurried off to the bedroom.

"Slow down before you fall!" Chasidy yelled at her. "Yur fresh outta collarbones." Chasidy took advantage of this moment to make sure her guest was faring well. "How are you coman' along Mrs. Peterson?"

"I haven't enjoyed Christmas so much in twenty-four years," she answered.

"I know this is probably a stupid question, but…"

"Yes. I miss him a lot," she answered before Chasidy could ask. "You're probably wondering what I miss about 'im. But there are times when he really is a sweetheart."

"I knew there must be some good in 'im for you to love 'im so much," Chasidy said. "I'm sure this must hurt."

"It does. But I'm certain he'll see the error of his ways."

"How are you so sure?" Chasidy was curious.

"I miss Jeffrey like I would miss my right hand if it was gone, and I have all these lovely people and your beautiful babies around me to keep my mind off of 'im." She smiled a melancholy smile. "He's in that big old house all alone with reminders of me everywhere and me nowhere in sight. He'll come around."

"I hope so, Mrs. Peterson," Chasidy said sincerely.

When Mic entered the room, Al began talking right away. "I'm glad yur back. My son has deserted me."

"Well, if you feel bad now just wait until he gets his present. We'll have to put his bed in da stables." Mic teased. "And don't you start gettin' used to that special second sense you've developed, I'm still waitin' to see those handsome ambers starin' back at me."

Alan joked, "I'm smilin' right now. Can you feel it?"

"Yes," she answered, "I actually can. Wanna smile some more? Lis'en to this, Catherine Grace."

"That's beautiful. I thought we were leanin' towards Lois Grace."

"Catherine is her mother's name."

"It is?" he asked excitedly. "What else do we know about 'er?"

"Nothin'. All I asked about was da name. Do you want Rob to do all da work for you or are you gon find some stuff out on yor own?"

"Yur right. This is my quest." he said.

"Yur wrong," Mic corrected, "This is our quest."

"I'm smilin' again," he said.

"Man, yur so silly," Mic said laughing. "You want me to go wrangler up yor son?"

"Naw. He's been with me non-stop. He's earned some time off."

"Whatta you think our potluck dish should be? Chasidy already has her sweet potato pies in da oven."

"I wish I didn't have to pick just one," he said like he really meant it.

"Let's go with yor three-cheese mac dish."

"That's exactly what I was thinkin'," she laughed. "We're gettin' more and more like Chasidy and Rob each day.

Chasidy started her baking right after Rob left hoping the little ones would let her finish. They must be in the Christmas spirit also because she was able to get two sweet potato pies in the oven before they started waking up. After that she concluded, "two will be plenty," feeling very accomplished.

"Can I help?" Mrs. Peterson asked.

"Sure," Chasidy said gladly, handing her the baby.

"Now which one is this?"

"This is Michelle," Chasidy answered. "She's named after Rob's first wife Rebecca and Mic. So, we call her Remi. Sometimes you may hear Rob call her Becky."

Mrs. Peterson had the most confusing expression on her face. "Was it your idea to name her after your husband's first wife?"

"And my best friend, yes," Chasidy chuckled. "Let me explain. Rob was so in love with his first wife, he thought he would neva fall in love again. He neva evan dated anotha' woman. Twenty-six years later, he met me and all of that changed. This is my way of showan' my appreciation to Rebecca for holdan' him captive until we met."

Mrs. Peterson burst into laughter. "That's a lovely story!"

"What's a lovely story?" Michelle asked walking back into the room.

"Hers and Mr. Barlow's," her mom answered. "She was telling me about little Remi's name."

D.M. Williams

"Yeah, that is a pretty sweet story," Michelle agreed. "Al and I tried for years to hook Rob up with someone. We even nominated him Most Successful Eligible Bachelor hoping someone would catch his eye. But it didn't work. He had to come all da way out here in these back woods to find da woman of his dreams."

They all laughed. "Chasidy's version sounded more romantic," Michelle's mother said. Then she noticed the babies' names on the beds. "There's one named Alan too?"

"Yes," Michelle answered. "We call him Third Al."

Mrs. Peterson burst into laughter again. "That's too adorable." Looking at Chasidy, the babies and then Michelle, she said, "You really do have a beautiful family, Michy. I'm glad da Lord put you in da midst of such good people."

"Me too, Mama," Michelle agreed.

Michelle's motherly instinct caused her to search out her son anyway even though Al had given him a break. When she couldn't find him in the house anywhere or The Grove outside his room, she asked Chasidy if she had seen him. "I haven't. He's probably with Rob."

"Where's Rob?"

"Don't know. He didn't say where he was going."

Michelle texted him: *Is my son with you?*

A one-word text came back: *yes*.

Continuing her conversation with Chasidy and her mother, she said, "they must be shoppin'."

"Most likely." Chasidy agreed. While they were talking, Third Al started asking for lunch.

"Let me do it, please," Mic pleaded.

Chasidy quickly replied, "Girl, you don't evan have to beg."

With Mic and Mrs. Peterson doing nursery duty, Chasidy used this opportunity to wrap Rob's gift that had arrived shortly after she started the pies. Michelle noticed the handsome cross with the name rings attached to it. "Can I see it?" she asked.

Chasidy moved closer to show her the White Gold Cross pendant with a large ring dangling across the top of the cross with his and her names engraved on it. Attached to the post of the cross were four smaller rings with each child's name engraved on them. "Rob's gettan' baptized," Chasidy explained. "There's one more part that goes with this."

"He is?" Michelle was shocked. "When?"

"Don't know yet. We're gonna discuss it with Pastor Christmas Sunday. We're attend'n Christmas Service and later he's coman' to dinna'. Y'all coman' with us, right?"

"I'll run it by Al. I can't see 'im sayin' no to church though."

"Mums da word on da baptism. Let Rob mention it to ya," Chasidy requested.

"I haven't heard a thing," Michelle agreed. "What's da oth'r part?" she asked.

"A limited-edition study bible. He says he can't learn enough about God fast enough. I'm tryan' to help 'im along."

"I can't b'lieve you guys are still at it. I wonder what sentimental gifts he's got stored away for you." Chasidy chuckled. Mrs. Peterson thought to herself, *this isn't a cult. This is pure love.*

Wanting to make sure she had what she needed for her famous mac-n-cheese, she asked Chasidy what she had in the kitchen. Chasidy had plenty of pasta shells, but Mic was out of luck with the cheese. She texted Barlow with a short list of ingredients to bring for her.

Will do. He texted back.

"How's yor injury?" Chasidy asked. "You gonna be able to pull that off?"

"Chasidy, this is turning out to be da best Christmas I can r'member Al and I ever havin'. I know Ethel's gone, and Al's eyes are full of foolery, but I'm b'lievin a Christmas Miracle for that. Being here with you, Rob, and my mom, and Rob being happier than I've ever seen him, I wouldn't miss out on this for da world. I can even feel Al's contentment. So yes, I can pull this off."

Her mother added, "She can always use both of my arms. Both of you can."

"There. We've got it all worked out," Michelle concluded.

Chasidy felt the same way for many of the same reasons. But the one reason that was most special to her was doing it all in her Grandma's Pecan Grove. "I totally agree, Mic. And we're doing it all in da most beautiful place there is in da backwoods of Mississippi."

"It is at that," Mic agreed.

With all those sentiments out of the way, Chasidy wanted to make certain that Mic was all set for Christmas gift exchange. "Did you get to finish your shoppan? You have all yor gifts?"

"Yeah. I did a lot of it in Florida. Da rest ov'r da phone. I'm good."

"They w're able to r'cover everything from da accident?" her mom asked.

"Every bit of it."

"Wonderful!" Chasidy said. "I did da phone thing too. We can chill now and wait for Rob to burn up da turkey come Christmas."

"Don't play like that," Mic said seriously.

Perfect Gifts

oth AJ's and Al's phones were lost in the accident. AJ wanted to get his dad another one. Along with the phone, he bought him the latest PlayStation game system. His purchase was accompanied by a tease from Uncle Rob. "Are you sure that's for yor dad or is it really for you?"

"Uncle Rob. He has to play with somebody," AJ defended. When he finished shopping for his dad, he made a confession to his uncle. "Uncle Rob. I don't know what to get Mom."

Barlow offered his expertise. "Take a minute to think about what she likes. What's makes her smile? Jewelry? Perfume? Bath oil? She likes to do something when you and Al disappear. What've you heard 'er talk about?"

"She doesn't talk about anything except making me and Dad happy. She never asks for anything. I've never heard 'er say, '*I wish I had anything.*' I don't know how to shop for 'er." AJ couldn't think of a single thing except .... "Uncle Rob, what's on that chain she wears around 'er neck?"

"A picture of her parents, yor grandparents."

"Oh." That got him to thinking. "Can we go by a jewelry store?"

193

D.M. Williams

"Sure. There's one right up da street."

At the jewelry store AJ saw a gold necklace set that included a heart shaped pendant with a diamond just above a keyhole and a key attached to a gold bracelet also with a diamond accent that read: *The key to my heart*. AJ knew the moment he saw it that's what he would get for his mom. It was a pricey set and AJ had just spent nearly that much on his dad. His cash flow was a little low. Good thing for him Uncle Rob liked that gift also and thought it was just perfect for his mom. Barlow suggested a lovely ruby bracelet for his grandmother.

#

Chasidy wanted to check on the little ones in the bungalow so she asked Mic if she would watch the babies while she took a short walk. She could hear Sam's voice and child's laughter as she approached the door. Then she heard him trying to quiet him after she knocked on the door. When he opened it, she said, "I could hear you guys walkan' up to da door. It's a good thang Mic doesn't come this way."

"I'm sorry. I'll be more careful from now on," Sam apologized.

"Nonsense. Nothan' to apologize fa. I'm glad he's adjustan' so well. Has he been askan' fa his mom at all?"

"Yes," he said. "Mostly at night or nap times."

"Unfortunately, that's normal," Chasidy told him. "Where's Sherry?"

"In the bedroom changing Baby Jane."

"I imagine he's pretty attached to you by now. He may not wanna leave you when it's time," she said on her way back to check on Baby Jane. "May I?" asking permission to proceed to the back.

"Of course," Sam said.

During Alan's alone time, he tries desperately to move his eyelids. He misses Mic's beautiful face and AJ boyish smile. He loves Christmas and yearns to see what Chasidy has done to the house. The smell of cedar mixed with a hint of apples and cinnamon fumigates the house in a festive aroma. His imagination runs wild with him as he tries to imagine what magic Chasidy has performed on the place.

He watched Rob runoff to be with God over the past months during each traumatizing event, spending hours at a time in the chapels at the hospitals. He knows this God. He's been communing with Him long before Rob has. He asked himself why he hasn't asked God's help with his eyes before now? The good thing Al knows about God is that it's never too late. From that moment and every other moment thereafter he had to himself, he asked God; "Father forgive me for not comin' to you sooner. Please open my eyes. Let me see my family again."

That night before going to bed, Michelle asked Al if Rob had mentioned to him about his desires to be baptized. That had stayed with her all day since the time Chasidy mentioned it to her. For some reason she was intrigued by it. "He hasn't said a word about it," Al told her. "Why would he keep somethin' like that a secret?"

"Maybe it's not so much a secret as it is precious to him," Michelle tried to reason. "He hasn't talked with da pastor yet, so Chasidy asked me not to mention it to 'im until he mentions it first. I'm askin' you to do da same."

"I got cha Baby. I won't show you up," Al agreed.

"Thank you. I'm goin' to bed. I may sleep through tomorrow and Christmas and…"

Al joined in with her, knowing what she was about say… "and get up in time to receive our babies." Michelle wishes she could see the excitement in Al's face. But for now, just knowing he is excited has to be enough. "Good night, Sweetheart," he said.

"Good night, Baby."

Likewise in the Barlows' bedroom Barlow wanted to be certain that Chasidy was in a good place with her Christmas shopping. "I know it's been difficult for you to get out with da babies. Do we need to ride out t'morrow so you can pick up some things?"

"Rob. There ain't no way I'd wrestle with that crowd t'morrow pushan four babies around and someone stoppan' us every few minutes to make googly-eyes ova 'em. Don't get me wrong, I love da attention they get. But that would make for a long day of shoppan that's already long enough by itself."

Barlow added, "You fa'got explainin' that they're not yor grand kids."

"Honey, yes!" Chasidy agreed with laugher.

Barlow added, "I can understand that with me. But yur as young as you are beautiful."

"Keep it up and I'm gonna tell my husband this old man is always flirting with me," she teased.

"And make sure you tell 'im there ain't a darn thing he can do about it," Barlow played along with her. "I know what you mean though. It took AJ an eternity taday to get done," he exclaimed.

"Un hun. But you enjoyed every minute of it, didn't you?"

"I'd do it again in a heartbeat," he said proudly.

"I know it meant a lot to 'im," Chasidy told him. "He thinks Uncle Rob can move any mountain left that his dad didn't move."

"It meant a lot to me too. I didn't mean to leave you stranded so long with da babies though."

"Don't pull yor hairs out ova that," she said looking at a pretend watch on her wrist. "Night shift starts right now." He couldn't help but flash his handsome smile at that. "But you *have* had a pretty busy day and I've had plenty of help with Mic and her mom, so maybe I'll help you out with night shift t'night, just this once". She thought briefly about her night shift duty in Georgia. "I just experienced what you go through in Georgia. You deserve something special for that," she teased.

"You got somethin' in mind?" he asked hoping she was ready for a little talk.

"Yeah. Sleep. Go to bed," she ordered.

"Thank you. I *am* beat," he said realizing that wasn't about to happen.

#

December 25th Christmas Day

Christmas Eve came and went uneventfully, and Christmas Day is finally here. Third Al and Remi's biological clocks were working right on schedule as they summoned their parents for their twelve-twenty am feeding. They both awakened within twenty minutes of each other. So, Chasidy and Rob were able to get back to bed fairly quickly. But it was Christmas morning. A morning that took its own sweet time about getting here. Sleeping was not on Chasidy's mind. While Rob romanced his daughter back to sleep, she prepared herself for her own early morning holiday gift giving. She had purchased a festive red semi-sheer nightie that showed off her silky legs and left very little else to the imagination. She lay on the bed propped against the pillows waiting for him to reenter the room. "Merry Christmas," she said in a voice he hadn't heard for way too long.

"For me?" he asked in the voice she deems her own.

"Not if yur just gonna stand there and stare."

"Don't under rate staring. But I'm definitely joining you." Much like their wedding night in his signature style of ultimate lovemaking, he took his time and enjoyed every inch of her and she him. She has missed him so much; she can hardly get enough of him. Having four children at one time conveniently puts all of that baby business to rest. She never wants to wait to make love to her husband this long ever again. They laid there in each other's arms in the quietness of the morning. "I've missed you too much," he told her.

"Un unh. I've been doing da missan'. When you would walk around me with those black jeans on that looked like they were made just for you, Mr. Barlow you nearly drove me crazy. I had to hide those britches."

"Britches?" he repeated.

"Yes. Britches. Don't try to act like you don't know what britches are."

"I know what they are. I just don't see ma'self as a britches-wearin' man."

"Baby don't shortchange ya'self. You look good in britches. And it seemed like you wore them every day. I had to fix that."

"I wondered where they got off to. You actually hid them from me?"

"I sure did. I was tryan' to keep my sanity intact."

"So, those are da only britches I look good in?"

"No, but you know there's always that one outfit that you know you look betta in than any of da othas'. You probably have one you like seeing me in. And I would bet it's yellow if I was a bettin' woman."

"I do. And you would win that bet too. I like da way it hugs yor waist, stops just above yor knees and curves up yor left thigh." He drew her an outline on her body as he described her dress.

"I knew that."

D.M. Williams

"How?"

"Cause, we *talk* a lot more when I wear it."

"Yes, we do. All I can think about is *talkin'* when I see you in it," he said smiling.

"But now that we're talkin' again, can I have my britches back, please."

"On one condition," Chasidy bargained.

"What's that?'

"You have to wear them every day."

"You might get tired of talkin' to me so much," he teased.

"Rob, that's a conversation I will neva tire of," she flirted.

"What if I wear them out?" he asked playfully.

"Then I'll start wearin' my yellow dress," she answered playfully.

"You have it all figured out, I see," he said. "But since I'm a whole week worth of years older than you, I'm gonna need my rest. So why don't I wear my britches for three days and you wear yor dress for three days and we rest da one day in between," he bargained.

"Bet," she said. They shared a quiet grin.

He reached into the drawer of the nightstand and pulled out a gift and handed it to her. Merry Christmas, Beautiful." She let out a loud joyous laugh when she opened it. He had to ask, "What's so funny?"

She went to her chest of drawers and pulled out one of her gifts to him. *And his black jeans.* When he opened it, he immediately saw what was so funny. He had given her a white gold necklace with a heart-shaped pendant with their names engraved on each side of the heart. Attached to it were four white gold rings with each child's name engraved on it. The only difference in his gift and her gift was the cross and the heart pendant.

LJ and Remi were kind enough to give them some time together before they demanded some Christmas morning attention. Before long everyone had been satisfied and Christmas Day was off to a good start.

It was four-thirty. There was no point in going back to sleep. Christmas services start at six-thirty. She and Barlow went to the kitchen to prepare breakfast. AJ was the first one up, smelling the bacon all the way up to his room. He made his way straight to the table after a pitstop at the tree. "Didn't find anythan'?" Chasidy teased. "You must've been a bad boy."

"No, they just didn't get a chance to shop with da accident and all." *That was such a grown-up answer filled with obvious disappointment*. She thought.

"Sit down and eat," she said. "Who knows? Maybe da day will get betta. It is Christmas, ya know?"

He had only taken two bites of his bacon when they heard Mic squeal. They all ran to see what was wrong. Even Mrs. Peterson came from her room to see what was happening. They could hear her crying, but they couldn't see Alan because she leaning over him with her arms around him. "Mom what's wrong with dad?" AJ asked scared silly with tears forming in his little eyes.

"Mic, what is it?" Barlow asked also. She beckoned for them all to come closer, too filled with joy to speak. Then she backed away so that they could see his eyes wide open. A true early morning Christmas Miracle. Still unable to talk, Michelle cried like a newborn baby. When she was able to stop herself, each time she looked into his handsome ambers, the sobbing started all over again.

"Dad, you can see me?" AJ asked.

"I can Son," Al said reaching for a hug. "Merry Christmas."

"Merry Christmas, Dad. This is the best present ev'r."

"Tell me that again later when you get your real present."

"You got me something for Christmas?" he asked excitedly.

"Me and yor mom, yes we did."

"But you guys were in da hospital?"

"Little Guy," Al said, "we had yor gifts months ago."

"You did! Thanks Dad! Thanks Mom!" AJ said giving them both a hug.

"I think we should give her a minute," Chasidy said.

"Yeah," Barlow added, "I think this is a good time to give 'em somethin' else too." They went next door to retrieve the children and invite Sam and Sherry to breakfast and church later. They both gladly accepted breakfast. Sherry had plans at home for Christmas.

When they made it back to the bedroom, Chasidy opened the door slowly and peeped in from behind it. "Are you still cryan' in here, girl?"

"No. I'm good now. I'm in control," Michelle said, taking deep breaths and fanning herself with her hand.

"Oh," Chasidy said. "Well let me see if I can't get you started up again." She walked in with Catherine Grace in her arms and right behind her was Barlow with little Charles.

Alan sat up in the bed. And Michelle started crying all over again. "Merry Christmas guys," Barlow told them. Mrs. Peterson stared in amazement.

"When did they get here?" Al asked.

"Da same day you did," Chasidy answered.

"We thought they'd make da perfect Christmas gift," Barlow added, "aft'r you gettin' yor sight back that is." Little Charles didn't have any problems attaching to his new family.

He sat in Al's lap comfortably like he knew he belonged there. "This is yor new brother AJ."

"I know. We've already met," AJ said.

"You have?" Mic asked.

"Yeah, we've been playin' t'gether over at Sam's since we've been back." Al just stared in wonderment at his friend, speechless.

"These are da babies from da accident?" Mrs. Peterson asked.

"Yes," Michelle answered. "Yor new grandbabies."

"Oh my!" she cried. "They are just da cutest things. May I?" she asked reaching for Catherine Grace.

Barlow and Chasidy left the family to their morning. "I'll bring in breakfast and then we've gotta get ready for church. It starts at six-thirty." Barlow told the proud new family.

"We'll be ready," Mic said not lifting her head from playing with Catherine Grace in her mother's arms. "Aren't they beautiful, Al?"

"They sure are," Al agreed. "Now aren't you glad we did this?"

"Baby, it's da best idea you've had yet. Thank you."

"Merry Christmas, Mic."

"Merry Christmas, Al."

#

Service had already begun by the time they all arrived. It turned out to be more of a challenge than expected to get six babies and three partially disabled older people ready to go. The ushers helped them to pews in the back for easy exiting access and less disturbance to services. Pastor acknowledged them from the pulpit and how big their family had grown referring to all the babies. The sermon like every Christmas Day sermon was on the birth of Baby Jesus and its purpose. Chasidy noticed Barlow trying to soak in every word. Al noticed it also. When service was over, Pastor made his way to them with open arms. "What have you all been into since I last saw you?" he asked referring to the babies and the braces. He turned to Chasidy and Rob. "It's not difficult to see what you two have been up to. Congratulations on your beautiful family. To all four of you."

"Thank you, Pastor," she and Barlow responded.

Turning to Al and his family, he said, "I heard about yor accident. We're happy you made it through that as well as you did." Looking at the new babies, he continued. "I feel like there's a special story behind these little guys. Where's Ethel, and who's this lovely lady?" It seemed like Pastor was trying to get all of his questions out of the way at one time, bunching them all up together like that.

"Mrs. Peterson, meet Pastor Bishop. Pastor, this is Michelle's mom, Mrs. Valerie Peterson and why don't we save da rest for dinner conversation this evening?" Chasidy suggested.

"Four o'clock, you said?"

"Four o'clock, we eat," Chasidy clarified.

"Understood," Pastor answered. "I'll be prompt."

On the way to the vehicles, Al told them to follow Sam. They were going to make a stop by his house first. He was anxious to see AJ's reaction to his gift and everybody else's. He instructed Sam to drive around back to the new stables.

Because he had to walk slowly, AJ had patted all five horses before Al and Mic made it to the stables. There were nametags on each stall just like in the babies' nursery except these were turned backwards. Al announced, "you have to guess which one is yors b'fore turning da nametags around."

"Rob and I have one too?" Chasidy asked.

"Yep. Merry Christmas guys," Al and Mic told them.

Chasidy went straight to the Appaloosa with beautiful black and greying spots against a silky white coat; a slightly gray mane and a long flowing white tail complimented her beauty. Rubbing her head, she said, "I don't know whose name is on this one, but if it ain't mine, I'm changan' it. She's absolutely beautiful." They all laughed when the horse nodded her head and grunted as if she was agreeing with Chasidy about her beauty.

Barlow walked several times between the American Chocolate Paint with large white patches, a multicolored brown and white mane and tail to match and the German Forest Work Horse which was a gorgeous dark chestnut with a flattering black silky mane and tail. He was taken with both of the handsome creatures. However, stopping at the work horse he said, "This looks like me. And if not, what Chasidy said."

Michelle wasn't really an animal person, but since she had to choose, she chose the one Barlow didn't choose. The Paint. It was already obvious which one AJ chose. Once he made his way to the handsome Black Stallion, his little feet were planted, and he wasn't budging which left a mesmerizing White Friesian to compliment AJ's black one.

Al had the hint of a grin on his face. "Looks like I see a smile trying to break out. Does that mean we made da right choices?" Barlow asked.

"Flip yor tags and see for yorself," Al said. They all let out joyous spirit-of-the-holiday laughs when they saw their names attached to the horses they had chosen. "I know you guys pretty good, don't I?"

"Buddy I'd say more than pretty good. You pegged us just right," Barlow added. "Now let's get you home so you can sit down. And rest that neck."

"Yeah." Everyone agreed. AJ and Rob walked with Alan back to the Bentley. Mrs. Peterson wished her husband could see the love they all had for one another. She was completely awestruck with their special relationship.

Before they helped him into the Bentley, AJ gave him a long hug squeezing him as tight as he could. "Thanks Dad. I'm gonna take really good care of 'im. I can't wait 'til we can ride together."

Barlow and Chasidy lead the way home. They took the road through The Grove to get to the other house which hid the view of the front yard until they were rounding the corner of the house. The scene couldn't have been more perfect as they drove up. Three stylish vehicles strategically parked facing the house with the ones on the end pointing slightly towards the one in the middle. Barlow looked at Chasidy and she back at him both smiling until their faces hurt. "Merry Christmas again," They both said to each other. Barlow had bought Chasidy her very own special-order Pearl colored Bentley with factory rims to match accented with black down the middle of the vehicle. The inside boasted pearl colored Persian leather seats accented with black trim.

Chasidy eyes filled with tears. "When I ordered that, I didn't know we we're with child," he told her explaining the near white seats.

"Don't worry about that," she said, "da Quad is riding in da station wagon until they can appreciate her beauty."

"I don't think they make station wagons anymore," Barlow told her.

"Then we'll have to special orda' one just fa them," she teased. "Thank you. I love it."

"And you already know, I love mine," he said grinning. "We gotta stop reading each other's minds," he said in reference to the handsome pearl colored Denali fresh off the assembly line itself and equipped with all the 'Barlow' technological necessities.

"Or not," she protested. "They're wonderfully matched. I figured da black one could use a break once in a while. Yur wearing da tires off of it."

But their reactions were nothing like Al's when he saw the shiny new ruby red Silverado parked on the other side of the Bentley. It, also fully equipped with every necessary piece of technology on the market and a few extras, including a movie system in the back for AJ and now their other children. Al became weak and had to sit back down for a minute. Staring endlessly at his wife, unable to speak, to even say thank you.

He closed his eyes as they filled with tears. That was thanks enough for Michelle. "Merry Christmas, Baby. Let's get you inside." Rob and Sam helped him in the house.

He wasn't ready to go back to the bedroom yet. He wanted to spend time with his new family and old one on Christmas. They perch him in Chasidy's recliner just in case he became tired and needed to lay down. He wouldn't have to move to do that.

AJ took Charles over to the tree to open some presents he saw his name on. Al thanked Barlow in his own way. "You didn't miss a beat, did ya?"

"I couldn't with him. He's at da perfect age to enjoy this day," Barlow responded. "AJ's pretty well grown out of it now. You should've heard 'im in da kitchen being all grown up about not havin anythin' under tree. Chasidy saw he was disappointed so she hinted that he might get somethin' b'fore da day was gone."

"Yur right about that," Al agreed. "He's my little man now." Shifting his attention to his wife. "Can you believe Mic, man? That truck? I think she's learnin' new things from yor wife."

"I think we're all learnin' new things from my wife. Those horses. That's a phenomenal idea," Barlow commented. "Did you see how she made her way straight to da Appaloosa. She didn't evan see da oth'r horses."

"My first glance at her Rob, took me immediately to Chasidy. I knew she would love 'er," Al told him.

"Movin' on to da subject of Mic," Barlow said, "Honestly Al. I didn't think Mic would ev'r wanna see you in anoth'r truck again. She nearly lost her mind da first couple of days y'all w're in da hospital. They had to put 'er to sleep to calm 'er down. I don't think she could survive if she ev'r lost you."

"I hope she nev'r has to find out," Al said. "AJ told me how he was there by 'imself until you and Chasidy got there. He was a real trooper."

"Yep," Barlow agreed. "Nurse Tammy fell in love with 'im. She stayed with 'im until we got there."

"I'm definitely gonna have to send her a thank you," Al concluded.

"You don't know it, but it was Chasidy who convinced Mic to visit you in ICU," Barlow told him.

"Really? You mean she didn't wanna see me?"

"First of all, she thought you w're gone," Barlow started. "That's how they came to sedate 'er in da first place. She heard da words *code blue* and lost it. Well, she had just come out of sedation and learned that you w're still alive and she wanted to know how you w're doing. I didn't know how to explain to 'er that you w're all bandaged up with a brace attached to your head but doing ok. I didn't even want Chasidy to see you like that. But she had offered to help me talk to Mic and she insisted she had to see you if she was gonna do that."

"So, what hap'ened?" Al asked.

"While Chasidy was holdin' yor hand and talkin' to you she felt a slight squeeze on 'er hand. Do you r'member that?"

"No," Al said, "I don't."

"Right aft'r that she put yor hand in mine and asked you to do it again. Then you squeezed my hand," Barlow continued the story.

"I did?" Al asked smiling.

"Da staff tried to make us b'lieve that it was all just coincidental, a process. But Chasidy knew it was da interaction, probably from when she was in a coma. When we got back to Mic, Chasidy made her understand that you needed her in there with you, encouraging you to get bett'r. She told her to channel all her fears into her strength and go be with her husband. And she did."

"Man, I'm glad we married her," Alan said. Barlow laughed.

"Not as glad as I am," he added.

"So, what hap'ened next?"

"I had gone back to da hotel and da next day late eve'nin about eight o'clock, Mic called Chasidy in tears tellin' 'er how what she said to her was right. That you w're respondin' to 'er and they w're movin' you into da room with 'er. They had released AJ, but Mic asked me to bring 'im back so he could see you. Again, I didn't want 'im seein' you like that. But Mic insisted."

"She did?"

"By then she was bound and d'termined to bring you back this way. She said *if Al will wade through hell and high waters to bring me home; he'll pry open da Pearlie gates to get back to his son.* That was her plan. Al, I tell you, when AJ walked in that room he ran straight past his mom and right to you. He didn't see bandages. He didn't see a brace. All he saw was his dad. He perched his little self on that bed beside you and stayed there until you woke up."

"Are you serious?" Al asked gleaming inside. "I r'member him being da first person I spoke to aft'r I woke up."

D.M. Williams

"Yeah. We all spent da day with you talkin' of good times purposely so you could hear, hopin' it would help you along. And it did, by God's grace that is."

"Wow! What a story! I'm so glad you told me. Thank you."

"I'm glad it turned out that I could tell you about it. I don't know that I could've handled it any oth'r way ma'self," Barlow confessed.

#

Michelle watched as AJ showed Charles how to tear into the wrappings to get to the good stuff. It took only two gifts before he got the hang of it. When he lost himself in playtime Chasidy and Mic made their way to the kitchen to prepare a place for the food that was on its way. Chasidy saw that Rob was enjoying Al's company so she and Mic with her mom's assistance helped with his part of the potluck and cooked his turkey for him.

All of the babies were in the nursery away from the noise of the big people of which they won't be able to avoid come later on. Mic and Chasidy could hear them through the monitor making happy baby noises like they were talking to each other. One of the babies started crying. Chasidy looked up at Mic who never stopped stirring her pasta. "Mic," she said. "That's not one of mine. But it might be if one of 'em decides to join 'er." They both went to check on Grace, by which time she had stopped crying. They found her in Al's arms waiting for Rob to bring her bottle.

Alan teased, "Is this yor way of r'mindin' me that I got you into this?"

"No, Honey I'm sorry," Mic apologized. "It's my way of getting' used to havin' a new little person in da family. It won't hap'en again."

"Mic," he said, "calm down. I've got 'er."

Mom offered her assistance. "Are you comfortable with her, Al? Do you want me to take 'er?"

"Thanks Mom. But I really am good." They went back into the kitchen to finish cooking.

Chasidy laughing at her friend, told her, "He's right. All this will be second nature b'fore you know it."

"Yea, I guess I'm still in a state of unbelief," Mic explained.

"Well," Chasidy said, "that will change too." Both ladies thought how it was only a few short months ago that the tables were turned.

206

But it was Chasidy who mentioned it. "R'membar' how not very long ago I was da one who needed advice."

"Yeah, and I was da one who gave it," Michelle finished. "Life's funny, isn't it?"

Mrs. Peterson reminded Michelle. "I can stay as long as you need me to, ya know, until you get used to little people being in the house again," she said it teasingly but meant it fully.

"I'd love that, Mom."

#

Barlow, being in a talkative mood, after handing him the bottle; went on to share his other thoughts with Al. "I've been doin' a lot of thinkin' ov'r da past months."

"About what?" Al pretended not to know.

"Gettin' baptized," he said. "That's why we invited da pastor ov'r. So, I can talk to 'im about it."

"That's great Rob, but what got you thinkin' about that?" Al asked him.

"I don't know exactly," Barlow replied. "I don't think it was just one thing. It was more like everythin' that's hap'ened even b'fore da kidnappin' when Chasidy would talk about her God to me. Throughout everythin', I just kept gettin' a deep'r and deep'r urge to be clos'r to Him."

"I don't think Mic was ev'r baptized," Al shared.

"Really?" That surprised Barlow. And the fact that it came out of the blue.

"I mean we go to church and all, but, well, none of us have been under da water," Al confessed.

"Maybe it's time to start thinkin' about that," Barlow suggested. "But I've learned that decision has to be personal."

"Maybe," Alan thought. The idea had crossed his mind on an occasion or two, but he never really seriously thought about it, nor had he and Mic discussed it. He was thinking especially since the accident, *maybe it's time they did.*

A Higher Calling

Barlow has always had quite a bit of influence on Alan. Not only did Alan love him like a brother, but he respected him also. Knowing that Barlow had become so serious about his relationship with God made him rethink his own. He began pondering the idea of baptism himself. But if he went under the water, he wanted his family to go with him. He would speak to Mic about it the first free moment she got. Being that it's already close to company arriving, he wasn't sure if it would be possible.

Alan was still limited in his movement even with the less invasive neck brace. Feeding Grace for the first time worked out ok, but he didn't trust himself trying to burp her. He was happy Barlow was there. "You want me to do it?"

"I imagine yur an expert by now," Al said accepting his help.

"I'm gettin' there," Barlow bragged.

#

The twins were anxious to see the babies again so, for the first time in the history of family gatherings, Terrence and his family arrived first. That and the fact that Terrence was anxious to see how his favorite uncle was fairing. Antonio and Caitlin drove up right behind them with Grandma Rosalee. They all took notice of the shiny new vehicles parked in the yard. Each one of them had something to say about them as they entered the house with their part of dinner.

Chasidy and Mic heard them pull up and came out to greet them. "Hey everybody!" Chasidy greeted, "Merry Christmas!"

Caitlin broke the Christmas ice. "Thank y'all so much for da Bentley," she said to Chasidy and Barlow. "I knew y'all loved me. Until now, I had no idea how much."

"Yea," Terrence added, "Imma look good styling in Pearlie. Throw some twenties on that baby and she'll be straight."

"I ain't really no truck person, but red is my favorite color," Antonio joined in. "I can roll with that."

When they ran out of vehicles, Jasmine was left with only her feelings. "If that's the case, then I guess y'all just forgot about me all t'gether. I'm feel like I'm feelin' a little somethin' b'hind this," she pretended.

Barlow comforted her, "Yors was so special, its takin' them an extra day to get it ready."

They all had stopped in a bunch just inside the family room. Rosalee was kind of stuck behind them. The door was left open and there was a chill in the air. Chasidy rescued her. "Y'all come on in and let Mama sit down." Once her mother was safely inside the warmth, Chasidy could address them properly. "First things first. This is Mrs. Valerie Peterson, Michelle's mom. Mrs. Peterson, my mom, Rosalee and my children and grandchildren. Just call 'em da gang until you learn everybody's names." She introduced them quickly, making extra moderations over the twins. Then she addressed Caitlin's comment. "Cait, I didn't know y'all had made additions to yor house."

"We haven't," Caitlin told her.

"Then you'd betta' get started," Chasidy continued.

"Why?" Caitlin asked, "You know somethan' I don't."

"Yeah. I know that da only way you drive off in da Bentley is if da Quad and I are with you. And you know we ain't leavan' Rob b'hind, so you gon need a lotta room, girl." Rob touched and agreed with her. "We're already orderan' a station wagon for da Quad. They can't even ride in da Bentley until they learn to appreciate her beauty."

"A station wagon. I'm sure that's child abuse in some country," Caitlin said.

Terrence made a different point. "Riding in a station wagon is everybody abuse." Everyone was tickled by that.

They looked like they were comfortable standing there holding their potluck and carrying on. But Michelle thought the kitchen was a better place for the food. "Y'all gon stand up and eat or y'all gon bring da food to da kitchen so we all can get some?" Then she added. "We don't have a turkey taday. Rob fa'got to cook it."

"Hot dang it!" Rob shouted. "Why didn't somebody r'mind me?"

Chasidy sided with Mic this time. "Well, Sweetheart, nobody had to remind anyone else. You really should've stayed on top of that. You can't cook a turkey in thirty minutes," she joked.

"I am so sorry y'all," Barlow apologized.

"Wait!" McKenzie said. "We ain't got no turkey! Who has dressing without Turkey?"

This time McKenna agreed with her sister. "Yeah. Somebody needs to do somethin' about this even if it's wrong." Terrance actually thought that was funny, so he didn't scold them this time.

"Don't worry about it, Mr. Rob," Jasmine said, "I brought a ham." And then to her girls, "You can eat ham with dressing."

"Yea," Caitlin added, "and I brought meatloaf. So, we've got plenty of meat."

"You ladies are life sav'rs," Barlow told them.

Alan could smell the turkey cooking most of the day while he and Rob talked. He was trying to figure out if Rob was playing along or if he really believed the girls. He just had to know for sure. "Rob?" He got his attention. "Are you serious?"

"About what?" Barlow asked.

"About da turkey. You didn't smell da turkey cookin' while we w're talkin'?" Alan asked.

Barlow looked up at Chasidy and Mic. They both were grinning and nodding at him. "Alright, y'all got me that time. Thank you, ladies, for bailing me out." After that, Barlow looked at his watch. It was almost three-thirty.

Chasidy noticed. "Don't worry, he'll be here," she said. But she had her own concerns about a different business.

Terrence made his way straight to Alan extending a handshake and a hug welcoming him home. And then to Barlow. Alan is completely taken aback by Terrence. Antonio and the girls followed suit after they put their potluck in the kitchen.

This would be the only time Alan would have to talk with Mic about the baptism. He had wished he could do it more privately. By a stroke of grace, he was able to do just that. When Chasidy went to the kitchen, Caitlin and the other ladies followed. The twins latched onto little Charles and went to the nursery to see the babies. AJ took Antonio and Terrence over to the stables to see the horses and Rob sat out on the porch to wait for Pastor Bishop.

"Mic," he said, "Come h're for a sec."

"Somethin' wrong?" she asked.

"How do you feel about being baptized?" Mic immediately began to smile. "What's so funny?" Al asked.

"I already knew this was comin'. You and Rob are as hopeless as Rob and Chasidy," she told him. He joined her in an invisible smile.

"Well?" He persisted.

"I think its way past due," she told him. "Our accident was a close call, an eye opener. I think it's time we gave our lives to da Lord. He's been too good to us."

"I was hopin' you'd say that" Al told her. "Maybe we can talk to Pastor taday too?"

"For sure," Mic said.

"Should we ask AJ or just tell 'im we're doing this as a family?"

"AJ's probably already been thinkin' about it. He loves his bible study with Chasidy. He would just read to her sometimes when she wasn't feelin' well enough for class."

"It's agreed then." After that he concluded he and his family would follow Rob's lead and get baptized. "Thanks Baby. I hear a vehicle. That must be him now."

"Rob is out on da porch. You wanna join 'im?" Mic asked Al.

"Not unless he asks me," Al replied. "He's made it clear this is between him and God. I respect that."

Chasidy heard the car pulling up too. On the way to the porch, she inquired about AJ and the others. "He took them to da stables to show off his horse," Mic told her. "Can you call and ask 'im to head back for dinna and come through da back door please."

"Sure," Mic said. "Do I smell anoth'r Chasidy surprise brewin'?"

"Yes, you do. Hopefully two. Any minute now. I don't want them to see it."

"Alright then I'll keep 'em in da kitchen when they get here."

"Thanks Mic."

"I'm waitin' on one myself for Al. I'm gettin' a little nervous. It's not h're yet."

"Don't worry," Chasidy said. It'll be h're."

But it wasn't Pastor Bishop driving up. It was Mr. Peterson. Barlow stood to greet him. "Hello Mr. Barlow. I assume its ok that I'm here. Your wife invited me. I'm awful glad she did," he spoke solemnly. Chasidy looked at Barlow. He nodded once. Then she called for Michelle's mother to come. "What is it, Chasidy?" She immediately stopped talking when she saw her husband standing on the porch.

Barlow said, "We'll leave you two alone."

"Wait, Mr. Barlow. It's actually you and Alan I wanna talk to first."

"Alright, follow me."

As Mr. Peterson walked past his wife, he gave her a hug. "Will you excuse us. I'll play nice." he promised. They made their way back to the kitchen to finish setting up for dinner. Michelle turned to Chasidy, "This was yor oth'r surprise?"

"Yes," she answered.

Michelle watched the men from a crack in the door. She couldn't hear what they were saying, though. Mrs. Peterson asked her, "What made you do this?"

"I couldn't think of anything to get you for Christmas. You couldn't be da only one without a gift from me," Chasidy answered. "Merry Christmas."

Mrs. Peterson gave Chasidy a long hug. "Thank you. I dreaded the thought of him being alone on Christmas."

Mr. Peterson poured his heart out to Alan and Barlow trying to explain his actions as opposed to making excuses for them. He explained his jealousy towards the men because of the relationship they shared with his daughter, with his grandson and even with each other. He explained how those feelings likely derived from the pain of losing his own three-year old son. "I knew you weren't no kingpin or cult leader, Mr. Barlow. My pettiness just wouldn't let me accept you fellas for who you really are. I'm glad you've been a part of Michy's life, taking care of her. I'm truly sorry for the way I've acted towards you both. I'm asking for your forgiveness. Sincerely, this time Alan."

There was a brief moment of silence between them. Then Alan reached out his hand for a forgive and forget handshake. Mr. Peterson not only shook his hand but gave him a long hug as well.

"Mom," Michelle called. She walked out of the kitchen. Her mother and Chasidy followed her. After Mr. Peterson let go of Alan, he immediately latched on to Barlow. He was hugging him when AJ and the others walked in.

"Grandpa!" he yelled. "Whatta you doing here?"

"I came to spend Christmas with you and my family if that's alright," he answered looking around at everyone.

AJ ran over to his dad. "Dad, is it alright?"

"It's more than alright, Son. It's anoth'r Christmas Miracle."

Mr. Peterson walked over to his wife and began to speak, "I'm…"

"Not another word," she said. "I've already forgiven you. Merry Christmas, Darling."

Michelle's concern was abated when her surprise for Al finally arrived. He was completely blown away when he saw his temporary parents, the Marshalls, approaching him. Papa Stan and Mama Kelly came to spend Christmas with their son. They were unable to reach him in the hospital because his cell phone was lost in the accident. Neither Rob nor Michelle had their number. They called while AJ was wrapping his new phone, one of his gifts to his dad. It was during this call that Michelle invited them for Christmas.

When they heard the next car pull up, they knew it had to be Pastor Bishop. Chasidy stayed only long enough to acknowledge the pastor and to let Rob know to be on the look-out for a delivery. "Do you want me to hold dinna 'til yur done talkan'?"

"If that's not too much trouble," Barlow answered. "I'll walk in with you." Stopping where Al was seated, he asked, "Al is it too cool for you on da porch?"

"Not at all. It's just right," Alan answered. Barlow helped him to the other rocking chair on the porch. Al was glad he was including him in the conversation.

"Mr. Peterson, yur welcome too." Barlow didn't wanna hold dinner up too long. They could always finish their conversation after dinner. So, he got straight to the point. "The reason we invited you ov'r Pastor is b'cause I wanna get baptized. Chasidy and I talked about that, and she said you w're da man to see."

"That's wonderful, Robert. Praise the Lord!" Pastor told him.

"But what I haven't talked to her about is why I really needed to talk to you. Everybody's been noticin' how I've been lost in my thoughts lately. Even my buddy Al here." Al listened attentively. "Since I first met Chasidy, she started talkin' about her God and what He means to 'er. Long story short, it wasn't easy, but I've developed a zeal for God. It seems that aft'r each trauma he brings me through, that zeal gets strong'r and strong'r. Now, I can't know enough about Him. But that's just da b'ginnin'. I wanna share what I do know with oth'r people. That's da part I wanted to talk to ya about. Somethin' keeps tuggin' at me to spread da word about God." The pastor looked on in fascination as Barlow spoke. "I guess what I'm sayin', Pastor, is that I wanna preach. But I don't feel like I know enough. Chasidy does a wonderful job in her teachings but even she'll admit at times there are things she can't explain. So, I'm reachin' out to someone who knows. I'm askin' you to teach me."

Alan couldn't believe what he was hearing. Pastor, however, was elated. "Robert, you may not b'lieve this. I've been struggling with assigning a co-pastor for da church ever since my co-pastor passed away a year ago. Every time I had someone in mind for da position, da Lord wouldn't let me proceed with it. Now I'm not saying He's holding that position open for you. What I am saying is I'd be glad to take you under my wings and see where da Lord leads us from there," Pastor Bishop explained.

This whole time Alan sat speechless, listening to Rob bare his soul and Pastor Bishop opening his heart to it. He knew Rob was serious about this because he had watched him spiritually grow over the past two years. He was proud of him.

Pastor Bishop taught Rob his first lesson. "Robert, da first and most important thing you should know as pastor is that you can never lead too many souls to Christ. Saying that, he turned to Al and asked, "What about you brother Al?"

"Well, Pastor, my wife and I just had our own conversation about this same thing taday. Chasidy has been having bible study with our son AJ and sometimes she sits in on it. He's been sharing what he's learned with me as well. We attend church once in a while, but we haven't seriously given our lives to da Lord. This accident was a real wake up call. We haven't talked to AJ yet. She doesn't think he'll protest. We would like to get baptized also as a family."

Pastor praised God again. "Looks like I have a prospective new pastor and a new deacon on board. What a blessed Christmas Day!"

Barlow couldn't have been happier. "Fellas, we've held up dinn'r long enough. Let's go eat," he told them.

The dining room was filled with happy chatter. Everyone was pitching in preparing the table for dinner. Barlow seated Mr. Peterson, Al, and Pastor at the table, and he joined in with a helping hand. Chasidy scolded him. "Whatta you doing? You sit down with yor company. We're about done anyway." Barlow elected to let the professional say grace this time after which the happy chatter started up again while they enjoyed their meal. Barlow, much like during Thanksgiving, looked around the table at his family giving thanks silently for each one. Especially the four new members at the table; the Petersons, Sam, Charles, and the youngest additions in the nursery. And the second new beginning of Mic and her parents.

Chasidy noticed him lingering in that place again. "Rob," she got his attention. "You've talked to da pastor, what's this distance about now?" she asked.

Barlow began smiling at her. Then he got everyone's attention by tapping on his glass with his fork. "Everyone I have an announcement to make." He reached for Chasidy's hand. She gave it to him. He kissed the back of her hand and squeezed it just a little bit. "I'm getting' baptized and I want all of you to be there with me when I do." Caitlin was the first to congratulate with a hug and a kiss. Everyone else followed suit. Barlow continued. "Wait, wait, wait. Don't sit down. Y'all have to do it all ov'r again." He looked at Al.

Al said, "Yea. Mic I, and AJ are gettin' baptized too."

AJ blurted out excitedly, "We are!" He got up and started hugging his dad and then his mom also. Once again everyone joined in.

Mrs. Peterson was completely blown away. "Oh Al, Michy, I'm so proud of you!"

"Yes. Both of us are, son."

Barlow was still smiling as everyone gave their congratulations. "Wait y'all," Chasidy said. "I feel like my husband isn't finished."

His smile got even bigger. "Yor feelin' is absolutely right."

"What is it?" Chasidy nudged.

"I b'lieve da Lord has called me to preach. I have this overwhelming desire to teach people da things you've taught me and so much more. Pastor Bishop has agreed to take me und'r his wings and let me shadow 'im. Al is gonna be one of his deacons."

Tears formed in Chasidy's eyes. She had once thought that just his wanting to be baptized was the best Christmas gift she could get, but this tops that by a mile. She stood up from the table excusing herself. When she came back, she handed Rob a box and kissed him on the cheek. Then she handed the other one to Alan, kissing him on the forehead. "I was gonna wait until gift swap ta give you both this, but I think this is a betta time," she said.

Barlow had his gift opened first. He lifted the lid to reveal two bibles. A large beautiful black and gold lined bible with a place in front for family heritage information so that he could start his own family tree. The other one; a handsome smaller study bible with a commentary section for easy understanding.

Then she made her way to Alan. Alan had the exact same gift in white plus something extra. Chasidy asked to borrow AJ's seat just for a moment. Alan pulled out a sealed envelope. "What is this?"

"I'm learnan' some new things from my husband," she started. "With today's technology, you can find out just about anythan' you wanna know. Rob told me how being an orphan haunted you as a child. This envelope has information about three Ferguson families in da area where Rob grew up. I started there since you two met really young." Chasidy paused for just a second. "Sometimes it's ok to let da past rest. But if you desire, one of these families I think you'll find very interestan'. It's yor choice to open this and continue yor family research, or you can start yor own legacy with da beautiful family you have right here in front of you." Al reached out his arms to Chasidy. She happily gave him the hug he was asking for. "Eitha' way, I thank you'll be very pleased." She smiled hinting that the information in the envelope was good news."

Al, not being able to get away from the norm of things, replied, "I'm so glad we married you. You w're just what we needed. Thank you. I love it."

Making her way back to Barlow, she winked at him and sat down to finish her dinner. With all that on his mind, he couldn't really eat very much. When the pastor was finished, they excused themselves to finish their talk. Al was ready to rest but didn't want to miss out on the surprise Chasidy had planned for her family. Rob perched him back in her recliner so he could have a short nap.

Chasidy heard the clamoring outside and knew her surprise was here. She urged everyone to take their time finishing their dinner so that Al would have a little more time to rest. She left Mic in charged to make sure that happened.

Mrs. Peterson was happy her husband was seeing the close family interactions she had been seeing since she's met them. She watched him hoping he was receiving it all for what it truly is. Family Love.

Chasidy went outside to instruct the setup of her surprise. Then she came back inside to get things ready. At the table, she handed out clue cards and when everyone was done eating, they procceded to the living room.

Mic hated to wake Al, but this kind of thing was right up his alley. She knew he didn't want to miss it. "Al, Baby. Chasidy's about to get started." A sleepy Al adjusted himself. Barlow waited in anticipation also. Even he didn't know what his wife was up to.

"Aunt Chasidy," AJ asked, "Can I give my gifts before we start the game?"

"Absolutely, Sweetheart," she said.

"Help me Uncle Rob," he told his uncle. He grabbed his dad's gift first while Barlow placed the other gifts on top.

Michelle, knowing her son, commented, "I'll bet that big one is for yor dad."

AJ grinned and said, "Don't worry Mom. Yur gonna like yors too," insinuating that he knew his dad would love his gift. Michelle felt appeased when she saw the beautiful message of the necklace. She beckoned for AJ to come closer, then she showered him with kisses all over his face. He giggled. "Mom, cut it out." Mrs. Peterson grew teary-eyed when she opened her box that housed the beautiful Ruby bracelet. "Do you like it, Grandma?" AJ asked.

"Come help me put it on," she said. When AJ came over, she followed suit behind Michelle and showered him with kisses over his face. "I love it!"

"Grandma!" He tried to pretend he didn't like it.

Alan opened his small gift first. "Thanks Buddy!"

"Ours got lost in the accident," AJ explained. Then Alan opened the big box. He laughed when he saw the electronic game system.

Michelle had to tell off on him. "You w're pouting 'cause he had deserted you and he was out buying stuff so y'all could spend more time t'gether."

"I'm smiling inside," Alan said, "best gift ever Little Guy. When my neck brace come off, I'm gonna kiss all over yor face too."

AJ then turned to his other grandparents. "I'm sorry, Grandpa. I didn't know y'all were coming. All I have left is a hug."

"That's quite alright, Son. A hug will do just fine," his grandpa told him.

"That goes double for us," Mama Kelly agreed. But Al and Mic had that covered too. Mic handed them a card with tickets to India to hike the Himalayan Mountains to continue on their world travel quest.

"These are perfect. Thank you." Stan said.

Once they were done, Chasidy passed a jar of straws around for everyone to pull one. Then she asked, "Do we wanna start from da shortest or da longest?" The shortest got the most votes. She instructed everyone to hold up their straws so that they all would know what order they were in. "Game rules," Chasidy started, "you have to read yor clue out loud and try to figure out what yor gift is. If you figure it out, I tell you where to find it. If you don't figure it out, you have to go on a scavenger hunt here in da house ta find it yorself. That's it. I encourage everybody to help out with clues so Al can participate. He's tired. We'll need to get him to bed soon. So, help each otha."

Antonio pulled the shortest straw. His clue read; "Blazing hot hits the spot. On the trail I go." He repeated it over and over.

Barlow teased, "I hope all da clues aren't this easy."

Antonio replied, "I don't see what's easy about it." He recruited help. "Hey. Mama said y'all can help me." But they didn't get it either.

"Since you w're such a big help to me when we w're in Georgia, I'm gonna help ya out," Barlow told him.

"Aw ight," Antonio said, "I sho' don't wanna have to hunt for it."

Barlow said, "Blazing trail."

"It still took Antonio a second to process what Barlow said. He repeated, "Blazing trail." Then he said questionably, "Trail Blazer?"

Chasidy teased, "Caitlin, where w're you baby? See how da *old man* figured that out. Thanks to yor dad you don't have to look fa yors. You've been walkin' around it all eve'nan on da dining table. Red box."

He ran to find the box and came back dangling a set of car keys in his hand. "Wow! Thanks, y'all!"

He started outside to see the truck. Chasidy stopped him. "Nope. Not until da game is ova'," she said. "Let's make this quick," she expressed again. The game was easier from that point on now that they had seen how it was played. They all were anxious to see what they had so they eagerly helped each other figure out their gifts.

Jasmine had the next straw. "Hi-ho, hi-ho. Off and away I go." she was grinning as she was reading it. "That's gotta be a Tahoe," she said.

"Yep," they all agreed.

"Oooh! My turn, my turn!" Mckenna said, excited to get her gift.

"Can I get mine first?" her mother scolded.

"Da cute little bag hanging on da fireplace," Chasidy said softly laughing. "Okay Kenna, go ahead."

"If beauty had a price, what would it be? Grandma, why you give me da hard one?" she complained.

"I didn't give you da hard one," Chasidy defended. "Think about it. What are you foreva' doing wheneva' I talk to you?"

McKenzie answered, "getting' her nails done." McKenna looked at her grandma still confused.

"Whatda you need to get yor nails done, Baby?"

"Money!" Everybody screamed.

"Oooh fa real, grandma? Where?"

"Hanging on da tree," Chasidy told her. "Yor name is on it."

"Thank you, grandma!" she said.

It wasn't McKenzie's turn yet, but she skipped ahead of her dad. "Grandma, you may as well tell me where mind is cause me and Kenna always get da same thing."

"You don't know that's what I did this time." Chasidy tried to fool her. She wouldn't be fooled.

"Grandma. Really?"

"Alright little feisty missy." At least read yor clue so everyone can hear it." Barlow was tickled silly at McKenzie and her grandmother.

McKenzie read her clue, "What thirteen-year-old girls want. And then answered it, "money."

"Under da tree. Green box. Smartie pants," Chasidy told her.

Terrence said to Chasidy, "I'm sorry Ma, but you should've let Dad and Uncle Al do da clues." They all laughed. Then Terrence read his clue while McKenzie rumbled through the packages under the tree. "I'm like McKenzie. You may as well tell me where mine is too. Cause I already know what this is."

Alan commented, "You should've let me, and Rod make these clues."

"Yeah," Barlow added, "they nev'r would've figured 'em out then."

"Is there anybody who hasn't informed me of this? If so, speak now or foreva' hold yor peace." Chasidy playfully protested.

"Read yors," Al said.

"Don't Blink. You might miss me," Terrence read.

Barlow looked at Chasidy and said, "Chasidy Sweetheart, everybody in this room knows what that is."

Chasidy responded, "Well until somebody says da word, I don't have to tell 'im where his box is."

Everybody shouted, "motorcycle!"

"Here it is Daa!" McKenzie shouted, still rumbling under the tree.

Caitlin followed suit with her brother. "Mom, I know what mine is too. You really should've let Dad and Uncle Al…" She started to tease Chasidy grinning. "I'm just playin'. I do know what it is though, fa real."

"Alright McKenzie Jr," Chasidy said, "at least tell everybody what da card said."

"Man is in the forest," Caitlin read. "That's from Bambi. Bambi is a dear. Dear are related to Impalas. Da Impala is my favorite car. So, mind is an Impala. Mine is an Impala. Holla, Holla, Holla! Mine is an Impala." Caitlin sang her answer to a snappy tune while doing her happy feet dance.

"That was pretty cool detective reasonin'," Barlow said. "And a good clue too," he said smiling at Chasidy.

"Thank you, Baby," she said proudly. Since everybody wanna play gang up on Chasidy, this was a last-minute thang. If it weren't for Al, y'all would've been huntan' for everythan'," she defended herself playfully. Then she said to AJ. "Ok, AJ, "Yur up Boo. Last one."

"What twelve-year-old boys want." Thinking about the twins earlier, he asked, "Aunt Chasidy, is it money?"

"Yur supposed to be tellin' me," she said.

"Money," he said positively.

"Nope!" she said, disappointing him.

"What do twelve-year-old-boys want?" he asked. Nobody said anything. "Dad, Uncle Rob, help."

Mr. and Mrs. Peterson had enjoyed the game up to this point, but quite naturally they took a special interest in AJ's turn. They listened carefully to see if they could help him figure it out.

The only thought Alan had was that it was likely something he could share with him. Mic had that same thought. She said out loud what Alan was thinking. "It's probably somethin' you can do with yor dad. Whatda you like doing with Al?" she asked him.

"Everything," AJ said without even thinking about it. Alan basked in that answer, though no one could see it.

D.M. Williams

Barlow thought about how she made each gift personal. How she used each one's personal interest to make their gift special. He agreed with Mic. He remembered how much he enjoyed their fishing trip. And how Chasidy instigated that. His guess was that it had something to do with that.

Chasidy felt compassion for him. "Since you really do have da hardest clue, I'm gonna help you out."

"No. Don't help 'im yet," Barlow said, "I think I got it."

Mic said, "Rob if you figure this one out, then you and Chasidy really are soulmates. There ain't no way you know what this is."

Al disagreed. "Mic, you know Rob and Chasidy have been thanking alike since they've known each oth'r. Have you forgotten da matchin' vehicles already that neith'r of them knew the oth'r had gotten? He could very well have this figured out."

"Al," Mic said, "You are too right. They have matchin' necklaces too. Have you seen 'em?" Then she turned to Rob and said, "Go ahead Rob, tell us what it is."

"Tell me Uncle Rob," AJ pleaded.

"Tell him Uncle Rob. Soulmate," Chasidy nudged, professing her faith in him.

"I think it's fishin' gear. That's something he can do with his dad. He really enjoyed da first trip," Barlow told them.

"Is that yor final answer?" Chasidy asked smiling at Rob.

"That's my final answer," he said smiling back at her.

"Little guy, do you think Uncle Rob is right?" Chasidy teased to build suspense.

"I hope so. I had fun fishin' with him and Dad."

"Yor gift is under da tree. Blue box." Chasidy didn't say if Barlow was right or wrong. Everybody was waiting on pins and needles to find out. When AJ opened the box, he found some papers in it that he didn't understand. He took them to his mom.

Mic couldn't believe what she was reading. "Well, it ain't no fishin' gear, but I know you didn't buy this boy a whole boat," she blurted out handing the papers to Al. Barlow pasted the biggest grin on his face.

Chasidy added, looking at her soulmate, "Are you sure about that, Mic?"

"I don't see any fishin' stuff in this box," she argued.

Chasidy asked, "Al, is a boat fishan' gear?" she toyed with them.

Al's answer was indefinite. "I suppose it could be. You do need a boat if yur goin' out on da water."

"Rob?" she asked for his definition. "Soulmate, please tell me a boat is fishan' gear."

Having every confidence in his wife that they are true soulmates, he knew there was fishing gear somewhere, so he answered, "No. A boat isn't fishin' gear."

Michelle couldn't help but challenge her. "Awe. What a sad Christmas Day. It looks like you and Rob aren't soulmates after all. I think I'm gonna cry."

"Hold up on those tears," she said never breaking her stare from Barlow. "AJ," Chasidy said, "you have one more box under da tree. Sit in yor mom's lap and open it."

AJ sat the box on the floor in front of Michelle because it was too big for him to sit in her lap. "Fishin' gear!" he screamed once the box was opened.

"Not just a boat," she defended, "but a whole rack of fishan' gear to go with it, including reels on da boat." Barlow let out the most joyous laughter. Alan laughed his first laugh also since the accident; even if it did make his jaw hurt. Even Mic was happy she was wrong. "You w're so excited when you got back from yor first fishan' trip. And Rob said you guys had so much fun that it would become a regular thang for you guys. I just had to."

"Thanks Aunt Chasidy!" AJ started hugging her and didn't want to let go. "Yur da best Aunt ever!"

"I am, aren't I?" Chasidy agreed. "Of course, it helps being yor only Aunt." She too showered him with kisses all over his little face. The twins' green-eyed monster surfaced, so she summoned them for their own shower of kisses.

It was Pastor Bishop, however, who made the proclamation, "Well Mic, they must be true soulmates."

The rest of the gifts were hand given including Chasidy's mom's gift. She brought the huge box from the tree over to her and sat it down in her lap. She opened it to find the most elegant three-piece royal blue and white fleece coat and jacket set with stylish accessories of gloves, hats, scarfs, and boots.

D.M. Williams

Sam's gift was from both Barlow and Chasidy, a special thanks for his recent help in Georgia. His eyes grew big, and his smile grew wide when he found open tickets for him and a companion for a three-week vacation to Turks-n-Caicos whenever he was ready to travel. Chasidy handed Mr. Peterson an envelope with tickets for a family Disney Cruise for him, Mrs. Peterson, AJ, Michelle, and Alan. Hoping that a relaxing trip would re-seal an old *and new* bond. Then she gave everyone permission to go outside and claim their gifts.

Pastor Bishop wasn't left to the wind either. Barlow handed him an envelope as well. "Thank you for joining us today, Pastor. This is our first family Christmas t'gether. We're glad you could join us. This is from Chasidy and me."

Pastor opened the envelope to find two generous checks, one made out to him and another with the greater amount made out to the church. "Y'all included everybody, didn't you? Thank you. I, and da church thank you."

She and Barlow stood on the porch arm and arm watching the children make moderation over their claims. Caitlin and Antonio were trying to figure out how to get their new vehicles home. They heard Terrell say, "I don't know what y'all gon do, but I'm ridin' mine."

He said to Chasidy as they watched, "Next Christmas, me and Al are definitely makin' da clues."

"Oh, we're playin' this game again next Christmas?" she asked. "I'm sure Al will be well by then," she joked.

"It looks like a Barlow-Ferguson family tradition to me," he said with a chuckle.

"In that case, why not just make it a full-scale scavenger hunt?" she asked.

"Chasidy," he said looking down at her, "this was so much more fun than a scavenger hunt. Everything you did taday was amazing, right down to bringing Mic's dad here. This was by far my best Christmas ever." Then he added, "But we won't have to help out with da clues next year though. Everybody's on their own."

"Bet." She agreed. Then she said, staring back at him completely satisfied, "I'm glad you enjoyed it, evan though I thank my soulmate is a little biased."

"And he is," he agreed.

Barlow Redefined

Pastor, Barlow and Al made the plans for their baptism, after which, Barlow escorted Al to bed. He had enjoyed a full glorious day, but it had taken its toll on him. He kissed little Grace and Charles welcoming them again to his family and made good use of the bed that waited for him, falling straight to sleep having enjoyed one of the best holidays ever.

Barlow wanted to begin his spiritual journey as soon as possible. But he and Al had been doing things together since they were boys. He didn't want to start leaving him in the wind now. Al was set for a doctor's appointment the second week in January. They set the baptismal for the third Sunday, hoping he would be free of the neck brace by then.

There was a different feel for New Year's Eve and the Barlow and Ferguson families ushered the new year in at church instead of a party like Barlow and Al usually did. Chasidy's family touched Barlow's heart when they all asked what they had planned for New Year's Eve. When Chasidy told them Rob wanted to go to church, they said they were going with him. Chasidy had never been able to get all of her family in church at the same time. Barlow had accomplished unknowingly what she had always hoped to accomplish. She hung up the phone looking mysteriously pleased at Barlow. "Guess what?" she asked.

"What?" he replied.

"My entire family has committed to coman' to New Year's Eve Watch Meet at church t'night. This is da part I'm in my feelans about; to see da new year in with you and Al," she told Barlow.

"They said that specifically?" Barlow asked.

Chasidy made it clear. "Caitlin said that they all had talked about it, and they wanted you and Al to know that y'all were their family now and they wanted to celebrate Christ with da two of you," Chasidy explained. "If I wasn't so happy that they wanna come ta church, I would be jealous. You have no idea how long I've been tryan' to get Terrence and Antonio in church."

"I'm glad they're willing to support us like that," Barlow said.

"I think it's more than that," Chasidy told him. "Neitha' of them have had positive male influences for most of their lives. They see that in you and Al. Da way you guys interact with AJ and now yor new children, they admire that. I b'lieve they see you guys as role models that they're lookan' forward to followan'."

Barlow was flattered. "I hope that's true. If it is, I hope they will join church so we all can attend t'gether."

"That would be wonderful, Rob," Chasidy agreed. "We are still in da Christmas Miracle season. Who knows?" Barlow was excited to share even that much with AL.

#

The young gang were gathered at Caitlin's house for New Year's Eve playing cards, laughing, and doing what young people do. Caitlin noticed that her brother hadn't had an alcoholic beverage all evening. Antonio had a glass of white rum with Caitlin but not much more than a glass. Caitlin couldn't pass up an opportunity for a teased. "You must have used up all yor get-outta-jail-free cards."

"Whatta you talkin' bout?" He asked her.

"I haven't seen you drink anythan' all day. You tryan' not to get a ticket?"

Terrence chuckled. "We can't go to church wasted tonight," he defended.

"Just b'cause you drink somethin' don't mean you have to get wasted," Antonio told him.

Terrence chuckled again. "It does fa me." They all laughed. Then he added in a more solemn tone. "Da twins are thirteen years old. I think I've only been ta church with them about three times." Then he looked at Jasmine. "I think I wanna change that."

"What you sayin'?" she asked him.

"I'm sayin' I wanna get baptized too with Dad."

"For real!" Jasmine squealed. "Baby that's great!" she said hugging him. "Wait 'til I tell Mama!"

"No. Don't tell 'er. They like surprises. Imma surprise 'em t'night at church."

"Let's all surprise em," Caitlin said, "and join church tonight."

They all liked that idea. "Yeah, let's do that," they agreed.

#

Barlow helped Chasidy get the babies ready for service. When he was done, he went into the bedroom to see if Al felt like going out tonight. Al responded, "Don't ask stupid questions." Barlow laughed lightly at him throwing his own answer back at him.

"That's good cause I know somethin' you wouldn't wanna miss out on."

"What's that?"

"Chasidy's children, our children, are comin' t'night to support us," Barlow told him.

"Us as in…." Al asked.

"You and me. They want us to know, and by us, I mean mostly you, that they're our family too. That boy of hers has really latched onto you."

"Man, Rob. This holiday just keeps getting' bett'r and bett'r," Alan told him.

"Al. Da only way it could get bett'r from h're is if they all joined church with us and we w're able to attend as a family."

"Well, we're still in da Christmas Miracle season," Al told him.

"That's exactly what Chasidy said."

"Does Mic know?" Al asked.

"Chasidy's tellin' her now." As they were loading up in the trucks, Sam came around in the Bentley. Barlow didn't think to mention to him that he was driving Al's truck tonight. "I'm sorry Sam. I forgot to tell you Al wanted to go in da truck."

"I know your vehicles are quite full," Sam said, "but can we make room for one more?"

"I'm sure we can fit one more in, somewhere between three vehicles," Barlow told him. That's when he noticed the headlights coming up the drive.

"Ms. Sherry will be joining me tonight." Barlow along with everyone else smiled surprisingly at Sam. Sam continued, "As the young folks say, we- hit- it- off."

#

Watch Meet on New Year's Eve is a short service and then dinner and games afterwards. It was during the service the children made their announcement. They had already spoken to Pastor Bishop in private. He agreed to help them surprise their parents. They all sat together taking up three pews. The pastor informed the church that there would be a baptismal ceremony on the third Sunday and a fellowship afterwards. He invited the candidates to the front so that the congregation could meet them. Alan was excused from standing but had a seat on the front pew.

After he had called Barlow and the Fergusons to the front, he continued on to the surprise. "It's a rare thing when a man can have such an influence on a young person that the young person has a desire to learn from that man and follow in his footsteps. It's even rarer if there are two such men. These two men confessed their faith in Christ on Christmas Day and upon attending church tonight their family came also in support of them." He asked the young families to stand and come to the front to be with Barlow. "Stand right here beside your father," he said to Terrence and Antonio. Jasmine, Caitlin, and the twins sat on the pew with their arms around Al. Mic and AJ were standing with Barlow. "I can't express how it makes me feel to see this family here tonight. Sister Chasidy has expressed to me many times how she wished she could get her family in church. Sister Chasidy, your children have something to say."

Antonio knew Terrence had the biggest news, so he elected to go first. "Mom, you've been inviting me and Cait to church with you for a long time. We decided earlier this evening that we're joining church with you, Dad, Uncle Al, and Aunt Mic. Like pastor said, we do wanna be like them. They're da coolest guys ever." Chasidy held back the tears in anticipation of what Terrence was about to say. It wasn't easy, she was already overjoyed.

It took Terrence a minute to start. He looked at Alan sitting on the pew for a long time. He stepped over to him to shake his hand. Then he turned to Barlow. He seemed to be stuck as to where to start. When he did, he said, "I've neva met anyone I admire and respect as much as I do da two of you. You guys *are* da coolest. So, if yur gonna get baptized, I wanna get baptized too and learn what you wanna teach about God."

It was more than Chasidy could handle. She jumped out of her seat running to the front to hug her children, beginning with Terrence. Sam was right on her heels. He extended hugs to everyone also. But he too had an announcement to make. He walked up to Barlow who was flowing rivers of tears by now and said something to him. Barely being able to speak himself, he said clearing his throat "Pastor, Sam has somethin' to say."

Chasidy was holding Caitlin by the time Barlow spoke. The church quieted for Sam. "Pastor, I desire to be baptized also with my family."

Barlow and Chasidy were more than elated. They were speechless. Two strangers joined together to make one; in the end secretly shared the same desire, to worship God as a family. And God being the Sovereign Entity that He is, gave them the desires of their heart because they desired first a work in His Kingdom just like He promised. When the church was quieted again, Chasidy made her way to her husband and asked him, "Do you know what it says in Psalm thirty-seven, verse four?"

He answered, not surprising her in the least by now, "Yes, I do." He recited; *Delight thyself in da Lord, and He shall give thee da desires of yor heart.*"

"Are yor heart's desires fulfilled, Rob?" Chasidy asked him.

"Desires I didn't even know I had until I met you," he responded happily. He shook hugged his sons and walked with them back to their seats.

#

Before going to bed that morning after the Watch Meet service, Mr. Peterson had a ton of emotions tumbling around in his heart. He was thankful that he had been a part of such a spiritual event. Having lost connections himself with God, after losing his son, he's beginning to rethink his own spirituality.

He had gotten a chance to see up close and personal this man he had once accused of operating a cult, interact with his family. He hadn't done anything different from previous encounters with him. But Mr. Peterson has seen him in a different light tonight; even over the past few days. His family didn't hoover around him because he ordered them to. Or cling to his every word because he insisted they do it. They didn't honor his wishes because he demanded it of them. His family had a perpetual desire for him, an admiration that could only come from the love they felt for him deep inside.

When he spoke with his wife before retiring for the night, he shared a confession. "This man that all of you have fallen in love with, he's a blessed man. I can see that now. Wherever he goes, love will follow him. Unfortunately, because there are men like me, who refuse to see the good in people, so will hatred."

"Do you still hate him?" his wife asked him.

"Sitting in that lonely house while you were here, thinking on how you and Michy took up for him, defended him and how he did the same for his friend, my son-in-law, I realized there must be more to him than what I was allowing myself to see. My jealousy of him and Al kept me from seeing the truth. Michy loves them both so much. And then you fell in love with them. Well, I did some serious thinking behind that. But I must be honest. It wasn't until Mrs. Barlow called me without her husband's knowledge and invited me here in an unconventional way that I realized the error of my ways."

"What did she do?" Mrs. Peterson asked.

"As soon as I answered the phone, she started talking. She said: *'I know you miss yor wife. She misses you too. She's da only reason fa this call, so don't talk or I may change my mind. Rob is a compassionate and fa'giving man. He likes yor wife a lot. So, if you showed up on Christmas Day to be with her, he wouldn't deny her that. And he would welcome you in spite of yorself.'* Then she hung up the phone. I realized I must have been such a jack whenever I opened my mouth."

Mrs. Peterson didn't comment. "You haven't really answered the question," she persisted.

"No, I don't hate 'im." he said. "I concluded that both my girls couldn't be wrong. When I stepped up on his porch and he extended his hand to me after all I had said to 'im, I saw the man you and Michy sees."

"In that conclusion, you gained a grandson," she said. He chuckled, looking back to just a few days ago when AJ received him with open arms.

"That's the darndest thing, isn't it?" he said. "That little guy wanted nothing to do with me as long as I was at odds with his dad and his uncle."

"I'm glad you came to your senses. Michy told me how close AJ is to his dad. She said as long as you resisted his dad, you would never be able to make a connection with him."

He added, "I'm glad they're forgiving people and allowed me to be here with you. I couldn't have made it through Christmas without you."

"Happy New Year, Jeffrey."

"Happy New Year Val."

#

Alan's appointment wasn't until next Tuesday, so Barlow made the trip to Jacksonville to lend his support to Gonzales on his first supervisory assignment. Barlow didn't use his usual charismatic appeal on his men to insure they gave Gonzales a fair shot. Instead, he stayed quietly in the Office Trailor behind Gonzales and let him speak to the men on his own. Many of the men didn't even know Barlow was in the office. The few who did, didn't care.

They had gathered just outside the office for their usual kickoff meeting that was attended just before beginning a project. Mr. Miller was standing beside Gonzales. Gonzales spoke like a true Barlow Inc leader. "Today's a special day for me," he started. "First of all, I'm proud for this opportunity to head this project with you all. Let's thank Mr. Miller for the opportunity. (They all clapped.) As you know, we should have started two weeks ago. But Mr. Ferguson thought enough of us to give us that time off to be with our families for the holidays. Let's show him how grateful we are by playing catch up and getting this project back on schedule. He and Mr. Barlow have made big promises to Mr. Miller. And we all know Mr. Ferguson would be here to see to it those promises are fulfilled if he could. It's my understanding, he's gotten much better. We thank God for that." The men clapped again in agreement. "This is our opportunity to show him and Mr. Barlow how much they can depend on us. We're the best in the business. So, let's do what we do best."

One of the guys yelled, "We got cha Gonzales."

Another one, "Yeah, we won't let you or Mr. Ferguson down."

All of the men clapped and yelled positively agreeing with Gonzales as Mr. Miller cut the ribbon to begin the groundbreaking of his new children's special needs hospital, St Michael's Hospital for Little Angels. Barlow left right after the crowd cleared without ever showing his face. Except to Mr. Miller.

#

Alan was having dinner when Barlow made it back from Jacksonville. "How'd it go?" he asked Barlow.

"Smooth as a calm river," Barlow responded.

"B'cause you w're there?"

"Nope," Barlow said, "b'cause we have da best team in da country on our payroll. They nev'r knew I was there. They gave young Gonzales da utmost respect and support. And they promised him they would do a job pleasing to you."

"Are you kiddin' me?" Alan asked.

"At da end of his speech, Gonzales said 'we're da best in da business. So, let's do what we do best.' And their response was "we won't let ya down Gonzales or Mr. Ferguson."

Alan looking proudly at Barlow, nodded once. He then said, "I think we'll add that to all of our ground breakings." It was Barlow's turn to nod once in agreement.

#

Alan, Mic, and AJ had appointments on the same day. Alan was more anxious about his appointment understandably due to his limited movement. However, he had no doubt he would hear good news. He didn't feel any more pain. And his neck was no longer swollen. He felt healed and believed he was healed and so expected

233

to leave the doctor's office unattached to a neck brace. He and Mic were up bright and early in anticipation. Mic even prepared breakfast for everyone. Her mom refused to allow her to do it alone though. "Sit and keep me company, Mom. I've got this."

"I will not. I came to help and help I will," she demanded.

"Thank you," Michelle said.

"Your father and I would like to drive you guys to your appointments if you don't mind," she offered.

"We'd like that," she said. And then added playfully, "so would Sam."

#

AJ and Mic saw the same doctor. He poked and prodded and gave them a thorough looking over and finally concluded that they were as good as new. Being from the country and a fan of old wise tales, he warned that they might be able to predict the weather from now on because of those injuries. Once he explained to AJ what he meant by that, his boyish imagination received it with anticipation, blatantly evident in his response, "That's what's up!" while nodding his little head." Mic, however, could think of better things to look forward to. Like her husband's neck brace coming off. Soon she would know if she anticipated in vain.

It was Al's first-time meeting Dr. Spencer. He was a short stubby guy who looked like he should be a cartoon character. For reasons known only to Al, he felt hopeful when he met the animated little man. It's befitting only of Al to find a reason to hope in a cartoon character.

Dr. Spencer asked him a rash of questions before carefully removing the brace. Then he asked Al to slowly move his head from side to side and up and down. Al performed like a rock star. Then he checked his eyes to make sure they were functioning properly. When the doctor finished examining Al, he then asked, "Now what was it you came to see me for young man?" Mic didn't think that was funny in the least, but Al let out a loud glorious laugh from deep down in his gut. Apparently, that's what the humorous little cartoon looking doctor was hoping for. He wanted to make sure Al wasn't in any pain when he laughed. He gladly pronounced, "young man, you're all healed."

Barlow nearly fell out on the floor when Al told him what the doctor asked him. Chasidy laughed more at Mic's reaction when Al told them she was ready to go immediately to see someone else. Anyone else.

#

The decision to make Barlow co-pastor was weighing heavily on Pastor Bishop's heart. He had such an influence on his family, surely a man of his character would be beneficial to his ministry. God's ministry. The baptismal was approaching quickly. He wanted to be able to make the announcement in service after the ceremony. He knew it was bound to cause an uproar. There were men serving under him long before Barlow came along who felt they should be named co-pastor. He had even considered one or two of them for the position. But it never felt right.

Robert Barlow felt right to him from the very day he said he wanted to be baptized and become a man of the cloth. Pastor Bishop hasn't felt a twinge of resistance from God from that very moment. In the end, he had to do what God wanted him to do, not what the church wanted. He did, however, feel compelled to discuss the matter with the congregation. He called a special meeting on the last Wednesday before the baptismal. Chasidy, being a member, was asked to attend but refused when she learned the subject would be her husband.

Chasidy has been on the phone more the past two weeks than she has since the phone was invented. She didn't mind. She wanted to be certain everyone was ready for their big day. She didn't consider herself a fashionista type. She would be the first to admit that it isn't important what you wear to church as long as your heart is right with God. But the baptismal wasn't just another day at church. It is just as important as a wedding day. In fact, she reasoned that it could be considered a marriage to God. She had decided within herself, if they were going to be baptized as a family, they would be dressed as a family.

She made a full celebration out of the whole event, arranging for a couple of popular apparel stores to come to the house the evening of the meeting so that everyone could decide together on what they would wear after being baptized. It doubled as a distraction to take her mind off of the meeting. Sam even invited Sherry to attend. Mic and Caitlin helped her prepare a grab and go bar with sandwiches, fruit, desert, and beverages. The grands had the fun part of watching over the little ones.

Once again, Barlow was blown away with Chasidy's tenacity to make an already special occasion even more special. Chasidy enjoyed watching the friction between the generationally gapped men debate over the style of suits to get. The guys were enjoying sorting out the differences too, voicing opinions why some pieces were for 'old folks' and others for 'young ramrods'. Neither of the boys knew what a ramrod was but only Antonio was courageous enough to ask. Alan didn't make it any clearer at all when he explained it to them smiling, "You guys. We just said that."

They were giving the store representative a headache. And Mic couldn't decide on her dress until the guys decided. Chasidy expressly suggested that her dress complements their suits intricately. The store rep finally proposed a solution. "Why don't we do this?" he started. "Each of you pick the suit that you want either in the same color or a different color, but all of you wear the same color shirt as Mrs. Ferguson's dress."

They all liked that idea. Mic had picked out some interesting colors though all very attractive. Chasidy was a little disappointed. She really wanted them dressed alike. In the end, when everyone had chosen their outfit and made it completely their own, the ladies were all in awe at how good they all looked standing there together modeling and posing for pretended cameras. None of them realized that Mr. Peterson had a real one.

Michelle had chosen a lovely Fushia sheath that gathered at the waist to her left side with large ruffles flowing down her hip that complemented her adorable hourglass figure perfectly. Al and AJ were dressed exactly the same in a handsome black double-breasted suit. Sam chose a stylish two-piece with only a blazer and pants. Terrence elected to sport a dashing deep grey vest with black slacks and Antonia a black and grey pullover vest with black slacks. But it was Barlow who stood out among them all. It was as if he was saying, this is my family. I will lead them, and they will follow me. The black and grey pin-striped double-breasted suit demanded that all eyes be stayed on him. As head of his family, he quietly demanded they take their place beside him in the company of God.

When everyone was satisfied, Barlow directed his attention to Chasidy and the other ladies, "Now whatta y'all gonna wear?"

Michelle added, "Yeah cause y'all can't walk in embarrassin' us."

"Chasidy on the defense, said, "I'm sure that's not what my husband meant but," she looked at Caitlin and Jasmine, "we may as well pick somethan' out too." Caitlin, Jasmine, and the twins chose attractive Fushia dresses suitable to their ages to complement Mic's dress. Caitlin helped her grandmother Rosalee pick out a nice two-piece pant set in soft Fushia. The Petersons were reluctant at first, but Barlow assured them that they were family too. Mic, Al, and AJ were more than happy to assist them, suggesting the exact same outfits they had chosen. Chasidy chose a lovely two-piece black and grey pin-stripe suit to complement her husband and a Fushia blouse to coordinate with everyone else.

Sherry was elated when Barlow invited her to choose an outfit also. Sam was happy he had included her as well. After she had chosen her lovely Chiffon dress with a flowing overlay, Barlow smiled and said, "My family is ready for church. Now who's gonna pay for all this?" The two store reps didn't think that was funny. The family thought it was hilarious.

That night before going to bed, he expressed his gratitude to Chasidy for making his day more special. "I don't know how you come up with these ideas, but they're always right on target. Thank you for a wonderful eve'nin'. I enjoyed it so much."

"So did everyone else," Chasidy said. "Isn't it crazy though, how the younger generation can't buy into suits anymore? Toni and Terrence looked like two little old men aging backwards in their vests." She giggled. "In my younger days, my brothars w're proud of their suits."

"What's even crazier is how da set up they picked is perfect for 'em," Barlow added.

Chasidy laughed. "I know right. They w're so handsome. Everybody did good."

D.M. Williams

"Thanks to you." Barlow just had to say one more time. "I love you, Chasidy."

She waited a moment, not answering right away. She just stood staring at him with an expression on her face he had never seen before. "I love you too, Rob," She finally said.

"What's that look about?" He asked her. "I thought I had seen all of yor expressions."

"You have," she said. "This one is completely new." She kissed him tenderly giving him a loving hug behind it.

"Now you really have my curiosity piqued. Are you gonna tell me?"

"This is my *'I'm so proud that I'm gonna be da wife of a preacher'* look. Somethan' I've wanted all my life." With that answer, he hugged her also, in return.

#

As it turned out Alan had decided to use the information Chasidy discovered for him to continue his search for his lost parents. He and Mic began the search together when one of the files Chasidy gave him had a familiar ring to it. *An infant whose parents had been killed in an automobile accident was adopted by the people involved in that accident. Five years later they too were killed in an automobile accident. The boy was placed in a foster care facility.*

Alan was so fascinated with that story that he had to pursue it. He remembered running away from a children's home because he wanted so desperately to find his family. He ran into a kind couple, the Marshalls, who had taken him in and cared for him for the next two years until he left that place also. Shortly after leaving the couple and two years after leaving the children's home, he met Barlow, and they became instant friends. Late Friday evening before the baptism, he received papers by messenger with some unexpected results.

Just before the papers arrived, everyone was enjoying a relaxing evening in the family room. LJ became fussy and Chasidy began singing *Hear the Wind Blow* to him. As she sang, Barlow began to take notice. He had actually heard her sing it before, but it never registered until now. "Chasidy," he said, "what is that song. It sounds so familiar."

"Hear da Wind Blow," Chasidy answered. "I used to sing it ta Caitlin when she was a baby."

He started singing the words realizing that he knew them. *"How do I know this?"* He was actually asking himself.

Chasidy answered him instead. "Maybe yor mothar used to sing it to you."

"I don't even r'member my mom," he said. "How would I r'member anythin' she sang to me?"

"That's how da mind works sometimes," Chasidy told him. "You r'membar' somethan' about 'er. Yor memory just has to be jarred to know what that is."

Mic and Al listened with attentive ears. They've learned over the past couple of years that when Chasidy spoke of the mysterious, it would be wise to hear her. AJ was playing on the floor with Charles listening also. And the Petersons were all ears as well.

"I wish I could've spent more time with her," Barlow confessed.

"You did," Chasidy said. Everyone looked at her in astonishment. The Petersons thought she was actually joking.

"Whatta you talkin' about?" A confused Barlow asked.

"She was with us da few months before da Quad was born," Chasidy confessed. "Berta was yor mothar," she said blatantly. Barlow was dumb founded. She began to explain. "She appeared to me in a dream right after da babies were born. I hadn't seen them yet, but she said they w're beautiful. She asked me to sang this song to them fa her because she used to sang it to you when you w're a baby." The room was whisper quiet. AJ came over and sat down in the chair beside Chasidy. "She wanted me to tell you that she was with you and that she wouldn't have missed that for anythan."

"But..." Barlow began, "that was Ethel's spirit in Berta. Even AJ..."

AJ interrupted, "I never said she was Grandma Ethel."

Michelle remembered the conversation at the hospital that she walked in on. "AJ, at da hospital right b'fore she left, I heard you call her grandma. Rob's mom wouldn't be yor grandma. That was Ethel, Baby."

AJ looked at Chasidy with pleading eyes and then at his Uncle Rob. "Uncle Rob, do you believe me when I say she was grandma?"

"Is that what she told you, AJ? That she was yor grandmother," Barlow asked him.

"Yes," he first answered, then he remembered, "well what she said was, I can call her grandma."

"Then how could she be my mom, Chasidy?"

"Aunt Chasidy, do you believe me?"

Chasidy smiled at him and said exactly what he wanted to hear. "I certainly do, Little Guy." Then she asked Barlow, "Do you thank that if yor mothar was here in place of Ethel and Alan showed up at her doorstep that she would turn him away? That she couldn't love him da same as she loves you, like a son?" Everyone shifted into thought mode.

"She said I could tell you who she was when da time was right," AJ continued.

Chasidy smiled at him. "She told me da exact same thang, Sweetheart."

AJ continued, "She told me a lotta things. She told me Aunt Chasidy would need my help with all of my cousins. She told me I was gonna have a brother and sister named Charles and Grace. But she didn't tell me about the accident."

Barlow, Al, and Mic were all ready to have AJ and Chasidy committed to an asylum when the messenger knocked on the door with Al's research results. It was a needed distraction from their present conversation. Or so they thought. At first glance of the papers, Al immediately looked up at AJ and Chasidy. Then at Mic and Rob. "What does it say, Al?" Mic asked. They all had Michelle's mom and dad's complete attention. They had never heard such strange talk before.

"I'm glad I've got this in writing or y'all would think I'm as crazy as we think these two are right now." He started from the beginning, which everyone knew except Barlow. Once he was up to speed on the information Chasidy brought him, he began reading the papers the messenger left with him. "*The parents of the infant that were killed in the accident were named James and Patricia Barlow. Alan and Jade Ferguson adopted the infant legally giving him their name along with the father's namesake. James Barlow was previously married to Roberta Louise Barlow but left her and her son for a Caucasian woman whom he later married. It was the child of that union that was rescued from the accident and adopted by the Fergusons. Young Ferguson ran away from the Chiricahua Children's home where he resided and was never recovered by the state."*

No one spoke a word. Everyone was trying to process what they had just heard. Al, still in shock from what he had just read, got up and went out on the porch to try to wrap his mind around it all. Chasidy and Mic looked at Barlow, expecting him to follow him. When he didn't, Mic stood to go see after him. Chasidy stopped her, "Mic," she called to her, shaking her head for her not to go. "I think I hear Grace cryan'."

All of the babies were resting by now. Mic didn't understand. All she knew was that her husband needed her. Again. "But..." she began to talk.

"It sounds serious," Chasidy continued, "I'd go check on 'er if I were you." Michelle was frozen where she was. She knew Grace wasn't crying. She knew what Chasidy was trying to do. She looked once more at Barlow. Chasidy continued, "Robert knows what he needs to do. I'm sorry girl, but it's not you he needs right now." She stared once again at Barlow as if asking *whatta you waiting for?*

He finally said, "I think I hear Grace too. You go check on 'er. I've got Al." He took a deep sigh and joined Al out on the porch. Mrs. Peterson went with Michelle to the nursery.

Alan was gazing out into The Grove. "Do you think Ethel knew?" He asked Barlow.

I don't know. I think she would've told us if she did," Barlow answered.

Alan thought back to the day Ethel passed. "Do you r'member da day she left us, da words she spoke to us both?" he asked.

"Yes, I do," Barlow said. "She said *'take care of yor brother'.* Thinkin' back now, it sounded deliberate, like she was tryin' to tell us. I'm thinkin' now, maybe that's why she fought so hard to win yor love. She wanted to keep us t'gether," Barlow reasoned.

"Have yor feelin' changed towards me?" Al wanted to know that he hasn't lost his best friend.

"Why would they?"

"My mom broke up yor mom's marriage."

"Our dad broke up my mom's marriage," Barlow corrected. "Al, I 've watched women practically throw themselves under you. And b'cause you w're so in love with Mic, you nev'r turned 'em a look. Our father had that same option. Feelin' da way I do about you right now, da way I've felt about you all these years, I can't even be angry at 'im for that. Yur da best gift he could've given me."

"I'm glad nothin's changed between us?" Al told him.

"I didn't say nothing's change. Yor wrong about that. Everything's changed," Barlow told him. "My best friend that I've loved all my life and called 'im broth'r truly is my broth'r. This is a story that only God could write."

Alan slowly shook his head, thinking back on what bits and pieces he could remember. "I don't even know how I came to meet up with you. I just knew that when we met, I was where I was supposed to be. Nothin' could pry me away from you. I admired you and loved you from da day we first met. And I didn't wanna leave you." He looked at Barlow with tears in his eyes, seeing the tears in his brother's eyes also. "I still don't. When you and Chasidy would disappear out here for weeks at a time, it nearly drove me crazy. Like part of me had disappeared with you. All of that makes sense now."

Barlow nodded once and said, "And I don't want ya to leave. Broth'r. It broke my heart knowin' you were livin' a und'r a railroad trussell. I knew then I was gonna take care of you for da rest of our lives." Alan smiled. "Da first time you visited me out h're, I didn't want you to leave that day eith'r. It both'red me for days. Chasidy's radar homed in on that. That's why she came up with da plan for us to be neighbors, so we'd nev'r have to be separated again. Watchin' you drive away that day felt like I was losin' my best friend." As many times as they've hugged before, they've felt nothing like this one. Barlow hugged his brother for the first time in fifty-two years. A hug he never could have anticipated.

After all the sentiments were over, Barlow and Al re-entered the house. They had regained their composure from the most wonderful shock. Mic was waiting for him, "You ok, Baby?"

Al kissed her on the cheek answering, "Yes, mam, I am." He started laughing softly to himself.

"What's so funny?" Mic asked.

"If anybody ever wonders if God has a sense of humor, I can tell them He does. I spent my entire childhood wonderin' why I couldn't be with my family. And I was with 'im all along."

#

Barlow didn't get a bit of sleep that night and the babies had nothing to do with it. Chasidy wasn't sure how all of this was affecting him, so she left him to his thoughts and assumed the late shift for the night. He was still awake when the first of the Quad awakened for his feeding. Chasidy was rocking Third Al and humming their song when Barlow walked in to keep her company. He started warming the bottle for Remi. "Sometimes I think too much about stuff," Chasidy told Barlow.

"What does that mean?" he asked her.

"All of this started with a Christmas gift," she answered "I feel like I need to apologize, but it's just so wonderful. You and Al, real brothars," she said still in unbelief shaking her head.

Barlow couldn't believe she said that. Not his Chasidy. The woman who once told him that nothing sneaks up on God. Nothing is a surprise to Him. "Now I know yur human just like me." She chuckled. "How can you feel guilty about that? It was you who told me that nothin' is a surprise to God. That He already knew what hap'ened today would hap'en. He put this in action long before you came along. In fact, yor part of da plan was to ensure that it hap'ened just like it was supposed to. Yor belief in Him is so solid, He knew He could trust you to do just what you did."

"Is that why yur sittan' up all night, because yur *not* havan' any feelans' behind this?"

He smiled, "Oh, I'm definitely having feelins behind this. But they're all good." Just then Remi started to wake. "And I'm going to sleep as soon as I feed little Becky." Third Al had already fallen back to sleep. "You don't have to wait for me though. You can go lay down."

"Um," she sat still rocking him, "I'll wait on ya."

#

Saturday morning, Barlow was helping Al and AJ tend to the horses. The grandfathers went alone just to hang out with the guys. AJ was a little pro by now, but it was Al's and Barlow's first time.

He got a kick out of showing them how to brush them down. Alan didn't have to ask him to take care of all the horses, AJ really enjoyed doing it. While they were there, Barlow received a phone call from Pastor Bishop. "Good morning, Brother Robert. I'm just checking to see if everybody is all set for tomorrow?"

"Yes Pastor, we are. And anxiously waiting. My family and I are extremely excited about t'morrow."

"That's wonderful! Just what I wanted to hear," Pastor told him.

"We're all havin' dinn'r here tonight if you wanna join us," he invited.

"Thank you, but by then I'll be in meditation before tomorrow's service. That's something you'll learn about during our mentorship."

"I'm truly lookin' forward to it Pastor." Barlow went on to share about him and Al and how God has shown Himself to him in so many ways lately. The more Pastor Bishop heard, the more he was convinced that Barlow would be his new co-pastor. "We'll see ya t'morrow Pastor. Eight am sharp."

#

After the baptism, the family was officially inducted as members of the Christian faith. Pastor had made his decision about who his co-pastor would be. He was met with much resistance in the Wednesday evening meeting, not only from hopeful perspectives but from some members as well. They felt leery of bringing someone in, to pastor them whom they had never met. Pastor Bishop hoped his congregation would have more confidence in him as a leader. He was now certain in his spirit that Barlow was the man God has chosen for this position. But he wanted the church to get the same feel for him that he has. He asked Barlow to share a little bit of his story with the church as they all stood awaiting the *Right Hand of Fellowship.*

Barlow had so much to say. He had never spoken in church before, he wasn't exactly sure what *a little bit* consisted of. "I'll try to make this short. But please bear with me if I speak just a little too long. Just over two years ago I was a very different man than what I am today. I lost my first wife when we w're very young. I had a difficult time gettin'' ov'r that. We had only been married six years. I didn't care much for God and hearin' people talk about how good

He is. I couldn't see past my pain to understand that. Then I met Chasidy. She was always talkin' about her God. She began to soften my ears towards Him. He began to soften my heart towards Him. He's blessed me through so many tribulations. Chasidy's and Mic's kidnappin'. I'm sure a lot of you have heard about that. Chasidy was in a coma for months. Chasidy's near death in childbirth just recently, four beautiful children to join with da wonderful children I've gained through marriage, my best friend, and da man I've called broth'r, Al, and his family in what could've been a fatal accident. He brought da three of them through that, alive and well. My beloved Ethel passin' assurin' me in her passin' that God is still with me. But brand-new blessings from just this week have really shown me how amazin' God truly is. Many of you won't believe this. My deceased moth'r who died so long ago that I can't even r'member her; visited me briefly just before our babies arrived. She stayed two months with Chasidy and me. She took care of Chasidy during da pregnancy. She revealed herself to my wife and my nephew. They revealed it to me, Al, and Mic just da oth'r day. Then He blessed me in anoth'r totally unexpected way." Barlow began to cry. He put his arm around Al's shoulder and finished talking. "I found out that same day that this man, my best friend since childhood, da man I've called my broth'r for all these years has turned out to be my real biological broth'r. Al was orphaned. He nev'r knew his people. He always yearned to know them. Chasidy," he reached his hand out for her to join him. "This wonderful woman who makes everythin' she touches special, gave 'im some information on Christmas Day that could help him find his parents. He found out that he and I have da same fath'r. Chasidy once told me that God had ordained everythin' that's hap'ened in my life. Lookin' back at some of the things that's hap'ened, I realize how right she is. No one else but God could've written my story. I love Him, I thank Him, and I praise Him for being in charge of my life and blessing me with da family that He knew I always wanted but nev'r once believed I could have. I pledge my devotion to Him for as long as I live and reverence Him as God of my life and Jesus as my Lord and Savior."

When Barlow finished speaking, the church was as quiet as a mouse. He had said things that Pastor Bishop hadn't even expected to hear. When Pastor Bishop stood in the pulpit looking over the church in complete awe of what he and everyone else had just heard, he was no longer wavering about who he would appoint as his co-pastor. He officially pronounced Robert Lewis Barlow co-pastor of the church. The whole congregation applauded and affirmed their support in Pastor Bishop's decision. When he asked the church to extend the Right Hand of Fellowship to Barlow and his family, the two men who were hoping for the co-pastor position were the first to welcome him and his family to the church family. The entire church welcomed them with open arms. Even Mr. Peterson gave him a good long hug.

#

After the service, during fellowship celebration, Chasidy watched her family enjoying themselves. She could have never imagined that over two years ago, the tall handsome stranger she met in her favorite home improvement store who captivated her with his magnetic personality, kind nature, handsome smile, and iconic laughter could have made all of her dreams, even from her childhood; come true.

During this same time Barlow, while sitting with the men of the congregation glanced over at Chasidy laughing with the other ladies who were making moderations over the babies. He remembered how when he first met her, he longed to see her beautiful smile; not realizing that she would be the woman to cause dreams he never knew he could dream, to come true. He thought he would forever be Robert Lewis Barlow - widower. Society had deemed him Robert Lewis Barlow - *Most Successful Eligible Bachelor*. God ordained him Robert Lewis Barlow - a beloved servant of His Kingdom. Redefined a man of God, like David: *after God's own heart.*

###

Thank you for purchasing *Barlow Redefined*. I hope you enjoyed it. Find out what it was like for Barlow, growing up in the small town of Amory with his best friend Alan Ferguson in *Trestle Rat-The Story of Al*. And I would greatly appreciate it if you would leave a review where you made your purchase so others will know how much you enjoyed it too.

TRESTLE RAT
THE STORY OF AL Book 3
By D.M. Williams
It All Begins with Al.

Family is everything to Alan Ferguson. Find out how it all started in:

TRESTLE RAT THE STORY OF AL…

when an unexplainable love at first sight formed between two boys ages twelve and thirteen that lasted an entire lifetime. Alan Ferguson ran away from a children's home at the age of ten in search of his family. People who looked like him. Born to an interracial couple, he didn't meet many people who did. A nice couple found him and took him in, but his heart yearned for his real family. Two years later, he met Robert Barlow and was instantly attached to him. So much so, that he left the good people who took him in and the comfort of their beautiful home to secretly live under a train trestle, just to be near him. It didn't make sense to him. Rob Barlow looked nothing like him and yet, he stayed. *GET THE TRILOGY!* Available in e-book, hardcopy and paperback.

THE BARLOW TRILOGY

BARLOW

DEFINITION OF FLAWLESS

By D.M. Williams

Losing Becky was the worst pain he had ever experienced. Doused in guilt drenched with unforgiveness over the death of his beautiful wife, Robert Barlow had no desire to fall in love again. A self-made multi-billionaire, he built his empire on the pain of losing his beloved wife, and with the help of his lifelong friend, Alan Ferguson. Ever since devoted to a life of hard work, he has now decided twenty-six years later to retire early, leaving it all behind in the hands of his trusted friend, and pursue his dream of traveling the world over. Barlow was perfectly content with sharing his world travels with the only woman in his life, his cherished mother-figure, Ethel Middleton. But then…,

HE MET CHASIDY!

Available in paperback, hardcopy, and e-book.

ABOUT THE AUTHOR

D.M. Williams

A Mississippi native who loves to write about the beauty of nature, the southern culture, her home state, faith, God and the wonderful miracles He still performs. Williams writes engaging family saga page-turners filled with spiritual phenomena, humor, relatable issues, love, joy, sadness, and romance from cover to cover. She often voices her discord with issues like bullying, domestic violence, child abuse, and racism cleverly crafted inside her pleasantly entertaining stories. Even though her stories are realistically relatable, as a hopeless romantic, she always finds a place for every girl's fantasy and always a happy-ever-after ending.

Please visit her blog, Buszy Hands Write at Buszyhands.com. Stay in the know, join her fan club and get a FREE SHORT STORY- Clover Valley's Storm- A enemies to love romance.

Email: donnamarie@buszyhands.com